# The Operations of
# SUBWAY
## and Its Soldiers

# THE OPERATIONS OF
# SUBWAY
## AND ITS SOLDIERS

By L. A. Williams

XULON PRESS

Xulon Press
2301 Lucien Way #415
Maitland, FL 32751
407.339.4217

www.xulonpress.com

Printed in the United States of America
Paperback ISBN-13: 978-1-66282-643-6
Ebook ISBN-13: 978-1-66282-644-3

# Table of Contents

# Preface:

In 1944, a short time after the end of WWII, some of the world's superpowers decided to create a testing site for the advancement of warfare. Nothing was off limits except explosive payloads greater than fifty feet. They needed a place to test new weapons, vehicles of land and air, body armor, and highly experimental equipment not yet ready for mankind. Sometimes things were placed on the island so they would never be seen again. The governments made sure to place it in a location away from prying eyes—an island with unknown coordinates. It was big enough to have all terrains and weather conditions.

The governments would get their data results from their "commanders." Most of the test subjects were forcefully selected. Haven't you ever wondered where some of the missing people actually were?

# 1
## Let's Get This Started...with a Bang!

**H**ave you ever had one of those weeks where everything starts off perfectly—so perfect you are soaring at some point above the clouds, and nothing could go wrong? Yes, I know gravity usually kicks in at some point, but I like to stay optimistic. My month started off that way, a half a week with bliss. I had finally proposed to the woman I've been in love with since the day we met, though I've never told her that simple truth. It took many years for me to tell her how I feel. I had finally befriended her brother, which, in all honesty, took longer than it should have; he's a little overprotective, and I was finally going home after being gone for what I assumed was ten years or more.

I was about to get my life back. Well, as you can tell, my life was going great. Of course, no matter how optimistic you try to be, physics teaches you that whatever goes up must come back down at one point or another. Unfortunately, life wanted to collect on some late fees. Now the rain is falling on my face from the clouds above. I am bleeding to death flat on my back with a big hole in my chest where my heart used to be. All I can do is wait for Old Bones in his black cloak and scythe to take me to a final resting place, though I hope he never shows.

How did I end up in a position like this? That is a question I have asked myself many times, every day, even now, as I feel the raindrops falling on my face. Where did I go wrong? Was this outcome avoidable? The only way to know the answer is to start from the very beginning, when my life really started to change.

My story started at sixteen years old. Despite my age, I had just graduated from Barstow High School. Yeah, that school—the school from a town you almost never hear anything good about, but it wasn't all bad, at least not while I was there. It was June 10, 2006, and the time was eleven o'clock. I was at home with a sweet tooth that just wouldn't be satisfied, and I also felt as though I was cooped up in the house and needed to go somewhere. I convinced my mother to let me go for a walk, since Dad had the car and there wasn't any other way of transportation except to walk. My mother always said in the past not to go walking after dark, but you know how we children can get: "I've done this countless times in the past...and I can do it again. Nothing can go wrong." My mom must have felt something was up because she really did not want me to go. However, with persistence, she broke and finally let me go. Before leaving, I told her I was going to a local food mart named Food 4 Self or something like that. It was the closest store to me, and the only one open until one o'clock in the morning. I grabbed my wallet and left eagerly.

There's something about taking a night stroll to get your mind off life. Though I could have taken a slow pace, I didn't want to take too long of a walk, so I sped up to keep it short. I planned to walk from my house to Armory Road to Barstow Road, turn down Virginia Road, then go down Muriel Street and back down Armory Road until I hit home, to create a route that made a complete circle. This was so I didn't have to worry too much about being followed without someone seeing it happen; I thought it was a good plan. I turned down Virginia Road, the sidewalk that I was on, crossed in front of a swap meet, which was on my right. I remember seeing a calico cat run away from the swap meet into the street. I thought it belonged to one of the two gated communities across the street. I didn't think anything else of it at the time, and I continued walking. Then I heard gunshots coming from the swap meet.

My heart started racing, and I ran away, keeping my head low, trying to avoid any stray bullets by following the three-foot wall that separated the parking lot and the sidewalk. I thought about moving from my location to the gated communities across the street, like the calico, but I realized I would still have a chance of being shot—even more so because then I would be out in the open. Not only that, but the gate might have been locked, and even if I managed to get inside, I would have increased my chance of being arrested by the police. I continued until I reached a nearby apartment complex parking lot that was on the same side of the street but hidden from the main road. It was the only place to hide from any surviving shooters nearby. As I hid behind the building, I tried to calm my breathing as much as I could so I didn't attract attention. I wanted to wait at least twenty minutes, so I could give those shooters plenty of time to vacate or the police time to show up, though that might take an extra ten minutes. I heard footsteps running from my current position; the gunshots had stopped firing long ago, and the only thing I could think was it was almost over. I just had to wait a while longer.

While I waited, I heard and felt a slight change in the wind. It was as though someone had passed me. I used one of the car's windows in the parking lot as a mirror, but nothing reflected from the streets. I looked around me, and the only thing I saw was a store bag drifting in the wind. "Today might be the last time I get to see my mom," I whispered. Then I saw the area in front of me was a small distortion. It didn't match the way it was supposed to. This caught my eyes, and I looked at it harder to be sure I wasn't going crazy. It was so bad I thought I needed glasses. I heard a voice laughing where the deformation was, but I assumed it came from one of the homes. I remember saying, "Someone must have heard a funny joke or something." The distortion fractured, and a weak light appeared around the cracks, giving an outline of something about seventy inches in height. The wind started blowing the and cracks opened a bit faster. The first thing revealed was the tip of a gun. As the cracks fell apart, the second thing I saw was an arm holding the gun. The rest of the body became visible as a strong gust of wind blew.

"You just ran out of luck tonight," a man's voice said. The guy was wearing some futuristic armor. I wasn't sure what type of metal it was, but it shined like chrome, despite being black. I could tell it had no exposed areas, so even if I had a knife, it would be useless. His helmet had a visor covering the eyes. The only thing that would ever come close to describing it is a sci-fi videogame. I'd never seen anything that came close in real life. "Looks like you're headed to the morgue, as my other victims did." My heart felt like I had dropped it out of place; the feeling swept up my body and rushed to my head. "Any final words before you meet your Maker?"

"Why me, I didn't see anything? I don't even know who you are, for crying out loud," I pleaded.

His helmet retracted and showed me his face.

I replied quickly, "I still have no idea who you are. Even if the police put you in a lineup, I still couldn't pick you from another fellow off the street." I became teary-eyed.

He laughed. "Do you really think that I fear you identifying me in a mere lineup? It does not scare me as much as you are afraid of me right now. Besides, if you were to die right now, I would still get away with the crime without a witness."

"As true as that is, I have not witnessed anything to hold against you in any court. In fact, I'm forgetting your face even as we talk," I pleaded.

"It's too late. This is the beginning of the end for you." He pulled the trigger. In the milliseconds it took the bullet to leave the chamber, I thought about how my whole life, I had done nothing to achieve any goals or anything that came close. Too bad, right? This made me see just how unimportant and insignificant my life really was.

All I could hear was the fuzzy sound of voices. I could not move, and I felt as though I was in a daze. I then felt as though I was hanging from my arms and legs. It was about five seconds later that I felt something hard hit my head.

I woke up and realized my arms and legs were tied to something, and my body was swinging right and left. I slowly opened my eyes, and the first thing I saw was a fuzzy pair of legs walking in some direction. I couldn't tell whether it was forward or backward because I was still in a complete daze. The language was different from English; it seemed like they were speaking an Indian language. I looked up and saw some special kind of clothes. As my vision finally returned to me, the carriers had seen me waking up and then injected my body with something that put me back to sleep. The one question going through my head was, *What kind of afterlife is this? I must be going through some kind of new afterlife initiation ceremony thing.* Whatever was going on, I knew I'd find out sooner or later.

The next time I woke up was because my body demanded food. My stomach roared like an angry lion. When I opened my eyes, I realized I was inside an empty tent. Standing over me was a girl with hair the color of pure gold. Her hair shined even where the light wasn't directly on it; it was long enough to reach her lower back. She was taller than the average girl, my age. She had an athletic build, but it wasn't intimidating. Her eyes were a beautiful emerald green. Around her neck was a golden necklace with a hawk hanging from the chain; she wore no makeup and had beauty I couldn't describe. There was something about this girl that made her different from any others I had seen before, but I didn't realize what it was. All I knew was my eyes couldn't look away from her. It almost scared me; she leaned over and looked down on me. I could only describe this feeling as love at first sight.

"I know, it's my eyes; they are teal," she said, touching my forehead with her hand. "Well, you're no longer sick with that fever, and the swelling has gone away." She moved her hand and walked away.

"Fever? What are you talking about?" I asked.

"Yes, you had a fever and a near-death experience. From our reports, you've had it for almost a week now. It might be from all the traveling; it didn't seem like it was getting any better until yesterday. That might be why you're so hungry."

"What were you saying about your eyes... wait, what? I almost died, but how?"

"Yeah, it was a fever with some pretty heavy stuff, likely from the drugs they used to keep you under. All my parents told me before they died was that my eyes turn blue when I am mad." I looked at her as though she was crazy from how fast she was talking. "Well, they turn green when I am in a great mood."

"You did mention I have been traveling for about a week. Could you tell me where I am right now, or how far I am from home?"

"Honestly, I don't know how far you are from your home. I have been out of touch with the outside world since I was younger."

"Alright then, can you tell me your name?" I asked. Her eyes looked a beautiful green, but maybe they were teal. It wasn't very bright in the room.

"Oh, right, duh. How rude of me. My name is Laura Midnight. The people here call me the 'Translator' because I speak over nine different languages fluently. Oh, you must be hungry, my apologies. I would be hungry too if I hadn't eaten in three days." She picked up a bowl of food and held it close to my face before pulling it away. "Say, what is your name? You never told me." At this point, I knew she wasn't going to let me eat unless I told her.

I looked at her and looked at the food. Any other time, it wouldn't have looked that good; I must have been really hungry. She could have offered me a plate of bathroom cleaner and I wouldn't have complained. I looked at her, then back at the food one last time. I sighed.

"Leonardo is my name. So, can I eat now?" I could have sworn something was swimming in the bowl. "Well, it's better than nothing," I whispered. It tasted like the best thing I had ever eaten; it was so good I could eat the bowl as well. "If you speak nine different languages, how did you guess to speak to me in English?"

"You talk in your sleep. Not to mention, the Webmaster said you come from America, a country that speaks primarily English, so it wasn't too difficult. Now, you should go ahead and eat up. You have a very busy day ahead of you." Laura sat down and waited until I finished eating.

"So, is this what you people normally eat?"

"No, that is food that everyone has to eat to detoxify the body; the octopi tentacles just makes it go down easier. It is similar to san-nakji. I honestly didn't think you would eat it."

When I finished eating, another woman walked into the room. It wasn't until she entered I noticed I was inside a hut and not a tent. I also noticed I was chained to the floor. Luckily, I was too weak to attempt going anywhere because I was sure they would have killed or maimed me. The inside of the hut looked like it was made from plaster. There were no windows, likely so I didn't know what was going on outside. Nothing was in the room but a bed across from mine.

It wasn't until the lady spoke to Laura that I truly understood why they called her the Translator; the language they spoke was completely different from English. Then Laura walked up to me, saying, "The leaders of the Boundless Control Center, also known as the BCC Group, will see you now. She will be your escort. You will follow her wherever she leads you."

The lady handed Laura some gauntlet, and Laura handed it to me, saying, "You are going to have to put this on." I gave her my arm. "I recommend not doing anything stupid, especially while this is on you." She clamped it on my arm. At first, it was loose to the point it could have fallen off. But then it tightened itself to a firm grip. Laura then removed the shackles. "Please follow us."

They took me out of the hut, and there were women all around me. But this wasn't a typical male fantasy, where they would feel up his muscles, flirt, and give him goo-goo eyes. Every woman had her own gun, and there were five towers with shooters in them. At least one shooter per tower was targeting me. I'd prefer just listening to them. What a dream come true, right?

"Hey, Laura, who is the leader of BCC?" I asked.

"The Webmaster."

"I know you mentioned her once before, but you never told me why they call her the Webmaster?" I whispered.

"It is because she is a human dictionary. Not to mention, she is very wise and well connected. By the way, if you haven't guessed, the thing on your wrist is a lot worse than any shackles they could put on you. The gauntlet is a behavioral correcting system. It was a tool created by Gloria Van Heart. She was originally a teacher in the backwater parts of Ohio. She originally made it to replace disciplining prisoners. She put it on the worst of prisoners, and the plan worked almost too perfectly. However, before she could mass produce them, one of the gauntlets malfunctioned and forced a prisoner into a coma, so they stopped using them and destroyed anything to prove ever using them. And we have gotten our hands on the remaining ones."

"Why wouldn't they just kill someone? Wouldn't that make more sense?"

"They might kill you for defying them. There was a slave who decided to defy their orders, but then again, Braiden was an idiot. They gave him a choice, and the fool chose death."

"What was the other choice?"

"Asking the neighboring village for equipment; nothing harmful. Not only that, but he was also an unpredictable worker. No one was ever sure if he was going to go crazy one day."

"How long was he here?"

"Two months. The Webmaster thinks it might have come from the cryo-freeze, but I doubt it. I think it might have been something else. At first, they thought it was my fault as a translator, but the Webmaster confirmed it wasn't." She paused, then said, "Don't worry, you seem smart enough not to get caught up in a similar situation. You don't have to worry too much."

When we stopped moving, they took me to what seemed like an abandoned temple. When we got inside, it was filled with books upon books that made a path we had to follow, almost like a small maze. We continued walking for another ten minutes. When we reached the end of the maze, there were ten thrones. Sitting on two of the thrones were two young women. One was in her mid-twenties; she had red hair and wore glasses. She looked like a busybody. The other woman seemed to be in her late twenties. She was blond and also wore glasses, but she was reading a book before I walked in. She wore what I considered a winter outfit. It was cold in the room, after all. Also, in the room were two women kneeling toward the throne.

The one with the book spoke, and Laura whispered the translation. "So, do you want to explain why you interrupted me in the middle of my reading time?" the lady asked in a soft tone, but no one dared to answer.

I thought I might be the reason, so I raised my hand and said softly, "Excuse me, ma'am."

She quickly switched over to my language, saying, "First off, I know why Laura brought you here. I am referring to those who came before you. Second, 'ma'am'? I am neither a queen nor a princess. So, is there anything you are implying?"

"No, ma'am."

"Your parents raised you right. I understand you are saying 'ma'am' as a sign of respect, but here on this island, your actions show how much you respect me. Either call me formally by my name, or since I know you don't know it, you are to call me Webmaster. Do you understand?"

"Understood, Webmaster."

She stood up. "Since we are still focused on you. Remember, it is rude to interrupt people when they're talking to others. When I am talking to you, I will use your language. This is the first and last time I hope this happens." So, she continued speaking to the women at the throne for the next few seconds, then looked at me. "As you were saying?" She walked over to me as if to hear me better.

"I apologize for earlier. Could you tell me what is going on and what I am doing here?" I asked as respectfully as I could.

"Let me see if there is a way I can say this so you can understand." She took a deep breath. "You were kidnapped, then sold into slavery somewhere in the southern parts of South America. While you were transported to South America, I received a request from your sister Kat to acquire you; if we were to find you, it was good. She had a picture to make it easy to spot you. Sadly, I didn't have the resources to send you home right away, and instead, you were sent here. Once a servant is purchased, they are sent to the buyer right away. I did this to avoid you transported to that slave facility and be sure I received you and not another. This is how the slave trade works on this island."

So, the Webmaster bought me to save me. That was an interesting concept, but understandable. It helped, but I was still unsure what they expected of me.

"This happens a lot; usually, they will grab somebody from one of the mainlands, either from a crowded city or a town nobody has ever heard of—in your case, Barstow. As far as your role here, you are a worker in the village until we are completely reimbursed by your labor, until you die, or until we no longer have a use for you. If you have any questions about what is going on, Laura will explain to you the events that are occurring around you."

She walked back to the chair. As she walked there, I asked, "You said you knew my sister?" Kat was my second oldest sister, loved by all, and kept to herself. Honestly, I felt as though she looked for someone to let her become her own hero or someone to look up to her, at the very least. She had a thing about personal space, almost to a fault. Though she was willing to help others, she didn't like to accept help for herself. I wasn't sure if it was pride or stubbornness. And before I was taken, I had a sneaking suspicion she was growing an addiction to caffeine. No one had ever told me about her having a double life. Then again, she did keep stuff like this to herself. I thought this would have been pretty cool if she'd told me about it.

"Yes, Kat. She worked for me a while back. Her situation was very different because she was able to give one of our associates help while Mr. Trotter was out. Since she was a big help and he was tired of traveling, he offered your sister a job. Mr. Trotter no longer has to go to Georgia, and your sister goes in his stead. As for what she does, you will have to ask her the next time you see her. Last year, her job concluded, and one of my daughters has agreed to go." When the Webmaster was behind the desk, she grabbed a book and gave it to Laura to give to me. "You are to read that book. It is one of the few we have in English. It will tell you a few things you will be doing here if I am unimpressed by your work ethic."

I took a look at the book's title, *So You Just Found Out You're a Slave? What to Expect While in Captivity!* It was written by Tyler Worthy Watt.

"You will read a chapter a day until you are done reading it, no exceptions. For every day you don't read this book, you will be disciplined." The Webmaster picked up the book she had been reading. "You can leave now. Please behave yourselves.

When outside, Laura explained we would go meet the grand elder who lived in a different part of the village in a building that looked like a big temple, up a sizeable staircase. However, that wasn't the worst part. The worst part was hearing a small rock fall from the top of the stairs to the bottom. Right away, I knew it would be a long walk. On the way up, I asked her about the Webmaster and why she only wanted to be called the Webmaster. To put it simply: one, it made her anonymous; you didn't know another person just by hearing their rank or title. Two, it was easier to make a title last longer and spread so that everyone knew who you were and what you represented. Three, it was a business tool, so even if you saw the Webmaster, you wouldn't know.

The explanation I received was a lot longer than this. So, what she did was a tactic and nothing more.

When we finally made it to the top of the mountainous staircase, I was huffing and puffing and trying not to complain. I fell to the floor and tried to catch my breath; I looked to the escort and Laura. "How can you walk up those stairs and not be tired?" I asked, gasping for air.

"You know, complaining won't change anything?" Laura replied, laughing.

"Yeah, but keeping it in is a man-killer," I replied, lying on the ground. My legs throbbed with my pounding heartbeat. On top of that, I had no shoes, so my feet felt the whole journey, and I mean I felt everything—thorns, temperature differences in the ground, and I thought I even stepped on an anthill.

"Hello, Laura," a voice said, but this voice was different from the ones I'd heard since waking up. It wasn't feminine, for one. "So, who's your new friend?"

"'Friend'? How did you know?" Laura replied. I turned my head to see a man in his early forties looking down at me. The interesting part was his clothing looked very comfortable, not formal, like you would think an elder would dress.

"First off, your green eyes gave it away. Second, you seem like you're having more fun than normal."

"That means nothing, Mr. Trotter." Thinking about it now, I think she was blushing. The gentleman's full name was Rodney Trotter. His history was unknown to most people.

I put my arm in the air, and waved, trying to say hello.

"So, you made him walk all the way up here from the bottom when he could have used the elevator instead?" Mr. Trotter laughed.

"I felt he could use the walk. He has been asleep for a while now; besides, I love the view along the path." I didn't notice it right away, but yes, the path was beautiful. If you like nature hikes, you could appreciate the beauty, as I eventually did because it was so green, and I am from a desert.

"I think this might be prisoner or even worker abuse." The man helped me up and continued, "I am sorry, young man, but she only walks up here to mess with the new help. Braiden was the last man dragged up here. I remember when she was a little girl, she tried to have her pet turtle go up the stairs, but I digress. The Webmaster didn't send you up here to talk, Laura." He looked into my eyes, still speaking to Laura, and said, "You tell her she has a good one for sure. In fact, he was also a good student."

"How do you know if I was a good student or not?" I asked, trying to figure it out myself.

He replied, "First, when it comes to self-worth, it is all in the eyes. Sometimes you can tell a lot about a person just by looking in their eyes. In your case, they tell people of your kindness and how much you are willing to help. It is a skill that is perfected with age." He walked away, saying, "I was also a substitute teacher for some of your classes a few years back. You can take him back down now, Laura, and take the elevator. That is one of the reasons it is there. Be sure to tell the Webmaster my thoughts on this matter. Leonardo, if you do everything right, you will be up here again soon, and we can talk then."

We walked toward the elevator. She smiled the whole time, but I couldn't figure out why. As the door closed, I noticed the escort did not follow us down. "So, why didn't the other woman come with us?"

"From what she told me, there were other things she had to take care of while she was in this area of the village. I am surprised you didn't notice her leaving while you were talking to Mr. Trotter."

"Hmm...So, can you tell me where on the planet I currently am?" I asked.

"Sorry, but I wouldn't know even if you gave me a map. I am too unfamiliar with the other places to make an educated guess. I know we feel the effects of all four seasons. If you want to know, you would have to ask the Webmaster or Anita."

"Anita?"

"Yes, she was the other woman sitting in the chair when we went to see the Webmaster. She doesn't talk much, but she is very reliable and scary good at her job. With those two working together, they are an indestructible force, one to be reckoned with."

"Are they the chiefs or something?"

"For you, yes. As for the rest of the village, they are more like very strong advisors, tacticians, and the spine that supports the rest of the people. The name 'Webmaster' holds a lot of power all around the island. Maybe one day, you'll see it for yourself."

"So, what will happen now?" I asked, leaning against the wall of the elevator.

"Now we place you in the middle of the city, where the council members who are present will decide what work station you will be placed at and whether it is a permanent or temporary duty station. It could be considered your lucky day, unless you get stuck cleaning after the animals. Then again, there is another woman who was recently promoted and placed on the council. With her there, it can go any way; she doesn't care for men in her work area, Mrs. Trudy Rogers."

"How many council members are there?"

"Altogether there are ten, but only four are in charge of your fate. Two of which you haven't met yet. Regardless of your fate, you will end up working for all four of them at one point or another."

The elevator stopped. As it opened, there were guards ready to escort us. "So, they trust me in the elevator but not in the open," I said.

15

"No, they had shooters ready to fire if you got out of line," Laura replied.

At the time, I could have sworn I heard war drums playing in the distance, but I couldn't see who was playing. I continued to walk and could feel my heart beating faster, my head getting lighter, and my legs getting heavier by the moment. I had just survived a near-death experience and be judged for some reason unknown. Until it happened, every moment would be treated like my last. I remember thinking, *Man, I hope this is all a dream and I wake up from it before they cut my head off or something.* When I saw where the path ended, my heart dropped, and everything seemed to spread apart before my eyes, for what I saw in front of me was a guillotine. Blood was all over the floor and on some of the walls. They carried me, because my legs forgot how to walk, placed me on the stage, then chained me right beside the guillotine. The war drum got louder; I could taste my own blood. This was turning bad fast.

"Leonardo, you have to calm down," Laura whispered. "Believe me or not, these are just procedures. But if you don't calm down, you are likely to pass out."

A hologram started to form then, and there was another woman with short hair. The woman spoke, and Laura translated: "Leonardo, you were considered a slave as of late. Because you were bought by our people and we do not have any use for slaves, you are going to be promoted to servant. It is because of your sister's excellent service to our people that you were even considered for this task. She once worked with us on a special project, and we have added this to our considerations before making our final decision regarding your fate. All council members will—"

Before she could finish the sentence, an explosion went off. In response to the explosion, the women drew their weapons and prepared for battle. Some had arrows, some swords, some even had guns, while others held objects I could only assume were some kind of stun rod. At first, it seemed unorganized, but upon looking closer, they were prepositioned for long and close-range fighting.

From where the explosion hit, out came another faction of warriors; the only giveaway was the way they were dressed. Maybe they were from a neighboring village. The first one to show his or her face was immediately killed. As for the rest, they didn't just run in, they enacted another plan. Some of the guard towers were taken down by planted explosives. Among the confusion, two guards and Laura were still by my side. The platform I stood on caved in, and all I heard was Laura yelling something in a different language. Then Laura yelled, "Get up, Leo!" I got up quickly, shaking my head. "Good to see you're still alive. We could definitely use your help." She stretched out her hand and helped me up.

When I got out of the hole, I noticed the two guardsmen were gone. Laura handed me a knife and rifle. I guessed these were her weapons. I put the knife on the ground next to me and held the rifle in my hands; Laura stood by my side. I had never taken a life, so I was not ready for the situation. The closest I had ever gotten to shooting any gun or using a bow was in video games. The only thing I could contribute was aiming and wishing I hit my target. *What do I do with this rifle*, I thought to myself. I saw one of the invaders attacking an unarmed villager who must have been unfamiliar with combat. I fired a shot; as the bullet left the chamber, it felt as though the rifle would break my arm off. Later, it was explained I was holding the weapon wrong. This did at least wound the enemy and force him or her to the ground. I made up my mind to assist only those who couldn't defend themselves, not because it was noble but because those who could were doing a great job at it, to the point it would be borderline friendly fire, not to mention, I didn't have many bullets.

The enemy continued to push for what I assumed was ten minutes, but the villagers did not give up their ground. I heard Laura yell. I heard the sounds of a horse running toward me. When I turned around, there was an enemy soldier upon the horse, sitting with a bayonet on the rifle in his hand. I turned to shoot, missed, and rolled out of the way. As I did so, I heard gunfire and watched as the horse dropped. The rider got back up, fired one shot, and began to rush toward me. I guessed he'd ran out of bullets. I fired again but could not stop him. As he approached, his gun was shot out of his hands. Though he was without his primary weapon, he continued to advance, pulling out a knife. Firing again, this time aiming for his leg, I realized I shattered his kneecap when he fell. I swung my rifle around my body because he was too close for me to feel comfortable using a long-range weapon in close quarters. I picked up the knife on the ground, preparing for hand-to-hand combat. When he approached, he missed me due to his lack of balance. I used my knife and stabbed him in his hamstring, then punched him in his face, knocking him out. After that, I lay on the ground to catch my breath, looking at the clouds above.

"This is a very stressful day," I said to myself. I saw Laura approach me and noticed the fighting had stopped, or maybe I was going deaf from the excitement. "What is going on?" I asked her.

Laura responded, "You did well for this being your first time." My attacker moaned. "You did so without killing him? This will not go well with these villagers."

"What do you mean?" I asked, trying to catch my breath.

"I mean this may be used against you. It could be seen as you conspiring with the enemy in order to attack us. You will not go unpunished unless the Webmaster can step in before these people do anything rash. I'd kill him before that happens if I were you. Since the enemy stopped, that means this is their leader."

"I can't do that; it goes against everything that I believe in."

"Then do you want me to do it for you?"

"No, taking a life is always going to be wrong. Besides, he is defenseless as he is right now. If I were to kill, it would only be in self-defense. I'd rather face the punishment then take a life without reason."

"Darn it, Leonardo." Laura walked away. Some of the Webmaster's warriors walked up, forcing me off of the ground. I looked around and saw the enemy had completely surrendered. They were escorted around the camp. The Webmaster's warriors dragged me in front of the people. I looked around and saw Laura being pushed to the front of the crowd, then in front of me. The ladies began to talk to Laura, their voices slowly getting louder. This continued for a little while until they stopped.

Laura said, "I told you these villagers would do this. If you would have listened, you would be something like a hero." They yelled at her, and she yelled back, "Because I am one of the few who speaks multiple languages, they are not going to let me leave until you can leave. You will be dealt with before you are delivered back into the hands of the Webmaster. Since you work for the Webmaster and Anita, you will not be put to death; however, this crime must be dealt with by the village customs. This is the purpose for the thing on your arm. If everything works right, no matter how bad it may seem, you will survive. The pain has always been described differently from person to person."

A young lady walked up to me with two chains, which she placed on my feet.

I asked, "What is with the chains?"

"Those are there to keep you from falling off the platform." Laura walked over to me, and I got a good look at her eyes. They were sky blue and nearly tearing up.

"Oh, crap!" I whispered, for I now realized she might not have been exaggerating this whole time. I realized that there was no way the gauntlet would come off. I looked for a safety switch that might have been placed on the gauntlet.

The young woman yelled, and Laura translated: "I will teach you what we do to those who work with our enemy. If you are a religious man, you'd better pray for mercy." I frantically continued looking for a button. Growing more desperate, I was going to bang it against the ground, but I remembered Laura said someone had died from it malfunctioning.

Laura said, "Three, two, one."

Once they got to one, the gauntlet turned on, and I felt my body lock up. I lost focus as the gauntlet took full effect. A numb feeling covered my body, starting from my wrist and spreading until it covered my whole body. All at one time, a series of pain surged through my body.

The pain was like nothing I had ever felt and would never forget. It was as though someone was giving me a billion small cuts, beating me with a spiked weapon, electrocuting me in twenty different places at once, all while stabbing me with thick needles, stepping on my body with cleats, covering me with fire ants, and beating me with a sledgehammer—this was just a small fraction of my pain. The pain grew more intense and didn't stop until I finally passed out. I think my heart may have stopped.

When I woke up, my vision didn't come back to me for a second. I saw a pool of my own saliva trailing to the ground. Finally, my vision restored slightly, and as I twitched my fingers, the gauntlet started up again. That forced me to pass out once again.

I woke up the second time and cried out, "No more... No more, please, just kill me, the prisoner, or both of us. Yeah, that'll work too; just stop this for the love of God! Please, no more; anything but the gauntlet again." I felt my heart beating.

Laura grabbed my shoulders. "It's over, Leo, so calm down before you hurt yourself."

I began to understand what predicament I was in. The room came into focus, and I realized I was in the Webmaster's courts, the giant library. I looked around and saw Anita standing in front of us.

"Leonardo, Laura has informed us of your situation. I am sorry that you were put in such a predicament. Sometimes the villagers lack common courtesy or sense. Nonetheless, that will be dealt with at a different time. We are glad you held true to yourself out there. I am also glad the enemy was brought before us to be properly interrogated. Sometimes I swear those people have no common sense."

I asked, "So why did they keep him alive if they were going to torture me for keeping him alive?"

Anita's response: "It was a custom rule. If one is willing to get punished, which was you, for another, that person being the leader, then that person must have some kind of value, no matter who it is. It is a very old rule, but it's still respected through the ages. I must leave for now because we are in possession of their leader, and the invaders are not allowed to be executed. I must now go give the prisoners an ultimatum." She walked away.

The Webmaster got up and walked to a bookshelf to replace a book. "Well, it seems you have met the villagers and have had a very eventful day. I must congratulate you on doing a wonderful job."

"What do you mean? I have done nothing at all," I asked humbly.

"Not true. You see, you unintentionally stopped a war between our faction and another faction. You have proven to be trustworthy and kindhearted to your enemies. You have a great reputation, and you have captured a traitor who will be returned to his leader and punished accordingly for making war. This will allow us to maintain peace with them, at least until our plans are complete or they decide to join us later down the road. Laura, please give him that item."

"Yes, Webmaster," Laura replied. "Mr. Trotter has given you this as reparation on behalf of the village. He said, 'I hope this will allow you to forgive us for the lack of manners.' It was a basket filled with fruits; the fruits were surprisingly tasty. If you continue doing good work, he said he will have another gift for you another day."

The Webmaster continued "Your duties and training will start tomorrow, so enjoy the rest of your day and have a good night."

Later that evening, Laura told me the reason she tried to leave was because she was trying to report the situation to the Webmaster. As for why there were no men, that was simple: apparently, couples needed some time apart from one another, and one week a year, the men and boys as young as three years old were forced to leave. Because I was new during this time, this did not apply to me. However, the following year, I was to help Mr. Trotter with whatever task he needed, such as making deliveries and cleaning. On our free time, we would reminisce about my old town, Barstow. I assumed it might have been a very long time since he had actually lived there at some point, so he wanted to know how it had changed, if at all.

# 2
## Nobody Left Behind... Until Now!

**F**our years had passed since I started working for the Webmaster and her council. At times, I would pay attention to their tactics, with the help of Laura's translations. To me, it seemed as though most, if not all, the predictions would come true, and it was amazing. From attacks and counterattacks to things like drought and weather conditions, things were just as they predicted. As for my job, progression wasn't too bad; I had to go and speak as a representative. I was never sent alone because of my lack of language skills; Laura would come with me to translate and make sure I didn't screw anything up. At the time, I didn't understand the reason for this other than the language barrier. Thinking on it now, I would have to say the job was preparing me for what was going to happen next.

The Webmaster once told me the only way for me to ever feel a little bit of freedom and acceptance from the people was to start proving my worth. It was difficult because I lacked knowledge about what was happening on the island during that time. From what I understood, generators placed in twelve different locations on the edge of the island cloaked it. This is what hid the island from the satellites and planes that flew overhead. As for the ships at sea, the generator sent out some kind of pulse to prevent anything from getting too close without permission from the inhabitants.

I think it was like a sound emitter or something, but I didn't know enough to make an educated guess about something like that.

Since I wasn't going to school, the Webmaster thought that nothing should hinder me from getting a proper education. I had proved myself competent with some of the tests she had for me, and based on my age, she estimated I was old enough to be in college.

One day, the Webmaster told me, "You should feel lucky because slaves wouldn't be allowed a proper education; that is why you were never given the title of slave but rather servant, and I will not allow you to be willingly uneducated. We have enough uneducated people in the world. Talking to them is like walking on nails... Now, don't think if you were uneducated we would let you remain that way, but we would be more tolerant of your ignorance."

I knew inside her meeting room were shelves upon shelves of books, but upon looking closer, I realized most were written in different languages. I am sure the books didn't all belong to her, but it was still pretty impressive. If someone were to look closely, as I had time to do, they would see most were novels, some manuscripts, and some educational. The Webmaster gave me a set of books to read. The books she had me read were all at a college level or higher. If I finished reading early, she sent me on errands.

During those four years, I learned a few things about the Webmaster and Anita. First, the Webmaster: her job was aiding in village expansion, forecasting battle situations, and preparing accommodations, but I knew there was more; however, these and the other things I have mentioned were all I understood. The Webmaster had three daughters. There was Tyra, the oldest, whom I'd personally never met, but I heard that she took care of all the business stateside. That way, they were not blind or deaf to the rest of the world's events. Tonya, the middle child, lived in the village. Her job was sur-veillance; she had her own team of scouts that knew the location of all the factions around the island, even if they moved underground. Then there was Tanisha, the youngest of the sisters. Her job...well, she was in training. I wasn't sure what she was training to be, and I never really asked, for every time we talked, we argued about something.

Anita did some of the things the Webmaster couldn't due to time constraints, but Anita's job was also very different altogether. She was a negotiator who tried to settle differences as humanely as possible. There was not one situation that wasn't resolved. I sat in on one negotiation involving domestic abuse. Anita was sent in, and I was told to follow. When the man wouldn't listen to what was being explained, he pulled a knife on Anita. She broke his arm and managed not to get cut. As for the man, he was banished and left for dead. She was calm during the whole thing and treated it like an everyday situation. This was one of the very few bad situations, and I might have done the same thing in her shoes. As for the other two assistants, they moved around too much for me to learn anything about them.

Looking back at it now, the Webmaster and Anita were overworked and underappreciated.

Over those four years, I learned that Laura was raised in the care of the Webmaster, and she had a brother seven years older than me whom I hadn't yet met. From what I gathered, her brother had left a year and a half before I showed up to make a living as a mercenary for the island inhabitants. I was told she still kept in contact with her brother, but I wasn't sure how. Mr. Trotter warned me not to take any of the women there lightly if I planned to live a fairly long life. I knew this to be true about all the women, but I didn't get that vibe from Laura. She just seemed harmless. So, I asked her about her past. She told me that as kids, she and her brother were only taught to kill to stay alive. She was born here on this island, unlike her brother. Her mother died from an ambush, her father from revenge. Before he died, he told her brother to run away and take her to the Webmaster. When they arrived, the Webmaster trained them to speak at least two different languages, but because Laura's brother was older, he continued to be one of the defenders, until he eventually left to be a mercenary. From what Anita told me, Laura would sneak out to tag along with him from time to time. When she tagged along, it was usually because she was stressed out or hadn't seen her brother in a while, so the ladies didn't scold her too much. This did explain why she would disappear for days at a time.

The day finally arrived when I was given a longer distance to travel for an objective. I was told this would be my first real assignment. Sadly, this day will never be forgotten. Even with my dying breath, I will remember everything that happened that day. For one, the breeze was exceptionally nice. It started when I was called to meet in the Webmaster's grand hall. When I arrived, Laura removed the torture gauntlet. They must have realized there was no reason to have me wear it anymore; they'd only had to use it those two times. Heck, even once was good enough for me to realize where they stood and how to behave. After she removed the torture bracelet, whose creator was probably a complete psychopath, Mr. Trotter gave me a new gauntlet, but this time, it looked more like a gauntlet wristband made of metal. Metal then expanded around my body and took the shape of armor when it was complete.

"So, what is going on?" I asked.

Mr. Trotter replied, "Well, I did promise to give you a gift if you kept up the good work, I am sure you remember. Well it is this new gauntlet."

Laura continued, "As for the first woman you saved, she and her family wished for me to thank you, she wanted to be here herself, but she has just given birth. She named her daughter Leona in appreciation of you."

"Well, that is sweet," I replied. Then I realized I had no idea how to take off the armor. "Hey, by the way..." As I was about to ask how to take off the armor, it went back into the gauntlet. "Umm...never mind."

As my armor was removed, the Webmaster said, "Leonardo, I am sending you to a military outpost toward the center of the island. This will be your first official mission, meaning we will not be giving you things to say. You will be doing it all on your own. When you arrive, you will see a woman guarding the outpost. Her name is Caroline. She will be wearing a pearl-like necklace, a pair of sunglasses in her right breast pocket, and a knife in her right leg pocket that is very hard to miss. If you still can't find her, then you will also notice she is the only one in black. Laura will accompany you on this little quest, but she will not help you negotiate or interact with the locals unless it proves too difficult. When you get there, she will tell you what to do next."

"May I ask why is Laura coming along if I cannot use her to talk to the people? Couldn't this be extremely dangerous? This would logically be no place for a translator." I was concerned for Laura's safety, nothing else. Thinking about it now, it wasn't how it came out.

The Webmaster spoke, "Because she wanted to spectate and see how you do on your own. Laura defeated you in those sparring matches every time you two fought. Besides, the other reason is simply because in the past four years, you have only learned one thing in our language, 'I have to use the restroom.' Everything else she has had to say for you."

That was true because every day, their language would change, and it became really hard to keep up with anything. I assumed it was just an X chromosome thing. I say this only with the facts, for when the men returned at the end of the day, the primary language was always the same, but it was one I never learned because I heard so little of it.

"That's not really my fault because men and women naturally speak two different languages. If someone says that is a really nice blouse, a girl will say, 'Ah, thank you,' while a guy will try to figure out what a blouse is and whether it's edible. Then when someone tells him what it is, he'll say, 'Why don't they just call it a shirt?'" Yes, I understood this wasn't a good or valid point, but I decided to try to go with it.

The Webmaster continued, "That is why I am sending her. On top of everything else, she is more of a people person. She will be your comrade. Be sure you don't leave her behind, for if she finds you did, I will not be responsible for what she will do. So, remember to protect your translator, and you'll go far. Please remember, if this were to ever turn into a military-type operation, you always need the translator because you don't speak the native language."

Laura walked up to the Webmaster, who handed her a letter. I was expecting her to hand me the letter. It was after Laura received the letter that I began to worry. Maybe it was a kill order, like what King David did to that one guy in the Bible. When we left, the sun was beginning to set. Nobody left at night, not even the birds or bats, for that matter. As we walked out of the city, it was as if the ground was shaking.

On our way out, Anita gave us two cases that had our names on them. We headed down the mountain. With the mixture of the full moon, flashlights, and a few naturally-lit water spots on the ground, it was surprisingly easy to see. As we walked, Laura and I said nothing. The reason I didn't speak was because I really didn't want to say anything stupid. I mean, she was beautiful, and this was the first time we were alone. Usually, there was at the very least a sniper. I couldn't think of anything that wasn't at its core flirty, and the beautiful scenery didn't help. The bright moon's rays reflected off the ground, the dew glittered, and the flowers bloomed.

"So, Laura, do you know what Anita gave us as we left?" I asked. Then I realized it had slipped out and retraced my steps to figure out what I had asked. I guess I was trying to break the silence; it was a little overbearing.

"Hmm...based from the weight of my case, I would say a custom sniper rifle with an SAATO scope, a silencer, about four extra clips of ammo, and Anita's mother's homemade tomato soup for good luck." Laura explained to me later SAATO was short for smart auto-adjusting thermal optic scope. There was a reader inside that adjusted to your eye's target; if it detected even the slightest strain, it adjusted accordingly. As the name declared, it had thermal optic abilities but lacked night vision. Laura used this rifle to go hunting.

"All that from just feeling the weight?" I asked. "Now I kind of want to be surprised, but I also want to know. I guess we can wait until we get there to find out." We walked across a flat plain field. This was the first time I had ever been this far from the BCC base campsite, so I wasn't too sure what to do. As I progressed, a thick mist seemed to cover the ground, making it very hard to see. I also remember it being very easy to lose my footing; it was as though my legs were vibrating. When this stopped, my legs gave out. But Laura paid me no mind and instead laughed a little. "So, is this normal?"

"What are you talking about?" Laura turned around. "Are you afraid or something?" There was no way she didn't feel the ground shaking. I suppose it was just one of those things that was better I didn't know or would take too long to explain. Heck, she could have just had a rough day.

"What, no. My legs are just a little weak.

"Well, that is too bad. I guess we can rest here until you can gather your strength." Laura sat down on the ground behind me. She placed her back against mine so we both had back support.

"So, why are they forcing you to tag along? I am sure you have better things to do."

"You are correct, but I would have followed you here even if they hadn't told me to. If you really must know, since the day we met, I knew there would be a fork in the road along my life's journey sooner or later. I could either go with you and see what was on your side of the fork or remain where I have been since I can remember. Besides, if I didn't leave with you, it would only be a matter of time before I joined my brother with his work. At this time, it seems as though you need more help than he does."

I sensed that wasn't all she wanted to say, but it was enough to get her point across. Besides, asking for any more information would be prying into her life.

"Why didn't you want me to come along? We both know I am more than capable of defending myself," she said.

I thought about it, and what she said was true; there was no denying the facts. I replied, "If I had to give a reason, I would say, truthfully, I don't want to ever see you go berserk."

"Now you are just being stupid." Laura stood up, and then forcefully got me up as well. "I believe your legs should be up to the task of continuing."

As I stood, I realized Laura was right. So, we continued to travel. After about five minutes, the wind picked up and the fog cleared. We walked only about fourteen miles before we came upon the military base.

"All right, we are here. We will stay at a distance and approach in the morning," Laura said.

"I am guessing it is because if we approach now, we will look like invaders," I stated. "So, how will we go about setting up camp?"

"I do not recommend using any kind of campfire, for we might end up causing unnecessary conflict. I think it will be OK if we go one night without a fire source. Besides, it isn't that cold, right?"

I felt good; the slight breeze wasn't half-bad, so I replied, "Makes sense to me."

"So, we should be fine, and the animals won't attack us. They normally don't bother humans here." It was almost like taking a nice stroll in the park. When the time came for us to finally sleep, we kept a respectable distance from each other.

When I woke up, Laura was already sitting up and eating the tomato soup. "So, how was your nap?" Laura asked.

"Nap, are you telling me I didn't sleep long?" I replied, getting up.

"I'd say you were asleep for only three hours," she said. "Since the sun rose, I would say there has been lots of movement in and out of the base. I am guessing there must be something going on. I have seen some troop movement and five loads of supplies."

"Are you saying they are moving to a new location?"

"No, what I am saying is they must be supplying their front lines or supporting another base elsewhere. In addition, I haven't seen this Caroline lady anywhere, so we can assume she is still inside. And your food is sitting right next to you, in case you are hungry."

I ate; if I remember correctly, it was eggs and rice. After eating, we headed down to base.

The guards outside the base were waiting for us with their weapons drawn. "Freeze. Drop your weapons and anything else you've brought with you." I felt uneasy, not only because of the loaded guns pointed at us, but also because there were two tanks pointing their cannons at us. I also remember a single helicopter circling overhead. It was as though they wanted us to move.

"So, we are definitely in the right place," I said, trying to ease the tension.

The other guard yelled something in a different language. I think it was French.

Immediately, Laura began to speak. "She wants to know what we're doing here."

"Tell her we were sent here on official business to talk to a woman named Caroline."

Laura yelled back to the lady. Two of the three helicopters began to survey the immediate area around the base. The French-speaking woman yelled back. Then Laura translated in English: "I will go and retrieve Caroline. As far as I know, Caroline is not expecting you, so please wait there and I will get her for you. While you wait, please don't make any sudden movements. We've had past experiences where someone tried and was blown to chunky pieces."

Laura gently fell to the ground. "So, tell me again about your brother."

"What, that is completely random," I replied, looking at Laura.

"Not really as random as you would think. This might take a while, and this way, we have something to do to kill the extra time."

I knew she was right. "What did you want to know about him?"

"Well, you said that he died, but you never said how."

"I am sure we discussed this at least once."

"You must have been talking to the Webmaster. I would remember a story like that."

"I was in the fifth grade going to sixth, for the summer was about to begin. My mom was at work, like she always was, to provide for the four of us. My dad...well, he was returning home after being gone a while. Not too sure where he went, maybe a train ride, maybe a tour of France, at that moment, I didn't care. As long as I knew he was still alive, I was fine.

So there at the house were my two sisters. My oldest sister, Cheryl, was babysitting us. Kat, she was doing some project or another. Then there was my brother Melvin, the youngest, and myself, which you have already met." I sat down. "I wasn't sure what triggered it, but Cheryl was talking to him about something. Then he just started getting louder, so I went to see what was going on and make sure everything was OK. He was known to be a bit of a handful when you paid too much attention to him—he loved receiving attention; it didn't matter whether it was good or bad. When I followed his voice, it led me to my parent's room. From my understanding, he'd grabbed a pair of scissors and trapped himself in the closet. He was yelling things like nobody loved him...he would be better off dead...stupid things like that. I remember the more he talked, the angrier I got because I did care; I did love my brother, even though he would act like a selfish brat from time to time. I tried to talk to him. My sister called one of the local church members to help us because we were not strong enough to open the door and didn't have enough experience for that situation. After the call was made, I remember hearing his voice getting softer. I thought it was because he was calming down; however, after a while, there was nothing but silence. When they arrived, they opened the door, and we were too late. My brother had already taken his own life. He used the scissors to stab himself in the wrist several times before dying from the loss of blood. I have run that scenario over a thousand times, trying to figure out what I would do differently, but I had no answer considering how I was. I still have nightmares about that day. It took a few years before I could go back to being somewhat normal." I paused one moment. "I did tell you this story because I remember your blue eyes tearing up and you saying that if your brother ever did anything like this, you would bring him back to life to beat him to death for giving up on life."

"Yeah, I remember. I thought I could take the story without being sad this time, but I guess I was wrong." She then tried to change the subject by pointing to the sky, saying, "Hey, doesn't that cloud kind of look like a lion?"

I slowly stretched out on the ground. I was more than willing to help change the topic. "So, where do you see this lion cloud?" I asked.

She pointed, and then I saw it too. We observed the clouds until I eventually fell back asleep.

An hour had passed before Caroline finally woke us up, walking toward us with twelve other soldiers. They followed her with their guns drawn; four pointed their guns at us, and the others aimed in different directions. I sat up and began to stretch.

Caroline spoke in French. As Laura began to translate, Caroline said in English, "Oh, Michael told me you speak French. I will have to talk to her later about this. Michael said you had business with me. I would have been here sooner, but I had a meeting concerning the base's budget and distribution." She stood next to me. "Who are you and what did you need from me?"

"My name is Leonardo, and the woman with me is Laura," I replied, getting off the ground. "We were sent here by the Webmaster—"

She interrupted me with a confused look on her face and said, "Until now, I thought the famous Webmaster was a myth. If the rumors are true, then she must have sent you down here for some kind of mission. Please correct me if I am wrong." She paused for a second. "Hold on, I just came from the mission brief, and, well, I hate to be the one to give the news, but I have to inform you there isn't anything like what you were sent here to do. We are supplying a sister base, but other than that, there is nothing going on. However, we are a little short-staffed. I'd like for you to join us, especially as people who worked under the Webmaster. We'd be more than willing to accept you. Well, to be more exact, you won't be working with me; instead, you'll be working with Captain Boo." The captain's full name was Susan Angela Boo. "I know you have a lot to consider, so take your time. We will be here if you choose to take me up on my offer. The Webmaster has a very keen eye for great potential, from what I've heard. Rumor has it she once sent a mercenary to work down here, and every time someone hired him, they never lost their battles. I have learned that through every fable, there are still facts to be had, so I am willing to see what you are made of."

"What do you mean? If I work for the Webmaster, then I already have a job." I asked, confused.

"Look, I heard all the rumors about this island, including one where they have sent scouts to look for her village. According to said rumors, the place you came from is completely gone by now. If you want to see for yourself, grab one of our jeeps and go. I can assure you, the whole village has up and gone."

"Is this true, Laura?" I asked.

Laura sighed, and from her blue eyes, I knew it was gone. "Yes, what she speaks is true. If you were to turn back now, everything and everyone will no longer be there. There will be no signs of life." *So now where was I going to go?* Laura continued, "The Webmaster told me to give you this letter, and it should explain everything."

I looked at the letter. It read:

*Dear Leonardo,*

If you are reading this, you must have just found out about your current situation. We regret to inform you we could no longer let you stay here with us. It seems some of the council members took offense in us keeping you a year longer than normal. We tried to plead before our council, but it

fell on deaf ears. It seems that since Mrs. Ramona stepped down last year, someone thought it would be a good idea to start something more extreme. However, due to Mr. Trotter, we were able to set you free rather than the alternative. You could consider that payment for your service over the last four years. There is one last thing I want to tell you: please take good care of Laura and continue being a "good egg." We hope you make it back home.
*Godspeed,*
*The Webmaster and Anita*

Their council was made up of thirteen when everybody was there: the Webmaster, Anita, Julian, Jen, and eight others. Mr. Trotter advised the council to provide an outsider's perspective, as he was raised in the United States and part of Canada for a while. He wasn't technically on the council, but his opinion was as valuable as three of theirs, so they would listen.

"I hope the letter was a better explanation than anything I could have given."

"Yes and no. Why didn't anyone tell me about this until now?"

"It was the quickest and most effective way to have you leave without unnecessary attention. I was restricted from telling you. Because of a new policy, we were told if you were still there by sunrise, you would be executed for knowing too much. Because you worked with the Webmaster for so long, you had access to locations normal people wouldn't, so logically, some of the villagers see you as a threat." I could see where the people were coming from. In Laura's case, she was raised there pretty young, and the village had learned to trust her. But I had only worked there, and as such, was more likely to betray the village, though I wouldn't turn on my friends or allies unless I had a proper reason.

At that moment, sarcasm got the best of me. I remember thinking to myself, *Could this be the reason she called me a good egg, because she was planning to kick me out of the nest like a bird and expect me to fly?* Of course, if they wanted to, they could have done this much sooner. Honestly, it wasn't like she left me up a creek without a paddle. She gave me everything I needed to survive, so now was the time to make good use of it. But I still wondered, why Laura? If she traveled with me, she was an unpaid, overqualified, full-time babysitter.

Laura asked me, "So what is your next plan of action? You don't have to go to this base if you don't wish to. But this will be the first real decision you make, and it could very well affect the way everything plays out in your life. Know that you are the one who must make the final decision, and I will follow your lead. The Webmaster wanted you to spread your wings out on this blind spot of the world, at least until you can go home."

"What will you do, indeed? I would like to know whether to invite you into the base or not." Caroline asked.

Choosing wasn't really all that difficult because I trusted the Webmaster and Anita's decision on this. I had to consider this my place of residence until I was finally able to go home. I finally spoke aloud. "We'll stay until we feel we are no longer needed here." Caroline's guards lowered their rifles to their sides and walked around us, engulfing us in a circle as they escorted us into the base. "So, may I ask why you have so much security?"

"Yes, that is a good question," Caroline said. "Last week, we had an individual surrender to us. We dispatched a small group to collect the soldier, but as they approached, our troopers were ambushed. Long story short, they didn't return. The next day, the ambushers attempted to sneak into the base disguised as our soldiers. They nearly succeeded, but they were wearing the clothes and nametags of our missing comrades. Luckily, the guards were paying attention, and the second attack was stopped at the gate. We were fortunate they weren't expecting their first plan to work, so they were not truly prepared for the second. However, even with their low numbers, they could do a significant amount of damage, for the base was undermanned until two days ago."

She escorted us through the base, giving a brief tutorial of where everything was. As we talked to her, she showed us our rooms and explained that we would follow Sue's orders and under her direct command while we remained. She gave us the remainder of the day to rest. That night, I wondered what I would do next, where I would go, and whether this was what I really wanted to do.

Morning came, and there was an older lady in my room with a southwestern accent. As I looked at her face, I had noticed she was in her late forties. Her hair was barely turning gray, and she reeked of cigars.

"Good, you're awake," she said. "Today, we are going to test your ability to think on your feet and know if you are worth my time."

"Test my what?" I replied, not sure what that meant. All I knew was it wasn't good because it usually never was.

"Meet me at the shooting range. I trust you remember where to find it. The both of you will be fighting me and whoever else I select to fight with me. I just hope you survive; the last ones who challenged me proved to be a waste of time and died within two minutes." She left the room, and as she did so, Laura got out of bed and opened the package she had received from Anita. Laura smiled, pulling out the rifle. I proceeded to open my case. Inside were two pistols, everything custom made, from the handles to the barrels. I went to pick one up, and it weighed about seven pounds. Each magazine was filled with bullets. Underneath was a change of clothes. There were also packed meals reminiscent of MREs, but they tasted tons better. Laura walked out the door. After she left, I grew nervous, second-guessing myself, all this while changing my clothes. I later realized that if it were my time, there wouldn't be anything I could do about it.

When I finished and exited the tent, I noticed Laura waiting outside. As we left, my heart beat even faster, to the point I felt lightheaded; this reminded me of the time my stupid brother broke our car windows by throwing rocks, and I got into trouble too because I was supposed to stay in the car. I just knew my mother was going to kill me. It was the same feeling. "Oh my God!" I whispered.

As we approached the shooting range, upon closer observation, I noticed once you got inside the range, it was big enough to be an arena. I suspected it was because it was built into a subbasement. The reason for this was likely so they didn't draw too much attention from their enemies. There was a man waiting for us to enter. He stopped us and told us to give him one bullet from each one of the guns we would use. We did, and just from seeing the shapes, he gave us ten special bullets and preloaded them inside the magazine, saying, "While you are in there, you are not allowed to use any other types of ammunition, so if you run out, you run out; you must make do with what you have." After which, he proceeded to let us in.

The arena was like an open plain. As we entered through the doors, the man at the entrance exited another door, giving us no way to escape or turn back. From where we were, we saw Sue and some young man with a sniper rifle laid across his arms. I wasn't sure how good he was going to be with the rifle, but if he was as good as Laura, then we are going to be at a big disadvantage, for there was a big gap between my skills and Sue's.

As we got closer, I saw Sue holding a pocket watch. She said, "Simple rules: you will have three minutes to find a spot and hide. If you are still alive after ten minutes or you somehow manage to defeat us, then I will allow you to work with me. If you fail, I want you to get the crap out of my base, do you understand?"

Not having anywhere else to go, I nodded my head and put my pistols in the holsters. "Anything else?" I asked.

"Yes, try not to die in the first minute. It downs the excitement of the hunt."

As soon as she finished, Laura and I turned and walked away. "So, Laura, do you have any ideas?"

"Until we know what we are dealing with, our only option is to split up. I am not sure about the sniper's skills, but if I see an opening, I will take it. I will be watching over you, so do not worry. For now, we are going to burn the clock."

"All right, Laura. I trust you," I replied. After finding a spot, I realized there was nowhere I could actually hide that they wouldn't know where I was. The ground began to change shape. I lost sight of Laura. With her gone, I was certain this was not going to fall in my favor. I panicked and decided to lie on the ground. What was once like sand was now hard as rocks. Snow fell gently; looking at the scenery was actually relaxing. I figured I might as well enjoy it before I died in a training accident. I remember thinking, *I wonder how Laura is going to be covering me if she can't see me.* According to the rules, we were only allowed to use the guns with the bullets they had provided. So, there was no way she could use explosives. Lying down on the ground to enjoy the view, I realized it was quiet. I didn't move and hardly breathed, trying not to attract any attention to myself. I felt as though this training was a waste of time.

Two minutes of absolute silence passed. And during those two minutes, I continued to think of my family back home. I could guess what they might be doing, well, except my dad. In my opinion, he was too stand-offish, so I really didn't know too much about him. Another two minutes went by, and there still wasn't anything going on, so finally, I got tired of waiting for death to find me. I slowly raised myself, quietly pulling out the guns at my waist. I walked around the ledges where the cliffs were to try and get an advantage. Even as I moved, I heard nothing going on, but I couldn't shake the feeling I was being watched; however, if they could see me, they would have just killed me. Right? The silence continued until someone spoke: "Leonardo, we have your woman. Come out if you want her to live."

I made my way to the top of the mountain, which was more than likely where they were. I knew I was going to have to do this covertly. If they saw me, I would be putting my life and hers in danger. Of course, my logic was justified; if they killed me, there was no guar-antee they wouldn't also kill her. So, I climbed up the mountain as fast as I could. When I got to the peak, I planned to keep out of sight and try to sneak up on them. However, I kept low. Sue's partner had already approached her. "Stand up slowly." I put my guns into their holsters. Placed my hands in the air. I knew I'd failed, so why didn't they just shoot me?

I walked toward them, thinking, *Maybe I should have stayed with her; that would have made more sense than splitting up, but then again, I didn't want to slow her down.* I tried to think of how we would get out of this alive, but everything I thought of failed.

As I walked toward Sue, Laura's body began to turn to dust. As I approached, Sue aimed her gun at me. "You lost to an illusion. Now it's time for you to die." She proceeded by shooting me; I closed my eyes and heard the gunfire. It was at this moment my body began to get lighter. I opened my eyes, thinking I had hit the ground, only to find Sue holding out her arm. "Hmm...

what was that?" Sue shot me again, but this time, I watched as she fired; the bullet hit something, bounced off of me, and shot her in the foot. Next, I heard a body drop behind me. So, I looked behind me to find her friend lying on the ground. I wasn't sure if he'd shot the invisible wall as well. Sue tried to limp away to find some cover. I heard a beeping go on around the arena; the mountains began to sink into the ground, shifting down into a grate in the dust. "It seems your ten minutes are up," Sue said.

I saw Laura walk toward me. "Did you really think they could capture me? You've seen firsthand in combat they would have had to kill me before I got captured. You should at least be able to trust me." She placed her hands on my shoulder. I noticed I was wearing armor, and she added, "And was that a tear I saw forming for me because you thought she had killed me?"

Honestly, I didn't even notice my eyes get watery, but if I had to give a reason why, she was right. It was because she was like my best everything. But because I didn't like the idea of looking or feeling weak, I lied and said, "No, the dust got in my eyes." I rubbed my eyes and accidentally got sand in my eyes, which was kind of poetic justice.

Laura walked over to Sue, helped her up, and walked with her toward the exit.

Sue then said, "You passed my test. Welcome to SUBWAY. Tomorrow, you will begin your training." Sue's assistant had gotten up and was holding onto his chest.

I asked, "So what kind of training room is this?"

Sue turned around. "It isn't a training room, it's actually our new gardening area for the vegetation. What we were testing was the climate control and adjustment area. That was the reason we did not allow you to use your own weapons inside."

# 3
## Umm...What Did You Say This Button Does?

**S**ix months had passed since Sue tested our skills. Within those six months, I met the rest of the people involved with SUBWAY. The young man who was with Sue on the initiation day was Daysen Michaels; he was, overall, what most called a lady's man. He was the nephew of Liz, the general and head operator of SUBWAY. She was almost never seen, but she was good enough at her job, no matter the situation. She worked at our sister base. Then there was Darnel, an elder gentleman who was an example of a man who never grew up. There was also Caroline, the one who brought me in, but she was relocated to the sister base. Then there was also Judith, who was Sue's best friend and second in command of our unit. Sue was in charge of our unit. Last but not least, there was our commander, Conner O'Neal.

During this time, I never met Conner O'Neal, but I did hear a lot of different things: how he was so cheap, and how he was always yelling at his subjects. The best example I could give of both was one day, there was a unit behind enemy lines that had requested supplies by air drop. Though he had the resources to deliver, he refused to do so because of the price of jet fuel. Instead, he sent in a small tactical unit to deliver the supplies by jeep. Before the resources were delivered, the unit was intercepted and beaten to death. About a week later, through all the odds, there was only one survivor. When she returned to base, she was chewed out and pinned for not having returning the unused supplies, possibly killing her whole squad in a fake ambush, and accused of conspiring with the enemy to take SUBWAY's operations. She was then sentenced to death by firing squad. A day after this trial, they dispatched a team to recover what really happened. It turned out they had never received the supplies; the only reason she could escape the ambush was because she had ambushed them out of desperation for food. She claimed it was her and another who remained to attack the enemy, but the woman was killed taking a bullet for her. According to what was recovered, all facts were proven true. When reported to Conner by Sue, she was yelled right out of the office, and, overall, the summary was the worst part; she was going to be used for a public spectacle. She was killed one week from that day. I watched as they killed her, knowing they had killed an innocent young woman. After the incident, Sue explained the situation to me, after which I began to understand Sue a little bit better, for it was her unit who did the investigation. To most of the others, Sue seemed very angry, but she wasn't. In truth, she was one of the sweetest people you could ever meet. When possible, she chose to expose injustice.

During our time spent there, Laura and I were officially accepted into the team. We were to learn under Sue Boo until she knew we could do everything ourselves, or until she could trust us. If you included us, Sue controlled a pretty small but powerful force.

One day, Sue came out telling Laura and me that we had a special and simple mission; we were going to have to play escort for a young prince named Rogan Otis Vasconcellos VI. This was before I had ever met the man, but he used to send people to the Webmaster's village to negotiate. Laura did know him, and she described him as a man of great importance in his province. Because of some circumstances, he was hidden away from his small village, but due to his father's sudden death, he would be promoted to chief. As for the mission, he wouldn't be the only one we were to escort. According to the mission briefing, we would be dropped off by helicopter to meet up with his group, and once we met up with them, we would walk the rest of the way to his village.

So, the night before the mission, Laura and I talked about my role for the mission. Because of the armor, I wouldn't move with everyone else. I would have to work more closely with Chief Vasconcellos to serve as a shield if something went wrong. Laura looked at the map and realized the path we would go along was completely exposed and could be easily ambushed. She told Sue, but Sue already knew and had prepared accordingly. Laura came back and told me Sue's plan was to use the main force as a decoy hiding as sheepdogs in sheep's clothing.

The chief, Laura, and I would take a completely different path from everyone else. Laura was used as a recon unit or sniper if need be. Because we would be in the field, Sue decided to give us code names. My code name was Cross, Laura's was Serenity, Daysen's was Mustang, and Sue's was just Captain, nothing fancy. Since Sue already had a plan, there was no real reason to ponder; after all, I didn't have a choice in what my objective would be, so I cleaned my pistols while I thought about everything that could go wrong. Laura looked for alternative routes and locations so she could keep full control of the area if a battle broke out.

The next day came, and Laura and I were already in the helicopter before the pilot himself showed up because Laura insisted we do so. I sat there waiting for the rest of the team and fell asleep after I strapped myself in my seat.

As I woke up and turned around, Sue was already talking to the group. She ended with, "So, does anyone have any questions?"

I didn't want to look like an idiot, so I replied "No, ma'am," just like everyone else.

"Good, I'd hate to repeat myself. Remember, Leo, you have the most important role, so don't screw this up. I do understand you're new to this, but that will be no excuse for failure." Sue then sat down and began to polish her machete.

I looked around and mumbled the word "Crap!" under my breath.

That was when Daysen handed me a piece of paper with Laura's signature on it. I retracted my helmet to read the note:

*You are to basically stay with the very important person (VIP) until we get to our destination. Caroline would have joined in on this mission, but there was an enemy attack west of our destination. Since they have the highest threat, a lot of our forces were sent with her, and that is why we have a skeleton crew for this mission. If anything goes wrong, it will automatically be your fault. I'll be covering you every step of the way.*

She walked to me and convinced Daysen to switch seats with her. "You have that puzzled look on your face. What other questions did you have?" Laura asked.

"So, did she explain why we are walking? I know these aircrafts, though cheap, could outrun many different missile and rocket types, so the odds of us getting shot out of the sky is pretty nonexistent."

"Though it is true it would be faster and more accurate to fly, our intel states Mr. Vasconcellos can't fly because he is traveling with too big of a group and would cost us more than if we were to take the safer route. And we all know Conner O'Neal wouldn't mind sacrificing his men just to save some money."

I leaned back and tapped my head against my headboard. "Cheap-wad. He'll be the death of our unit."

"I know," she replied as the ramp doors opened. "I guess we are here."

I looked out of the ramp and saw a beautiful meadow in the middle of the forest. "Well, this will be a nice view."

She put her visor on her head and her magazines in the rifle. I put my helmet back on. This was the first time I experienced leaving an aircraft with the engines running.

Sue stood on the edge of the ramp, yelling, "All right, guys, girls, and rejects, you better remember your roles or you're going to die by me if the enemies don't kill you first." She left the plane. Waiting outside of the ramp stood a small group of about thirty people. I stood up, began to walk out, and noticed they were all wearing casual clothing, like T-shirts and jeans. I walked over to Sue, and she was yelling on the radio to command. I sat down under a shady tree and watched as our ride took off.

"This is bull!" Sue yelled. She walked over to Daysen and Dave. "Our intel was wrong, and we could have fit all of these civilians on board with us, but the pilot couldn't wait because he had orders to go on an escort mission to bring in a high value target (HVT) to base, after which he will be at our extraction point to pick us up. I have Serenity searching the area to make sure our position is clear from any unexpected guests here. I will have to find the young ambassador, so stay where I can easily find you."

A man in his early thirties wearing a T-shirt, slacks, Gator shoes, and sunglasses, all white, walked behind her and said, "I think I am the man you're looking for."

Sue grabbed him by the throat, saying, "Who are you, and why shouldn't I kill you?"

"I am Rogan Otis Vasconcellos VI, known to you as Mr. Vasconcellos, the new chief. I am the one you are here to protect," he said, unbothered by the way he was being treated.

She let him go, leaving a slight bruise on his neck. She walked a few steps away to light a cigar and said, "So, Chief, where is the rest of your group? I was told we were traveling with more civilians, at least a hundred and fifty."

"I didn't travel with them here. I sent that message to your superiors at least two days ago. We have been waiting a while; since then, they made their way to the village." Him waiting wasn't surprising to us. Sue warned me about Conner being cheap. It was very likely he was holding out for more money or better trade.

"Sorry about our field team leader—she doesn't like to be surprised," Daysen replied and proceeded to ask, "Then who are these men?"

"These are my new followers," Chief Vasconcellos replied. "We are currently going to meet up with the rest of my villagers."

I got up and saw some of the chief's council members gathering the rest of the followers around us. I noticed someone who didn't look as though they belonged in the group. I was going to approach the person, but Sue stopped me.

"All right, the current plan is for you to travel with Vasconcellos using a more straightforward route to a destination," she said. "We will be traveling a totally different route with these followers. Your support is Serenity. She is going to be traveling out of sight from you."

We started to leave, going toward the forest. Laura said, "I got eyes on you, Cross. Don't worry, I will be watching you the whole time. There will be no way you could screw this up like the last mission." On the last mission, she had decided to use me as bait; that back-fired because there were more enemies than expected, and I had gotten overrun, but that is life.

"Thanks for the comfort, and I'd prefer to forget about that if I could," I said.

"So, you're the famous Leonardo. From the way Mr. Trotter and your sister talked about you, I thought you'd be bigger."

"How do you know my sister?" I asked, then I thought a little more. "Wait, why did you assume I would be big?"

"I heard you had a pretty big sweet tooth. And your sister Kathrine used to work for the Webmaster for a while. In some cases, she would actually come and visit the Webmaster. Because my village is allied to the Webmaster's, we eventually worked with your sister."

As we walked further into the forest, I noticed there was a man sitting down on a log. I pulled out my pistol.

"He's not here for me but rather to see you," Chief Vasconcellos said.

I looked at the man and noticed he was the same person hiding in the crowd earlier. The man seemed to wear fresh rags that covered his clothing. I looked at his face and saw he was looking at the ground. Putting my pistol away, I noticed he was drawing something on the ground.

The chief continued by adding, "A young man who uses the alias 'Lightning Bearer' has informed me you still need to learn how to use your ability, so I have asked one of my contacts to try to teach you a little something."

"Serenity mentioned something about rumors about these custom suits and hidden potential. So your Lightning Bearer is correct to assume this...By the way, do you know who he is?" I asked, following him.

"He is my contact who knows more about the situation than I do. I can tell you only one thing about his situation. He is contract-bound to whomever he makes a contract with, no matter what the contract is or how difficult it will be to complete. He also has no loyalty to any one faction."

"So, you're telling me he is like a mercenary?"

"Something like that, but money is not always going to work when hiring him. He is too much like a wild-card. He is quite impressive because he always completes the missions, no matter what the task is. The difference between now and how this normally happens is, this time, he came to me to get you here." Chief Vasconcellos spoke with great respect for the man.

"Sounds intimidating. Is that all the information you have on him?"

"Sadly, that is all I can tell you. This is all the information my people have on him—other than the simple fact that he wears black armor and could actually kill anyone without a problem. Enough chitchat about him for now; we need to focus on training you to better use your suit's abilities; nothing too advanced—just the basics and how to better use your abilities to your benefit."

Normally, I liked to challenge people's intelligence, but this was the one time I couldn't help but agree... especially if it would help me survive on this terrible waste of space of land. "I agree with you. So how are we going to do this?"

The black-armored warrior stood up. "Mr. Cayden, the fire user here will be the one to initially train you in this matter, and both of you will be escorting me through the forest while the rest of the group will be following the trail. If your sniper is as good as I remember, she will tell us if our people are in trouble. And you can move more freely to save them."

"Why are we staying in the shadows of the forest when we could stay with the group?" I asked.

The chief responded, "Good question, but too obvious. It is to avoid getting caught in crossfire in case of an enemy ambush. Your team doesn't know Cayden is here, and we don't need to cause people down there to believe you are an inexperienced rookie and don't really know how to use your abilities. This would cause more harm than good, don't you agree?"

Of course, the more I thought about it, the more it made sense. So I nodded my head.

"Good, so are you ready to train, Water Boy?" Cayden said. "I will teach you all the basics you need to know."

"Water Boy? What kind of stupid name is that? I hope you are not referring to me." I scoffed and threw my hands up.

"Let's go, and I will explain along the way." He walked away, and the chief followed.

"Go with them!" a stern voice said on the radio, as though my radio were slowly changing its frequency. We walked for five minutes until we reached an opening. Along the way, Cayden gave me a brief description of the suits we wore and how there were nine different types, two of which were just rumors. Now, to explain what the armor's metal is made of, I would have had to pay attention, but I didn't. Besides, I usually skip the tutorials in video games. Knowing the material is one thing; knowing how to use the material is something different.

In the opening, there was a small lake about a half-mile wide in the middle of the forest. The lake, I later found out, was called Lake Sapphire because of how blue the lake's colors showed with the sun reflecting off the water. It was pretty well known and one of the few places seen as a landmark. This was one of the places people went to make treaties, for it was an unwritten rule that no combat could be performed at Lake Sapphire. Well, at least that was what Laura told me after when we got back to base; she could have been exaggerating because that was the first I heard about it. This location was picked for me because my suit had a filter in it to keep it from contaminating the water. I saw Chief Vasconcellos turn to the side. Walking close to the lake, Cayden pulled out a shotgun and fired it a point-blank range into my chest. As he pulled the trigger, there was an explosion, but there was no blast. I thought I was dead and fell to the ground. After I realized there wasn't any damage, Cayden walked up to me, saying, "Are you done jerking around? You know I'd rather be doing something else right now?"

"What happened? How come I didn't die? Why was there an explosion?" I asked.

"Seems like I underestimated your defensive wall. It seems higher than others. Since I shot too close to you, it caused my shotgun's barrels to explode because the bullets and blast had nowhere else to go. Please note: if I wanted you dead, I wouldn't use bullets on you. I need something further so I can get a more accurate reading."

He held up his left hand with his index, middle, and pinky fingers in the air. I stood, trying to figure out what he was doing. Two ripples similar to water formed in front of me and wrapped completely around me. I heard a loud bang off in the distance. Something small appeared about two feet in front of me, almost as though it were launched through a vortex. At first, I assumed it was a very fast fly because they were the only creatures I knew that could move that fast. Then I noticed it was causing a ripple around me as well, but this one was more continuous. It looked as though it were caught in place. I got a closer look and noticed it wasn't flying but spinning. The ripples stopped, and the bug fell. I caught it only to find out it was a bullet.

"In its dormant state, your armor still does its job. As you see, the water caught most of the bullets. The parts that would have missed would have just bounced off you anyway and fallen to the ground. It should stand up to just about anything. This is very similar to what happened with the shotgun's barrels. First off, you need to know your armor is going to protect you from most things, and if it doesn't, it is also bulletproof to most bullet types."

"You could have just told me like a normal person."

"Yes, but where is the fun in that?" Cayden said.

Sue's voice came over the radio. "Serenity, what was that?"

Laura replied, "My weapon discharged. I think it overheated and fired on its own. I looked around and saw no casualties. I'll cool down the remaining bullets to prevent the same situation."

"All right, we don't need anyone knowing we are here, especially with the few people we have."

"I'm more of a show-n-tell kind of teacher," Cayden replied. The shards of the shotgun caught a blaze, melting into nothing. Cayden opened his hands, and a ball of fire ignited. "You see this ball of fire? This is a fraction of what my ability allows me to do." The ball of fire moved around him as though it was an electron and he was the nucleus of an atom. The ball sprouted wings, flapped beside him, and grew a beak all while keeping the atom's pattern around his body. It grew to half the size of his body, then flew straight up, launching like a firework, sound and all. When it exploded, the flames shaped a flaming tiger.

Sue contacted me on the radio. "Cross, was that you?"

"Yes, ma'am. The chief thought he could confuse some of the enemies if we launched a loud firework."

"What does he think he's doing? The point of the operation is to stay covert, not to tell the enemy where we are, not to provoke them, not to intimidate, just escort them from point A to point B. We could have made this easier if that stupid penny-pincher of a boss gave us a vehicle to use instead of having us walk up there."

"Yes, I know, and I'll tell the chief to stop using the fireworks. Serenity, can you go on ahead and see if the road is clear? We don't have an advantage in this area because the trees surround the path."

"Copy that, Cross. I am moving ahead."

Chief Vasconcellos laughed, "I see you were trying not to lie but not telling the full truth either, all while trying to talk to two different people, Sue Boo and me. I guess what I heard about you was actually true."

"Shall we continue?" Cayden asked. "You can do the same thing, but of course, the difference is yours is water-based. Now, to pull this off, you must do what I tell you to do. Mentally, I want you to focus on one thing and only one thing. Imagine a horse standing in front of you."

Luckily, I had a good imagination, so I could tell this part was going to be pretty easy.

"You need to see it as clear as day for this to work," Cayden said.

Water from the lake rushed in like a title wave. When it cleared, the one thing standing there was a transparent horse made completely out of water. I watched as it dissolved into the sand.

"Very good. Now you just need to learn how to focus to keep it the way you want it."

"Was that it?" I asked.

"No, there are three more things you must learn." He looked up and saw there was a small cloud overhead. "I want you to pull that cloud down, forming it into a ball."

I focused on the cloud like I did the lake. The ball formed and came closer toward me; as it did, I felt my hands locking up. I kept compressing it, and then my forearms locked up. I compressed it until it was a complete ball of water, then the rest of my arms locked up. I pulled it down toward us slowly until it was right over the lake, and lastly, this was when my chest locked.

"Now I am guessing by the fact that your arms are locked the way they are, you must have realized the suit's potential and that you shouldn't try to use it on anything but water itself. This does include if you were going to try to use your skill on ice; however, if you were to try it on ice, it wouldn't lock up as fast. If there is 70 percent or higher humidity, you can use the ability without worrying about it locking up."

"You need to learn to use your words," I stated.

"Yeah, and ruin the learning experience? No thanks. For your next lesson, I will just have to tell you first because I can't show you without getting hurt in the process, and second because I can't physically show you. I am sure you must have figured out the suit keeps you protected at all times. This is really true when it comes to anything fire; however, it's only true about lightning if the water around you is not directly attached to you and is strong enough not to let anything electric pass through it. If the lightning even slightly goes through and makes contact with you or your armor, you will feel twice the amount of pain any man would. For instance, if you were hit by two volts, you will feel four, thirty, sixty, and so on."

"So, what is the final thing you need to tell me?" I asked as I felt my armor began to slowly release.

"The last one you will learn in time. But for now, keep practicing. We'll meet again. I believe this concludes our business, Rogan." Cayden walked away from our group.

"It seems we have arrived at our destination." I looked around and saw people coming out of the ground. I pulled out my pistols.

The chief pushed my gun down, saying, "These are my men."

I put my weapons away, and they surrounded us, talking in another language. As they spoke, subtitles displayed on my visor—from their language to mine.

"Sir, what do you want to do about this intruder?" one of them asked.

"You will do nothing to my escort," Chief Vasconcellos said. "He's no threat to us. Besides, if I know our enemies, then our allies are currently in trouble."

"Cross, we need backup. Our forces are currently under attack by an unknown enemy," Laura said. "You can find them two and three-quarters of a mile north-west of your current position."

"You should go help your unit before they end up in more trouble," said the chief.

"I am going to go out on a limb and assume you're safe. Thank you for your help, and please tell Cayden I thank him as well."

Because of the distance, I had plenty of time to think along the way. I remembered a day when my brother and I were outside sparring in the front yard on a low brick wall; we used a metal rod and some sticks and tree branches. Now that I think about it, it wasn't the safest thing we ever did. The objective we had set before sparring was that whoever fell off first would be the loser...

*"Melvin, come on, you need to keep your defense up. What will you do if your opposition is attacking you and you leave yourself open?"*

*"It will never happen."*

*"You're not immortal, remember that, Melvin."*

*"There is more to fighting than having a great defense, Leo."*

*"True, but there is more than just attacking."*

That was a little before we were introduced to a video game of old famous strategists like Zhuge Liang and Sima Yi.

"Leo...Leo, are you there? Can you hear me?" Laura said on the radio.

"Yeah, I was remembering something. I'm good now. I am closing in on their position. Do we at least have a plan?"

"I have examined the scene, and we should arrive from the east to cover Daysen's position."

"You know, this kind of reminds me of the video games I used to play."

"Are you an idiot? There is a big difference: if you die, you die."

"I know, I know. Sometimes I forget this is our everyday life." I arrived at the clearing, taking out enemies along the way. I ran out into the clearing, and the first person I saw was Daysen aiming in my direction. "East clear."

"Cross, you're late," Daysen said. "Where is Serenity?"

"South clear," Laura reported on the radio. "Mustang, I need you to cover Captain's position."

Five minutes after I had arrived, the area was clear.

"Where are the followers?" I asked.

Sue looked at the ground because she heard groaning and moaning from some of the bodies. She shot one of the prone bodies. "The followers are safe because I told them to stay back until I gave the word. Why are there still survivors? Mercy will get you killed out here."

"Yes, but mercy is the only way I know how to live."

Clapping echoed in the area, and we all turned around. Quickly, we aimed our weapons at a young man dressed in all-white armor that looked similar to mine. "You have done well so far, SUBWAY Task Force, especially you, Cross. Or should I say Leonardo? You were just flawless in your execution of the plan and showed up with enough time to stop the ambush."

"Who are you, and how do you know who I am?" I asked.

He disappeared, and we heard Laura gasp behind us. When we turned, he was holding Laura in his arms. "First of all, I am not your enemy, so you can put your weapons down." He put her down. "Second. I was only sent here to give you words of warning. By now, you must realize you are not the only one with special armor. The other users will show themselves in time."

"I take it you are also one of the other armor users," I replied.

"There are at least six more of us, not including myself."

"Why wouldn't you include yourself?" I asked.

"I take it he is one of your friends," Sue stated.

"You have no idea." He took his helmet off.

"Tim, how did you get here?" I asked, surprised.

"I was lucky enough to receive the time armor from this timeline's current user, and I was asked to check on you in this time frame."

"Captain, go on ahead. I will catch up."

"Fine, but make it quick; we don't have all day," Sue said, giving everyone the signal to move out.

As everyone moved, I turned back to Tim and said, "You really must have the time armor because the last time we talked, I was older than you, and now you look older than me. Tim, could you tell me what's happening on the mainland?"

"Hmm...I am restricted from telling you too much about what is going on, but what I can tell you is the current year is 2011, and your family is doing well. Sadly, I am restricted from saying more than that. I was told I could only tell you the bare minimum. I apologize."

"So, what have you been up to? I haven't seen you in about four years."

"I am doing well. I joined the Army when I was seventeen. Luckily, I had this armor before I left. At first, the effects of time were very strange. I'd watch as time came to a complete stop. It was always random. I'd be shooting, and suddenly, things would stop. Sometimes I would see bullets stop in midair. If I approached the bullet or explosion, time would rewind, but if I moved away, time would continue. When I returned from my first tour, I had asked the one who gave it to me if there was something else I needed to know about it. He then informed me about the armor that came with it."

Laura stood off in the distance. I said, "I think she is waiting for me. Let's walk and talk."

"So, what have you been doing since you've been here?"

"Well, from what I understand, it has been four years, I have been a personal servant to several young ladies.

The Webmaster, who goes by no first name, Anita the viceroy, Julian the accountant, and Jen the...I forgot what she did, but it must have been important. I met Laura, who is the girl from earlier, while I was under their care." We continued catching up until we could hear the propellers from the helicopter.

"I don't want to keep you longer than I should. I hope we can meet in my timeline," Tim said, and then he disappeared into thin air.

I ran up to Laura and realized that I was not that far from our destination. We made our way to the escape point and noticed the helicopter was going for another pass. As we arrived, our ride was just landing. Once it was on the ground, I immediately got on board. While I waited, I began to form and play with the suit's abilities over water. While I did this, Laura was nowhere to be seen, Sue had to fill out some paperwork, and Daysen was communicating with the village ladies. I looked around and noticed a cage. Inside was a man chained to his seat with shackles. He was a young man with a goatee, his clothes were surprisingly clean, and I could tell that he surrendered without resisting. With as much restraining protocol as they had for him, I was surprised they hadn't gagged his mouth. I walked toward the cage and sat down.

"You must be the VIP," I said, looking at him.

"VIP," he replied, looking at the ground. "I don't think that title suits me. I am more of a prisoner of war (POW) if you can't tell by looking at me."

"Huh? I guess you are right. Well, I wish you the best of luck in whatever you must endure." Little did I know what would happen next.

According to reports, Caroline was the reason for the capture of the HVT. Afterward, she had only submitted the paperwork to the pilot, but was not retrieved with the POW. She instead turned in her resignation. Laura had gotten a hold of the form and read it to me later:

*I've had a taxing few years working for this organization known to the surrounding public as SUBWAY. To all those who may read this letter, let it be known this will be my last mission for that Crotchety old fart Conner. If any of you have the ability to leave, then, by all means, I recommend leaving as soon as you are able. Sincerely,*
*Captain Caroline*

Rumors traveled, and I heard she somehow got off the island. I just hope the rumors are true and that she was able to return to her home in Mackenbach, Germany. She had a daughter she hadn't seen since the daughter was seven years old.

Godspeed, Caroline, godspeed.

# 4
## Are You Friend...
## or Foe?

**F**ive months had passed since our last mission, and our missions were always the same. We were sent on basic training missions—I guess they wanted to familiarize us with their equipment or, at the very least, were expecting us to fail somewhere along the way. Our mission was usually surveying the area or providing support fire. There weren't any real threats.

As for the prisoner, he hadn't given us any important information. Over those five months, we learned that his name was Rayshawn, he was about twenty-seven years old, his favorite color was red, and he was the only male child in a family of five. He loved to flirt with any attractive woman as long as they were of age. As far as if he took life seriously, I wasn't too sure. Based on Caroline's report, it looked like he was spying on our base and was reported to be trespassing, so she captured him. He reported he was only looking for one of his sisters, who was last seen in our area. Since he was close to our base, I understood why we immediately fired upon him, forcing him to flee. We had no idea if he happened to be working for another group or not. No matter what we did, and no matter how much time passed, his story never changed. Sue was going to set him free. But Sergeant Dave Tappet refused to let him go, for according to him, Rayshawn was still withholding information.

Like Sergeant Tappet, I didn't believe what Rayshawn was telling us; however, my reasoning was more... direct. Why would someone share this much information about himself so willingly? Not only this, but his story was too crazy to be true and too specific to be made up. Maybe it was my problem with trusting new people. Heck, I thought Laura was going to poison my food the first few times we argued about our difference in opinion. Yeah, she was that kind of person, or at least she seemed to be. However, Laura completely trusted the POW. She was the one who managed to get his name and most of the other information gathered.

During that fifth month, we received information from a group known as Dark Siren, an organization with a grudge against ours. They requested to meet in an area of their choice and directed us to bring the prisoner in exchange for a rare item. We knew meeting them would give them an advantage if this were to turn into a battlefield. We had to plan accordingly so we could have at least an ace up our sleeves. Sue recommended we have one of the helicopters come to cover our tracks as we made our escape, just in case. Conner, of course, refused to approve the backup; something about inefficient costs and how wasteful this would be. Unfortunately, we had to do without any type of real backup. As we continued planning, I saw different scenarios where something could go wrong.

The day of the transfer finally arrived, and because Conner was too cheap to supply us with the means to survive, the only thing we could do was hope we weren't walking into a trap. We were permitted to use a helicopter to get to the area but not for any other reasons. Along the way, we would have to try to avoid any likely traps. On this mission, Laura and I were tasked with prepping the prisoner.

Before we put him in chains, Laura handed him a map and said, "So, you told me before that Dark Siren is not your ally. However, you have seen their camp before and know the basic layout." Rayshawn nodded. "Good. Then in your own opinion, where is the enemy most likely to hide?" I didn't understand then why Laura trusted him; maybe I never will completely understand her.

"Hmm, let's see..." Rayshawn said. "They would more than likely be hiding in the northwestern trees because those trees have the strongest fortification and could hold the most weight. Also, I would avoid the waterfall; it is just a deathtrap. Lastly, avoid being herded into traps; I saw some animals and even other people falling into the traps, and the end results can only be described as overkill. However, if you look carefully you will see the traps."

I watched as he identified all the possible targeted routes and traps he remembered. It was possible that she used some kind of mind game with him. For him to identify as many traps as he did and still be considered an enemy, I could only assume one thing—maybe he had Stockholm syndrome. After, I proceeded to cuff his hands and shackle his feet. From there, we escorted him to the briefing room, even though our orders were to wait at the chopper. I didn't want to disobey my orders, but no matter how much I refused, Laura just wasn't having it. She was so intent on taking him to the briefing room despite how stupid Dave would act, and I had no choice but to give in. By stupid, I mean Dave would try to turn people on her. I assumed it was because she was a better soldier than he was. Then again, she was better than most of the people there, and she proved it at the shooting range one time when she used a broken sight and compensated. After the third shot, she hit the mark every single time, and it was Dave who tried to sabotage her.

When we arrived in the room, it seemed like everyone was about to leave. Laura walked up to Sue, saying, "Sue,

I think we are about to run into an ambush. I have been talking to the prisoner, and he has confirmed what I assumed would happen. Look at the map and the placements of the traps along the route that he has taken. He drew himself entering toward their camp from the east and leaving to the west. Since he was unarmed, it is possible that they didn't see him as a threat and was the reason they let him go. He has also confirmed all the locations I picked for possible ambushes. There would have been more if he was going in and out frequently."

As they talked, two people took Rayshawn to our helicopter.

"Sorry, Laura. I have a last-minute mission I must attend to. Trudy will be in charge of your operation, so you will have to pass all concerns to her."

Dave walked over to Laura, laughing. "It seems you're willing to believe just about anything anyone tells you. I am sure if I tell you I am an all-powerful and all-knowing warrior originally born in the late 1320s, you're so gullible you might actually believe me. Just because you are good with a gun, you think you are this ultimate warrior."

Laura shoved the map into Dave's chest, saying, "Dave Tappet, born in North Europe. You were born into a poor family and given to a rundown orphanage. Later, an upper-class family raised you. By the age of fifteen, you were hitting on girls of every age. At age eighteen, you were hitting on everything that moved as long as it had two X chromosomes. By age twenty-one, you had been incarcerated eleven times and had killed three victims because they refused service. After that, your foster parents disowned you. You had nowhere else to go, so this was when you were offered a job from SUBWAY. I know enough information about you to have you buried."

Dave tossed me the map. "You have a good informant, but there is no way the enemy would ever help out his enemy."

Looking at the map, I tried to put it all together. I noticed some of the locations actually made sense, so I added, "Unless he was never the enemy to begin with."

"Have you also found our guest's story believable?" David asked.

"No, but I'd rather you not assume our plan is any better. Taking extra—" I was interrupted before I could add, "extra precautionary steps wouldn't hurt."

"See, even your boyfriend doesn't believe the prisoner. So, young lady, why don't you keep your false intel to yourself? If you want to help out, why don't you teach the new girl something? Becky is still new here. Go keep her company or something."

I knew Laura's ideas were going to be undermined, and her reaction wasn't going to be a good one. I grabbed her arm, gently, for fear she might break mine, and whispered, "Come now, Laura. We both know this will not end well."

She turned around, and we headed out the door. Exiting the threshold, she stopped and said, "By the way, there were many different things wrong with what you were saying. If you were all powerful, you would be a leader instead of a man who is still feeding on your mother's breast milk. If you were an all-knowing warrior, you would know who you are talking to and just how bad it would be to make me angry. And even if you were originally born in the 1320s, you'd still have died years ago. The water on this island only slows down your aging process by about half. No, Sergeant, you are the gullible one here. I am surprised you are not dead, honestly."

Normally, Laura would have been reprimanded, but everyone knew it was time someone said something to him.

When we walked outside, I asked her, "May I ask you why you believe Rayshawn over what everyone else says?"

"Because he's not lying to us," she replied. "Call it a sixth sense, and I am not usually wrong about these things."

I leaned forward to look into her eyes. I knew what color they were going to be because she was getting frustrated, but I wasn't expecting it to be a midnight blue.

"Do you still not trust my judgment after six and a half years of being around me?"

It wasn't that I didn't trust her; we had been friends for years, after all. In fact, I have known myself for many years, and I trusted her more than I trust myself.

"You have seen the facts laid out in front of you and still refuse to see the bigger picture," she said. "Tell me, would you like to go with information that has a small chance of being true, or would you rather jump into a battlefield you have no current intel on? Look, that POW has been with us for months. Why would they wait this long to try to get him back?"

"I don't know, maybe they forgot about him until recently." I realized how stupid that sounded after I spoke.

"I pray to your God you are not really that stupid," Laura said. I could see she was getting even more frustrated with me, for she began to clinch her fist.

I raised my hands as though to surrender. "OK, Laura, that was not thought out very well. I do trust you, and I am behind you one hundred percent, but to trust another person in extension is ludicrous. If you're wrong about this guy, then..."

She interrupted me to add, "I will personally shoot him myself, take complete blame for everything that goes wrong, and will never make another choice again." This wasn't what I wanted to hear, but I really didn't have anything else prepared. "If I am right, however, you will eat a salad made with only the fruits and veggies you hate when we get back."

After hearing these two choices, I looked at her with disgust, as though I could taste the radish and celery. "Umm...I guess, but why would your terms be so cruel?"

"To make sure you never doubt me again," she smiled.

The hardest thing about this was trusting someone other than myself. I had been double-crossed too many times to count. "I feel like I'm going to regret this either way. I feel even more so that I don't really have a choice."

"Good, now let's go. We will be leaving pretty soon."

We walked over to the helicopter, and the only thing I thought was, *I hope she's wrong because the salad will be the worst thing I have ever eaten.* We walked to the helicopter where Judith was standing guard over Rayshawn.

"May we talk to Rayshawn?"

"You can talk all you want," Judith replied. "You two are escorting the prisoner to his destination."

"How come you're having me and her play personal bodyguard?" I asked.

She replied, "Sue knew Laura had concerns and felt this was the best way to resolve them. This is, until the moment you all drop him off."

"Good, this will give us the time necessary to prove my theory right or wrong," Laura added.

Since we were already at the helicopter, I sat down and re-examined the map, considering all Laura's arguments and connecting the dots. How did Laura really come to trust this total stranger? I knew she could be trusted, but I didn't know this guy, so I had nothing to go on.

One by one, everyone else arrived. The first to show up was Lieutenant Lizzie, who was on her computer. Lizzy was our official officer; she used to be a hacker and was wanted in most countries. Her purpose was to give us official logistical support; her field name was

Mage. A few minutes later, Becky and Daysen arrived, holding each other's hands. Becky had ended up in juvenile hall after beating her boyfriend half to death; her field name was Dos Equis. As for Daysen, he was brought to the island with the promise of some kind of scholarship to a mechanic school. Becky and Daysen had recently been...seeing each other. Last to arrive was Trudy, an ex-pilot who was field-named Habanero, and Sergeant Tappet, or Devil-Dog. As they approached, Trudy led the way. You could tell just by looking at Dave that he had an alternative motive for being behind her. They sat down, and so it happened that he sat next to me. The first thing he said was, "Man, it doesn't matter how many times I get a look at those thighs, a look at her breasts, or even the way she swings those hips of hers, it still has me going for a double take."

It wasn't like I really cared; she wasn't my type, mostly because she was older than me. She was cute for her age, which was maybe thirty, but Dave was the kind of person who always had something dirty to talk about. I wanted the conversation to be over as soon as possible, so I replied, "Yeah, totally."

The helicopter took off, and the only ones going were Trudy, Dave, Lizzie, Becky, Daysen, Laura, Rayshawn, and myself.

"Becky has some nice features, but she is too childish and too skinny for my taste," the sergeant continued. "The only thing Lizzie has going for her is her spunk and her glasses, but her acne throws it all off."

"Yeah, that's great, Dave," I replied, giving him two thumbs up, hoping it would be enough to end the conversation. I wondered why he was talking to me in the first place.

"Now, Laura, though still young, has a very hypnotic body..."

"Oh my God! I get the point!" I yelled. "You do know they can hear you?" I leaned my head on the door, hoping it would open so I could get the conversation over with.

We flew to our extraction point, and from there, we were forced to walk the rest of the way. It actually wasn't too bad; we were only three miles away from the waterfall where we had to meet.

As the helicopter took off, Rayshawn said with desperation, "We need to turn back now while we still have control over the battlefield."

Laura explained, "There is nothing you can say that can make them change their minds now."

As we walked, all we could hear was the wind slowly moving through the trees and birds chirpings, creating a natural atmosphere.

"So, young lady, do you see anything out of place?" Dave asked.

"Of course, there is nothing out of place here," Laura replied. "This is the extraction point. If we don't have a safe haven when landing, then we wouldn't have landed. Let's just move on."

"I know what it is I am talking about, and this is a simple trade." Sergeant Tappet continued.

We moved to our objective. We traveled for about a mile, and there was clearing that led to a river. Rayshawn looked around. "And now we are at the point of no return," he said.

I asked, "What do you mean?"

"We have been spotted by two enemies, and they will be cutting off our retreat," Rayshawn said. "If you are creative enough, I am sure we can still turn around." By the way he was talking, I began to seriously wonder about our position. "If we go any further, soon, there won't be a way out if this turns out to be a trap."

"Enough out of you!" Sergeant Tappet yelled, pulling out his pistol and aiming at Rayshawn's face.

My reaction was to pull out my pistol, but it was gone. I looked at Laura and saw she was holding my gun in her hand. I am not sure exactly how or when, but Laura had disarmed me. I looked at Rayshawn, but he did not seem concerned with the pistol in his face. I looked around and saw Laura, Daysen, and Lizzy were also not concerned.

"Let me hear one more word out of you and I will blow your head clean off your body," said Sergeant Tappet.

From his left, Trudy punched him in the face, knocking him down to the ground. "When did I put you in charge of my op?" she asked calmly, shaking her hand. "The last time I checked, I was the one who was still leading this op. My second in charge is Lizzie, then you. Are we clear?"

Checking his jaw, Dave replied slowly, "Yes, ma'am." He was bitter, and everyone knew.

Trudy leaned over with her arm out. He reached for her hand to try to get back up. She said, "Disarm. You are now going to be stripped of all your weapons, except your pistol, for the remainder of the mission. When we return to base, you will be punished for endangering the mission objective." She helped him up and watched as he disarmed; making sure all he had was a pistol. When he was done, he wasn't even armored up. She gave the armor to Rayshawn and the weapons and ammo to everyone else. "Next time, I hope you think twice before putting the mission objective in jeopardy. David will now be point man. Let's move out."

We started to walk away, and Rayshawn, almost under his breath, said, "Are we really going to continue regardless of what I am telling you people?"

"Yeah, seems like it," I replied, grabbing his shoulder. I suddenly noticed the birds were no longer chirping, but I thought it might have been because of all the commotion.

We finally arrived at our destination. Looking around, it seemed as though we were in front of a bigger water-fall. There were five men dressed like assassins who had covered their faces. As they saw us approaching, four of them walked away, and the fifth one just stood there. As we got closer, the waterfall began to split, revealing two statues with crossing spears. It seemed we were standing in front of an ancient shrine. Blue smoke rose from the ground. Out of the smoke came a man wearing a midnight blue business suit and a blood red tie.

"Have you brought our companion for the trade?" he asked.

"Of course," Trudy replied. "Do you have what we have agreed upon?"

"Yes, our agreement was a prototype healing armor. Was it not?" the man replied, walking toward us.

"Bring forth their companion," Trudy said.

"I am not their ally. You realize this is all a trap," Rayshawn said to Laura, for no one else would listen. "The moment you send me over there, they will kill your unit, torture me for a few days to get intel that doesn't exist, and then they will leave me for dead in a pit."

As we brought Rayshawn forward, they sent a representative to send over the prototype.

"What do you want to do now, Laura?" I whispered.

"We can't do anything until they fire the first shot. Otherwise, they can say they were provoked."

Rayshawn finally reached the exchange point.

The man in the blue suit, the courier, yelled, "It just occurred to me I might want to keep both for myself."

I used the water from the falls to free Rayshawn from the chains and immediately formed a shield around us with the same collection of water. Trudy threw Rayshawn the shotgun she got from Dave. Rayshawn shot the courier, who was close enough to be inside the shield, grabbed the package, and returned back to us. Thanks to Laura's thinking in advance, we started to move along the escape route she had prepared. Unfortunately, there wasn't a way we could escape without casualties; we were forced to split into groups of two. We were to meet back up with each other along the way to the evacuation point.

The plan was for Daysen and Becky to stay together. Laura was to go with Lisa, Dave with Trudy, and as for me, I was to travel with Rayshawn. We looked around and saw what we thought was our helicopter coming in. As it got closer, Dave ran out of cover and tried to flag it down. It turned around and began to open fire; we thought it was providing fire to cover us, but the bullets got closer until it was firing directly on our position. Dave was torn to shreds. As his lifeless body oozed blood, the hailstorm of bullets never ceased. At first, I thought it was just shooting us at random, but as the ground caved underneath us, I knew this was no accident. The fall forcibly disabled the shield. Underneath us was the waterfall, and as we fell, we fumbled to gather by grasping at one another's limbs or clothing so the suit could break our fall. As I stretched and fumbled to grab ahold of Lisa or her clothing, I realized she was too far away from us. She died, crashing head first into the water at full force. As for the rest of us, we quickly sank to the riverbed. I, once again, created a barrier so we could breathe and catch our breath without getting shot.

Rayshawn asked, "What is going on here?"

I answered, "We are currently underwater in an air bubble big enough to escape the bullets above."

"Is this similar to what you were using up there?"

"Yes."

"Is this safe?"

"The bubble? Yes. The bullets? Since they are aiming at us, no. I thought that would be obvious."

Boulders began to rain down from above, most likely from the falling through the ground. The bubble was strong enough to hold up, and I pushed them right and left as we headed downstream as though we were part of the water. Finally, they threw an explosive into the water, but when I saw it, the barrier released us and wrapped itself around the bomb, making the current stronger and harder to control. As we were pushed away, I looked in the direction of the explosion, which was so big it went straight back up the waterfall. I looked around, and the only one I saw was Rayshawn. So I grabbed him and swam to shore.

"I hate being in situations like this," Rayshawn said. "All right, considering that is the norm, what is the plan now?" He began placing shells in his shotgun.

"We have to meet at the evacuation point and collect any surviving team members on the way," I replied, and walked away. "You can come along if you want, but the choice is completely up to you. Heck, if I were in your situation, I would run for freedom the moment I got the chance."

"Why don't we hold position here and wait for reinforcements to arrive?" Rayshawn asked. "More than likely, your forces will come looking for you, right?"

"No, Conner would rather proclaim us dead than send out a rescue team. It is cheaper for him to be rid of you than to try to keep you around. Laura might, but knowing her, she would say this is some kind of survival training."

"How long would that take?"

"Five days minimum, if she is feeling nice."

"So, then we are screwed?"

"Yeah, pretty much—unless we can rejoin our team and make a plan from there. Hopefully, they will have a better plan than 'try not to die by getting detected.' What do you think?"

"Is it too late to say I told you so?" he asked me.

"No, my friend, it is too early. If we survive this, then you can tell me and everyone else who doubted you."

We walked into the forest to keep out of sight, but stayed close to the water to make sure we kept the advantage. I used the radio to contact the others.

"Serenity, Mustang, do you copy?" No reply. "Dos Equis, Habanero, are you there?"

"I don't see how we survived all of that," Rayshawn said, keeping his voice low. "Neither do I see how anyone else would have. Shouldn't we consider them, you know, gone?"

"No, optimism is sanity right now," I replied. "Besides, it is a possibility their radios might just be broken or out of range." I wondered what was going to happen with troop morale being so low. If what Rayshawn said was correct, then with the troops we had left, the odds were looking like twenty-five enemies per one of ours.

We continued walking. We started to hear bushes move; we hid behind the trees so whatever was in the bush wouldn't see us. Rayshawn and I began using sign language. Rayshawn was to cover me while I was to charge in to keep the risk of casualties to a minimum. I charged the bush using the nearby water as a shield in front of me. I leaped over, drawing my pistol. As I leaped through, Laura had already drawn her rifle and was aiming it at me. Seeing there were no enemy threats, I put my pistol away. Trudy was also hiding behind the bush. I stood and flagged Rayshawn to clarify the scene was safe.

"I'm glad you weren't the enemy," Laura replied.

I looked at Trudy and noticed she was holding a magnum in one hand. With her other hand she was holding her side. I asked, "What happened to her?"

Laura replied, "She has three cracked ribs, one broken rib, minor spinal damage, a sprained ankle, and a collapsing lung."

"How do you know all of that?"

"When I would spend too much time...with my brother, the Webmaster would be sure that I studied medicine. That way, if being a combat translator didn't work out, I could choose medical as a backup career. I am surprised I never told you. It was my father's request before he died."

Rayshawn walked up, his head low, and whispered, "Your helicopter is currently hovering overhead. What kind of tech does it have?"

"It is a standard helicopter," Trudy replied. "No modifications were done except the anti-heat sensor, to avoid heat-seeking missiles, and the anti-marker, to avoid laser markers."

"You know we can't call for extraction while they have air support."

"Nah, really? Next, you're going to tell me snow is just frozen rain," I replied sarcastically. Normally, I wouldn't, but it was too obvious.

He replied, "No, next I was going to tell you—"

"Calm down, boys!" Laura said, putting her hands over our mouths. "There is no reason to play alpha male. Apologize, Leo. I understand you are stressed out, but you have less to worry about than the rest of us."

"I'll do it later," I replied, mumbling.

"Fine. Look, Trudy and I have devised a plan to take down the helicopter. Hopefully, we can take it down without them knowing where it is."

Rayshawn replied quickly, "It can't be done."

"He's right," I agreed, and then I remembered the map layout of this location. "Rayshawn, can you escort Laura and Trudy southwest of our location? There should be a good defensive ground position to cover. I'll catch up if and when I lose the enemy."

"Sure, do you have a plan?"

"I hope."

Laura replied, "All right, but instead, I will do the escorting. If what I know about you is true, then you only know the two ways out of here, and they should be patched up by now. You take Trudy; it will be easier for you to carry her than if I were to."

I held my position for one minute, giving them a little time to clear the area. I walked to the river, putting my hand above the water. I wasn't sure exactly why I did this; maybe it was a way to calm me down. Maybe I was trying to practice control over the water. Whatever the case, I was planning my next move. I began to whisper.

"Up until now, I have been only using the suit's abilities over water in a defensive way. If I want to destroy the helicopter in the sky, I will need to be more tactical and offensive. Shielding will only get me so far."

As my hand was over the river, I formed a circular saw blade from the water. I flicked my wrist and it began to spin. Then I threw it and chopped two of the trees. I felt my right shoulder getting hit. It was like a punch in the arm. I look at my shoulder and saw there wasn't even a scratch. "Must have been a sniper," I whispered. I dropped down, once more putting my hand in the water. Then, as the next bullet fired, I placed another shield up, which deflected the gunshot. I pulled out one of my pistols and fired in the general direction of the gunshot. Then another gunshot was fired from a different location, but it didn't hit me. I shot in that direction as well. This process continued three more times. Then two appeared at the same time, then three. I was eventually overrun. Then I heard the sound of a loud whistle. I turned to block whatever it was. As expected, there was a loud explosion, and the only sound I could hear was water, as though I were sinking. I didn't move for a few seconds; I assumed I had died. It wasn't until I hit the bottom of the river that I realized this wasn't true. I remember thinking, *So, I am still alive. That's a relief. Man, this suit can take a lot of punishment. How did I end up in the river? Well, there is no time for that. I have to get back to the top so my team can get out of here safely.*

I started to swim up, which was surprisingly only about twenty feet.

"Hey, Cross, this is Mustang. If you are still alive, Dos Equis and I will be giving you fire support when you get out of the water."

"I copy, Mustang." I reloaded my pistol and jumped out of the water like a person using a water jetpack. This time, I only shot when I knew I had the shot, unlike before. When I was running low in the chamber, I dropped back down and reloaded. When I rose back up, I saw Daysen and Becky waiting for me to surface. I landed next to them. "So where is the enemy?"

"They started to run away," Becky replied.

"Is that so? Well, that can't be good," I said. "You two should get out of here as well."

"All right, we will be heading away from where they were," Daysen said. "You should keep an eye out then; they might be coming back this way."

"All right," I said.

As they ran off, I heard the sound of the helicopter approach. As it got closer, I could hear the sound of the gunfire from above. I took cover behind a nearby boulder. Upon approach, it chipped away at the boulder I was hiding behind. That they knew my position was surprising because of how high it was and the number of trees in the area. The constant firing was destroying the nearby trees, which was unfortunate because they were keeping me hidden. I sprinted along the river, trying to avoid stray bullets. The whole way I constantly looked for an opening. When I found one, I collected water in my hand. I formed it like a disk and threw it like a Frisbee. I aimed it at the propeller; if it hit any part of the propeller, it would have cut that part off and made the helicopter lose balance. If nothing else, it would at least make it harder to fly. I missed, for it slowed down just long enough to let the disk pass by. It then continued to open fire. It cut off my movement, and I was forced to hold my position and form a shield around me. It began to get dusty, which made it hard to see. At that moment, I knew I was caught between a rock and a hard place, and I couldn't move. It stopped firing for a moment, I guess due to the lack of visual.

"Cross, don't move," Daysen transmitted.

So I stayed still, keeping my shield up. Then I heard a gunshot from a rifle. I watched as it passed by, looking at the dust swaying.

"Their spotter is down; you are now free from their sight. Becky and I will be going on ahead; you should take down that chopper while you have this moment. Its location is directly above you."

I leaped into the air but didn't go very high. I prepared another disk, throwing it at the helicopter; this time, the pilot was unresponsive. The water cut loose the propeller, forcing the helicopter to come down. The blade, I don't exactly know where that thing went. When the helicopter crashed, my first instinct was to reunite with my unit, but I realized the best move was to draw attention to myself a while longer to be sure they got away. I next heard a loud whistle above me, and saw a shadow with great speed pass by. I looked around and heard gunfire. Pulling out my pistol, I waited to see if it was a friend or foe while also trying to figure out my next plan.

"Cross, did you take out the air support?" an unfamiliar female voice asked on the radio. "It won't be easy to send in backup if they still have air support."

"Yes, the air support is down. Go ahead and send in backup."

"Good, a unit is moving to your position now."

I heard another helicopter in the air. Then a shadow flew overhead once more, but this time, I heard a high-pitched whistle that got louder. I prepared myself for an explosion by dropping to the ground, bracing for impact. I heard a crash and saw more dust picked up.

When the smoke cleared, there was a giant man about eight feet tall holding a turret over his shoulder. From the way his armor looked, it was very similar to mine, minus the color and the size; his was green and tall in stature.

"You must be Leo, aka Cross, the water user," the giant said in a German accent. "My name is Peter Collins; you can call me Tank. I have just been told your allies have been spotted and will be rescued shortly."

"Which ones?"

"A young man and his female companion; they are just a short distance from our current location. They were the ones who contacted us while we were a little ways away. They also requested we send help to your location."

"Mustang and Dos Equis. I guess that is a good thing. Those two are the ones who possess the package we were originally after."

"You guess?" he replied. From his voice, I could tell he didn't understand.

"Those two need not be rescued; they would make it back to base regardless. She is a Russian spy trained to assassinate targets, and he was trained to use his body as a weapon, only when absolutely necessary, by some unknown master." He wasn't unknown; I just don't remember his name. "Good to hear I was able to buy them some time. So, where is extraction?"

"We will call it when we have the rest of your party. I think there are three of them. Please follow me; I have their last known location."

So I followed him, asking, "How will they get in close enough without getting shot down?"

"Susan made sure it would be quick with the drop ship, and we have medical personnel on board just in case."

"All right, that should make things go more smoothly. The last time I was with my group, we had someone who was injured."

He then wrapped his arm around my waist and picked me up. "They never mentioned you had a fallen comrade. We must go to their aid quickly before things get worse. If we wish to get there to aid them, we are moving too slowly. So I will be running." He broke into a run, which was five times faster than my pace. As he ran, he dashed through everything in his path. When he finally stopped, I realized he must have already known their location, for we heard gunfire as he put me down. He pulled his turret off his back and slowly started to walk into the gunfire. I am sure he intended to draw gunfire off from our allies. I heard one gunshot and looked around for the origin of the sound. When I found it, I ran to the location. When I arrived, Rayshawn was providing cover fire while Laura was patching up Trudy's wound. Peter walked into the opening from behind, still firing in the opposite direction. I ran to them, giving them support fire.

Rayshawn looked at me and said, "Glad to see you finally showed up. What's with the walking tank? Is he with you guys?" I looked at Rayshawn's arm as he put his shotgun down and saw an anime girl tattooed on his arm.

I replied, "He hasn't tried to kill me, and he is currently shooting at our enemies. I feel that I can safely assume he's on our side."

Then I opened fire on the immediate threats I could see. After a few minutes, Peter picked up Trudy and threw a beacon on the ground. He said, "Get ready."

Immediately, a jet from above began to hover down. As it came down, everything underneath it began to slowly deteriorate. Our job at this point was to keep them back. The way the drop ship was made, it only would destroy environmental things so people and metals would be safe. As it made contact with Peter, the hanger doors opened underneath the ship. It landed, and inside the plane, the medical personnel quickly grabbed Trudy and put her on a stretcher. Laura was next to go up. When we had all gotten on, we quickly took off. The first person I saw was a girl dressed in a gold and silver leather outfit with knives from her shoulders to her toes. She was leaning against the wall; I guessed she was also new to the team. Strangely enough, as soon as Rayshawn saw the girl, he was the first to rush over to her and began to hit on her. I looked around and saw Peter, standing in the pathway, telling me to follow him, so I did. He led me to the back of the ship where Sue talked to Daysen and Becky. The way the conversation went, she was briefing and debriefing them, so I had to wait.

While I waited for Susan, Rayshawn approached. I said, "I noticed there was a tattoo of some kind of anime girl on your right arm. What's up with that?"

"It's from another time," Rayshawn replied. "I was the very definition of an otaku."

"How did your relationship go with that girl?"

"Ah, she said that she was already in a relationship. So it was a no go."

"So what are you planning to do now? I am sure with those witnesses around you, you've been cleared of working with the enemy."

"Well, you might be right. I don't have anywhere I have to be. I think I will stay with you guys for the time being if you guys will allow it."

Before I could say anything else, Sue interrupted, "Come in, Leo. We need to begin your briefing and debriefing,"

"Well, good luck my friend," I said, leaving him in the hall.

Most of the things Sue told me were pretty basic: the real mission behind this operation, the true reason we went in with little to no intel on the enemy, and the fact she knew the pilot of our helicopter was going to stab us in the back. Due to these odds, she had decided to send in her most trusted, which I was now part of, apparently. The one thing she told us, as a group, was the airship MOTH, also known as a Military Operations Transporter of Heavies, was never officially there, as she was never given permission to take it. The purpose of the MOTH was to carry either fifty passengers and a few light vehicles or twenty-five passengers and a tank. It couldn't fly very high, but it had excellent speed, even with the cargo. The "heavy" in its title came from the protection on the outside.

Under the Mission Objective Category, the mission was a success. We managed to keep the POW alive, get whatever it was that we were sent down there for, lower the number of enemies, and dispose of one of the moles they had in our fold. Under Mission Overall Morale, how-ever, we lost two of our comrades on the battlefield; we lost Trudy, who died from internal bleeding on the way back to our base, and we ran into an ambush that could have been prevented. It was after that mission I began to worry about what SUBWAY's operations were really about. As for the POW, when he returned, he joined our team while under complete watch.

Within two weeks, I had seen Sue reading a book, *Cecilia's Overwatch*. It was one of the first books you would see upon entering the building; that was when she wasn't reading it. I don't remember what it was about, but it had me thinking. I asked Laura about her relationship with the Webmaster because I was curious, and I'd never really asked her before. She replied by saying, "The Webmaster was a genius without equal. She wanted to learn; eventually, she learned all that she could. Now she just reads for fun. With what she learned, she wanted to better humanity. But when she wanted to share her plans, someone wanted to prevent her plans to make profit and install fear; this is how she came up with idea to come to this island that govern-ments were hiding in plain sight, choosing to better humans from the shadows rather than just making a quick buck; because of this, I highly respect her for it." It did explain the Webmaster's personality, not to mention the book maze that she had stored away.

# 5

## While The Troops Are Away...
## The Enemies Will Play

**S**even months passed, and Rayshawn and I became good friends. Laura, however, would leave when the two of us got together. I never figured out why; even to this day, I don't understand the reason why she left. My theory was she wanted me to have more than just her as a friend. Sue and Judy went on more of our missions to ensure success and prevent what happened with Trudy, and there were fewer casualties because of it. As for Peter, he wasn't so much the strong silent type I took him for; he was actually very friendly to everyone, and maybe a little too open about his life. As far as his strength, he could lift a tank completely off the ground using only one finger with great ease. The woman with the knives, her name was Kristy. She was more likely to use a blade in combat than any type of gun. In fact, she would only use a gun when she ran out of throwing knives or if her sword broke or dulled, which wasn't very often; she performed constant upkeep on them to prevent this. She was generally a nice person toward other women; as for guys, she could have been a little nicer, but I could understand her attitude toward us. Just based off of how attractive she was—she was always getting hit on. Rayshawn would hit on her four times a week. I wouldn't hit on her because of two reasons: One, I couldn't talk to a woman with any alternative motive. Laura was my prime example of why. Two, she reminded me a lot of my sister Kat, which was a little awkward. We had one more recruit show up named Jonny Flowers; he was an explosives expert. Jonny almost always talked to a girl or about blowing things up. I later discovered these three were no more than mercenaries, guns for hire found by O'Neal.

Becky and Daysen announced their plans to consummate their love through marriage. Laura thought it was cute, but Rayshawn and I thought it would be more of an annoyance than anything. They were always kissing, hugging, flirting, and talking dirty, regardless of who was around them, none of which should ever be spoken in public. I think it was God's way of getting back at me because of what I did around my friends when I was a high schooler with a girlfriend.

As far as the package we picked up, we had experimented with it. We never figured out its potential or what it was exactly, but we were sure they needed volunteers to conclude the rest of their experiment, and it was said to unlock some kind of power. Daysen was their volunteer, so he was the only one who knew about the project further. During that time, I learned how to better use my suit's abilities beyond just the basics. Some of that help was thanks to Peter, who was actually very resourceful.

One day, Judy received orders from command, stating she had been reassigned to another base; because of their sister-like bond, Sue requested she be Judy's escort to the next base. The ladies would use this escort mission as a way to say their final goodbyes, for the odds of coming back were unfavorable. They took Peter with them and left Daysen in charge.

Laura had just finished modifying some weapons; after five days of nonstop fiddling with the equipment, she finally went to sleep. As for the modifications, she was making a sniper rifle strong enough to shoot through three consecutive tanks full of people without any obstacles blocking the path, but this was not why it took her so long to finish. She had to make nonlethal bullets for it. So, if someone were to get in front of the bullet, it would switch to stun. She never told me how she made it, but she did tell me how the bullets worked, but I can only take so much information. From the way she described it to me, the bullet had four different sections, three of which were exactly the same. The way I understood it, the bullet would pass through the tank and scan for the point with the most amount of people. If it found any, it would stun them for about an hour. Though its purpose was to be used on heavily armored vehicles, it could also be used on an open battlefield. Its max target was twelve per section. Because it was so powerful, its nonlethal aspect could never be used at close range.

Laura slept for about three days; she only woke up to eat and use the latrine in a near-zombie state. This was pretty typical of her when she was passionate about her projects, but she only did this like once a year. The last time I saw her do this, she had worked on the Webmaster's ABOFNYS project. I didn't ask what it was and hadn't thought about it until then.

Ray and I sat down in the center of camp, playing cards with Jonny and Kristy. We waited for orders to go anywhere or do something, and so we made sure we could be found. Daysen, who carried two envelopes, finally approached us after two hours and thirty-seven minutes.

"Guys, ma'am, I have just received your new missions. Kristy and Jonny will be going to the location sealed in my first envelope. Rayshawn and Leonardo, you will be going to the location sealed in the second envelope; Conner's orders. Have fun," Daysen said, handing over the envelopes.

When I looked, I saw there was something different about this mission, but I couldn't figure it out. Our mission was to take place in a nearby desert at a nearly abandoned outpost. We were to stay until we were given orders to return. This would leave our base in the hands of the two lovers, one sleeping sniper, and a whole lot of rookies, at least until Susan returned. I couldn't shake the bad vibe I had.

When Rayshawn and I finally arrived, I would look for something to do, but our destination was literally in the middle of nowhere in the sandy desert. We walked into the watch station, and I noticed there was nothing to do. That was when Rayshawn pulled out the cards we played with earlier. So, we decided to sit down and play poker.

We reminisced about the past and our families. That was when I found out he'd been on this island for six years longer than me, both him and his sister. He was also raised in Barstow, California, like I was. He informed me he was at the DMV with his sister when they drugged them, and when they woke up, they were here, sitting in a boat with the smell of gunpowder left on their clothing. I asked him where his sister was, and he told me they were separated from each other around the time he was captured by us. After about an hour, we were bored of playing cards. "Rayshawn, I know you have been here longer than I have, so what does SUBWAY stand for?

"I am assuming money can buy everything."

"No, I mean the acronym."

"Oh, umm maybe Sudden Underqualified Betatesters Without Actual (Y) experience; something like that."

So, he pulled out a laptop, which he had "liberated" from Dave's room after his passing, and decided to hack into SUBWAY's operation systems and data history, and gave me a satellite dish.

"Rayshawn, what are you going to be looking for?" I asked, sitting in a chair and holding the satellite dish.

"We are going to use this to look up our current history and see what is really going on at our base while we are away. That way, if we are under attack for any reason, we'll be the first to know."

"What about those who are already there? I am sure they could handle an attack even without us. Besides, they have Daysen and Becky there, two of our top soldiers. They will be fine," I added.

"Will they?"

"What do you mean?"

He paused, looked at me puzzled, and responded, "Do you really trust Daysen, bro? He's been acting quite shady lately, him and Becky. They have been that way ever since he volunteered for O'Neal's little project. Don't tell me you haven't noticed. Besides, this is much more interesting than sitting down and playing poker with someone who doesn't know how to play."

"Hey, that is not my fault! My mother was against all kinds of gambling, so I am more than just a little rusty; more like corroded, if you will. However, you are onto something. Daysen has been acting weird since he volunteered. I couldn't figure out the reason why, so I just assumed it was me being paranoid."

"Trust me, I've noticed, but that is why we are going to find out what is going on behind the scenes." He opened up some folder on his computer and hacked into the system, page after page popping up. The program he used answered every password and security question correctly. Through everything that popped up, surprisingly, nothing actually stated what SUBWAY stood for; it was just something I noticed.

"What kind of program are you using that could get this kind of intel?" I asked, letting go of the satellite dish and looking at how fast he typed.

"Well, the program came from a man who calls himself Augustus. He was a pretty well-known programmer."

"So, how does it know what to put in for the passwords?"

"Well, from what I heard, it copies the information from the slots either most frequently used or the data last entered in the required areas. So, going through the secure areas is a simple task."

"You know you could just plug a USB into the port and it would be much faster than what you're doing now."

"First of all, I never received a USB. Second, using a universal security breacher would work, but it is much too sloppy, especially when you want to leave no trace you ever hacked the system. It is more for when you are in a hurry. Besides, I think we are almost through. Who do I talk to about trying to get one of those?"

"Well, I got mine from Laura. She told me not to lose it."

"Hmm...if Laura gave it to you, it might be a custom-made USB. So, I take it you have it on you? We might be able to combine the two."

I took off my necklace, which was shaped like a cross with a pistol and a sword crossing the cross, and handed it to him. He took it from me and examined it.

"So, which side do I plug into the computer?"

"Wrong kind of USB—the way Laura explained the universal security breaker, all that is required is placing the device right next to the computer or electronic locking device, and it will be able to unlock it, whether you are hacking or just picking a digital lock."

He was about to hand it back to me when the computer flashed from one screen to another rapidly.

I continued, "I guess you never realized we haven't been locked out of any building during our missions for more than a couple of seconds."

Finally, it stopped, and the only thing it displayed was a screen saying, "If caught, who will take the fall?" It was ready for us to type in a name. So, Rayshawn typed in the name, "Lo-Lo," a name with no attachments to it, and pressed enter. The next screen said, "Welcome, Lo-Lo." We looked at the information and then saw the name "Behavior Monitor—Project Immortality: Subject Daysen." We opened the file.

As we opened the file, I noticed someone off in the distance limping toward us. I picked up my necklace, put it around my neck, and walked over to this person. As I got closer, she began to look familiar. I signaled Rayshawn to follow me. When I was a hundred feet away, I saw it was one of the new recruits. Her name was Britney Kasey. The main reason I could remember her was because she told me she was working on an experimental cell phone, which would have been the only way to contact anyone from the outside world. When I looked at her, she showed all the signs of dehydration, so I used the suit to give her some water. Then I placed water on the edges of her face to cool her off.

Rayshawn leaned over her body and noticed she held something in her hand. So, he tried to get it from her just to have her wake up and spit out the excess water. After coughing, she asked, "Have you seen anyone else with me?"

"What do you mean? You are the only one we have seen," I replied, helping her up from the ground.

"There were three of us originally. I guess they didn't make it. Kristy told me to deliver this to you and made me promise I'd give it to you no matter what." Britney handed me the paper, and I gave it to Rayshawn. He read it out loud:

*Gentlemen,*

*I sadly doubt you'll ever receive this letter; however, if this does get to you, I have disturbing news. Your mission was nothing more than a ploy to get the base's internal defenses down. I believe our comrades are in serious trouble. You must hurry and return to base so*

*we can fix the problems. Please meet us one mile west of the base gates so we can take back what is ours.*
*Kristy*

"Crap! I can't believe our enemy could have set all this up, right under our nose," I stated.

"Yeah, to lower our troops' morale and scatter us so easily without ever shooting off a single shot," Rayshawn added. "I knew we should have hacked the surveillance system instead of the security system."

The tower beeped and blared, "Missile Alert!" It could only say it one time before the missile hit and obliterated the tower. I shielded the three of us from the blast. When the dust cleared, I put my shield down and left in its place was an outline of the shield. We pushed slightly against the mud, and it opened our path. The tower had been completely consumed by the ground beneath it. I looked around and saw our vehicle was completely destroyed.

"Is everyone all right?" I asked, still looking at the tower.

"Good here," Rayshawn replied.

"Crap, now we have to walk," I replied, making sure Britney was all right.

"I think I might have a plan for our ride out of here," Rayshawn said, walking away.

Although I was helping her, I couldn't help but worry about what might have happened to Laura. I began to overthink what might have happened to her, and the more I thought, the more I realized she was fine and felt more pity for anyone who messed with her. Knowing Laura, she also managed to secure herself in our room.

"I'm done. I can't take it anymore, I never agreed to any of this crap," Britney quietly said with a blank stare on her face.

"What are you talking about?" I asked.

"I went to school to become a veterinarian with a secondary training to become an accountant." She continued, "Neither of my jobs trained me what we do here. So, that is it, I am done. I can't take this anymore. People shooting each other, killing without a real purpose, reverting back to their primal instinct."

I couldn't disagree based on everything I'd seen. "You know, it isn't like you signed a contract or anything, so you can quit anytime you want. No one will pursue. The only thing I recommend is changing your clothing before you go too far. If you wish to return to a somewhat peaceful life, you should talk to Laura. She might be able to arrange something. If you wish it, I could talk to her on your behalf and see what can be done."

"If it wouldn't be too much for me to ask of you."

"No, it would be my pleasure. Hopefully, she can find something better than this."

The ground started rumbling, and Rayshawn drove up to me inside our first-generation ROACH Humvee. It was radiation-proof and could last up to three hours without a power source. It also had six individualized tractors, so if one broke, it would still move. Sadly it was solar-powered, and when the sun was on, it would stop all operations to absorb power if it was nearly out, but this time, the chargers were too dirty to even charge from the sun. I carried Britney to the Humvee and placed her in the passenger seat, then sat on the backseat. "Where did you get the ROACH from?" I asked.

"It is a spare tank. Sue told me it was here as a backup. The maintainers come for its upkeep once a month. It was placed here in case we were ever attacked from this section or if our second-generation tanks malfunctioned."

Honestly, this literally was the first time we were able to use it. We had never seen an instance where we actually used the vehicles—not that we couldn't use the firepower; however, Conner never approved us to use them because the ammo shells cost too much, or so he stated in his reports. He would rather we just wash and maintain the tanks. Truthfully, it would have been easier to just get rid of them; they were just eyesores if we couldn't use them.

As we drove to our next location, my concerns about Laura's safety resurfaced. My mind was preoccupied with thoughts, like: *What if they burn down the building she is in? What if Daysen and Becky give up her position?* I got impatient and stressed myself out imagining these and other concerns like them.

"Hey, we are here," Rayshawn said.

When we all got out of the vehicle, Jonny approached us, and Kristy used binoculars.

"You know we are not that far from base?" Rayshawn said.

Jonny replied, "Yeah, we are about fifty yards out and hiding in the cliffs south of our base. A surveillance detail already passed by this sector three minutes ago, and another's not due for twenty or so. Before you got here, Kristy had just finished scouting the area."

"How did that go?" I asked.

Kristy replied, "Sadly, I found no weaknesses in the base's defense. It was like whoever is in charge has been planning this for a while now, so much that we have our own working with them. With that said, we are going to be forced to assume that everyone in the camp is hostile. Our options are limited without the skills of Laura. So, we need to come up with a plan that maximizes our chances of survival with the limited manpower we have. This is proof we need to train more snipers."

After a few minutes, we came up with something. We left Britney with Kristy; they were to hold position until we gave them a signal. Part of their instructions was to move and remain hidden in Laura's secure area until the signal was given. We drove the tank around and approached the base from the opposite direction to keep them from being detected. Next, we sent the tank to drive through the gate. Before it ever reached the gate, it was filled with bullet holes, and as it drove through the gate, it was blown off of its tractors. Seconds after it cleared the gate, it blew up spontaneously, causing a trail of fire until the tank reached a wall and stopped. From my understanding of the first ROACH models, though radiation proof, they were not properly bulletproof. We had all used the provided distraction to sneak into the base through an underground path Rayshawn had created to retreat from the base. The reason he built the underground tunnel was to escape in case there was a massive assault on the base, a massive food shortage, or, even less likely, a zombie attack.

As we approached the underground area, it took Rayshawn a few minutes to find the actual location we were looking for. As it turned out, he'd hidden it under a flat rock near a pond. The rock looked as though it would not budge. When he lifted the rock, it looked just effortless. I assumed he was just very strong until I saw the rock was hollowed out. As we entered the tunnel, I saw the ground was made of really soft sand. The tunnel was tall enough for a short man to comfortably stand up in; Rayshawn had used old lumber we had laying around to hold the ceiling up. After taking a second look, I could only admire how well it was constructed. It explained why he was always tired on a daily basis. As we continued through the tunnel, I thought it ironic we were using an escape route to get inside the base.

As we exited the escape tunnel, it led into Rayshawn's tent. We loaded our weapons and prepared to do some recon work. Luckily, I could use my suit's abilities to make myself blend in better, but it could only give a mirroring effect to cover the both of us. The plan was to do as much recon as possible. Or, this *was* the plan; it was, unfortunately, short-lived. As we walked outside Rayshawn's tent, I saw Kristy flagging Britney to follow, but as she ran by, there were two scouts who observed her. Before they could start shooting, I shot the two guards. This gave up our position before we ever actually got into position. When I thought about it, this really was a stupid idea because my weapons were not silent, and Kristy was more than capable of protecting Britney, but on the plus side, the girls got away without being detected. Rayshawn saw someone approach and punched him in the face. We were now approached from all directions and surrounded.

"I think we could take them, Leo," Rayshawn said.

After he said this, I calculated the odds of us winning with a few causalities; sadly, the odds were still very low, even with my water manipulation ability.

From behind the troops, there came a giant figure wearing a mask, cape, and some unknown armor. "Leonardo and Rayshawn," it said in a deep voice, as though it were trying to roar. "Surrender now, or I will put you to death."

When I saw the giant, I holstered my weapons and wondered if I was looking at Peter. Rayshawn followed my example and dropped his gun to the ground, kicking it away. The reason I wasn't trying to fight wasn't just because of the casualties, but because this might be the way we could find out who the key players were. They escorted us to the general's living quarters, which was one of the four biggest buildings in the middle of the base. They didn't even bother binding us because they knew I could just break out.

As we entered the building, I began to look around for possible gaps in their security. I knew it was easy for me to escape, but I could be placing Rayshawn's life in jeopardy. Not to mention, with the information provided to me, I was limited in what I was allowed to do. Oddly enough, the security was most definitely flawless for a group that took our base within a couple of hours. I also noticed the building interior was run down; it looked like a building that was about to be torn down by a construction crew. It was at that moment I was really glad to be living in the tents, for the only thing going for the building was the air conditioning. *So, where are the base's casualties?* I thought to myself. There would have been many more dead bodies if they were killed, and the tents would have been better guarded if they were there. I didn't see any of them in the rooms along the route they led us on. The only place I could think of was the prison cells, but those cages were not that big, and I couldn't tell who, if any, of these people were being held against their will. I was intrigued.

Rayshawn then whispered, "Have you noticed a weakness in their defense?"

I replied, "No, the only thing I've noticed is whoever this might be is very cocky since he is using our biggest building as a main keep. The security here is very high, but it seems the rest of the base, though secure, is lacking in comparison."

They opened a door, and we entered. The room we entered shined with polished gold that was close to blinding. It was the first time I'd seen something like this with my own eyes. Some trinkets reached higher than the ceiling; others were laid on the floor, possibly to keep them from tipping over. Directly in front of us was a thick veil. I tried to see through it, and from what I could make out with my eyes, I saw a man in an even shinier suit of armor.

"Let's not forget he also has an obsession with the color gold," I said.

"No kidding."

The man behind the veil stood up. "Do you really think all of this is mine? Why would I risk having this much gold on the frontlines? With this gold, I could probably buy a small island."

"I thought that was a little off," Rayshawn replied.

Having time to think about the situation, I came to a different conclusion. "So, I take it that all of this junk belongs to O'Neal?

The man answered, "Yes, Mr. Conner O'Neal. The same cutthroat tyrant you work for. Did you really believe him when he said he didn't have any money to upgrade any of the things you were in need of?"

"How did you know about that?" I asked.

"There are spies from all different organizations that have people pretend to be devoted soldiers. Heck, if someone had enough money, they could easily pay for loyalty from an enemy's organization. Congratulations, by the way, you two. Surviving a missile attack is a great feature. It seems your chances of survival were higher than I originally thought. It also seems harder trying to keep those who are off the base...off the base than keeping those who are here from escaping. I promised not to harm anyone if they didn't try to escape, but there is always someone. To be more direct, there were ten. The original plan was to try to convince the four of you to work for me. We couldn't ask that woman who is always around you because we didn't know where to find her. Our intelligence claims she didn't leave with you or with the other unit. We have searched the base thoroughly, and there is not even a trace of her." My guess was they'd planned to use her to blackmail me. "Now you have to choose. You will either serve me, or I will have to dispose of you two as an example to those who are planning to rebel against me. The choice is yours and only yours to make. So, choose wisely."

Rayshawn instantly replied, "Hmm...That is an easy question to answer, hands down. I mean, really, spending even a fraction of my life serving someone or dying a slow, painful death? I'll take death."

"Yeah, death is so much easier than working for someone I don't even know," I replied.

Ray and I fist-bumped while he added, "We bros fight together and die together."

"If that is your final answer, then so be it. The giant behind you will escort you to the execution grounds."

I hadn't forgotten about my suit's ability, I just didn't feel as though there was a real threat or any real reason to use it. At the time, I was just trying to make sense of the situation. The thing that stopped me from making any sudden movements was a simple matter of me not knowing if the man in charge was an electrical user. I'd rather not make a big mistake like that. Reflecting on it now, by this time in my life, I had come across many near-death experiences, so many that the Grim Reaper had my number on speed dial; I just never picked up.

They escorted us to an open platform located in the middle of the base. They lined us up in front of a firing squad. As I watched, I noticed it took three minutes for them just to find the people to execute us. I remember thinking that if they were going to kill us, then why did it take so long? I also looked out for possible signs of Kristy; there was no way she hadn't found out about this situation. I looked around and noticed the surrounding people watched us. Right in front of us, they had placed a camera on a tripod. They possibly recorded this so they could use us as an example. The whole time we waited for the firing squad, we made jokes back and forth.

The sun set, and the firing squad was finally in position.

"Well, I can't think of a more beautiful sight to see before I die," I said, looking at the sun setting.

Rayshawn said, "I am just glad we finally can get this over with."

A brute walked up to us. "Have you changed your mind?" he asked insistently.

"Why would I change my mind now? I've already made it this far," I said.

"Very well then. Squad, ready your weapons!" the brute commanded.

"Hey, Leo, do you think this plan of yours is going to work?" Rayshawn whispered.

"So far, half of the plan will work, but there will not be any guarantees of the other half working. Without Kristy in position, there is no promise the other part will work out so smoothly."

"Aim!" the brute continued.

I saw a shadow walk past, blocking my view of the sunset if only for a second. I thought maybe it was Kristy getting into position. "I think all of our pieces are on the board, Rayshawn. So, make sure you're ready," I said.

"Fire!" the brute continued.

I immediately formed the shield in front of us, stopping the approaching bullets. I heard static, as though something charged up. I threw Rayshawn one of my pistols, "Remember, you can't shoot until there is a break in the shooting." Once they noticed we were shielded, they fired more desperately.

"Prepare to fire. I am going to try to create an opening," I said. I formed a ball of water to try to use a sideways geyser to make an opening for us to return fire. I threw the water like a baseball, hoping to cause it to expand and make an opening; at the very least, I could use it to make a distraction long enough to allow Kristy to make her move. The brute had leaped out of the way. Before I could make it explode, a flash of light struck the ground, making a sound of thunder. After the thunder cleared, there was only the sound of surging electricity. The only one standing was some guy in all-white armor. Lightning circled his body. Besides minor details, his armor closely resembled what Peter and I wore.

"Hey, Ray, do you know who that is?" I asked.

"No, bro, it must be one of theirs," Rayshawn replied, shooting. Rayshawn shot him three times in the back.

As this guy turned around, Rayshawn shot him once on the head, which emptied his clip and reloaded.

Because I also didn't know who it was, I could only assume he was here to help the other team. I saw no way this was possibly an ally of ours. I prepared to fire as well, but as I aimed down sights, he had disappeared just to reappear right in front of me. Somehow, he got through my shield, placing his hand on my gun. He sent enough voltage through the gun to forcefully make my hands release.

"I take it you must be the Lightning Bearer," I said, taking out my knife with my other hand. I went in for the stab, only to have him catch my hand and flip me.

He held the knife to my neck and whispered, "That is strike one! How will you waste the other two?"

I tried to move my hand, but the more I squirmed, the tighter his grip seemed to get. Rayshawn fired at the Lightning Bearer. As the bullet made contact with his armor, it just bounced off. Then the Lightning Bearer launched a bolt of electricity, knocking the pistol right out of his hands.

"If I were you, I wouldn't push my luck. You are already on your second strike. Now that I have your attention, I am the Lightning Bearer that you have heard of. I was hired from one of your contacts to assist your party in retaking the base. If you don't know by now, I could easily kill you by forcing enough electricity through your body to stop your heart from beating; there's enough water in and around your body from the nanomachines to drown a whale six times over. So, the electricity would easily spread." The Lightning Bearer loosened his grip.

"All right, you've made your point," I said.

The Lightning Bearer let go of me. He focused lightning into the knife and threw it. I followed its trajectory with my eyes. I saw a trail left behind, and the brute coming at us. The charged knife had enough force to make the brute fall to his knees. Rayshawn picked up the pistol he had dropped and aimed it downrange; he tried to fire only to realize he was out of bullets.

"Hey, bro, I am out," Rayshawn said.

"Crap, I just realized I don't have any more bullets," I replied, standing up. The brute ran at us again, but I held him back using the pressure from the water. "Hey, Mr. Lightning Bearer, you never told me what you originally came here to do."

"The original plan was to watch the base from afar unless there was an incident, in which case I was to intervene after collecting the survivors who were not involved in the situation. My contact is one of the young ladies here who has been requested by a woman you call Susan. If you two idiots weren't trying to fight me, I could have finished this a long time ago. By the way, have you seen another one walking around? I just don't believe this one is the brains behind this."

"Yeah, there was a gold one. So, what is the plan?" Rayshawn asked.

"I will be helping you two to take down this brute. Then we can turn our attention to the other one."

"What if he's escaping as we speak?" Rayshawn asked.

"Then he will be blown out of the sky. I had your demolition expert rig each aircraft with explosives. So, if he were to run away, he'd die before he knew what was coming to him. I have both of those females looking for him. The first place they were to look was the motor pool. From there, they were to look in the surrounding tents until they made contact with us."

While the Lightning Bearer talked, he sent electricity with the water to see if he could halt the brute's advance. But it was all for naught. It was almost like the brute wasn't affected at all. "I will have to do something else. You two will have to keep him busy until I come back." With the sound of trickling electricity, the Lightning Bearer disappeared.

"Well, I doubt we could keep him busy for much longer," I said under my breath. I turned to Rayshawn and yelled. "Rayshawn, go around back. See if there is a weapon lying around. That might buy us the time we need for him to come back. I think he has a plan."

So, Rayshawn made his move; it was about five seconds before he fired on the brute, but it didn't cause the brute to lose any concentration. As I saw his hands break through the water, I prepared to get out of the way. I made a pothole about knee-deep. It would give me just the time I needed to escape. If the brute's strength was like Peter's, if he managed to grab me, it would be game over for me. So, I moved backward. As he reached to grab me, his foot fell into the pothole. Next, I grabbed a rifle from one of the bodies on the floor, thinking I could shoot out one of his eyes, only to realize there were no bullets left in the magazine. As I released the magazine, the brute got out of the trap and headed straight for Rayshawn, so I proceeded to create a shield right in front of him.

I heard the Lightning Bearer returning from where ever he was. He appeared between Rayshawn and the brute. From where I was standing, I could tell the Lightning Bearer was holding a big weapon, but I couldn't see what it was.

The Lightning Bearer said, "Everyone get down!"

I dove to the ground and heard a very loud bang. It was the loudest bang I have ever heard. I wasn't sure of the reason at the time, but I noticed a bullet, and as the bullet hit the ground, it separated into three different parts. The brute fell to the floor, coughed up blood, and fell, placing one hand over his or her stomach and the other over his or her mouth. The armor retracted and his or her face became visible, though from where I stood, I could only see her blond, braided hair. I got up from the ground and walked over to the girl. I took a look at the face of this girl. When I saw her face, I could tell her face was remodeled. I next noticed her face had been so swollen and disfigured that you couldn't even tell she was a woman if you didn't already know.

"You know what he is capable of, and yet you all still work for him. O'Neal is just going to use you...until you no longer have the strength to fight. You could have joined us...I guess, to the winners..." The brute said, bleeding out.

I looked away because watching a person die was painful. As I looked away, I saw the Lightning Bearer holding a sniper rifle. Upon closer inspection, I noticed it was the same one Laura had made. "Hey, what are you doing with Laura's sniper rifle?" I asked.

The Lightning Bearer replied, "I am only borrowing it from her." He pulled out a paper and gave it to me.

I took the paper and noticed it was completely signed by Laura to allow him to borrow the rifle; I couldn't question what he was doing. "Do you know where she is then?"

"Young Laura? She is currently resting in your room." That was a big relief on my heart and mind to know that she had been safe during the conflict. "You will have to see her after."

Rayshawn took one of the rifles he had on the ground and placed the butt of it on the brute's neck.

"What are you doing?" I asked.

Rayshawn replied, "I am checking her pulse. I would do it with my fingers, but her muscles are too thick."

"You two should go after the gold one. God only knows what will happen if they get away. I will be fine; trust me, bros," said Rayshawn.

"Let's go!" the Lightning Bearer said, throwing me something that had been on the brute's wrist. When I caught it, it turned to dust.

"What was that?" I asked, following after him.

"Nothing now. You must have broken it." He fiddled with the radio. "Team Two, what is your location?"

"We have intercepted the gold target at the helipads. We will need backup; nothing we are doing is stopping him. I am not sure if Team Three has our surprise ready for him or not, and if he gets away, he may return with a stronger force."

"All right, we will be there shortly."

We had a chance to finish off the leader, but the quickest way to regroup with Kristy was to run into the enemy's stronghold around the base. As we ran through the stronghold, all of the enemies had already been slain. I wasn't sure by who, or what, it could have been.

"Where are you, Leo?" Britney yelled on the radio.

"We are on the way to your location now."

"Hurry it up; we can't hold out much longer. He's too much of a match for us here."

"Understood," I replied. Then under my breath, added, "Yeah, no pressure." I ran the rest of the way. When I approached, I saw Britney reloading her weapon with her teeth; I could tell she had been wounded in her right arm. I ran past while the Lightning Bearer stayed behind. He tended to Britney's wounds. As I approached, I saw Kristy was severely wounded with shards of what I could only assume came from her own blades covering her own body. I heard an engine turning on for one of the helicopters. I looked around and saw the propellers on one of the helicopters moving.

The gold man yelled out of the window, "You should have joined me when you had the chance. We would have been unstoppable, but now I will crush you on my violent return."

I started collecting water and charging the helicopter. When I was underneath the aircraft, it was already thirty feet in the air. As I was about to throw the water into the propellers to jam up the gears, Jonny walked up to me, laughing. He threw me a detonator.

"Hey, Leo, you remember that favor I owe you for assisting me with the explosive containments on our last mission? Consider it paid in full." He ran away. "I'll be taking care of Kristy; you take care of our uninvited guest."

I pushed the trigger and saw the explosion was shaped like an emoticon with a tongue sticking out like the ones I used in my emails back home. As it got closer to the ground, the three blades on both propellers were forcefully and simultaneously ejected; one was launched straight into the air, the other five broke into many nonlethal pieces, keeping the damage around the base to a minimal. The helicopter fell to the ground, and their leader crawled out of the wreckage. He stopped when he knew he was clear of the flames, but as he stopped moving, the vehicle had a small implosion, which caught onto his legs. This crushed the leader's feet inside the destroyed helicopter, but this did not kill or cripple him. He was perfectly fine; he just could not completely move his legs, for it had warped around both of his legs.

I began to walk toward him, saying, "Now that was just completely overkill." I leaned over. "What have you done with our allies?"

"What do you think? The ones who refused to join me, I tormented until they changed their minds, and those who still refused to listen to my command were killed. Those who tried to escape were killed immediately, but it seems as though I couldn't get all of them. So, which are you talking about, and do try to be less vague?"

"Becky and Daysen!"

He laughed. "It seems I overestimated you. I guess you really don't know what is going on here, do you? No, you couldn't, that would be the only way to manipulate you. The truth is..." A flash of light blinded me, and I felt myself being pushed. I got up quickly and rubbed my eyes to see. I saw the Lightning Bearer stand over me. I looked back over to the gold mystery man and saw the propellers sticking out of his chest.

"SUB...WAY...will...consume..." He exhaled, and then he died.

"I must have forgotten to plant the last explosive on the blade," Johnny yelled, helping Kristy off the floor. "Let's hope the information he had wasn't all that important."

I leaned over to check for his pulse and the device on his wrist, much like the device the Lightning Bearer had thrown to me, turned to dust; the armor he wore slowly rose into the air like burning ash. As the armor turned to ash, the leader's face became more visible. When I got a better look, I noticed it was Daysen.

Rayshawn walked up beside me. "Hey, bro, I've got some bad news. It seems the brute was—"

I interrupted, "Becky, yeah, at this point, I am not even the least bit surprised."

"So, I take it the other one was Daysen? Hmm...What a mess we have been tangled into."

"Ray, we are going to have to clean this mess up. We will be using Sue's emergency protocol Alpha-One-Lemma-Nine-Sigma. It might take all night to do, but it might be the only way."

"Already on it. What about Becky and Daysen?"

"They will be treated as Bravo-Three-Lemma-Five-Trident."

"Sounds good, bro."

Alpha-One-Lemma-Nine-Sigma could easily be broken down. The first letter was to show the importance, hence Alpha; the first number indicated the order of the mission; if you had two Alphas, one would be more important than the other, hence the need of the number. The second letter told you what job needed to be completed. The second number dictated different areas that needed to be taken care of. The third letter, Sigma, represented the hours it needed to be done in, also known as "no later than." In short, we needed to take care of this right then; whatever you were doing before needed to be put on hold. The base needed to be absolutely spotless, and the places that could not be fixed would be made to look like we were under attack by some other force. We had nine points to clean and nineteen hours to make it all possible.

The Lightning Bearer walked up behind me, saying, "There was nothing we could have done to save your comrades. Those test model suits will corrupt and manipulate the minds and hearts of all who wear them. Even if we were to take it off, their minds were too far gone."

I took a deep breath. "What are test model suits?"

"The best way I could summarize is they are practice suits to make the armor we are wearing possible." I noticed his voice scrambled up a little bit. "It seems we will co...tin...this con...ion later. I think the explo...damaged my voice filter...next time." He turned into a bolt of lightning and vanished.

I noticed where he had stood was Laura's new sniper rifle. I picked it up so I could return it to Laura, but it wasn't as heavy as it looked. I saw Laura barely get up from her sleep.

"Laura, I am very happy to see you are doing well, but I am going to save the pleasantries for later. We have an Alpha-One objective." On the inside, I was truly relieved.

I had honestly wished what we had dealt with was an invasion rather than an internal conflict. But you can't have everything you want, so you have to make up for the shortcomings. Within the time frame set before us, we had the base running efficiently. Those who had conspired with Daysen and Becky were eliminated. Coming up with our story wasn't too difficult; if they asked about what happened, we said Daysen and Becky had run off, eloped, and taken a helicopter and the ROACH with them. As for the damage, Becky flew, and we tried to stop them. As we approached their room to look for clues on their location, there was a note that said they were running away to the far corners of the island. Sadly, I couldn't lie, so I avoided being asked, for in truth, we took their bodies and buried them together right outside of our camp. We burned their belongings out at sea. Susan returned right after we finished cleaning. She didn't notice the story was untrue, so she returned to her tent. As for Britney, she had left our base the moment her injuries were completely healed. From what I heard, she was also able to return home because of some strings the Lightning Bearer pulled for her. As it turned out, her father was a doctor who worked on some vegetarian soy experiment that would allow vegetarians to get all the minerals and proteins needed to survive without ever eating meat, but I don't have all the details on that. Conner never found out what happened because no one cared to tell him, and if he were ever really there to be a leader, we wouldn't have had so many problems. As long as money wasn't noticeably affected, he didn't care. In fact, the lack of maintenance saved him money in the long run.

# 6
## I Can't Believe... This Is One of Those Stories

After about three months of sending out search parties for the lovely couple, we were given orders to count them as a lost cause. This wasn't before sending out a bounty on the two. Due to lack of troops, I was surprised it took so long for them to stop the search. The people they used to search for the two were from Conner's other base, also known to us as Alpha Base, the base Trudy was currently stationed at. We called it Alpha Base because it was better manned and maintained than where we were stationed previously, plus, if we ever looked for Conner, we could usually find him there with something to complain about. The ones who went out to search never returned, and because of this, Conner needed to temporarily relocate some of his troops between the bases. It took four weeks before the relocation process was finally done. Somehow, I was caught in their rotation, which gave me time to realize just how much of a difference there was between the bases, mostly on how much better they were at being prepared for a combat situation. Their weakness was with their chef's oven-heating system always breaking down and their leadership never seeing eye to eye. However, they would request our base to precook some of the food, and as for the leadership, since they had an abundance of people, it really didn't matter. When I returned, Flowers had left us, taking another contract for a black market that he later became the leader of. Peter and Kristy sparred against each other to improve their skills. Peter was to assist Susan with the night operations, while Kristy was to take point during the day.

Cold winter nights were now upon us, and snow completely covered the ground. When I was still in California living in the desert, snow was a rare thing to see. I didn't see much of it back then. It wasn't too bad because, sadly, I hate the cold too much to enjoy the snow. One of those days on the island, I remember just lying bundled on my cot, listening to footsteps crunching in the snow, thinking about what my family would be doing this time of year. When I saw them again, would they recognize me? How old was my nephew? Did my sister, Cheryl, have more kids? Did my mother's cooking still taste the same? Did my dad still cook his famous fried chicken? Did my sister Kat even talk to our family, or did she still disown us? Did anyone still visit the cemetery where my brother's body lay? Most importantly, did they miss me? While thinking of these things, Laura walked in, talking to someone. I didn't bother looking; I just wanted to stay warm.

"Yes, ma'am, he is right here with me," she said. "You told me you needed to talk to us together about a personal mission."

"Yes, please place the device down somewhere." The voice reminded me of someone I had not seen nor heard in a while. I would take a look but it was just too cold. I heard her place whatever device she used on a desk right in front of where I lay. "You did make sure the room is one-hundred-percent clear of nearby eavesdroppers? The last thing I need is some unexpected guest waltzing in to stop our conversation shorter than the time I already have."

"Every time you say anything, the people outside only hear a chirping bird," Laura replied.

"Very good." The voice paused. "Leonardo and Laura, I am very happy to see you two still alive and kicking. I don't normally ask for favors, but, sadly, I will need one now." I finally got up to see who was talking; when I looked, I saw a hologram of the Webmaster calmly sitting down in her chair. "One of our neighboring villages have agreed to merge our two villages together, and we can finally live peacefully as one community, but there has been a problem. Their leader has gone missing. We need her to make it official to merge; no one else can approve or disapprove because she is the one in charge. The kidnappers will more than likely try to use her as a way to hurt the two villages, or they may just have other plans for her; we need you to stop them at all costs. She is in a tall tower covered by armed guards and land mines. So, the ground is not a route you should take. Air will be your only way in. Normally, we could easily handle a situation as easy as this; however, some of the people who are opposed to the idea of the merge have hired a hit man to execute the young lady before she can sign the treaty. I have already arranged a mode of travel for you two to arrive there with little to no problems. Your ride will be here shortly if you accept. What is your answer?"

Because the Webmaster was like a second mother to me, I agreed. "I'll take the job," I replied. Laura nodded. I continued, "Just tell me how long until our escort gets here so I know how much time I'll have to get ready."

My tent started to flap from a strong gust of wind coming from outside.

"He will be ready to leave in about fifteen minutes, so you have ten to get ready. Laura will be waiting aboard the drop ship."

I felt cold touch my cheek; when I looked, I saw Laura holding the snow in place with a smile, saying, "You heard the lady, let's go." Laura walked out of the tent, taking the projector with her. I got ready and walked outside. The drop ship was right in front of my tent, so I just walked aboard. When I sat down, I noticed our pilot was flying the chopper; Corporal Samuel Lee was his name.

"Leonardo, how's it been going? I haven't seen you for about a year."

"It's all right," I replied. "So, where are we headed?" Corporal Samuel Lee was a freelance pilot. He would work for SUBWAY from time to time, and work against us as well. He was actually famous around the island for his piloting skills.

We went up, wasting no time.

"Well, if you can't see it now, you'll see it as we get closer. It is quite hard to miss." The snow lightened up as we took off; it might have been because the thrusters melted the snow.

"Laura, what else is there to this mission that I should know before we get any closer?"

"Nothing, really. The only information I have is the same information we were given in the briefing. I will keep you posted as any possible updates come in, Cross."

*So, we are already on mission basis*, I remember thinking to myself. Laura passed over the information to my visor's display; from what I could see, it was the layout of the tower we were headed to. I saw it was built like the Leaning Tower of Pisa.

"According to the layout of the place, there is an underground base. This will likely be populated with enemy forces; however, it might be an alternative exit if things get too hairy and we want to avoid getting shot down from the AA guns on the ground. How you maneuver up and down the tower is really up to you. I understand you might be able to get out using your water abilities as far as flying out of the area goes; however, it would be too risky to try any of the stunts you would normally go for. Besides, if what the Webmaster said is true and they are sending an assassin in, we don't know who it is. Wait☐we have new information coming in." Laura paused and started typing on the computer. "It seems the assassin is going to be the Lightning Bearer, so you might be a lot safer if you travel underground rather than above ground if he shows up." I nodded my head in agreement.

The snow picked up once more, causing mild turbulence. I looked in the distance and noticed something. It was like a tower, though it was kind of hard to see because of the snow. Laura looked too and said, "There it is. We will be there in twenty minutes." She sat back down and prepared her rifle for combat.

As we got closer, we opened the drop ship bay doors. "Hey, I don't see the tower," I said.

"That is because you are looking out the wrong end, for one. For two, the snow is quite thick, which makes it hard to see it," Corporal Lee replied. "All right, little lady, the dropping point you requested is coming up shortly. Brace yourself for impact and prepare yourself for drop. It may be a rough landing."

"You requested a special landing?" I raised my voice so she could hear me over the loudness of the open door.

"Yes, all landings have been prearranged. Some are more exciting than others."

The tower's defenses began to fire. I would wrap the drop ship with water to protect us; however, this drop ship needed the wind from every angle in order to fly right. Heck, even the rockets exploding would be more helpful than no wind at all. When we were a mile out, the signal for Laura to jump out turned on.

"All right, Cross, I'll see you at the completion of the mission," Laura said as she dove out of the door.

I watched as her parachute opened and she gently glided down.

Mr. Lee looked at me, giving a thumbs up, and said, "All right, kiddo, I am going to be dropping you off like a bad girlfriend. Remain calm and maybe we can survive the separation. Good luck."

"What is supposed to happen?" I asked.

Before he answered, we had already begun to separate. As we separated, I saw him flying straight up, moving about three times faster than when he had approached. I flew straight at the tower like a missile. Before the pod connected with the tower, a shielding covered me from the impact. I rammed into the tower, got out of the opened cargo bay door, and walked around. When I looked back, I noticed the part of the ship I arrived in was oddly shaped like a pod.

"Cross, are you in the tower?" Laura asked.

"I am in the tower," I replied. "Where is the VIP?"

"I'll let you guess. After all, we are talking about a person in distress and a giant tower. You tell me."

"From your sarcasm, I am guessing it is a safe bet she is at the top of this tower." I began going up the stairs. "Hey, Serenity, is everything all right? You don't seem quite yourself today. I also noticed you were avoiding me a little. Do you have some kind of history with the VIP or maybe even the Lightning Bearer?"

She sighed heavily. "History, no, I don't have any real history with either one. I never met the princess because she was appointed maybe two years ago, and as you know, we have both been here. I did, however, hear a few rumors about her. For one, she originally came from one of the main countries. They appointed her as a princess only to rival the Webmaster. She is at the very least in her teen years. Even though she is very young, she is also very talented and smart. She brought in new ideas and built better defenses, so they were also able to hold their own against invaders, and personally, if it weren't for her, they would have been killed off months ago. Though being young is her strength, this is also her Achilles's heel because she lacked experience. Since the Webmaster saw they were so desperate to have a leader they would take advantage of a non-native, she came up with the idea to merge the villages together so everyone would be a winner. As for the Lightning Bearer, he is a gun for hire. He's so good at his job he could easily kill his targets in a room full of people without ever harming anyone else. However, if you were to push his buttons too much, he'd attack you without mercy. He uses what he calls the three-strike rule."

"What, like baseball?" She gave no response. "Never mind, so did you bring along your custom rifle?"

"Yes, I didn't work on this bad boy for nothing. I will be using a drill tip on the end of the bullet. If my calculations are correct, it should be able to dig underground at great speeds and still hit its target up to a mile underground. Hmm...well, if I am being totally honest with you, I guess the Lightning Bearer and I do have a little history. In the end, he knows me better than I know myself. I couldn't explain even if I wanted to. By the way, my area is clear and I am set up with my rifle. I hope, for the sake of the mission, you are already going up the stairs."

"Yes, I am already on the move."

"Good, I will do what I can to help you. You shouldn't have to worry about reinforcements if they mistake the pod you arrived in as a missile or something. They may just look for a damage report and send in the bomb squad. This is considering you don't trip any alarms on the way up. If they do show up, I will shoot the grenades you left behind, which should activate the fire extinguisher, making a controlled fire. That way, they'll believe it really was a missile with a delayed explosion rather than an empty pod."

As I climbed up, I noticed how high this tower was; it seemed like an endless number of stairs. I wished they had placed an elevator in this tower or something to that effect. I heard an explosion coming from down below. After about a minute, I finally made it to the top floor. I saw the pathway was clear.

"Laura, do you think this old tower would have any pressure plates?"

"The tower really isn't that old; in fact, it was completed a few weeks before you arrived to the Webmaster. It only looks old on the outside, but the inside is actually pretty modern."

"All right, then it would be safe to assume the path leading to the POW is probably protected by motion detectors. I will be going up." I cut a hole in the top of the tower so I could go through the roof. While I was on the roof, I sliced along my path just enough to see where I was headed. When I was right above her door, I broke into her cell.

I looked around the room and saw a young woman wearing an all-white dress suit standing by a window, looking out at the snowy storm. Her red hair was tied in a ponytail reaching to the bottom of her shoulder blades. She turned toward me slowly. As she turned around, I noticed her eyes were hazel, she was wearing glasses, and she was very young, looking about sixteen or seventeen.

She said, "So, you must be the executioner," although it looked like she wanted to say something else.

"Why would you assume such a thing?" I replied, putting my sword on my back.

"First off, you are not dressed like the rest of the guards who have been bringing my food. Second, I was told by one of the guards there is an assassin on the way here."

"That would be the other guy. If I was going to kill you, I would have just destroyed the tower."

"Then who are you?" she asked.

"The Webmaster sent me here to escort you back home. If you must have a name to call me right now, it will be Cross for the time being. We need to get out of here before the other one shows up and kills both of us."

"Fine, we are good to leave then," she replied, walking toward the door.

"Cross, did you find the girl we are looking for?" Laura said over the radio.

"Yes, the VIP is no longer a POW." There was an explosion followed immediately by the alarm going off. "Serenity, was that you?" I asked.

"No, I am out of sight and too far for them to see me. I think the explosion of the pod triggered it; what a delayed response."

"I'll say, and you said it was modern. I guess the pressure plate doesn't matter anymore." I turned off the radio and pulled out my pistol. "Crap, we don't have time for this. I can't believe the alarms are going off now. Stay close, Princess."

"All right," she replied. I broke the door down, ran out, and headed down the stairway with my pistol drawn.

I noticed she wasn't moving as fast as me. "Come on, young miss, we need to get out of here quickly before we are overrun. If you can, stay within ten to twenty steps behind me. Any closer and you may be harmed; any further and we might not make it out of here in time," I said. "If you need to stop, tell me, and I will comply, and I shall expect the same in return." I headed down the stairs as quickly as I could, listening for her footsteps coming from behind.

"There are about twenty people halfway up, coming to you, Cross," Laura said. "I take it back, eighteen coming up. I am losing perspective position, so hurry up and get to ground level. I am going to be moving in shortly."

"We are moving as fast as we can. Is there any sign of the Lightning Bearer?"

"Not yet; he hasn't shown up on my radar."

"Good, then we still have time. Please keep me posted."

We continued going down the stairs. When we ran into our first enemy, they had already fallen to the ground. "Crap, I understand she is an experienced shooter. Sometimes it scares me just how good she is," I mumbled under my breath." It was at this point I realized how lucky I was just to have Laura on my team. I heard her voice over the radio, but all I could hear was an uncontrollable amount of static. It seemed she was adding information based off how long she was talking. "Repeat please, Serenity, that was not a good copy." More static. I stopped, turned to the princess, and said, "I might have lost contact with my partner. We will have to be extremely careful."

"Will they be all right?" she asked me.

"She has survived more than her fair share of battles," I replied. To be honest, I was more afraid for our well-being than Laura's. It wasn't because I was selfish, but rather, I'd seen Laura survive more impossible odds while she was half asleep, without even a scratch. We finally got to the midsection of the tower; the Lightning Bearer was waiting for us there.

Next, my communications restored, and I heard Laura's voice: "I repeat, the Lightning Bearer is in the building, and I do not have a clear shot. If you can, either make them visible so I get a clear shot or clear the building. Either way, hurry up and choose."

I heard the princess's footsteps behind me stop.

"Come down, Princess, I already know you're there," the Lightning Bearer said.

I raised my hand as if to tell her not to move. He raised his hand toward me, saying, "You have a valiant knight here, Princess, but please understand that if you don't come and accept your death, then he shall die along with you. You have three seconds to comply. Three."

I heard lightning rise sporadically.

"Two." Lightning focused in his hands, and I felt myself die a little inside.

"One."

"Wait!" she yelled, running down the stairs. I blocked her from coming down the stairs. "What are you doing?" she whispered.

"I don't take failure very well, Princess," I whispered back.

"That is strike one," the Lightning Bearer said.

I formed water underneath his feet and made it explode like a mini geyser. I heard a small current of electricity as it exploded.

"Strike two," the Lightning Bearer said, hanging from the ceiling. Though I provoked him, I also tried to move him without making it so obvious.

"Cross, I have the shot. What do you want to do?" Laura asked.

"Do you have anything to blind them?" the princess asked.

"Serenity, fire a flash bang up here on my signal," I said. The princess pulled the sword off my back. The way she held it, I could see the tip of the sword from the corner of my eye. "What are you doing?" I asked the girl. I watched as it changed shape. The snow around the building stopped in place, which did not stop it from collecting outside. I watched carefully as it melted. The Lightning Bearer did not notice the snow outside seize from what I could tell.

Laura said, "Message received. Firing to your current position. Two seconds until impact. Be sure to shield your eyes from the blast." I don't know how she received a signal to fire.

I turned around quickly and placed the princess's head down to the floor. When Laura's shot exploded, the tower also exploded. As we fell, I held on to the princess tightly, looking up to see if I could see the Lightning Bearer follow us, but I did not see him. I formed water below, but using my sword, the princess used the water to punch a hole in the ground level, forcing us to fall into their underground facility. When we landed on the ground of the cavern, I ran forward to avoid being crushed by falling debris. Then we ran to nearby cover. When I knew we were in the clear, I laid down on the ground and looked at the stalactites hanging from the ceiling.

"What are you doing, we need to go," the princess whispered.

"Do we, now? I don't like being too much in the dark, so I need you to explain what is really going on. Until you talk, I will be staying here."

"That makes no sense," she replied. I sighed and retracted my suit, even though it was cold in the cavern. "Are you seriously going to do this right now?" she asked.

"If you can't tell by now, I am not wearing my armor and quite bundled up, so the cold will affect you long before it will start affecting me." I took a deep breath. "You know it really isn't as cold as I thought it was."

Seeing I wouldn't move, she said, "OK, my name is Lilly Alexis Celestial. I am the granddaughter of one of the creators of the suits. To be more exact, I am the granddaughter of the lightning creator's suits. They made their suits with an override switch only blood-related family members could use without being official users. My grandmother and my dad told me this override would not go past the third generation. I was only on this island to visit my grandmother's friend who needed some materials for a new project he was working on. As I was about to leave this island, my escort was bribed ahead of time to bring me to see if I could fix an issue they had in the camp. Shortly after arriving, their leader became sick and because of how smart I was, they made me their leader. No was not an answer. They needed me to try and compete with the Webmaster's intelligence. I had a plan to unite the two lands so I could go home. While I was being transported between the two villages, my carrier was attacked and ended up here. The captors, from what I could understand, were to keep me here as a ransom. After we are done here, I need to go back to my grand-mother's friend so he can help me find a way to get out of here and return to Montana. If you would like, I could take you with me."

"What do you mean?" I replied.

"I can tell you don't belong here from the way you act. If you help me now, I promise to get you home. Do we have a deal?"

I was skeptical because I'd never heard of anyone ever leaving, just a few rumors here and there, but it couldn't hurt to try to leave this place.

"Fine." I raised my hand to make the deal.

She grabbed me by my arm and pulled me up. She then grabbed my sword and slapped me; from what I could tell, she grabbed the sword to nullify my water's shielding ability.

"If you ever want to make a deal with someone, you should always do it on your feet out of respect. Even if it is with someone like me, do you understand?" She didn't slap me hard, just enough to get my attention. Besides, it wasn't the first time I was told this, but it was the first time I was ever hit for not doing it. Last time, I was dropped in a waterless well that I had to climb out by myself; this was while I was learning to fight hand-to-hand from Laura while I still worked for the Webmaster. From what I was told, she needed to teach me some manners. It seemed insulting to someone who was taking time out of his or her busy schedule to help you. Though this was a very different situation, the concept was the same.

"So, do we have a deal?" she reiterated, keeping her hand out.

"Yes, ma'am," I replied. I thought about becoming angry, but I saw no purpose in doing so. After all, she was possibly my only way off this island.

"Can we please leave before we are discovered?" she asked me.

"Yes, let's go." As I was about to walk off, I noticed water leaking onto a stalactite. "If we follow the path of the water on the ceiling, the closest path leading us right out of here seems to be about three miles away. We will have to go there before the Lightning Bearer shows up."

"When did you survey the area?" she asked me.

"Did you think I was lying on the ground just wasting time?" I had gotten a good look at the cavern we were in and noticed the lighting was actually from crystals reflecting light from the surface. I thought for sure the snow would have blocked the natural lighting, but they might have removed the snow from the surface, possibly using fire as a substitute; either that or the clouds were gone. "We need to get going, Lilly."

"OK, let's go," she replied, keeping the sword handy.

We walked slowly, keeping our heads low. It seemed every time we heard someone's voice, it was always for just a second, and then it would go away. Though I could not understand the language directly, my suit identified it as an older Latin language and translated it as chatter for evacuation plans and which route they would take to make sure there was no one left behind. They would check using a search party of only fifty, who were checking by twos in separate areas of the cavern. Based on how they talked, they were not looking for intruders.

"What is our next plan to proceed? Twenty-five groups are a little more difficult to avoid," she said.

"We will have to play by ear. This will be the only way to avoid being detected." We continued a little further until we saw the scouting party walking by. Stopping, I asked her in a very low tone, almost like a whisper, "Why did you stop us from being on ground level where this would have been easier?"

"I don't know if you have realized it or not, but you do not have control over ice," Lilly stated. "If we had stayed on the surface, even with your armor, it would be very difficult to protect someone from an endless army on the surface when you cannot create a shield at the proper time you need it, and it isn't there. That isn't even including the assassin, who most likely survived as we have. As long as we were on the surface, he could collect electricity from the clouds a lot more efficiently than you could collect water from the snow. Considering the fact there's more water sources underground and he was also waiting for us at ground level, I think I made the right choice." As soon as she saw the coast was clear, she tugged me in the direction we were going.

This felt like the longest walk of my life, for the simple fact she didn't talk unless you asked her a question. She would answer, then it would go back to being... weird. I was surprised just how straightforward she was. Maybe she was telling me I talk too much. It was at that moment I wished the radio would come back on. Most of that time, I think I was just talking to myself. Yeah, so fun.

As we got closer to the exit, I saw Lilly getting tired and noticed an open door leading inside of a building. Once we were inside, I noticed all the doors were opened.

"Do you need a moment to rest, Lilly?" I asked.

She replied, "No, the sooner we leave, the sooner we are in the safe zone, so let's not rest until the mission is done. Besides, we do not know if they have checked this area yet."

We continued walking, following the water from the ceiling. We could feel the flow of air coming from the surface. It was then we came across their rally point, unexpectedly. There were guards standing on the wall waiting for their people.

"Cross, Cross, can you hear me? If you can hear me...I want you to know I am above your current position... Please respond."

"Serenity, oh, thank God. Yeah, I have a good copy. What happened to you? You sound like you are in a lot of pain."

"Yeah, while I was trying to avoid conflict with the Lightning Bearer, I seem to have rolled into a few cacti, so I have thorns jammed in my arm and the side of my abdomen. I got away, but I don't know where he is right now. How are things going with the VIP?"

"Things are going all right; she's not much of a talker. Hey, could you cause a distraction for us down here? But be careful, if you kill these targets, you may start an unnecessary conflict with these locals. From what I can tell, they don't know we are here, and if you kill them, they may discover us."

"You do understand you are asking for a large request? I couldn't help you."

On their radio, a voice began yelling, "Emergency, we have injured personnel in a collapsed building. All personnel required." The two guards threw their rifles over their shoulders and ran away quickly. We began to move.

"Laura, what did you do?"

"I didn't do anything. If you don't believe me, you can check my ammo when we get back. I could tell you where all of them went."

"Nevertheless, what is the status on the surface?"

"Well, after the Lightning Bearer destroyed everything up here and killed everyone, he disappeared. I think he might have a secondary objective."

"I wonder what it might be."

"You know, this is the third time he tore up the battlefield and left me alive. I am starting to think he has a thing for me," Laura said. It seemed as though she caught her breath.

"Who knows with that guy? Maybe he is trying to impress you. All I know is he has shown me no favoritism. Well, regardless, we could make our escape now."

I saw someone on top of a building looking down. "Hey, bro, what's up?" Rayshawn's voice said over the radio.

"Rayshawn, is that you?" I asked, using the radio.

"Yeah, I am right here."

"What are you doing here?"

"We finished early and heard you might need assistance. I was transported here from one of your contacts. Someone by the name of Rodney Trotter; he said he was going to pick you up. Hurry up so we can get out of here. The rest of the path is clear."

We ran to meet with Rayshawn, and as we approached, we saw the Lightning Bearer standing right next to him. I stopped Lilly. The Lightning Bearer walked toward us, saying, "It seems our game of hide-and-seek has finally come to an end."

"Rayshawn, move; he's not an ally!" I yelled.

The Lightning Bearer used enough voltage to stun him, from what I could tell. Then the Lightning Bearer threw him to the side.

"You people at SUBWAY are just too predictable, from the way you think all the way to how to manipulate you. He should be glad he hasn't tried to get in my way just yet. Now, surrender the girl, and I will let you walk out of this with your life!"

"Sorry, my friend, but I am not allowed to do that," I replied. He flashed in front of us with a shotgun to my throat.

"Do you really understand the position you are in right now?" The shotgun's barrels were cut off. Then he was pushed away by a wave of water. As the water pushed him, he used his sheer speed to split the wave and grab me by the neck. As he went to grip, he was pushed into the wall from the sword. The force looked like it was stronger than the wave Lilly had just formed. After he was pinned and realized he couldn't move, he sent an electrical shock into the sword. This forced Lilly to drop the sword. To keep him pinned, I used the water again, only to have the same incident happen to me. When the electricity hit me, I instantly fell to the floor and nearly blacked out. As I tried to roll over, my helmet began to retract, which allowed me to throw up.

"That was strike three," the Lightning Bearer said as he walked up to me. "I am a little surprised you did that, considering that you had just seen that happen to her. You seemed smart the last time we met, so what happened between now and then?"

"I don't know, reflex," I replied, rolling over to my back.

"So, are you ready to see if there is an afterlife?" he asked, charging his fist.

"Leave him alone!" Lilly yelled. "I am your target, remember?" She raised her hands to surrender, opening her palm. I took a look at her hand and could see second-degree burns.

"Wait there, your lordship, and I shall be with you in a second." He sent the electricity through his hands into her body and charged his hand once more. At this point, I could not even attempt to run away because my vision was fading in and out. I tried to stand up, but as I got up, the Lightning Bearer grabbed me with his uncharged hand. But as he grabbed me, he fell to his knees and let go.

"Rayshawn, report, did I hit the locked target?" Laura said over the radio.

"Yeah," Rayshawn replied. "The target is down. We should be wrapping up here very soon."

"It seems I didn't send enough of an electrical charge into your friend's body," the Lightning Bearer said, holding his hand over his face. I had noticed dust falling from the ceiling, which was an indication that the drill bullets actually worked like they were supposed to. "Maybe this is what I get for the crimes I have committed."

I looked over to the princess and said, "Grab Rayshawn and head toward the rally on his tracker. And get out of here before he regains his strength. I'll catch up as soon as I can. I just have to catch my breath. Hurry and get out of here."

I heard footsteps running toward where I thought Rayshawn was. I had to assume she left with Rayshawn.

"You understand that, without them, you have no backup to take me on, that you are defenseless right now." The Lightning Bearer said slowly as he got up and covered his left eye.

"Your mission objective is secured, and even now, you are still pursuing?" I replied. "You know you must admit defeat sometime in your life. What does your contract say, anyway, to make you so persistent?"

"Contract states I must kill the leader of the village."

"She's no longer going to be the leader. She's planned to leave them as soon as possible. That will be today. I am going to be sure they drop her off somewhere else so she can go home to her family."

"Is that what she told you? How do you know she's not just trying to use you?" he asked, standing over me.

"I don't really care if she's using me; heck, I'd help you if you asked. Besides, dealing with liars is something I've done since childhood," I said, trying to once again stand up. "My brother was a compulsive liar, so I know what to look for. Lilly didn't show any of those traits."

"Do you claim to be an expert?"

"Of course not; no two people are exactly the same."

"You seem like a man who has a lot of trust issues, and living in this part of the world, you must have trusted someone."

"Honestly, I've been placed in more than one uncomfortable situation where I've had to put my life in other people's hands. There was the Webmaster, Anita, Rodney

Trotter, you, and even my sister, who I recently learned had a secret life. None of whom I regret trusting. But the one I trust the most is my companion, Laura; the one who has stayed with me since the first day I woke on this stupid crazy island."

"Oh, how sentimental. You understand you are just another mission to her?"

"That might be true about you, but I don't feel that same way about her. I think if I had to be honest, I trust her more than anyone." I stopped talking, got to my feet, and put my helmet back on. "It isn't because she is so honest, nor because she is so friendly. It helps, but those are not my reasons, rather it is just because I feel I can. Though I don't know the princess enough to trust her, I can't see how lying to me would benefit her at all. My mission is to bring her back alive anyway, whether she told me her story or not. Don't you have someone you trust?"

"Trust...The only people I trust are the contractors who hire me to do these kinds of jobs and the one they call 'Big Red,' you know him as Cayden," he said as he walked toward me.

When he approached me, I thought for sure he would kill me. He reached out his hand. Knowing there was nothing I could do to really defend myself, I stood there and watched what he was doing. I then noticed he was waiting with his hand still out, so I shook his hand; it was at that moment I heard my radio shut off. He leaned over, pulled me in, and said, "I wouldn't place all my eggs in one basket, especially with someone like her. A woman like your friend has no reason to stay loyal to you. If the Webmaster were to order her to eliminate you, she would kill you without ever flinching."

"Why are you telling me this?" I asked.

"I am only giving a warning. She is more soldier than human. If I were you, I would seriously think twice before putting all my trust in her hands."

"I will trust her until I can't anymore. And when that finally happens, I will be stuck reminiscing and dwelling on the past." He let go of my hand, and the radio began to reboot when he let go. A bolt of lightning flashed, and when it was clear, he was gone.

"Hey, Bro, do you need someone to hold your hand?" Rayshawn spoke on the radio sarcastically.

"I'll be there shortly," I replied. When I finally caught up, I saw them waiting in an ANT, an all-natural terrain sentinel. The ANT was an armored truck not really made for anything but a brief retreat and recon. This vehicle, whenever we had, it came in bulk. But whenever we got rid of the bulk, we never held onto just one. Because of the bulk, they cost too much to maintain, so we would have to sell all of them again. Eventually, we just stopped using them. I was not sure how Mr. Trotter had found one without the excess, but then again, he was in the military long ago. I looked and saw everyone waiting for me. Even Laura was there.

On the way back, I talked to Mr. Trotter, planning, catching up, and telling him Lilly needed to go somewhere else. He dropped Laura, Rayshawn, and myself off. When we returned, I built an igloo and went to sleep in it to see if it would be warmer. Sadly, I couldn't test it out because a mission came up. When the mission was completed weeks later, the snow had melted and the igloo was gone. We also had two new recruits, Veronica and Victoria. Later, I found out why the base was so cold; it turned out there was a broken generator that was supposed to heat up the area to maintain a moderate temperature around the base.

They did not get to fix the generator until the snow cleared. The day after it was fixed, I received a message from Lilly telling me she was safe with her grandmother's friend. She went on to tell me she would be ready to leave in eight months. All I had to do was survive until the day I could finally leave.

# 7
## Oh...You Two Again

The months passed with few incidents at our base. From the way the seasons behaved, I assumed it was spring going to summer. After my mission for the Webmaster, they decided to give me fewer missions; I think because they felt they could not trust me completely because they saw me as a rogue agent, even a threat to their cause. As for Rayshawn, they piled him up to the neck with work. It got so bad he'd finish one mission just to immediately go on another because they needed someone who was there.

We began to collaborate with other factions. Conner thought it was a good idea; more than likely, he saw more of a profit than an actual ally. One of these allies thought it would be a good idea to assassinate me with all this confusion, but their plan was a failure. The bullet they used deflected off my armor and killed them on impact; I didn't even feel it hit me. I only found out because one of their people told me, but it didn't bother me. I would expect nothing less from the way the armor held up. The only thing that scared me was that the armor began to get cracks; based off what I was hearing, only the fake armors that corrupted the user were breakable.

During this time, it rained off and on. Peter, who normally kept to himself, finally talked to the rest of the group. He also showed interest in one of the new girls. I had also noticed because someone brought it to my attention, Peter never took off his armor even when he went to sleep. While we were on a mission, I saw his ability made him bulletproof. I only saw his skin bruised two times. Once, when he fell about a hundred feet to charge in behind enemy's lines, and another time when he was shot point-blank from a .44 revolver with armor-piercing rounds. During this time, Kristy was used for assassination missions. She would usually finish with her missions before the heat of the day. Occasionally, we would have to work together, and when we did, she complained about how slowly I completed my parts of the objective. Of course, I would rather be slow and efficient than fast and inaccurate. Honestly, I think she worked better alone with assassination missions. The times I would help her, I was at more of a risk of losing my life than she was. That was neither here nor there. The longer I knew her, the more she reminded me of my sister Kat in the way she remained distant. Even her features were the same. Of course, after the mission, she was generally a kind person. I couldn't understand how her personality was so different on and off the field. We had two new girls who joined our unit that stood out above the others. The two of them had ranked up rather quickly and blended in without any problems; they were just learning the ropes. These were the results of Sue destroying an enemy outpost, taking out the last of our immediate enemies. Peter went with Sue to give her support.

I had just woken up from a nap when I heard a lot of footsteps around my tent. I rolled out of my bed and saw Laura standing with her arms crossed, leaning on the doorpost, and looking outside. "What is going on out there?" I asked, covering my face so I had time to adjust to the blinding sunlight outside.

"Sue has returned, and it seems she has a captive with her."

"A captive? That doesn't sound right," I replied, standing up to stretch.

"Yeah. They must be truly skilled, or she is about to make an example out of them."

"Do you know for sure that it is only just one of them?"

"No, but do you see her taking more than one captive at a time?"

"I don't see her taking any of them alive. So, are you going to see the captive?"

"Maybe later. Right now, I have to take care of some paperwork on the other side of base."

Laura walked out of the tent, so I proceeded to do the same, but I did not follow her. I walked outside and saw Sue escorting the prisoner. Her ankles and wrists were completely shackled, and her face was covered in charcoal and ash. Her hair was so long I couldn't see her features.

Some of the people whispered and spread rumors, one of which was, "I heard she was the one who held her ground for twelve days before she finally surrendered. I think they said she ran out of ammo and was forced to surrender because of it."

That was uncomfortable. Sue didn't normally bring prisoners back because their loyalties might be messed up. I watched as they brought her to the center of the camp and forced her down to her knees. As they forced her to her knees, her hair was moved out of the way, and even with a quick glance, her face looked familiar. I walked toward the front of the crowd.

Sue yelled, "The rumors you heard about this young lady are true, and many of you might be wondering what I plan to do with our new guest. The truth is our manpower is low as of late. So we need capable warriors, and this woman here has proven herself more than capable to be one of us." They unshackled the young lady's hands. "Normally, I wouldn't do anything like this, but with her unusual situation, I have decided to bring her into our organization. You will treat her as though she were me."

Sue had left the area and walked over to me. As Sue approached me, I saw Rayshawn walking toward the woman on the stage. "Walk with me," Sue said, moving past me.

"What's going on, Sue?" I asked, following her.

She didn't say anything until we were away from the rest of the group. "Leonardo, I am going to be real with you right now. I have tried to talk to Conner about the upgrades we need at the base. I thought he might listen to me since I am his leading officer here. This would be so much easier if he weren't so cheap. I need you to tell Laura we can't pay her back for her blueprints, so there is no need to continue production. I have also been looking for a way to upgrade your rank in SUBWAY; what do you think?"

"Sue, I am truly grateful, but honestly, from where I stand, being in charge is more of a popularity contest than a position with responsibility, so I couldn't take that position seriously. If you need me to help in any way, don't hesitate to ask, but I couldn't ever see myself in that kind of position."

"I thank you for your honesty. We can continue to discuss this later; it seems your presence will be needed elsewhere." She walked away from me.

"Hey, bro," Rayshawn said, approaching me. "I would like you to meet someone."

I looked behind him and noticed there wasn't anyone there. "Rayshawn, there isn't anybody behind you, and if you're trying to tell me it's your new girlfriend, then we will have to talk about it later."

The recruit Sue had just brought in approached from behind Rayshawn. Looking at her face, I could see her head had almost literally just been removed from a tank of water.

"Sorry, Rayshawn, I needed to wash my face," she said.

I looked at her face. She reminded me of a girl I went to high school with back in California.

"Leonardo, is that you?" she asked.

"So, it really is you, Melena. How have you been? I haven't seen you since the tenth grade."

Melena was a girl I used to like back in high school. She usually seemed to be in trouble, but this seemed impossible because she was a very quiet person who didn't really do anything. I guess it is a possibility she only acted like that when I came around. I remember trying to help her turn her life around because I heard these rumors. But I remember one day in the middle of the school year, she just wasn't there anymore. I wondered if I started helping her too late. I must have started too late; she could have been afraid to change, or maybe deep inside, she never wanted my assistance.

"So, how did you end up on a forsaken island like this one?" she asked.

I answered, "I was kidnapped walking home one night and then sold into slavery. Fun, right? So, how did you end up here?"

"My parents went missing one day. My brother and I went looking for them."

"And I already told you how the two of us ended up here." Rayshawn said.

"That does explain why you didn't go to school anymore," I said. "So, why didn't you two stick together?"

"We are brother and sister," said Rayshawn. "Sometimes we get sick of each other, so we took a break; however, before I could track her down again, SUBWAY captured me."

Melena said, "Meanwhile, I was invited to the LARCS organization by their junior leader, Martin Corrine. He originally hired me because he was undermanned. But while I was under his command, he saw I had great promise, so he trained me to be a more efficient fighter."

Laura walked up behind me. "Hey, Leo, we have a mission coming in."

"Can you show me to my quarters, brother?" Melena asked.

"Sure thing. I will have to catch you two later," Rayshawn said.

"We can catch up more when you return from your mission. Good luck," Melena said.

After they left, Laura asked, "You know her?"

"Her name is Melena. She was my friend when I was in high school. I was told she used to act out while we were in school. To me, however, she seemed like a really kind person who didn't do anything bad. She was a really good friend of mine." I took a look at Laura's eyes. "Hey, are you all right? You seem a little down."

Though beautiful, her blue eyes were never a good sign.

"I'll be fine. Anyway, you have a message from a Kat Blanca. I was told to deliver it to your hands only. I wasn't even allowed to open it myself." She handed me a small data chip and began to walk away. I grabbed her shoulder.

"How did you get this?

"It was delivered by the Webmaster's personal assistant."

"She got another slave?"

"First of all, she buys slaves to give them a chance for a better life. Second, she only treats them like slaves when she first gets them so she can gauge them. Third, the delivery girl was the Webmaster's daughter."

"Victoria, I forgot she was there. Is she the reason you seem down today? Did she say something happened to your brother?"

"No, nothing like that. You have nothing to worry about from me. So, are you going to open the package you were given?"

"Yes, shall we open it?" I asked.

"We?"

"Yeah, sadly, I don't know how to use these chips. If it were a USB or a floppy disk, I know how to use those with little to no problem. But for some reason, I have never came across a chip of this sort. Besides, I would like to know your opinion."

We headed back to our tent because if the message was really private, we needed to keep it that way. Laura hooked the chip up to a projector, which projected a perfectly colored hologram of my sister, Kat. She was sitting down in a desk chair, signing a piece of paper.

"Let's just skip the pleasantries, little brother. This is a recording, so don't bother to verbally respond to anything I say. We all miss you, but we have a bigger issue going on here in the States. To be honest, if I had the time, I wouldn't bother you with such mundane affairs. Our sister's husband has been kidnapped. Looking at the evidence, I have reason to believe he has been kidnapped and brought to the same island. Everything is really unofficial, including your case. When this happened to you, you had a much better chance of survival, not just because you were under the Webmaster's protection but also because I know who you are. But our brother-in-law is not in the same situation.

"Our sister Cheryl has asked me to keep an eye out for him. From what I heard, he was doing research on the day you went missing, and then he went missing himself. Ironic, am I right? Anyway, you will need to go to the island's slave auction; he should be there. I would have requested this from the Webmaster, but she had already got a servant assistant for their village a few months ago, and if they were to get any more, it might attract some unwanted attention. I don't know how well you blend in with the locals, but I hear you know some of the locals on the island. You should convince someone you trust to escort you there if you haven't already.

"Before I forget, your friend Revaughnt is also there; however, my sources cannot prove this. You may want to look into this as well if you have the time for that womanizer. Please hurry up; the sooner we can confirm this, the sooner we can go about our lives. I don't expect you to do this for free, so I will forward you the money upon completion. All you are going to need to do is be sure he is there. Please be swift. Hearing our sister's worried voice is driving me crazy. When you find them, your mission is to get them back as soon as possible. Good luck. Kat out."

The hologram turned off.

"That was your sister?" Laura asked.

"Yeah, and not even a hello," I replied.

"Wow, why is she...why is she like that?"

"She is just busy; she has always been busy. Kat rarely had time for her own family when I was stateside, and when she did, she liked to keep it short and to the point. Heck, before I was brought to this island, she had become more and more distant. We used to be close, I guess, because we were both middle children, and she was the only one who mentally challenged me in my family."

"Do you know what happened?"

"I thought it was because of the death of our little brother, but that affected her more emotionally and did no real damage to her mentally. So, I don't have a clue. Let's do this as soon as possible, my oldest sister..."

"We...Give one good reason why I should agree to go with you," Laura stated, taking the chip out of the projector. By this point, I saw a little smile on her face. "After all, you have your new friend Melena, who was capable of holding her position for twelve days before she was forced to give up. Plus, it would let you catch up on all the time you two have been away."

I knew she was sarcastic, but I had to go with it. "I am sorry for assuming, I just thought you might be interested in going. As far as Melena, she is very busy. Besides, they might not speak the only two languages I speak."

"Your suit can translate every language except for old hieroglyphics, or so I was told by Peter. Just how serious are you about getting my help?"

I looked at her eyes and noticed they were turning green. Now at this time, I had so much I wanted to tell her, but I went with the least embarrassing thing: "I really need you to go because you are my best friend and I trust you the most. There isn't anyone else I'd rather have beside me. That and you are like a good luck charm to me." That caused silence for a few seconds. "That's not what I meant to say, although it is true. It seems as though every time I do a mission with you, even if everything goes wrong, it all seems to fall into place."

"You had me at and best friend and lost me at charm, but seeing as how I'd rather not let you go out and get yourself killed, I'll go with you because of our friendship. But you are going to owe me a favor."

"What is the favor?"

"You are driving."

"Is that really all you want?"

"Well, the way I see it, you owe me more than enough favors."

"Well, that is true. So, are we ready to go?"

"Yes, in a second." She pushed a button and I heard a car chirping, as though someone had turned on a car alarm. We went outside, and a car pulled up. Looking at it, I could tell it was like a black sporty limo with black rims. Of course, this attracted a lot of attention from all over the camp. Most of these people had never ever seen a limo in person, not to mention one like this.

Laura handed me a suit and tie. "Put this on before we get started."

I was tempted to ask her why, but it seemed like a bad idea. I went back to my room and changed my clothes. As I left my room, I kept my armor on so no one could see what I was wearing; however, as I entered the driver seat of the limo, I took the armor off.

I looked in the back seat and saw Laura sitting there, so I drove off. "OK. Now that I have changed my clothes, Laura, could you tell me why you had me wear this?"

"First off, I think it makes you look good, and I don't remember the last time you wore those clothes. I thought it was time you took them out for a day."

I always hated wearing dress clothing, and she knew it; I started to regret owing her so many favors. As we drove out of the gate, everyone stared at the limo.

"We are going to the desert area on the west side of the island," Laura said. She rolled up the divider so I could no longer see what she was doing. At first, I wasn't sure what she was doing. It wasn't until we reached the desert that she rolled the divider down. She wore a red dress with red shoes, with diamonds in the predictable areas, from ears to ankles. She sipped just a little bit of wine, but instead of drinking it, she gargled it, and then swallowed it.

"Why didn't you change when I did?"

"I wanted to see your face the moment I changed. From the fact you haven't taken your eyes off me, it makes me relieved I put a drive assist function in the vehicle. Please continue driving with your eyes on the road. The assist functions only compensate for some errors," she said as though she was trying not to laugh. She guided me the rest of the way after setting the glass she was drinking from in a holder. As we pulled into the lot, there was an actual parking lot there, which I had not seen since I came here. I looked around after parking the vehicle and saw a very elegant-looking building. Laura said, "We are here."

"Are you sure this is where we are supposed to go?" I asked.

"Leo, have I ever been wrong about these kinds of things?" I thought about it. "As I was saying, I will need you to open my car door and every door until we get back to the limo. The whole time, I will need you to stay no more than ten feet away from me. You must be completely emotionless, even if you see your brother. Do you understand? When you are ready, let's go."

I took a deep breath, got out of the limo, walked around, opened her door, and bowed my head. "Ma'am."

As she walked out of the limo, I thought about the last time I was here, when I slept through the transportation process. Laura told me I was placed in a medical observation room when I first got to their camp. We walked in, and the place looked like a hotel resort. I read the signs they posted, and slavery was not the only trade they dabbled in. There were drug trades, gun trades, food trades, and even vehicle trades. Each thing was, of course, in a different area. There were more people present than I expected, all going to different areas. Laura walked up to the counter, and a young man pointed her in the direction she needed to be headed.

As we headed down the slave pathway, the smell began to change to something more pleasant, which didn't make any sense, considering all the movies I'd seen. As we walked into the area, we saw the outline of people in pods standing straight up. They were frozen in cryo-freeze pods about ten pods high and a hundred pods long along both sides of the pathway.

"What is that smell?" I whispered.

"They clean the slaves and make them prepped and ready for buying. What they clean them with will keep them cleaned for one whole month. However, you didn't go through that procedure because the Webmaster hates the artificial smell. The last time she got someone with the smell, she complained that the smell was too strong, and she was able to get a free one. Because of the strength of the smell, they were forced to sweat the aroma off before they were allowed to ever come back into the village. Sadly, the smell never left them during those thirty days. In fact, forcing them to sweat was more like taking a shower."

"Why does the Webmaster buy slaves? She doesn't seem like the type."

"I already told you some of the reasons, so I will assume you are referring to a long-term goal or something. She has two long-term goals. One is to set them free, and the other is to send them home when and if she can. I heard in order to send them home, there would have to be a big impact that would happen if the person went missing; people like celebrities, military members, and investors with more than a million dollars in investments, etc. The reason she didn't send you home is because she couldn't. So, she did the next best thing."

Laura walked up to a young woman and began talking French to her; I couldn't tell what they were saying because I was not wearing my armor. She pointed to me, looked back, and then flagged me to come closer to her. I walked up to her, and she whispered, "Was your brother-in-law the III or the V?"

"III," I replied. It was then I began to be astonished because I finally understand why women were considered the best listeners of the two genders. I had only told her his name once, and she remembered. They continued talking. When they stopped, we stood in front of a pod at the end of the hall. The way the pods were set up, this one was isolated from all the others.

"She told me they isolated him because it was a special pod due to the aroma," Laura said.

Sadly, this did not surprise me because my sister told us he smelled all the time and hardly took showers. She opened the pod, letting steam release in the room; from the outside, all we could feel was the cold air leaving the pod, which actually would have felt better if we were still outside the building, but since we were inside an air-conditioned building, it was quite cold. I thought we would smell something from the outside, but the scent was sealed; now there was only the scent of cold.

"He was only frozen for a couple of days, so there shouldn't be any long-term damage to him, except the smell of new car," the woman said with a French accent.

"I want you to escort him to the limo and wait there. This won't take too long," Laura said.

I walked to the limo carrying him fireman style; I truly couldn't understand why the Webmaster hated the smell so much, but then again, this was the first time I had encountered a person with a new car smell. I walked him back to the limo and placed him in the backseat. I then waited in the shade for Laura to come out.

I waited only five minutes before she came outside. As she walked outside, I followed her to the limo, opened the door for her, and then went around to get in the driver's seat. "Laura, are we good here?" I asked.

She looked at me and said, "We will have a few hours to pay them in full; if not, they will send an assassin in to capture or kill the slave and us. Sadly, we are going to have to take the risk. We can't have this trip be for nothing. Don't you agree?"

"Well, yes." *Why would we take such a risk?* I wondered. This didn't seem like something she would do; it seemed out of the ordinary considering her characteristics. I wondered who she really was. The payment wasn't on our end of the plan. The rest of this was up to my sister. I didn't know how much it would cost for a slave purchase or even what was considered currency on this island. I drove away.

"So, what were you two talking about?" I asked.

"Nothing that would interest you. We were talking mostly about her husband and what he does here. He is a doctor who works in the drug labs. So, do you at least know where to find this friend of yours?"

"Revaughnt? Knowing him, he is surrounded by women somewhere."

"Hmm...women have gone missing in a mountain region not too far from here. We can check there."

Willie began coughing.

"Well, looks like he's finally awake," Laura said.

"What the heck is going on?" Willie said.

"You are being transported," Laura replied.

"Who are you guys? Last thing I remember, I was leaving my friend J's house. Wait, was this because I found out the government was tricking the population into eating pies so they could secretly test a new drug that would give the human population superhuman strength? Is it because I am a poor man who knows every conspiracy theory that is true?"

Laura laughed.

"See, you laugh now because you are blind to the facts. But when you find out it is true, there will be no denying it. I watched as a good friend of mine died from a heart attack after one of those corrupted pies."

I replied, "He didn't die—he was choking because he was eating too fast, and since you didn't know the Heimlich maneuver, you were lucky his wife did. You just blacked out and must have fast-forwarded to his funeral."

He paused, and Laura added, "I bet you never paid close attention to the roads you drive on and how it affects your body. The dividing lines that are used to separate traffic are also used to make you hungry, making restaurants' business go up by foreigners alone. The trick is using subliminal messaging. Whenever you get closer to an actual restaurant stop, the message will be there, depending on what lane you are in."

"Well...actually, I have, thank you very much. I just wanted you to think I hadn't and underestimate me," Willie proclaimed.

"Laura, please don't help him get going on these conspiracy theories," I said, now trying to avoid looking at the lane lines.

"Hey, Leo, has your brother-in-law always been like this, or is this a side effect?"

"Yeah, he's always been like that. My sister married a real nut case, right?"

"So, you're the evil organization that kidnapped my brother-in-law, Leonardo. He has been missing for a long while now. And now that I know it was you bastards who kidnapped him, I will take you all down and slaughter you and your loved ones."

I pulled over because I knew it was going to get very bad very quickly. Laura predicted the same, and before Willie could even move, she had him pinned to the ground and forced his head to look straight up. She placed her thumbnail under his neck.

I smacked my forehead. "Darn it, Willie can you go fifteen minutes without nearly getting yourself in trouble? Laura is the last person you should be messing with." I turned around and saw her whispering something in his ear.

"Would you really have me believe your driver is Leo?" Willie asked.

"Is there any denying what I am telling you? You can see him as clear as day in front of you," Laura said.

He looked closely at my face. "No way." He was caught speechless, as he had begun to look even closer. "I tried searching for clues but couldn't find anything to track him. I can't believe I have finally found you. Man, I have been investigating you going missing for years. What have you been up to?"

"You know, the same old things...I always do," I said before realizing that my life had changed a lot.

"Playing videogames. Man, you really haven't changed," Willie said, turning back around.

"Well, the shooter games I play now have better resolution. In fact, they seem real at times."

"So, is this the in-law you said had gotten in debt?" Laura asked.

"I have only one in-law as far as I know, and yeah, this is him," I replied.

"Well, I guess you haven't heard yet, but Kat is getting married in a couple of months. So, you'll have two brothers-in-law. And that controller your rats chewed on was not my fault, even though I snuck in your room to play video games while you were at school."

"Wait, Kat's getting married? Since when?"

"Hmm...from what I hear, it was very sudden. I want to say it was three months now."

"Man, am I really the last to know what is going on in my own family?" Heck, my mother would show everybody the house my family was going to move into, and I was always the last to know.

"Yes, but this time, you don't even live near them. So, I don't know how you would keep in touch," Laura added.

"Man, I do miss video games. Anyway, was there anything else happening in the family since I have been gone?"

"You've had two nieces since you have been gone."

While we talked, Laura changed her clothing using an auto changer the Webmaster had created. It unsewed then resewed the material into something else without any need to cover up. The product was still in the beta testing stage and only exclusive to the village. She then wore a tank top and cargo pants, both of which were still as red as her dress. She sat next to Willie and pressed a button, causing the limo to compress in length and expand in width until it turned into an armored sports car. It pushed her to the passenger side of the car.

"Since you're not going anywhere, I will drive and you can talk." She pressed a button that retracted the steering wheel from my seat to hers. The gauges were all projected on the window. "Willie, have you ever used any type of gun?" she asked as she pulled away.

"Not yet," he replied.

"Do you get the concept of point and shoot?"

"Of course."

"All right, I have a 12-mm Black Parana that might be suited for you."

"A what?"

"A pistol with an extended barrel, extended magazines, a single-shot grenade launcher, and a custom trigger that gives the bullet enough strength to behave like an armor-piercing round, whether you're using the special bullets or not."

"Yeah, I could learn to use one of those in no time."

As she was about to hand it to him, I realized that with most of her weapons, if you're not using special gloves to the resist the initial blast, the kick had a high chance of breaking the user's hand with a single shot.

"Wait, Willie, didn't you tell me you had a friend who was going to give you a gun, then he realized you were more likely to shoot yourself in the foot?"

"Well...um...that is beside the point. Do I look like someone who would shoot himself in the foot?

I paused. "Yeah, you're the kind of person who would set himself on fire lighting the pilot to a water heater." So, I gave him a map instead. "Try to remember the map just in case we need to split up." The map I gave him was holographic; it would show the user where they were. It was similar to a GPS, but instead of using satellites, it used towers that cloaked the island to locate where you were. Sadly, he couldn't figure out how to turn it on, so I turned to Laura and asked, "So, where exactly are we going, Laura?"

"Well, if you want a chance to find your friend, we will have to contact someone with the connections to the descriptions you left of your friend."

She called Rayshawn on the communicator. As she talked, I turned around and showed Willie how to turn the map on. As I turned back around, Laura spoke.

"Rayshawn's connections say your friend's location is possibly at Ruby's Peak. He will show up in case we need back up."

We drove to Ruby's Peak, and on the way there, I found out they called it Ruby's Peak because this location was an abandoned base whose commander's name was Ruby. Rumor said the commander held his ground for a year before he was overrun; the name was a way to commemorate the fallen commander. As we arrived, I looked around and noticed the fallen base was built like an older temple. We saw Rayshawn waiting where the road ended with his shotgun drawn, facing the temple doors. We knew people were inside because it was well lit, and we could hear the faint sounds of laughter come from inside.

Laura got out of the car and asked Rayshawn in a low tone, "Are you sure this is the right location?"

"I was told a young man fitting the description you mentioned earlier was seen living here over the course of three months. He was on a mission to do something. When he got here, he was talking to the locals to gather information. Well, until he started to pay attention to the beautiful locals. Rumors say he lives here against his will. Look, all rumors and trails end here."

Willie got out of the car holding the map. "OK, you do understand that just because I have a degree in computers doesn't mean I can read a map this advanced without any land markings to compensate for the lack of terrain?"

Rayshawn walked up, placing his helmet on his head. "So, are we ready to storm this temple like we did the enemy camp three weeks ago?"

I went up to Rayshawn. "No, since it is just the three of us, we will have to go in diamond formation. Willie is a VIP; we can't risk him being killed. So, he will be behind the rest of us. We can't have him injured." I pointed to Willie. "Before I forget, this is Willie, my in-law."

The way we charged three weeks ago, we bolted into a room without the risk of casualties because I took point. We normally worked in groups of three because of the lack of personnel and living space on our base.

"We are going to enter the base in diamond formation," I said. "I will charge in, taking point. Laura and Rayshawn will follow right after, watching my sides. Willie, you are to stay low and don't get shot. If we break formation, Laura, guard the exit. Rayshawn and I will fight through."

We gathered by the door. When we were in place, I used the force of the water to break the door down. As we entered the temple, we saw Revaughnt sitting down on a throne. He had one woman in his lap, another feeding him grapes, one massaging his body, another cleaning his feet, one trimming his hair, and the last one fanning him off.

Revaughnt rose slowly, walked up to me, and shook my hand, asking, "Leo, how have you been?"

"Hi, Revaughnt," I replied.

"Hey, bro, I am pretty sure the escort doesn't need us to rescue him," Rayshawn said, putting his gun down. "In fact, this looks like a man's paradise."

"Yeah, you said it; a real man's paradise," Willie added.

"OK, I am going outside to gaze at the stars. Call me if you need me," Laura said, walking backward.

"I'll be out in a minute. I apologize for my friend," I said. "Revaughnt, it has been a while. I would ask you how have you been, but I can see you are doing quite well for yourself. Sadly, I can see your lifestyle hasn't changed since we last met. However, since we are on a timed schedule, we are going to have to leave quickly."

"I don't know if you've noticed, but the sun is setting and going anywhere off of this peak is very dangerous at night because some of the natives attack unsuspecting travelers in these parts. So, we are not going anywhere. We are going to need to rest until morning," Revaughnt stated, taking his attention off of me and placing it on a woman who was walking by.

"I'll be outside. We'll leave at sunrise and no later than that, as we are pressed for time. Understood? You guys have fun." I was tempted to stay; however, I wasn't too sure what they would do, so I took my chances outside. I fell asleep looking at the stars.

When I awoke, I felt someone leaning on my back. I could smell perfume, so I knew it was Laura, so I didn't move. Instead, I thought of what I would do with Revaughnt and Willie and how I would get them home. As long as I'd been here, I have only ever heard rumors of people leaving this island. "What will I do?" I whispered.

"Don't worry so much," Laura whispered. "I'm sure something will come up soon."

"Should I have them work for our group?"

"I know you don't want them stuck there, so you shouldn't put them through that. An idea will come to you soon. So, go back to sleep."

It was then I heard an incoming voice message from Lilly, the ex-princess we had rescued. She said, "Mr. Leonardo, I know it has been a while since we last spoke. I am sending you this message to inform you that my contact has made reservations for me to leave back to the States. As I promised you, eight months and two days from the time this message gets to you. I have room for you and up to ten others you may want to bring on the aircraft. I will be leaving at sundown to avoid being shot down. My pilot used to fly F-15s and has agreed to fly us where we need to go. You will meet me at a hanger bay at an abandoned base. Transmission over."

"See, I told you something would turn out," Laura whispered.

I looked at the sky. "You were right. Looks like the sun is going to rise pretty soon," I replied. "We should get ready to go."

She took a deep breath and sighed heavily. "We probably should, so we can avoid a possible pursuer."

"May I ask why you had us sleep back to back?"

"Because I wouldn't want you to suffer from a painful cramp in your back from lying on the ground. I will get the car ready; you wake everyone up."

I woke everyone up from their sleep. It took about half an hour before we were finally ready to leave. While we did this, I had an uncomfortable feeling we were being watched. When we finally drove away, the feeling seemed to fade away slowly.

"Laura, I think someone is watching us. I am not quite sure who it is, so we need to be on our guard," I whispered.

"Who do you think it is? All of the enemies who know us from SUBWAY don't have a clue what we are doing," Laura whispered.

"I don't know, but the last time I had this feeling, it was the Lightning Bearer, and he made me throw up with how many voltages he put through my body. If it hadn't been for Lilly, I would have been killed."

Laura said, "Doubt it would be the Lightning Bearer, for the simple fact he is currently on a mission on a classified mission list. At least, that was what his mission board said."

"I heard through the vine you and the Lightning Bearer were great friends," said Revaughnt.

"Yeah, Revaughnt," I answered sarcastically. "He, Rayshawn, and I go clubbing every night. As for every morning, we go flying fishing every weekend. I raise the water, and if the fish don't fly..."

Ray added, "We have Leo launch the fish even higher in the air until it goes right up in the air without damaging their wings. If we can't shoot the fish before they hit the water, Leonardo breaks the water underneath so it doesn't kill or damage them..."

"...as the dead cannot reproduce. Isn't that right, Laura?"

Laura defused the sarcasm by replying, "Oh, that would explain where you go during those mornings. I thought the Lightning Bearer told me per every ten fish that land back in the water, you have to take a shot of vodka and sake."

"Now, that sounds fun." Revaughnt added, "I didn't see you as much of a drinker, but living on this island, that kind of makes sense. I couldn't go one week without living in grief."

Willie added, "I'm so proud. I thought you were going to be a church boy or something. I've tried to corrupt your manners for many years."

I sighed, "You guys are funny. Can we change the subject?"

Though Laura didn't give me much to work with, from the details she did give me, we could get there without getting lost because Laura knew this land very well. We approached the abandoned base, and from the writings, designs, and vehicle types, we could tell the base was once a German weapon testing facility and hadn't been used in quite some time. The base's gates were open but only enough to let a small vehicle fit through. As we drove through the base, we eventually came across the hanger bay. As we looked around, we didn't see a runway anywhere around it, but there were old jeeps, tanks, and Humvees in the parking lots like all the personnel had cut their losses and left in a hurry. I was surprised none of the other factions had tried to claim this abandoned base as their own after the Germans left it so many years ago. We approached the hanger and exited the vehicle.

"So, what is the first thing you're going to do when you get back home?" I asked Revaughnt.

He replied, "Live the life. I'm going to this girl's house. I think her name was Shelly."

Rayshawn asked, "How about you, Willie? I think your answer will be more original."

"I am going to buy a subwoofer for my car," he replied.

"Wow, you boys are simpleminded. Then again, most men are," Lilly said, standing behind us. "With men, it is usually food, cars, video games, and what girl has the biggest caboose. What will you do when you return home, Leonardo?"

"I will hug my mom and dad, visit my brother's grave, and say hello to my sisters. After all, I haven't seen them in years," I replied.

"Good answer; let's proceed," Lilly said, waving for us to follow. As we entered, we saw the aircraft and a tunnel leading underground.

Laura looked at the aircraft in deep awe. She touched the engine and said, "Hmm...a custom engine with the ability to break the sound barrier, and she, from the way the outside looks, could fly without being detected on radar. It is currently unequipped with any weapons, and even if it had weapons, we wouldn't see them anyway. It does have defense capabilities even without weapons, and if I am not mistaken, it should also be equipped with full autopilot."

"You can tell all of that from just looking it?" Willie asked.

"Yeah, Laura has always been good with machines and vehicles, including the armored vehicle we have been riding in," I replied.

"That sports car was an armored vehicle?" Revaughnt asked.

"Who is your contact?" Laura asked Lilly.

"He isn't one of my contacts, he is my grandmother's contact. I believe his name is. . . "

I noticed a laser aimed at Lilly's chest. I turned around and formed a shield of water, protecting the entrance so no one would be shot.

"I see you learned how to control your water abilities better. But you're not as smart as I was hoping you would be," a voice said in the surrounding area.

"Hurry up and get everyone on the plane. I don't remember who this voice is, but I do know it's somebody who is very dangerous."

Lilly ran into the plane, flagging everyone to fall in line behind her.

The voice continued, "I wonder who is going to be the first one I kill in your group?"

I walked toward the plane, moving slowly. There came an explosion from above, and the next thing I knew, I was pinned to the ground with a black saber to my neck, which forced my armor to activate. I looked at his face and saw it was Cayden.

"Hello, Leo, I guess today is going to be your last."

He set the saber on fire and laughed menacingly. Ray charged at him and swung his shotgun like a golf club, hitting Cayden, and forcing him to leap backward away from the plane. When he looked back at his shotgun, it was completely melted where it had contacted Cayden's face. Cayden threw a fireball and knocked Rayshawn to the floor.

"Leo, the unarmed people who came with you are currently already aboard the plane. We need you to get on if you're coming. This plane doesn't need long to warm up. If you take too long, it will just begin to take off," Lilly said.

"Lilly, it seems I cannot leave with you guys today. Just tell Willie to tell my mother I love her and miss her so much."

Willie responded, "I will, and when you get back, we are going to have to play some video games. You might be a little behind on the current stuff."

"All right...I'll be looking forward to that day. Hopefully, you don't suck that much when we play."

"Ha...Good luck, Leo," Willie said.

I looked back and noticed Laura standing between Cayden and me with a rocket launcher in her hands. "You are getting sloppy, little sister; it was obviously you."

"How did you know it was me?" Laura asked.

"Because you used our mother's name as your alias. And there is no one on this island who goes by the name Raquel, Laura."

"Brother, can you turn the other way just this one time for me?"

"Sorry, but you've already used favors for the rest of this season. I will let you live, but I will not allow anyone else here to survive. The mission comes first, my sister, and my mission instructs me to teach you a cruel lesson about lying to my clients. I will not stop you from trying to help them, but as long as you keep holding back, this will be a one-sided fight. Even though your friend can use water as a counter to my fire, he is too inexperienced to compete against me. Though I cannot kill with normal means, I can still beat him to death the old-fashioned way."

"No!" she yelled, throwing the weapon to the floor. She pulled out a knife and began to fight him. As they continued, sparks flew through the air. At first, I thought the sparks came from the suit and the knife, but I noticed the suit was like new and the knife got smaller. It was after the knife was half its original length that I noticed the sparks did not dissipate and still floated around the hanger. I prepared the water to protect Laura, Rayshawn, the plane, and myself.

When the knife had completely burned off, Cayden grabbed Laura and placed her in a sleeper hold. "How about I let you choose who I am going to kill first, little sister?" Sparks gathered around them and spanned around his body until they moved faster and grew in size.

"Please stop! I'll join you on your missions if you look the other way right now," Laura said.

The flame took the shape and form of a big lion that stood right beside them.

"Right here!" I yelled, pulling out my sword. "You want someone to kill, let's go!"

The lion charged at me, leaving behind a trail of flames. I used my water as a shield to trap the beast and extinguish the flames around it. I then formed a water geyser underneath Cayden's feet, forcing him through the roof and freeing Laura from him. Laura ran to my side. Rayshawn ran to pick up the rocket launcher, and we all waited for Cayden to return. The ground began to sink; this is when we realized where the launchpad was. Laura and I moved away from the plane, giving it less attention.

Cayden came back down from the ceiling. As he landed on the ground, Rayshawn launched a rocket toward his feet. When it exploded, the blast was absorbed into his armor. He opened the palm of his hand and made a flame that took the shape of the rocket that had just launched at him. "I think this belongs to you!" Cayden yelled, throwing the rocket at Laura. I formed a wall of water in front of her, but as it approached, it burned out.

"Save Rayshawn," she said, pointing to him.

I looked over to Rayshawn and noticed another missile headed toward him. I knew it was going to be too late to protect him. All I saw was Rayshawn pushed back and sliding underneath the plane while it was still stationary.

"Irene, foolish woman, you made me miss my shot," Cayden yelled.

As I watched the explosion, a pair of legs stood where the blast took place. The rest of the body quickly regenerated; we watched as all the body parts regrew, one at a time. As the skin grew onto the body, armor began covering it, except the head. The hair on her head began to tie itself back up in a Chinese twin hair bun.

"Please clear the active runway," said an automated voice. "Launch will not commence until the threat has been cleared from the circle of safety."

Laura ran beside Irene, readying her fists. I ran over to Rayshawn to check on him. He got up from the floor, checking his body.

"I think she pushed me to save my life, bro," he said.

"Good to hear, but we need to help the girls push Cayden away from the plane so the launch bay doors will allow them to leave. We are going to be forced into hand-to-hand combat to push him back. Anything else will annoy him and make him kill us quickly."

Rayshawn assisted the ladies in keeping him distracted. While he was distracted, I waited for them to give me an opening so I could push him back with the force of the water. I charged a ball of water in my hands when the team gave me an opening. I pushed him through the side of the hanger and quickly followed, giving the aircraft just what it needed for its circle of safety inspection. As I headed outside through the hole he left behind, I heard the doors open. As we went out, I looked back and saw the aircraft was gone. I looked off in the distance and over the bay, watching as my one-way ticket home left me behind. A flaming eruption came from in front of us. Cayden stood up and walked away.

"I'm sorry, but it seems my client has finally received their payment. So, my mission is complete. Hopefully, next time we can meet under better circumstances." He lifted his hand and was picked up by a helicopter that passed by.

The four of us who remained drove back to base. When we returned Rayshawn informed us Melena was promoted. Melena was ranked second to Sue from just her showmanship in the battle they had between each other. As for Irene, she decided to join our forces, claiming to be excited to join us. She claimed to be insprired by the battle we had with Cayden. I asked to hear her story, and she obliged to tell me. Apparently, she was from the year 2015. She acquired a corrupted time suit, which merged with her healing ability allowing her to go back in time. She used the new powers once and was sent five years into the past, and when she tried to return was sent back another five years. This happened four more times before she realized she was going to have to live out her thirty years to return to her original time. That would make her over forty years old and she didn't look a day over twenty. I came to the realization she was only here to keep busy until the present-day Irene goes back in time and she can avoid a time anomaly.

# 8
## We Were Once Enemies...and Now

Over the next four months, we were piled up with mission after mission, and each became more and more difficult. We fought against a fraction that called themselves Rising Flares, led by Lieutenant Commander Sari Juno. Both of our camps knew where to find the other. What they had in numbers, we made up for in strategy. Even with our strategy being so brilliant, our troops' morale was at an all-time low. We went through seven different leaders until Susan was forcefully promoted due to her time and service. Most people would pretend they didn't understand what happened to the other leaders, but I didn't blame them; it always had something to do with Conner stressing them out. They would either leave or make their death look like an accident; one even shot himself. This wasn't surprising, though; there once was a pregnant woman only days away from giving birth who was still doing missions; the day after she gave birth, she was back in the fight. It wasn't because she chose to be, and it wasn't because we needed her there, but because Conner threated to put a bullet through her head; within a week, she died from putting too much stress on her body. Laura took the child back to the Webmaster's village so they could care for them.

With Susan in charge of our ranks, she could stabilize troop morale and hold our own against the Rising

Flares. However, our conflict would never end as long as our enemies knew our location. Susan then put in a suggestion to Conner about a new base location.

We had finally pushed the enemy back. Before we could, they found a way to mess up our generators and destroyed any way to fix it. This caused the heat around our camp to rise to where we could barely think or even prep for combat. We knew it was the generators because when we walked off base, the temperature dropped drastically. As far as going inside the base, you would feel the force of the intense heat blowing in your face like a super hair dryer. Conner knew of this but did very little to fix the problem.

Susan finally came up with a plan to push the enemy off our land after that. We could easily fix the problem with the water; all we needed was one big push. Laura and I prepared for my part of the plan. At this point, I knew I was needed, but something was most definitely going wrong. I just couldn't be sure what.

"Laura, so where are we headed? We are positioned southwest of the camp. The objective is to set up an ambush with Melena's unit. Sue will use herself as bait. Peter and Kristy will cut off the enemy's retreat. Ray is part of Melena's unit. Irene will be helping Susan attract the enemy. Emily and Simone will be the snipers; when we hear their guns fire, we attack." As I spoke, I noticed my eyes began to blur, but it wasn't too bad. I then coughed up blood.

"Leonardo, is that blood?" Laura whispered.

"No, I think it is a pre-throw-up bile. It must be from the tomatoes I ate before the mission. It must have made me sick."

The only reply I heard was mumbled. "You are a terrible liar."

"What was that?"

"We need to hurry up before the operation starts without us." Laura walked away.

I look at my hands and whispered, "What a terrible liar I am. I didn't even eat the tomatoes."

We continued to the ambushing area. I saw Melena off in the distance giving me a thumbs up. Rayshawn walked up behind us.

"What happened to the plan?" I asked.

"We're still doing it," Rayshawn replied. "We are waiting for Emily and Simone. Susan is cutting off their escape point. Bro, I think you smell like blood."

"Don't worry, man, I am good. It must be my cologne I am using. You can try some when we get back."

"Nah, bro, I prefer not to scare ladies away with the smell of death. You may want to consider throwing it away."

"I'll consider it." I got the vibe Laura was watching me even more closely after what Rayshawn said. It was obvious I was sick, but I felt as though I was needed for this mission, and I didn't want to seem like a burden on my team, so I didn't say anything about it. Rayshawn returned to his position while Laura and I set everything up and prepared for our part of the plan. We finished about five minutes after we started.

I got on the radio and said, "All right, Susan, our unit is in position. Awaiting further orders."

Susan replied, "All right, your team was the last one. We have confirmation all teams are in position, and we are just waiting on the signal to storm the base."

An explosion was heard, and we started to ambush the area. Peter dropped from the sky like a missile. The next to charge in was Kristy, then everyone else, one by one. The battle lasted less than ten minutes because the enemy surrendered, dropped their weapons, and accepted their defeat.

When the job was done, my legs gave out, and I couldn't hear anything, not even my own body falling. My body felt heavy, and I threw up. My heart rate rose. I heard and felt my heart beating faster and faster to the point I thought it was going to explode. I whispered, and a red fine mist rose up. "What great timing, but I won't let this body tell me who's boss."

Finally, someone ran up to me. I couldn't hear the words they said, but from what I read on my visor, it was, "Are you all right?"

I could barely utter the words, "Yeah, of course." The world around me morphed like I was in a dream. I was in a wide-open field where grass covered the whole area. Then the field began to decay, and the rain came, and the plants didn't grow—instead, it just got blacker. The sky turned white as snow, and ash fell from the sky.

I then heard Laura's voice faintly. "I am leaving; we have no time to waste."

Another voice echoed in the background. "What do you want me to tell him if he wakes before you get back?"

"He should have listened to me, and I left, and he might not ever see me again, thanks to his stupidity and stubbornness." Well, it was along those lines. I wanted to speak, but I could not. Their voices faded into the sound of raindrops and lightning. In the meadow, Rayshawn, Melena, and Susan appeared and then faded to dust. The dust eventually returned, but this time, when it cleared, I realized I was lying on a bed in the medical room of the second tower of the second floor.

"Aw, I see you're finally up," I heard a voice talk, but I just laid there, trying to figure out who it was. "It was a real close call for a moment." I didn't recognize the voice, but I knew it was very familiar. "How long will you continue to lay there?" I realized I knew the voice. It belonged to a person I hadn't seen in a while; unfortunately, the voice had a vexing vibe to it. "After all, you and I haven't spoken since you pleaded for your life on Virginia Way, back in Barstow, California."

"You!" I yelled, rolled off the bed, and turned my arm into a blade of water, charging him and pinning him to a wall before I could sever any of his limbs from his body.

"At ease, Leonardo!" Sue yelled, forcing me to stop. "Mr. Muller has joined us. Anything you have against him now, you can consider it over, here and now!"

I looked at him and saw he had a smile on his face.

"It's because of you I am in this bloody mess, Muller. Did you really think I would forget something so wretched?"

"It seems you have fully recovered. But I am not forgetful. If there is one of us who has forgotten, I was the one with a fully loaded gun, and I chose not to kill you that night and to make better use of you, and even make some extra cash on the side. Yes, I sold you, and I'd do it again."

"Let him go, Leonardo. I understand you have been out for a few weeks, but it is no excuse to challenge a new officer!"

"What do you mean a few weeks? I feel as though it has only been a few hours," I replied.

I slammed his body to the wall then let him go.

"We'll let you be on your way. Let's go, Dave," Sue said, so they left.

I looked around the room and noticed Laura wasn't there; this wasn't normal. Usually, she was the first one I saw in the morning, with her beautiful smile. I knew it wasn't like we were married or even a couple, but it was nice to see her every day. I left the room, headed downstairs and out of the building. As I walked out of the building, the first one I saw was Rayshawn, who was standing inconspicuously looking at the nurses who were walking in and out of the building.

"Sorry, bro," Rayshawn said. "I remember everything you told me, so I tried to stop them from recruiting him, but he fit just what they needed him for. So, what is the plan?"

"We can't do anything; our fearless leader has already spoken. By the way, where is Laura?"

"Sorry, bro, I haven't seen her in a while."

"How long is 'a while'?"

"Maybe a week or two now."

"Crap!"

"Don't worry, maybe my sister or Simone knows something. You know how women talk to each other."

"Thanks, Rayshawn."

"I'll let you know if something happens."

"Thank you." I continued walking to where Melena and Simone loaded up some cannons. "What's going on here?"

"We are moving these cannons from here," Melena said. "As it turned out, the enemy might attack us from a different location, so we were instructed to move them to the east side of base to protect us there."

"Hey, ladies, have you seen Laura?" I asked.

They talked among themselves for a moment, and then Simone answered, saying, "Laura, I haven't seen her for almost a month, not even on missions. From what we heard, she has special duties elsewhere."

"Thank you." I could tell they hadn't seen her either. So, I walked away and saw Peter sitting against a tree, petting a lion. I then approached Kristy, who was sharpening her blades on the tree.

"Good to see you're finally up, Leo," she said. "I take it you are looking for Laura, right?"

"Yes, if you wouldn't mind telling me where she is."

"Yeah, she agreed to exchange contracts with the Lightning Bearer in exchange for his help in the upcoming battle."

"Why would they exchange contracts?"

"Since money isn't the real currency here, the way things really get done is through favors." The only time money was good in this part of the world was if you still had your footing somewhere in the bigger countries.

"So, where is she now?" I asked.

"Honestly, I am not too sure. I told you all I know. By the way, Laura wanted me to remind you to thank the Lightning Bearer for saving your life." Her head moved up a little bit, then back at me. "It seems we have new orders."

Susan approached with the rest of the squad; as they approached, I still looked for Laura, even though I knew she wasn't there.

"The team will be moving and attacking the Rising Flare's base located on the southwest beach," Sue said. "We will be storming the beach—not with numbers, but precision. Since the enemy already knows the location of the base, we will have to leave some personnel behind to protect it. If all goes according to plan, the enemy will not have the time for a counterattack."

"How do you know this?" I asked.

"Because this is an important mission, we convinced Laura to pull some strings to hire her old acquaintance, the Lightning Bearer. He will be joining you and Rayshawn."

"Why our unit?"

"For one, Laura isn't here, so you are short one person. The second reason is because I was told you three have worked together before and have shown great progress in the past. You don't have to worry about teaching him anything. Laura briefed him on what was expected and what to expect. Everyone else will follow under Melena and my orders as we see fit. I will not promise you it will be easy, but I can promise it will be done shortly. We leave at sundown; you have until then to be ready." Susan walked away.

Before she could go too far, I asked her, "So, who's in charge of my team?"

"Doesn't matter. Progress does. If you really think your team needs a leader, then you have roughly two hours to decide." Since I really didn't need to prepare for combat, I waited inside the helicopter as I had in the past. I realized how much I had taken Laura for granted.

As I waited, I heard the sound of knocking come from the door. "Are you busy?"

"What may I do for you, Lightning Bearer?"

"I am only here to talk."

"I am all ears."

"So, do you feel better now?"

"I just woke up after a long nap, and the first person I saw was the same man who sent me here to this death sentence of an island."

"What do you think you'd be doing if you weren't here right now?"

"Not too sure, honestly, but anywhere is better than here."

"You hate it here that much?"

"The island, yes, the people, no. Heck, if it weren't for him, I never would have met Laura. So, where is she? I was told you knew where to find her."

"She is doing some recon work for me so I can do my next mission."

"Is that all you are having her do for you? Seems like you're getting the short end of it. How do you know Laura?" I asked.

"I met Laura when she was fourteen years old. She and her brother were sent on a mission to protect a neighboring king. I, however, was paid to eliminate the same target, so, naturally, we were enemies. Luckily for them, her brother had acquired the flame armor, which kind of leveled the field. Though I had speed, he had cunning and could protect the target, causing flames so hot they melted all my external weapons. So, I had to postpone my initial attack for a different time." He sat in the seat across from me. "When I was attacking the second time, I couldn't set foot on the target area. Laura's reflexes were adequate enough to hold me back, so I had to postpone my attack for another day. On the third day, however, I was told by a higher up that I was to extract the brother and sister without killing them.

From what I understood at the time, the target they were sent to protect was corrupted; he was destroying his people from the inside. The pay, though not money, was quadrupled in value; I won't tell you exactly what it was I received because it is classified. As you know, it was pretty difficult to signal Laura without being shot on sight. So, I had to draw her brother out so he and I could...talk. It didn't take long before Laura showed. I saw the laser on my chest from the rifle she was holding. But by that time, the truth was already exposed. And he signaled Laura to get her finger off the trigger. Now at this point, they were supposed to leave, but instead, they collaborated with me, and we completely eliminated the leader and his elite guards. It was from that day forth we all became close."

"Why didn't you just charge into their camp?" I asked because I knew he had lightning-quick speed. Moving that quickly would be nothing to him.

"Yes, I could have, but I realized that might be like issuing a challenge, so I didn't. So, what is your relationship with your companion, Laura?"

"Now why would I tell you, someone I don't really know, when I haven't even told Laura, or even Rayshawn, for that matter?"

"We are just talking. After all, it isn't like I am going to tell anybody, most certainly not her. Whatever we talk about will stay between us, I promise."

He was right; it wasn't going to profit him whether he knew or not. Plus, this might help me collect my own thoughts on the matter, so I didn't mind sharing. "My situation with Laura has been a complicated one. I don't know where we stand. I had a chance to leave since the last time we spoke, but when leaving was a real possibility, I couldn't imagine leaving her behind."

"Leaving? Now, how were you planning to leave this island?"

"I was at the abandoned German base because I was to meet up with Lilly Alexis Celestial. She was the one with the plan to fly us out with the use of a jet. As the jet was about to take off, I saw we were about to be ambushed by Laura's brother. From the way things were going, I knew Laura wasn't going to board the plane, so I came up with the bogus excuse that I couldn't shield the aircraft from the inside, even when modifying the water was possible."

"So, you're saying?"

"I selfishly stayed so I could prolong my time spent with her. That is all I am saying in a nutshell. I would tell her, but I don't think she'd like that very much. In fact, I wish I could tell her. As far as my thoughts toward her right now, I fear I might be taking her for granted. It wasn't until the moment I woke today and she wasn't there that I noticed it. I can't really explain it. She's usually the first one I see when I wake, but today, she wasn't there. And I came to this realization at that moment. Heck, on the last mission, I basically lied to her because I didn't want her to worry about me. I was feeling sick two weeks before then and didn't tell anyone. Maybe I am too self-centered. What is your current relationship with Laura?"

"You will have to ask her when you see her. It seems our talk is over. I see Susan approaching with everyone else."

"All right, we are going now," Susan said. When everyone got in, Susan sat right next to me and continued talking to me. "I know Laura was mad when she left the base. She said she needed to blow off some steam, and this is one of the reasons. Just think about this as Laura having a 'me day.' So, she will not be on this mission, as you may have guessed by now, but you will see her again. Thanks to your last incident on the battlefield, she said you stressed her out so much she could not go on this mission. No need to worry about her; she'll be back before you know it."

"Thank you, Sue," I said, and leaned back in my seat. We slowly rose into the air.

"The mission is a simple one. We will push the Rising Flares back to the hole they climbed out of. Then, when they are out of our way, all we will need is one last push, and their main base will be ours for the taking. You who are all with me are squad leader material, and that is fine and dandy, but there will not be any others joining us today. I know some of you are still recovering; if it were up to me, you would get the rest you need, but Conner doesn't believe in more rest for his troops. You all know how he is, but once the mission is complete, we will finally get that well-deserved rest."

There was a continuous beeping that came from the front cabin. "All right, we are in position now and ready. Everyone, grab a parachute and land at point according to the chute color." This was the part where we got up and just leaped out; after all, the suit protected me, so what did it matter? Right after I did, Irene jumped out too for the same reason. As I fell, I closed my eyes and felt a raindrop on my check. I knew the water broke my fall, and I broke Irene's fall too. I turned my body to where my feet were going first. When I landed, I placed my arms out and caught Irene, holding her in my arms. The ground underneath us became like mud because of the built-up water.

"Are you two proud of skydiving without parachutes?" The Lightning Bearer said, throwing me a rifle. I caught it by the strap, and then placed Irene on the ground. "So, where is Rayshawn?"

"What, did you expect him to leap out the same way we just did?" I asked.

"I'll be back," the Lightning Bearer said and walked away. He went behind a tree, and all I could see was a flash of light; next, I saw a bolt leave from the surface to the sky. Then, it came back down. On the Lightning Bearer's shoulders was Rayshawn. The Lightning Bearer dropped Rayshawn and said, "Let's go, I have better things to do then just waiting here."

"All right, Lightning Bearer, lead the way," I said. I walked to Rayshawn. "Hey, Ray, are you all right?"

Looking around as though he had a panic attack, Rayshawn said, "What happened?"

"Looks like you were forcefully ejected from the aircraft. He went as far as melting the parachute you were using," I said, looking at his straps. "Are you all right other than that?"

Irene helped him up. "Heart rate high but sustainable; blood pressure high but balancing out; everything else is normal. He will fully recover in about thirty seconds." She turned around and walked away. "Your other friend is right; we don't have time to waste.

"How did she know that?" Rayshawn asked.

"If I understood correctly, the healing suit's other ability is to help the user when treating their patients so they can respond quickly and effectively." I handed him his shotgun that was on his back. "We better get going before they leave us behind."

We walked a mile into the forest and picked off the straggling enemy personnel. Once we saw a good place to set up our equipment, we were forced to kill any others in our perimeter. We held our position until the rest of our team finally caught up. The plan was to cut off the enemies' retreat from their main base. Our team split into two different groups; one group went to attack the base while the other stayed behind.

I went forward to help push the charge. Keeping the momentum going along with me was the Lightning Bearer, Peter, Irene, Kristy, and Rayshawn. The Lightning Bearer went up ahead, acting as our scout. He sent us the layout of what we got ourselves into. I noticed the outside was built like a bunker, but it was only three floors deep, so it just wasn't as deep. I would have asked how he received these plans, but knowing him, he just interrogated one of the enemies.

We entered the clearing and saw turrets aimed in our direction, so we stopped and took cover behind the nearest tree, but the turrets did not fire.

"Hey, is this your handiwork?" I asked.

I heard the Lightning Bearer's voice come from right beside me, which, I will admit, honestly scared me. "No, this is not my handiwork. Those turrets are automatic."

"Can't you disable those guns?" Kristy asked.

"I would love to, but they are using an electro-disrupter, possibly to keep the radio signal jammed, but it is also keeping me from using my guns or my speed. So, unless you can find the source of it, you are on your own. I am not as bulletproof as some of my counterparts."

I stood up and handed the Lightning Bearer my rifle. "All right, I will move forward and get the attention off of you guys, but I will need you guys to disable them. Rayshawn and Irene, look for the disrupter."

I ran forward, and then a turret popped out of the ground and began to fire on me. As the turrets came out of the ground, somebody would shoot them, disabling the firing systems. There were sixteen turrets that were triggered before I could even reach the main turrets I was focused on. When I did reach the main turrets, I clogged the barrel, keeping the bullets from leaving the chamber, eventually causing it to self-destruct. Peter charged at the door, breaking it down. I followed behind, shielding him and myself from whatever was on the other side of the door.

Peter tapped my shoulder. "The room is cleared, comrade."

"I confirm. All right, all remaining units, you are clear to move into the bunker," I said.

I surveyed the area with the water as I did when I was in the cave with Lilly, to look for the stairs or an elevator to go down further into the bunker. I heard footsteps come from another room a little bit further into the bunker, so I checked it out, signaling Peter to hold position. As I walked down to see what caused the footsteps, I saw other rooms, and nothing seemed out of place. I could not figure out what had caused the noise down the hall. So, I decided to turn back. When I turned back around, I saw Kristy holding a knife in her hands.

"Hey, I think your water thing has found the direction we are looking for. It started glowing on the ceiling for whatever reason."

"All right, I understand. I will be there shortly."

I saw Kristy walk away from me, so I turned back around and tripped over a body that had one of her knives sticking into it, so I got back up and followed after Kristy. After I regrouped with the others, we followed the water's path to the elevator that would lead us further into the bunker.

We exited the elevator and saw a room filled with women and children. "Where are we now?" Peter asked.

The Lightning Bearer put his gun down and threw something on the floor, said, "We seem to be at their shelter if we are considering the presence of their women and children. Looks like they forgot to block off this floor. Let's go to the next one."

"What did you throw in there?" Peter asked.

"Honestly, before I accepted this contract, I had accepted a contract to retrieve some people for extraction. Before you assume the worst, they are not going to be sold into slavery or anything. At the very least, they might be used as experiments, but their lives are not in any real danger."

The elevator doors opened, and there came a barrage of bullets, explosives, and gas. Luckily, before they started shooting, I had already formed a wall. The bullets were constant for thirty seconds. When I heard the gap between the gunfire, I lowered the shield, and we immediately fired into the room. After shooting for three seconds, we seized fire. I walked into the room with my weapon still drawn. I looked around the room for survivors, and I saw they were preparing for an attack, but not from us.

"Hey, Cross, I hope you can hear me," Rayshawn said over the radio.

"I guess this means those power jammers have been disabled."

"Yeah, but that isn't what I am calling you about. We talked to one of the locals who managed to survive. He said we are not the expected party. This would explain the lack of defense to a bunker this well fortified."

"Yeah, I've noticed." Peter gave me a piece of paper with the layout of the bunker. I glanced over it. "It doesn't look like we were supposed to find this bunker."

Kristy added, "Considering the fact that we are in a room with a dead general and the floor above us was filled with unarmed civilians, we were not meant to find this bunker. Even if we did, we got here too early for them to seal the survivors in there, and if we showed up on time, this was just supposed to be their last stand since there are only about twenty people in here, and the report says there are more. I will guess it is safe to assume the majority of their forces are holding off their intended enemy."

"Makes sense to me. Well, since we are all clear up here, we will be down there shortly."

The Lightning Bearer said, "Don't bother coming down here. We will have to come up to you." He went to a terminal and messed with the keyboard. When he finished, the bunker began to shake.

"What's going on?" I asked.

"We are just taking a shorter route to the surface. Nothing to be concerned about."

I noticed the walls rotating. After about thirty seconds, light shone through, and I could see the outside. Waiting as we finally got to the top was Rayshawn.

Rayshawn said, "This was kind of disappointing; it seemed we completed our objective before schedule, and it all took less than an hour."

"So, what will we do next? After all, we completed the main objective before we were supposed to."

"We can look and see if there is anything worth collecting," Peter said.

Rayshawn replied, "You guys enjoy going through all of their crap. I will try to go ahead and look for the remaining members of our team that might be in the area so we can start calling for an extraction."

"I will stand guard so we are not left unprotected." I walked toward the outer perimeter and just stood guard. As I walked away, I noticed Irene following me. "What's up?"

"I shall accompany you," Irene replied.

This bothered me because we had nothing to talk about. For whatever reason, she really didn't speak much when she was around me. I'd seen her more social with others but never with me.

After about thirty minutes, I heard the chopper start to arrive.

"Why is the extraction team here? The rest of our team isn't ready yet," I said. No response. "Darn it. Irene, we will need to regroup with our people because there is something going on, and we are not in the loop." Once we caught back up with our group, we saw Peter already packing things into the helicopter. I saw Rayshawn and asked, "What's going on?"

"New orders. We are supposed to pack anything that might be important," he replied.

"I didn't hear anything about this on the radio."

"Is it possible your radio died?"

"I didn't hear any indication of that happening."

Irene walked up from behind me and took the radio out of my ear to take a closer look. "There might just be a short somewhere that is stopping the battery from sending the charge. It needs a constant flow of electricity just to patch it up." She paused, putting the earpiece in my hand. "I used to be an electrician one or two lifetimes ago." She walked away.

From the corner of my eye, I looked at the tower and saw the second floor where those unarmed casualties started to float off. From what I understood, thrusters launched it straight up into the sky. I saw the Lightning Bearer walk up to me; he took my headphone and switched it with his, which was already in his hand. He said, "You can just use mine."

Kristy ran from the tree line and into the opening. She had been leaning against the tree, and the rest of the team rushed out. The next one to come out into the opening leaned against the tree on the other side, aiming into the trees. The team started running toward the chopper. After Kristy saw the chopper, she yelled, "We called for extraction and only one bird showed up. Conner, that son of a..."

"What are we going to do?" I asked.

"There won't be enough room for everyone. Too bad the Lightning Bearer didn't carry anymore thrusters with him." Susan sighed and lit a cigar. "All right, the first group of us who are going to be leaving will be Melena, Kristy, Peter, Emily, Rayshawn, Irene, and, of course, the spoils of war." This left Susan, the Lightning Bearer, Dave, and myself. "Hurry and clear the area. Let's go, you maggots, or else the maggots will feed off your corpses!" Susan flicked her cigar into a dry bush. That started a fire to help cover our escapes while at the same time giving the enemy our location.

Dave said, "There are enemy forces a half mile to the west, so we will keep moving east. We have about twenty minutes to get to our next evacuation point."

Sue said, "We will have to split into two. I will travel with the Lightning Bearer and let you two learn to get along. If, however, you don't, then I will kill you before the enemy will ever have a chance to. Any questions?" No one spoke. "Good, now let's go."

We ran away from the group with the rendezvous in our sight. We traveled without saying a word; we ran into resistance but never gave up. At that time, we were forced to use weapons without gunpowder. After a while, I caught onto Dave's suit ability and stealth because he just kept disappearing.

We got to our meeting point first, still not saying a word. The Lightning Bearer and Susan had maybe run into trouble. There was something fishy, something I didn't trust about him. With that thought, the two finally showed up. Next, the helicopter arrived, and Peter jumped out. "This position is completely compromised with enemies surrounding us. What's the plan?"

"The Rising Flares forces were more prepared than we expected," I replied.

"No, we stumbled onto our enemy's enemy. Unfortunately, they have more troops than us. We might be the special forces of the group, but we are far too outnumbered," Peter said.

The helicopter got low enough to the ground but never landed. Dave, Peter, and the Lightning Bearer all got into the helicopter. Before getting in, I waited for Susan, but she put a cigar in her mouth and lit it. She took a puff and said, "You guys go on without me."

"Susan, we're not leaving without you," I said.

"Normally, I wouldn't try to stop you, but today, I am. Leonardo, I don't know if you've noticed, but I am too old to be leading this unit. Project SUBWAY isn't for the elderly but the young. The way things are looking, your 'friend' Dave will probably be your next leader. I do apologize. It has been a real honor working with all of you. Tell Melena it is all in her, yours, and Rayshawn's hands."

"Let's go!" The Lightning Bearer yelled, pulling me in.

"I guess your secret will die with me, Lightning." The helicopter's door closed, and all I could do for her was bring the water underneath the ground to the surface, destroying the enemies' hiding position until there was an eighty-foot radius all around.

"Let's get back to base," Dave said.

There then came a voice over my headset on a private channel: "If you can hear me, Leo, get out now. Dave has set up a trap. For if you return to base, it will be waiting for you when you land. Sometime tomorrow, there will be someone you can trust who will meet you wherever you are." I wasn't sure who was speaking, thinking about it now, but I knew I trusted him or her.

I leaned forward, cut a hole around my seat, and fell out. When I looked around, I noticed I had landed in a desert region. I didn't have a lot of time and had to move quickly, so I used the water to dig a small trench and began to burrow a few feet. I waited in the trench for the helicopter to circle back around, but luckily, it never did. After waiting in the trench for fifteen minutes, I moved away from that location. I dug another trench, but this time, I had a stable covering. There had to be a reason why they didn't turn back around to pursue me; maybe Dave was turning this into one of his sick ploys—just like when we first met.

# 9
## Wait, You Brought Me Back...to Do What?

**T**wo weeks passed, and I set up camp under the desert sand with a cloth tent covered by sand to better blend in. I heard footsteps approach and I reached for my weapon, and before I could draw my weapon, I could feel a pat on my cheek and a grip on my hand. "What's wrong, Leo, are you getting complacent these past two weeks?" Laura said, wearing desert apparel.

"You really are a scary good tracker." I let go of my weapon and sighed.

"You should have left with your friends, you know that, right?" I nodded my head. "So, what will you do now that you are a wanted criminal by the same group you set out to help?"

"I will wait for another opportunity to present itself so I am able to leave this island," I replied. "Let's just say I don't have many places to go. So, what is your relationship with the Lightning Bearer, if you don't mind me asking?"

She paused, then replied, "What's it to you?"

"Well, he was telling me you two were old friends. I was just confirming."

"We were lovers long ago." When she said that, her eyes shined like emeralds, her face turned red from blushing, and I felt my heart sink. "I am just kidding;

he and I are old acquaintances who work together on missions from time to time."

"Can you tell me why you stay with me instead of him? After all, he can actually protect you."

"He is kind when he wants to be, but I think he is arrogant as well. I honestly couldn't tell you why I follow you; I never really thought about it. I wish I knew so I could tell you and give you some kind of answer. Why have you trusted me thus far? You know I am more than capable of killing you because I remember you told me you don't trust anyone."

"It is because of that I trust you. You have had many opportunities to kill me or have me killed, so I have no real reason not to. Honestly, if you were to kill me, I believe that you must have had a good reason." As I replied, a helicopter flew overhead.

"What was that?" Laura asked.

"Helicopters have been flying around this area since three days ago. I believe they are looking for someone or something around here. So far, they haven't found it."

"Are you certain it isn't one of SUBWAY's scouts?"

"I doubt it. From what I understand, there are three Js on both sides. So, it is a different organization altogether. Besides, I doubt they could find me here due to the fact I built an underground lair camouflaged with the desert's floor. If anybody were to walk by, they wouldn't see me. I am kind of surprised you found me; after all, I do keep moving to different parts of this desert."

"You do remember I used to hunt High Value Targets in snow and swamp, not to mention I was one of the people who taught you what you know. How long do they patrol the area, usually?"

"Honestly, the times between get longer and longer, but about five minutes on average. This one seems to have been here longer than normal."

She picked up her rifle and watched the entrance. I pulled out a pistol and dagger and did the same. I could faintly hear a small team load their weapons. An explosion blew the top of the lair completely off. The sand blew in the wind, leaving us completely exposed. They pointed their guns at us. I formed a shield to cover us from above; I spun it like a disk so I could more easily redirect any incoming bullets.

"Did you forget to refill the water in your armor?" Laura whispered.

"What are you talking about?" I asked.

"Haven't you noticed that under regular circumstances, there is usually some kind of water source nearby that you can pull water from? So, if you have been digging in the dirt with water, there will be water that will have been left behind."

"Dang, I didn't notice. It isn't like I ever get thirsty anymore. How do you know all of this?"

"My brother."

I looked up and saw one of the troopers yell to someone behind them: "Targets are confirmed as Leonardo and Laura. Ma'am, we found them. What are your orders?"

A familiar voice said, "At ease, troops."

The trooper replied, "If the rumors are true, they could kill us."

I could tell this was going to be a drawn-out stalemate; they didn't put down their weapons, and we sure as heck weren't putting ours down.

"They could kill you even if you were armed with tanks. Now, lower your weapons before I make you by force." I could hear the voice approach, and I watched as everyone lowered their rifles.

"Melena? How did you find us?" Laura asked, putting her rifle down.

"I knew you wouldn't go too far from Leo. After all, it's like you two are inseparable. I knew you would lead us to him, so I had you followed. We actually lost you, honestly. We searched for you in two other locations before we found you here."

"I take it you are here on behalf of that menace, here to kill me, and take the reward for yourself."

"You don't even believe that story because you know she is a much better person than that," Simone said, walking up from behind. "After all, you have known each other since high school, or at least that is what I heard. This strike was not her idea but rather mine. She wanted to leave you here in the desert. She told me this is the closest you've gotten to being home in a while, but we need you more than ever. As for your bounty, it was lifted due to being falsely accused of treason, espionage, and desertion. I take it you still don't believe me, or you think I am trying to set you up. I have no reason to lie to you. If you don't believe me, then check with someone you do trust." She threw a transmitter to Laura. Of course, I briefly lowered the shield.

Laura placed the transmitter in her ear. "Who's this?" Laura asked, and then paused for a second. "Understood." She now pressed my gun down slowly. "Leo, their story checks out. It's your choice how you wish to proceed."

I scanned the crowd, looking at their faces. Finally I retracted the water and asked, "What did you need me to do?"

"We will give you the mission briefing in the helicopter if you agree to join us," Simone said, dropping down to where we were. "So, will you lend us your power once more?"

Laura walked up and whispered in my ear, "To make this decision easier, if you join them, it may buy me the right amount of time to get you back home again."

"You make a good point, and I thank you, but I think I was going to join them anyways." I then spoke to Simone. "I will join you all once again, against my better judgment."

"Then, please follow us; we need to make this quick," Simone said.

So, we got out of the trench and into the helicopter, troops and all. After it was off the ground, Simone spoke.

"I hope you enjoyed your little vacation. It would have been longer, but in order for this plan to work, we will need your abilities. We were attacked around the same time you left. At first, we assumed it was you coming back for revenge, but after we captured then tormented the man, he informed us he knew nothing about you. Rather, he was of the Sand Wolves."

"What, those assassins? Those guys are trouble; they are the same ones that attacked our water supply, making the base hotter by like twenty degrees," Laura said.

"Yes, the most interesting part of what you just said is the fact they are doing the same thing as they did before, but this time, the heat is more potent. It is literally so hot you can see the steam rising from the outside of the base. From what we've observed, the water isn't poisonous or anything, so we can still drink it. It's so bad that Conner got involved, but that bastard is so messed up in the head. He expects us to run our base at full power. He hasn't been here even once since the heating problem."

Conner really was a cheap bastard. How he convinced anyone to work for him was beyond me. I remember the last time these people attacked, he just let the issue ride for about three months before he did anything. It was so hot the cooks wouldn't cook, and we didn't want them to. Frozen food stayed frozen for no more than five minutes. Simone said this time was more potent than before—that wasn't good.

Melena continued, "Simone and I both went before Conner and mentioned this to him. He wasn't thrilled, but he is in the process of creating a new base, one that's supposed to be built like a fortress. Your mission is not to stop the water flow. It is to lead troops to safety. You are the only one who can fly on suicide missions without regard for safety. Most of the other pilots are KIA or working on Conner's pointless missions. It's you and some of our new recruits."

"Wait, what happened to Kristy? She was a crazy good ally, amazing with her combat skills, and one heck of a better pilot than I could ever be," I added.

Melena answered, "She found a lead on her father being somewhere and left; before you ask, Peter is no longer with us either. He was sent on a mission to the south of the island to rescue Simone from enemy ambush, her and Emily. They left, and when the troops got there, all of the enemies had been killed, and Peter...was nowhere to be found. This was about three days ago."

"So, I'm playing escort?" I replied. "You ladies do remember what happened the last time I had to do a mission like that?"

Truthfully, I had never been good at escorting, not even once. Even when Laura was there with me, it just never went well. There hadn't been one mission where I played the role of defender that went well. The last time I did it, I was to protect a tank from enemy ambush. From what they'd told me, there wasn't anything special about the tank. Long story short, the tank was overrun, and somehow, one of the enemies snuck in and stole a chip. Upon delivering the tank, they told me the chip was actually of more value than the tank. Apparently, the tank had the ability to maintain itself automatically, including ammo and auto-targeting. Without this chip, it was nothing more than an expensive yard decoration. The purpose of the escort was to make certain the tank wasn't destroyed before it got to its destination. So, they had refused to pay Conner for his services.

"Yes, we do, and Conner is still very angry about that mission. Might be why he didn't mind the bounty being on you for so long. Not only did you get the chip swiped, but also the cost of the damages to the tank came out of Conner's pocket. Honestly, it might have been cheaper to destroy our own tanks, burn our food rations for three months, and put a bomb in our own base, but the mission was complete."

"So, how does Conner feel about my return?"

"If you want the truth, he didn't even notice you were gone until yesterday. Getting back to the point. We don't expect the helicopter to come back. So, do what you need to come back alive. I want everyone to arrive at our new base unharmed, and if they are lucky enough to leave this land, to return to their families in good conditions." She looked out the window. "It seems we have already arrived, and the last of the vehicles are being packed now. There will be someone to show you the location of the new base."

As we got closer, the air became thicker. The humidity rose; it was like sticking your head inside of an oven and putting it on broil. The helicopter came down but only hovered close enough to the ground for us to get out. Everyone began to get out of the chopper, so I proceeded to do the same, but the pilot told me to sit back down.

"Excuse me, I have something to take care of." Simone walked out of the helicopter with a briefcase. "This will be goodbye."

Melena, however, just walked to the back of the helicopter and grabbed a gun before jumping out. She said, "Leo, the pilot will take you where you are going. You will be away for about one hour. That's a round trip. Rayshawn is at the other base and will ride back with you to give you support fire. By the way, Laura wants you to meet her somewhere known as the wastelands after the mission is complete. I don't have a clue where that is; she said you would."

"Why didn't she just tell me herself, she was just here?"

"You know how she is about being vague."

"Thank you, Melena," I said. "I will see you when I get back."

"We will have those who are going on the first transport ready to head out to the new location." Melena walked off

Before the helicopter could take off, a young pilot jumped onboard.

"Who are you?" I asked.

"Get out!" she yelled.

"Now why should I do that?"

"Because I told you! Now get out before I make you get out!"

"I would like to see you try to get me out!" I wiggled into my seat. She reached out to touch me and reached for a knife. I broke the blade off, grabbed her by the hand, and pinned her to the wall of the chopper.

"You must be Leonardo. Just let her go. Topaz Stone-Heart has an attitude problem not even a mother could love, and because of this, she has been reassigned," said a voice from behind me. "So, just let her go, Water Boy. Because of her reassignment, we were forced to move you as well. Do you have a problem working with me?"

"I don't know you, but I would assume not."

"So, let's go!"

"Now why should I listen to you?"

"Because if you don't, you would have to fill out a whole lot of paperwork when we arrive at the new base; if, however, you were to kill her, I don't really have a problem with that. Better you do it now so no one else has to do it later."

I let go of Topaz and walked off the chopper. "So, why the sudden change?"

"As you can see, no one really likes the idea of working with her, so once they said I was going to be stuck with her as a partner, I quickly tried to break that plan up because if I were to get stuck with that

@#$*%&"—honestly, I am not too sure what she called her, but I know it was the insult of a lifetime—"I know if we were ever put on the same mission, only one of us would make it back alive. Once I brought up this fact to our leaders, they said if we could catch you before you took off, then the trade would be official. I hope you don't think you are the only one who doesn't like her. I don't think anyone does."

"Who are you?" I asked.

"How could I forget? My name is Amelia, Leonardo," she said. "Now, please follow me. We have to protect the camp until the enemy can no longer fight, or until the objective is complete."

"So, what exactly are we doing?"

"Our job is to protect and escort Simone. She doesn't know if she will have to take drastic measurements, so she's preparing just in case she does."

"What drastic measurements would she have to take?"

"I don't know, she never told me, and I doubt she will until the time comes."

I looked around and saw the base was all but abandoned. "Where are the others?"

"Well, they are currently being moved around until the next base opens up. All I was told is they are being moved to an undisclosed location, and we will be joining them shortly."

"It sounds as though they are slowly being killed off, if what you say is true."

"I never trust someone I just met; however, if I were in your situation, I guess I wouldn't have many choices. If you don't think that you are qualified, then I'll find someone else, possibly Laura. I wonder what she'll think."

"So, you know you told me we are doing an escort mission, but you never told me the why."

"Simple, our job is to ensure everyone here escapes."

"Why me? Can't anyone else, literally anyone, do this?"

"Based on what I have heard, you can do it. It must be something to do with your ability over the use of water. Many said they would trust you over any others who might be in their unit. Besides, you're the only one who is capable of pulling this off with little risk to your own life. You'll know when the mission starts, so just relax and keep your radio ready. Rest easy until then," she said, walking away.

Since I had time to kill, I decided to check on my old room, but when I got there, it was gone like it was never there. There weren't any imprints of the building, no discarded trash, not even broken soil, for that matter. It was definitely more than a little weird to me. Maybe they used me as one of those examples; who knows. I hoped they had at the very least moved everything to the new base. I sat down and was left to my thoughts.

I closed my eyes, catching a brief whiff of vanilla. This automatically reminded me of my mother. I could see her face and the faces of my two sisters. I walked up to her, then a beach formed in the background; both of my sisters were playing with kids. It was now that I heard my brother's voice: "So, were you ever going to come home? You know they miss you, right?"

"I miss them as well, but I don't know how they'll really feel about me when they hear of the things I have done here."

"Is that the only reason you missed the plane ride off of the island? Because there was plenty of room, and you could have easily protected the plane from the inside. Or was there another reason you stayed here? You know Laura is trying everything in her power to get you home. You can't be selfish with her."

"I am not...You're right, little brother; you're totally right. I think I am just afraid to lose her. I am not sure why I have been wasting her time. Why am I being so selfish?"

"That, big brother, is for you to find out. Hurry back, brother. Mom doesn't need to have two dead sons, especially not when one of them is still alive."

"Regardless, if I leave before completely finishing what I have started here, then it will not end well for anyone."

"Always trying to be this big hero. One day, it might just get you killed."

"Maybe you're right."

"Now if I were you, I would definitely wake up."

I heard an explosion and immediately woke up. I heard an alarm go off and a voice announce, "We are under attack." I rose quickly and saw everyone run to evade the enemies. I put my helmet on and ran into battle with my pistols in hand. People headed toward the evacuation points where the vehicles would pick them up. Some could leave right away, but they were few in number. They knew if they were not already in place to be picked up, they would be left behind. At this point, I knew my job was to hold the enemy back until backup arrived. So, I started holding them back, but it seemed the harder I fought, the harder they did the same. Some of our snipers helped keep them back to the best of their abilities. As for our other shooters, from what I could tell, their shots were not as accurate, and they didn't want to hit me in the process.

I fought there for about twenty minutes before the evacuation team showed up. Rayshawn jumped off with a light machine gun in his hands. Everyone else swarmed in rather quickly. Rayshawn ran up to me, and then we were back to back.

"Sure do get yourself into trouble without me," Rayshawn stated.

"No, they heard you were coming and decided to bring the party," I replied.

"So, did you enjoy your desert vacation? I heard you enjoyed it so much you tried not to come back."

"Well, of course, it was nice, but I guess all good things must end at some point and time. If not, then life would be too easy."

As soon as the transport was full, it took off.

"We'll play catch-up at the new base. For now, we need to get this battle over with," said Rayshawn.

Then, we fought enemy after enemy. Eventually, the machine gun ran out of bullets, so Rayshawn switched to his shotgun. Bodies piled up around us. Because I also ran out of bullets for my pistol, I was forced to use my sword. Normally, the sword would have expanded and water would circulate around it, but this time, it just opened.

"Hey, are the water reserves still flowing through the base?" I asked.

"Last time I heard, we never turned it off."

I slammed the sword to the ground to charge and noticed water begin to gather in the handle. Since I had no other weapon, I had to use the weapons on the ground from the attackers. I noticed that every time a bullet hit me, I felt the actual impacts from the blows, unlike before. Was it because I didn't have my sword on me, or was it because the suit was running extremely low on water, which I had recently learned was a possibility? I looked at the areas where I was hit, and luckily, there wasn't anything but a light dent, but I also noticed the armor looked like it barely held together. That might be where the last of the water was. This was the first time I had been thirsty in a long time. I couldn't play this as carefree as I normally would. So, I would have to be more careful, at least until the sword was finished charging. I noticed there was a lack of gunfire coming from the enemy.

"Rayshawn, how many of them do you count out there?" I whispered." He signaled at least thirty. "Crap! I take it that we don't have any explosives, so we will have to wait for them to get a little closer. If we can buy some time, it might just be exactly what we need."

"For what?"

"You're just going to have to trust me."

The enemy slowly advanced toward us. I again searched the dead bodies, looking for anything useful. All I could find was a grenade and half-emptied cartridges. So, I took the cartridges and handed Rayshawn the grenade.

"Hey, doesn't the MOTH have some kind of weapons on board?" I asked.

"Usually, yes, but on this one, the guiding system is broken. It was the only one Conner would let us use," Rayshawn replied.

As he finished speaking, I noticed I couldn't hear the enemy moving at all. I popped my head up to see what was going on, and I saw the enemy taking cover. There was someone loading a missile into a barrel. He prepared to fire, which was when Rayshawn threw the grenade. But before it went off, the missile released. The missile hit an engine. The damage wasn't too bad, from the way it looked; the engine was just exposed, but it could still fly. I heard a loud whistle echo in the sky.

"They're using mortars?" I asked.

At this point, I could not tell if they were trying to hit the MOTH aircraft or us, but I knew the next attack wasn't going to miss its target. I heard another pop in the air followed by a whistle. Rayshawn began running, as I did. I also ran by the sword to do a sweep and grab. As I grabbed a hold of the sword, the explosion hit the ground; luckily, it hit where we were. In my hand, the sword morphed into a shield. With the shield, I aimed it toward the enemy. As I did so, the enemies at close range began shooting and exposed their position. Immediately, a blue gas released; at first, I assumed it was concentrated water released into the air. Those who stood in front of me fell down. Their bodies shook on the ground as though they were having a seizure. I then noticed my visor display, stating, "Water at 100 percent. Release of all toxins completed. Water now purified and will be regulating through armor shortly..."

With this toxin in the air, we were able to slow down the enemies' advance on the base at least until they regrouped.

The transport was finally filled with people, and the engine was on once more, but the exposed engine was on fire. We walked to the transport to get ready to leave.

"Is everyone aboard?" I asked, looking inside.

"No, we were still missing two others, Simone and Amelia."

"Crap!"

"You two get in or I'm leaving you behind!" Topaz demanded.

"Leonardo, you're still at the base, right?" Simone's voice said over the radio.

"Yes, I am; where are you?"

"I will assume Rayshawn is with you. You two have new orders. One of you is to head over to the underground basement. I need your help with a little project; one last direct hit to cripple the enemy with. The other needs to distract the enemy away from our last escape point. There they will meet Amelia, who needs help."

I then yelled to Topaz, "All right, you bastard of a woman, leave. No one wants you here anyways."

"Bye!"

"All right, Rayshawn, you help Simone in the basement. I will play decoy. Good luck," I said, handing him shotgun shells.

"Thanks, but I will not be needing it. With just the right amount of bad luck, my days remain entertaining."

I couldn't help but chuckle. "I guess you're right." Rayshawn left. "Amelia, where are you?"

"I am at the front gate," she replied. I went to the location Amelia gave me. When I arrived, Amelia sat on the ground, reading a book. "You're late!" Amelia said, turning the page. "We are going to hold them back for as long as we can, slowly making our way to the escape point. When we arrive at the escape point, we need to stop their advance. By the way, thank you. If it wasn't for you, I would be stuck with Topaz."

"So, what are you reading?"

"Doesn't matter. Laura told me you hate reading. Telling you would be a waste of time."

At that time, I thought she wasn't being real; Amelia never showed her real emotions, not even when she was angry. I think she was like a soldier who only knew how to fight.

"So, why is the escape point here?" I asked, watching the last of our troops escape. I proceeded to retract my armor.

She replied, "Because of how easy it is to leave from that point. You might not know this, but I was told they are here for you, and if you had gotten on the aircraft, it would have been shot down. Since you weren't aboard, they got away without the taste of death. You would have been the only survivor. An elderly man by the name of Fredrick Knight told me."

Fred Knight? I knew a Fred Knight back in high school, and if she was talking about the same person, then he was the same age as me, if not about a year older. It must have been a coincidence. "Where is he now?" I asked.

"From what I understand, he was equipped with armor like yours; one made for time travel, so I guess this means he could be anywhere and whenever. I was told you might know him."

"If he is the same guy I am thinking of, then yes. He and I grew up together." I grabbed a grenade. "It seems more guests have arrived."

"That was sooner than expected." She closed her book, putting it in her inner breast pocket. She picked up a light machine gun and began to unload. While she fired, I held up a wall of water to shield us from incoming shots. Whenever her magazine emptied, we went to the next checkpoint, and so on and so on. Each checkpoint was about five hundred feet away from the last. It seemed like every time I tried to help, she would yell and tell me to focus on keeping the shield up. The final checkpoint was on the bottom floor of one of our towers.

"All right, go upstairs. When you get up there, you'll know what you need to do," she said.

I ran to the rooftop and looked over the cliff. I saw Amelia wasn't downstairs anymore. "Hey, where are you?" I asked.

A chopper rose from the ground; its pilot stared me in the face. I grabbed hold of my sword slowly. I could see the machine gun rotate; I would be forced to use it like a shield.

"Come on, bro, we don't have all day," Rayshawn said.

"Dang, Ray, you scared me. I was planning a play to shoot the chopper down and everything."

"Leo, you coming?" Ray said, raising the chopper. I used the water as rope to pull me up without causing the helicopter to lose balance. As I got up, I noticed there was a car in the cargo area. "Laura placed a car in the back. I guess she didn't want to leave it behind."

"OK, so what about the other two? What about the girls?"

"They'll be fine."

"Rayshawn, we've got to go back."

"All right, bro, but we only have enough fuel for one pass."

I used the radio and yelled, "Hey, ladies, we only have enough fuel for one pass. Please make your way to the evacuation points."

The first to reply was Amelia. "I copy you, Cross, I'll meet you at the top of warehouse three. I need you to get as close as you possibly can so you don't have to land."

Rayshawn replied, "That is a good copy. We will be there shortly."

"Simone, what is your current status and location?" I asked.

"I am taking care of the gift. I will have to meet you at the top of warehouse three as well," Simone replied.

We made our way to warehouse three. As we got closer, we saw Amelia run, then I saw her multiply, moving in several locations at one time. When I saw all of them, my first thought was that I was dizzy from the lack of sleep or something, but it was only Amelia who multiplied. Everything else remained the same, so there was something about her. I saw the building start to crumple; it was as though there were explosives placed inside the building. The ground under Amelia's feet began to cave in. I saw an enemy on the roof; he prepared to fire, but one of the many Amelias shot him and vanished.

"Rayshawn, can we get any closer?" I yelled.

"We can get closer, but this is as low as we can get without the Electric Magnetic Pulse shutting us down."

I watched as she multiplied even more. Eventually, there were about thirty of them. They all began to stack up on one another, but because of gravity, they fell down. The other eleven used the other girls as stairs, using their arms to give the others a boost. Cutting their numbers in half, it was now that I tied a rope around myself. Then another three used momentum and locked hands, spinning until they were no longer going up. The last two again kicked off the other's foot. It was now that I leaped out of the helicopter without hesitation. If she missed me, she could at least grab the rope. Oddly enough, I jumped a little too soon, so I fell down before her. She reached for the rope but I felt no tug, but as my weight swung, I was able to grab her hand and pull her up.

"Rayshawn, go!" I yelled. We were reeled in and watched the explosion underneath. "Where's Simone?"

"I think she wanted me to give this to you. It's a recording," said Amelia.

The helmet scanned and started playing the recording.

"This will be my last journal entry. Tomorrow, we will need to destroy our base with a self-destruct sequence that's already being prepared. Sadly, we don't have the personnel to make this a possibility. We have to find Cross by tomorrow morning if we want to have enough time. We have hit many different locations where he used to be, but there was no sighting of him, and we don't have a prayer of finding Laura. If we can find them, it will be a miracle at this point. Conner has already erased the bounty, but if he doesn't, this will be even more difficult. The only way to find him will be through Rayshawn. We will have to get the information out of him, one way or another. Honestly, even if we could find them, Leonardo will not like this plan. We will have to sacrifice someone, and I will volunteer myself. I am tired of working for SUBWAY, and with me being one of the leaders, there will be nowhere for me to run or hide. So, this will be it. Leo, if you are hearing this, then I am sorry. And I hope, in time, you can forgive me. This is Simone Goodman, signing out."

As the recording finished, the base exploded. The explosion was high enough to barely pass through the island's camouflage. I knew this because I watched as it temporarily malfunctioned from the blast, breaking through the top like a zit, and just as quickly as it broke, it repaired itself.

As we were still being reeled in, a cannon was launched toward the sky from the ground. It hit, combusted, and set the rope on fire. I used the water to form an umbrella protecting Amelia from the falling fire. I looked up and noticed the rope caught on fire, but I quickly put it out. I heard a gunshot and felt the rope broke; this, in turn, caused us to fall. Lucky for us, there were some trees nearby, and I tossed Amelia at a tree. As I was about to hit the ground, water formed underneath me, breaking the majority of my fall. I noticed we were in a swamp close to the fallen base. Amelia dropped out of the sky and landed right next to me.

"So, where are we going?" I asked.

Amelia replied, holding a digital map, "We are supposed to be heading west to get to the new base."

"It's a good thing you've been there before."

"Yes, but it seems the map has malfunctioned. The blast must have knocked out the feed. It might take an hour or two for the system to completely reboot. So, we will be walking around blind having to use the sun as our compass."

"Yeah, not a bad idea, but the sun will be setting before long. When it sets, the only thing we will be doing is waiting."

"For the comms to come back online."

"Comms are down too?"

"Yes. Let's go before it gets too late."

I followed her until we got out of the swamp, or at least I thought we were out of the swamp. The ground underneath felt rock hard, and the trees were longer stood. In my mind, I thought this must have been where the cannon fire came from. I smelled ash and cooked animals. The ash filled the air, and if it wasn't for the mask I wore, I might have died from that much debris in my lungs. We continued walking, and the ash cleared up. There, in the middle of it all, was a camper roasting a hotdog.

"So, you two finally got here. I thought this was going to take forever," the camper said.

A person faded in like a ninja in the wind.

"We've been waiting," he said. I walked closer for a better look.

"Mr. Knight?" Amelia said.

I looked at the ninja and noticed who he was, so I said, "Fredrick, it is you? I haven't seen you since high school. Your mother was a teacher at our high school if I remember correctly."

"Ah, you too, Leo. Are you here to help me, or are you here to get in my way?" Fredrick asked.

"In your way of what?" I asked.

"Of killing Amelia because she has a corrupted suit of armor."

"This does explain why she could do that multiplying thing back there. I was curious and was going to ask her about it when we got back. I just assumed it was a natural skill from being a super soldier."

"You need to lay off the comics," the camper replied.

"Normally, I would love to help you, but I have yet to see her do anything wrong."

"Yet...but I already knew this was going to happen. You have always been that kind of person. I would challenge you, but I have a huge upper hand here. So, to stop you from interfering, I brought with me a distraction." The camper stood with his back toward us. Armor started to form on him.

"Cayden?" I asked. "We don't have the time. We need to return to base."

Cayden turned around and dashed over to me, not putting his helmet on. He put two fingers on my chest and literally destroyed my armor, everything except for the power source. He held something behind his back. I thought for sure he was going to kill me and was holding a dagger or a sword behind him.

Cayden said, "Your armor breaking was inevitable. It was going to happen whether I did it or not. I might have just saved your life.

I felt defenseless at this point. He moved his second hand and offered me some food. I was left motionless, so Cayden picked me up and sat me near the fire, and then sat next to me.

"This was going to happen anyways. I know you're mad and maybe even scared, but this was going to happen. Let me guess, you've had that suit for two years?" he asked.

"No, it's been about four years," I replied.

"You must either be really careful or a pacifist. Mine took three months. It broke after I took five slugs to the chest. If it weren't for the bullet-resistant vest and the Lightning Bearer protecting me at that time, I wouldn't be here today. The wielders wanted to make our minds more like the elements, so in your case, the more like water you are, the stronger your armor will come back. To be honest, I believe there are two armor types. We have the Betas and the Alphas. Normally, the Betas are very easy to break and will usually corrupt the minds of the wielders, whereas the Alpha suits work with the wielders to achieve their goals. We—you, the Lightning Bearer, as he is called, and me—are part of the elemental class. Our armors' creators made these suits to eventually break, even shatter at some point. This is, of course, until the armor comes back. Then it won't ever go through the wear-and-tear process."

I noticed Amelia and Mr. Knight finishing their fight. They fought the whole time Cayden talked, but neither could lay a hand on the other.

When they neared the end, clapping came from behind.

"Man, I was right, this was a good show. One of the best fights I have ever had with a close friend; all this for a misunderstanding."

Amelia and Fredrick stopped and stood back to back, for they didn't see anyone there.

"No need to worry, I am not your enemy, more of a passive observer," said the voice.

"Cayden, take Leo and head to the wastelands. Someone needs your help. I need to talk to these two."

Cayden threw me over his back.

"Leo, all will be fine. You'll see," said the voice.

So, we left. Seconds later, I received an SOS beacon through the armor device in the direction of the wastelands. We got closer; it was like Cayden knew exactly where to go. When we arrived, he dropped me upon landing.

"So, this is where you have been," Cayden said. "You are indeed a very pride-driven woman, and that pride will get you killed one of these days."

"You worry too much, big brother. I see you brought Leonardo."

I heard the footsteps walk closer. At this point, I knew he was talking to Laura; I wanted to say something, but it was like all the strength in my body had left.

"If you are as fine as you say you are, then why did you send out a distress call to your unit?"

"That wasn't to the whole unit, just a very select few."

"You knew I was in the area, and you called your unit."

"It's called being independent."

"I don't know if it was when you turned eighteen or when you met Leonardo, but you have changed."

"Crap, Cayden, what did you do to him?" she asked. She quickly got down and started to feel for my vitals; it was later explained that because a small amount of my armor was still on, it looked as though I had slept on a grenade while wearing the suit.

"He's fine. I just broke the shell of his armor."

"I told you his suit wasn't corrupted. Why don't you listen to me for once?"

"Look, I might have saved the man's life. It would have been worse if it broke in an uncontrolled combat area."

"I don't know how we can be related when we are so different."

She shined a flashlight in my eyes, and then helped me up. As I got up, I saw what looked like an active warzone. We headed back to where the Webmaster's village was. On the way there, Cayden explained the mountains and plains they were built on rotated once a day; how much rotation wasn't always the same. It does this so gently it doesn't draw attention to itself. This was why it was hard for anyone to find the Webmaster. When I returned, Mrs. Ramona had left to get off the island and return to London. I stayed there for two months learning to make my mind like water; that way, I could have a chance to repair my armor.

# 10
## Chaos...
## within the Ranks

Approximately two months had passed, and Laura was the one going back and forth between the Webmaster's base and the new base to be sure they didn't believe we were dead. Mr. Trotter came to the village to drop off some supplies. We talked for five hours, and he told me I shouldn't worry, and having a mind like water wasn't as difficult as it sounded. He told me I was overthinking the situation, which was something I was known for. He said not to be afraid and that I should return to base, so I left.

As I arrived, Laura happened to have just left, and this was bad because I wasn't 100 percent sure of the new base's location; she had briefed the location was in our enemies' blind spot. They couldn't find it even if they looked. I walked off the moving land as I had before. I heard the sound of an engine approach, so I dropped low to the ground because there was a possibility it was an enemy attack. A car pulled up, and the passenger door opened; the driver was Cayden.

"Leo, my sister requested if she hasn't returned by the time you left, then she wanted me to escort you safely to your base so she wouldn't have to worry about you getting lost."

"Why you?" I asked.

"Because my sister knows that I can be trusted when it comes to sensitive information, especially when it comes to the Webmaster's hideout and the location of your new base."

I got in the car, and we drove, not saying a word. We got to the new base, and the only thing I thought was, *Although this was a new facility, it is the same terrible boss; still cutting corners and forcing his people to take the blame for his shortcomings.* Nothing would ever really change here, not as long as Conner was still here. The new base did have a futuristic vibe, although I hated to admit it, with a chrome-like appearance that shined brightly. I continued riding, and Johnny met me by the gate, which was where I was told to get out. When Cayden drove away, Johnny met me at the base entrance to show me around the new location. While I looked, the only thing I noticed quickly was the base was literally twice as big. They showed me to my living quarters, which looked more like a house than the tents and trailers we lived in before. I looked around, and all my stuff was already there.

Johnny left, saying, "There is going to be a mission for the whole team, but this will be nothing more than a practice run, so take your time."

So when he left, I familiarized myself with my room. From what I saw and heard, everyone was excited to be at the new base, but I could not feel the same way as them. I walked outside, and for some reason, I felt a faint presence. It was now I knew my new goal was to leave my current position on the globe and return home to California, either that or meet my Maker trying.

"God, why?" I whispered.

"Well, maybe it's just part of His plan," Laura said, walking in front of me.

"I wouldn't be surprised even in the least," I replied, looking up toward the sky. "So, what is the mission?" I asked.

"Well, it's not really a mission. This is nothing more than a test for the leaders to see if they're capable of leading in battle, and unfortunately, we must go. Amelia, Rayshawn, and Melena are on the scene already."

"Is there anything else?"

"Yeah, we are now in joint forces with another faction who call themselves Jx3."

"What does that stand for?"

"Judoka Jumpers of Justice, if I remember correctly. They were defeated, and as gesture of good faith, we merged factions."

Their helicopter was located on the helipad. After walking to the helicopter, we saw the pilot standing outside, leaning beside the helicopter as we approached. The pilot had a small stick of dynamite in his mouth, no lighter. He took it out and asked, "Are you on the right pad?"

"Does it matter?" I asked. "Aren't we all going to the same place?"

"I guess it really doesn't, but the condition by which you get there does."

"Wait, are you threatening—"

Before I could finish my sentence, Laura had covered my mouth. "I'm sorry, we missed your name," she said.

"My name is Joe Shorty. I am an ex pilot, originally from Russia. If you are going with me, just wear your seatbelt until I tell you otherwise."

He got into the helicopter and started up the engine. We had just sat down when a few others walked onboard. When all who were going with him showed up, he took off without ever closing the door. I looked around and noticed there were just a few of us with him.

"Hey, aren't we going to wait for more people to come before we take off?"

"No, most people are afraid to ride with me, so it is more of a punishment."

"Punishment? Laura, did you purposely pick this one?"

"Not for the same reason you might think, but yes, I did. I assure you, he is the best pilot this team has to offer. Besides, those J fliers are not as prepared as he is for combat."

"You expect to go into combat up here? I thought you said this was just going to be a training mission."

"It is; they need their training too."

"Alright, the exercise will commence very shortly," Shorty said, "so, if you haven't buckled in yet, you should do so now. From here on out, if you get hurt, it is on you."

I noticed those who hadn't buckled in just yet strapped in and grabbed onto their seats. We heard a beeping come from the helicopter's equipment.

"I hope you are ready. We are going to dodge the incoming projectiles."

I was going to shield the aircraft, but Laura told me not to. He proceeded to do a barrel roll while releasing flares. He proceeded to slow the rotors. As the helicopter fell, we gently rotated from the tail end. He quickly pulled up, scraping whatever was on the ground with the bottom of the helicopter. It still pulled up, but then we heard an explosion as the missile hit the ground.

"That was a little excessive, right?" Shorty said, pulling back up. "Going back up. All right, we will be over the drop zone in fifteen. Be sure to have all your belongings in hand; if you don't, then you will be without them for the mission. Drop in ten, nine, eight, seven, six, five..."

The missile alert went off again, and he dropped us. Laura aimed up to the sky. She fired her sniper rifle into the air, and the missile exploded.

As soon as we hit a certain height above the ground, our chutes automatically opened. When we landed and stopped moving, they refolded.

"Annie, I have marked the locations of the anti-air guns on the map based off of where they launched. I will continue to give you air support from up here." He paused, then continued, "This location will be clear shortly after the charges are set and ready for the leaders' landing as planned. Landing party, don't move too far or you might be killed from the explosion." We heard a loud whistle, and then an explosion followed by airplanes doing an airstrike. "All right, I will be landing shortly. Air combat training is complete."

As Shorty began to land, Laura turned to the landing party and yelled, "All right, you bunch of wannabes, our new commander is coming here. We need to prepare for Commander Kim Goldstein. Set up a perimeter half a mile wide. Now go! This is a simulation, but it is supposed to be treated like the real deal. If I see anything out of place, I will make you regret the day you decided to come to this island. Let's move it, people."

"Wow, Laura, I didn't know you had all that in you. This whole time I thought you were the nice one," I said. "So, what exactly are we supposed to do here?"

"Well, normally we are supposed to watch and make sure these people are actually doing their job, but because you are considered a special unit, your main concern is to keep the area safe, at least until we have left."

"So, nothing."

"I wouldn't say that. You have seen when things go south and what to expect, so just be ready." She tapped my breastplate, smiling. "Stay vigilant. Remember the incident with Rayshawn. Good men and women were slain because of their obliviousness."

Joan walked up, yelling at the new recruits, "Now let's hurry up!" The troops got even more riled up. "Let's go!"

I didn't know much about Joan, but from what I have heard from the people around me, she was usually very nice to be around. The people around her loved her. She didn't take crap from anyone, and very well educated. Just because she was small didn't mean she didn't know how to handle herself.

Joan walked up to us and said, "Can we talk?"

"Yes, he's all yours," Laura said, walking away.

"Well, now that she is gone, what did you need to talk to me about?" I asked.

"I want to know more information on the history of how SUBWAY has progressed since you first got here."

I calmly replied, "Honestly, it has only gone down more and more since I have been here. We had great soldiers die every day. Conner knows this and just doesn't care. To him, we are nothing more than an expense report. For every man he's lost, he doesn't even have a funeral for them; instead, he leaves them where they lay, except when they die in the camp. When that happens, he ships their body with fertilizer. I don't know if you noticed, but we are not even fighting a war, just a bunch of small battles. There is no final boss, no secret Hitler, and no terrorists; there is nothing but a meaningless war. With our weapons so advanced, I feel as though we are only here to test out the weapons for the other countries. That is literally everything crammed in a nutshell. Anything else?"

"So, with you knowing all of this, how do you still work for SUBWAY?"

"How does anyone stay motivated for anything these days? You have to find something to distract you." I referred to Laura. She made things more interesting, and watching her was fun. "If you can't find that, then this is a hard life."

Shorty walked up. "Hey, Ann, what are you up to this time?" he said.

"Just asking our friend here about his experience with SUBWAY."

"It is probably just as crappy as what we are going through."

"Sadly, yes," I replied. "If I were you, I'd try to get out while you still have a chance. I am pretty sure if you really wanted to get off of this island, then you would have to find someone with connections."

"Why, have you tried to return home?" Ann asked.

"Home?"

"Yes, from what Melena has told me, you are not from here, and you are actually from America. I ask my question again: why haven't you tried to go home yet?"

I paused, for I didn't actually have a reason. "I guess I have been a little too distracted. There was a time I wanted to try and make this place better, but once I saw there was too much corruption, I had no choice but to give up on that goal."

"That is sad to hear," Laura said, walking up. Everyone looked at her, myself included. "Oh, I am sorry to interrupt, but the rest of the team is here, and the new commander is traveling with them."

"Great, this oughta be fun," Shorty said. Next, he talked over the radio. "All right, the primary target will be here soon enough. Is my LZ clear?" For those who don't know, that is Landing Zone.

One of the scouts replied, "Yes, sir, LZ is clear."

"Good, I would hate for something to happen because you suck at your job."

The commander landed. At this point, I had never seen her, but I had heard all kinds of rumors, and none of them were nice. Apparently, Captain Kimberly Hobbs wasn't very well received. Kim landed with her helicopter; as the door opened, she came out along with three others wearing purple uniforms; I assumed they were the special unit from Jx3 squad. They were not fully armored and only had medical gear. All four of them approached me, and Laura stood beside me, kicked me in my leg, and then stood at attention. I assumed she was trying to tell me to do the same, so I did. The captain then stood in front of me.

"At ease; this is just an exercise, so no need to be official here." She shook my hand and said, "So, you must be the water user I've heard so much about. Isn't that something? I am glad you can be here. I suggested to Laura it would be a wonderful team-building experience if she could convince you to come along. The new personnel are still learning things, and they needed to train. And the best way to do so is by getting major personnel to be present for this. I know you don't want to be here." And she was right; I just wanted to rest in my room. "Later, Melena and Rayshawn will be here to replace you and your partner, Laura. Since you two have been there longer than anyone else, I was wondering if we could better understand what to expect."

I replied, "You can, but I have nothing to say that will be positive, so if you want to know anything, it might be better to ask Laura."

"Is that attitude I hear through the ranks?" a man said. "It doesn't matter what you want to do, you were told to do something."

Laura whispered, "That is Second Commander Cory Aaron. He is a bit of a prick."

He continued, "All that matters is that you're being told by your superior officer to do something. You should be honored."

I finally got ticked off dealing with everyone's crap, saying, "Honored, NO, you must think I am a slave or something. Your train of thought is extremely messed up. Honestly, you can go screw yourself. In my life, I have only worked for two people. Susan Boo, the old commander of SUBWAY, and the Webmaster."

"That may be so; however—" he tried to add.

"There is no 'however.' You can go screw yourself. It isn't like you can deduct my pay or anything."

I began walking away, and Kim added, "That's enough from you two. To answer your question, we will be here until the team can work as a single unit or until further notice. We have a new roster of rookies, so we have to make sure no one will run when the fighting gets too hot."

"Fine, but I'll not be a part of this; however, if you need me, I will be watching from a distance."

"Very well, and thank you," she replied.

I climbed up a tree and waited. I thought that Laura would train with them, but instead, she came to see me.

She asked, "Is everything all right?"

"I thought you were going to train the troops," I said.

"The troops are not my responsibility; you are. Besides, I wouldn't know how to start. I have trained, and every time, the people have to be retrained after."

It was true, though; she knew a lot of things but could never teach another person to do what she did. This wasn't to say she would never try, but her teaching method was a little more than rough. It was all kinds of confusing. I loved watching everyone's confused faces when she taught. Her do-it-herself attitude didn't help. Though she would talk to me normally, explaining things to others changed it.

"It's a real shame that you have been here that long and can explode like that. You do know it is unprofessional?" she said.

I sighed. "Yes, I know you are right; however, that prick had no right talking to me like that."

"Yes, he did; he is second in command." I knew she was right. "Maybe it is just about time we try to get you back home."

"Home? I have almost forgotten what it looked like." I wondered if I would know it when I returned. "So, what about you? What will you do?"

"Hmm...I never really thought about it? Up until now, you have been my responsibility. I guess I could always return to bother my brother. Heck, I could return to the Webmaster; she always has something for me to do."

"Why don't you return with me?"

"I have not been in regular society since I was a little girl. I don't think I know how to be with the people from your world."

"As I didn't know the people from your world, and you assisted in teaching me, so I shall do the same for you."

"Well, that is mighty kind of you, but why would you want me to come along?"

I knew she was either searching for some kind of confession or she genuinely wanted to know, so I answered to the former. "What about wanting to see the great sights or even the land you were born in?"

"You have known me for years. Have any of those things ever interested me?" Of course, I knew they didn't, for if she wanted to see a great wonder, she would either read it in a magazine or build it herself.

"They will have a variety of guns for you to use."

"I make my own, and they work so much better. Besides, we have plenty of guns here, and from what you told me, your mother hates them."

"That is true. Well, there are a variety of different food types you could have."

"I can do that here," she sighed. "Look, if it really means that much to you, then I will keep it under consideration for you, but we must still try to get you home safely first."

"Just tell me the plan and where to go, and I will be there just as quickly."

This place wasn't made for people like me, and I knew it even before I started; I didn't belong here. Even though Laura did, I felt as though she needed a new life outside of this, but in the end, it was her choice to make. I only hoped it would be leaving with me, as selfish as that was.

A week passed, and we were still there, and through the rain, snow, hail, heat, wind, flood, and mud, the training went on without a break. It was a very interesting week. During this intense week, Laura cooked for me an excellent full-course meal that reflected the weather each day. I think it was her way of saying, "If I wanted a full course meal, then I will make it myself." That was very true; she made food from the freshest ingredients, usually during missions.

It was then I heard little Kimmy had run away. She was a young woman, but it was like she was too smart to be working for SUBWAY, so I was happy for her when I heard she left. The training was finally coming to an end, and I only knew this because the team finally could follow directions, no matter if they seemed stupid or not. Commander Kim was about to finish the training after all this; oddly enough, she called Rayshawn, Melena, Amelia, Topaz, Joe-Shorty, Laura, and myself to partici-pate in the end-of-training event; I guess they wanted to make our job look better than what it really was, but dirt is dirt, burned is burned, and ash is ash.

So, Kim's plan was to have them against us. We would be outnumbered; for every one of us, there were three of them. We were forced to use stun bullets, so there was no risk of death. Joe joined in because he was bored. The match didn't last sixty seconds; we all took this as a real challenge, and I created a shield around us acting as cover.

Rayshawn, Melena, Laura, and even Amelia were quick to take action, pulling out their guns and firing in all directions due to the water. I was able to line the bullets accordingly, and as the bullets hit, the targets just fell.

Mission complete, but to Kim, it didn't show capa-bility of what they learned, though they did learn not to go against me. So, Kim got smart and did a show and tell. She took everyone out of the equation but Melena, and she won by seven soldiers. Next, they added two other generals and switched Rayshawn for Johnny; and Rayshawn and Melena tied because Shorty was on Rayshawn's team. Topaz, that stubborn young woman, refused to take part in these..."mundane affairs." Amelia felt up to the challenge and decided to take on all of those who participated in the challenge. Due to her suit's abilities, she could avoid being hit by everyone she went against. All this training finally looked like it would pay off. And with what would happen next, they could really test their knowledge and know-how.

At a distance, I saw flashes of light coming off from afar. I walked toward the flashes, and the next thing I knew, I was pushed into a tree, and then my armor retracted back into the gauntlet. I got off the ground only to see the new recruits panic. Melena, totally focused on the situation, stopped and told most of our forces to return back to base, this included Topaz, Anna, and both commanders.

Standing above me was Shorty, laughing. "Are you all right? That looked like something they did in those Hollywood movies."

"You're telling me," I said. "Yes, I think my armor took most of the impact. So, do you know who we have left?"

"I can find out, but I think there will only be five of us left if I heard correctly. Are you coming up with a plan?"

"No, this is Kim and Cory's op, not mine. If it were up to me, I would have Conner train the new recruits personally."

"You do know they are both leaving right now, right?"

"Not surprising." I then spoke on the radio, "Serenity, do we have a plan?"

"Negative. I wish we could contact my brother or even the other armor users, but nobody is responding," Laura replied.

"So, I take it we are going to have to rely on our team's natural abilities. I hope that we are ready. Do you think it was the Lightning Bearer?" I asked.

"No, I've worked with him before, and he doesn't attack without making a spectacle about it. I will be preparing a sniper's position and will take the shot when you are ready."

I replied, "I copy, Serenity." I turned to Shorty. "I need you to tell Rayshawn and Melena to prepare to attack, and tell Amelia she will be a backup sniper for Laura."

"And what do you want of me?" Shorty asked.

"Do what you feel is necessary. I don't know you well enough to tell you where to go in combat."

Melena contacted me. "All right, everyone is moving into position. Rayshawn will be heading your way."

"Please tell Anna to have an airstrike ready on the standby, after she drops everyone off."

"I already did."

"Amelia and two others will need to draw her attention to the middle of the field while you draw her closer to me. All units are ready. Just give the order. We just need to unarm him or her and destroy the device on his or her right arm. In theory, this should make them more rational and hopefully stop them from any senseless bloodshed; however, if we fail, Anna will be forced to drop an explosive on this location."

Everyone took formation, which was named "Corner," and looked exactly what it sounded like. We were supposed to corner the enemy from all sides. Usually, we need more people to make this work because we would fight more than one at a time, but with this case, there was only one target. So, we didn't need a big force, although it would be preferred. I could not charge in like normal; however, I could still do my part in helping, using a rifle instead of my two pistols. The reason was because I was almost certain the attacker was using electrical abilities. So, we began to fire upon the target, one by one, using the trees as cover; all of us but Laura, who was out of sight anyway. We tried not to fire in any pattern to avoid being predictable. But after sixty seconds, the team realized they were not doing a lot of damage to the armor.

Rayshawn said, "Does anybody have a better plan? Because at this rate, we are going to run out of bullets before we ever get close to killing the target. I am already on my third clip. What about you, big girl?"

Melena said, "I am on clip number five,"

Shorty said, "I am on four myself. Hey, Cross, have you or Serenity ever fought one of these things before?"

"I have, but the situation was different," I said. "I got help from one of Serenity's contacts."

Laura said, "I think I have noticed a pattern. Shorty, you do follow the rules concerning having spare parts aboard the vehicle, right?"

"Yes, ma'am, I do. It is because of me that rule stays in rotation. Do you think the boss really cares about safety?"

"Good, then I will need someone to gather the ones that are sturdy enough to go into the ground at least two feet."

Rayshawn said, "I am on it. I just need you to draw his or her attention away from me so I can slip out."

"All right, all who can hear my voice, stay in cover and close your eyes."

Laura fired a shot, and as the bullet left the chamber, I was in the process of closing my eyes. For whatever reason, the bullet left a trail and moved at about half the speed it normally would. My curiosity piqued; I squinted as the bullet connected then exploded into a bright light. It was almost like a flash bomb that lasted four seconds total.

"Open your eyes and disperse until you are given the orders to return to a new location. Cross, you and I will be keeping it busy," Laura ordered.

I could see everyone on the move, and the bright light disappeared almost like it was absorbed into this person. Afterward, I had a dark spot in my eyes as though I had looked into the sun for three minutes and decided to look away. The only way I could see the person now was if I looked slightly to the side. I saw even he or she was struggling to see, and the visor he or she wore had a layer of UV shielding over it.

"Darn it, Cross! I told you to cover your eyes."

I felt Laura push me to the ground. From the force of the push, I could tell she had fallen over as well.

"Serenity, are you all right?"

"Yes, I am fine, but you are not if you don't listen to me carefully. Right now, your eyes have just witnessed a light strong enough to strip your sight. Because you were not wearing any kind of visor when the blast went off, it can cause serious damage. You need to reactivate your armor and hope that it can return some of the moisture back to your eyes. Try to find a spot to hold like the rest until your sight returns. I shall hold him or her until then."

I heard her footsteps running away. "Crap!" I whispered, putting the armor back on. "She needed my help, and right now, she is on her own." I moved around the best I could, given my limited sight, and when I thought I was far enough away; I stopped and lay there on the ground. I could hear the gunshots going off in the opposite direction. I closed my eyes, and every few seconds, I would open them again to see if my vision had returned. I think I lay there for about five minutes before I could see effectively, but what was once black was now returning with all the colors a shade of red. "All right, Serenity, I can see, but everything I see is in the shade of red."

"It should only be whatever part of your vision was looking at the flash when it went off. It will have to do because we are making our way back to your location, so be ready to draw her attention away from me without using your suit's abilities. Otherwise, she will use the nearly invisible link you have made to electrocute you."

"'She'? How do you know it is a she?"

"Other than her movements and her constant heavy breathing, it is the frame of her body."

"How did you know all that stuff about the suit?"

"You were not the first person to use it. I had to use the armor on one of my missions with my brother before you ever showed up. It was a field test. Now, stick your head up when I jump over you and shoot in the direction I am coming from. Try to hit the target."

As she finished talking, I felt a rifle hit my chest, and I saw her jump over me. I grabbed the rifle because I assumed she wanted me to shoot the target with it. I aimed and fired at the target's head. Normally, I would be concerned about the target's safety when using one of Laura's guns, but with the gear she had and her ability to use electricity, I couldn't afford to waste time. When I pulled the trigger, the bullet left the chamber and the rifle exploded. She ended up moving to the side to dodge the bullet, but the force of the bullet as it connected, however slight, shattered the left side of the helmet and the shoulder of the armor.

"Good, now get up. We have to keep moving." So, I got up quickly. "Baby, darling, do you have my required rods?" Baby was the Code name given to Rayshawn after he lost a bet.

Rayshawn replied, "Yes, I have acquired them and found some of the recruits who were left behind. We are currently awaiting further instructions."

"OK, you are going to place them randomly around the area where the food was held originally. Elitist, please assist, Baby Ray."

"Moving now," Amelia said.

"Big Girl, you know what to do."

"Already on it. Brother, I'll take the rookie recruit with me. Have them ready to go."

"Sure," Rayshawn said.

It was at that moment we stopped running, but Laura still drew her attention toward us. I asked, "All right, what about me, you, and Shorty?"

"Shorty is already doing his part of the plan. As for us, we will be slowly luring our target to the locations required."

"That isn't much of a plan."

"I didn't see you suggest anything."

"I hate planning with lightning users; I almost died the last time. Besides, you are a heck of a lot smarter than me," I said. It was now I had noticed something. "While we've held our position here, you have only fired a single shot."

"Yeah, for one, I only have one bullet left, and all the others are those training rounds they gave us. I really wish you hadn't wasted that shot on the head. A head shot with this rifle can be fatal even with non-fatal bullets."

"So, why don't you aim for the shoulder? It is also exposed."

"Because she isn't moving."

I stuck my head around the corner, and from where I was, I could only tell she had short brown hair. From the way the sun shone on our enemy, I thought I saw her crying.

"Go to the point we discussed earlier. She will be on the move shortly."

Laura crept away. I ran back to the campsite; as I ran, the enemy followed. It didn't take long for her to catch up. "Ladies and gentlemen, I hope you're ready, the target is moving back your way."

"Understood, we are waiting to receive the package," Amelia said.

We were finally in the campsite, and the woman charged her hand to shoot a bolt of lightning, so I braced for impact. As the bolt was about to leave her hand, Amelia arrived with a metal staff and redirected the lightning into the ground.

"Cross, stop and hold position!" Laura yelled.

I stopped running, and in response, the target did as well. She charged another bolt and threw it toward me. As it left her hands, it was redirected to the right. She did it again, and the bolt went down. She then summoned the lightning from the suit's natural reserve; as it left the suit, it was as though it came out of the ground. The rest of my team appeared, one after the other.

"Don't move, Cross," said Laura. I heard gunfire fly through the air. The girl's gauntlet was destroyed with a clean shot from her sniper rifle. It shattered the gauntlet to pieces. The armor fell off of her body and dematerialized into nothing.

We heard the sound of inbound helicopters. "So, our reinforcements finally decided to come back," Amelia said, looking up.

"They're more than a little late," Ray said. "So, what are we going to do about the girl?"

I walked over to the girl to help her up. Looking at her clothes, I saw she wore what could only be described as rags. Depending on how long she wore the armor, she could have been anything from a scientist to a bum on the streets. The only thing apparent was it was placed on her, but that was just my own thoughts.

"Hey, I am waiting by the helicopter we came in. Do we need a tourniquet for her wounds?" Shorty asked.

"Negative, just come back. We will need to debrief before the official debrief," Laura said.

"Hey, girl, are you all right?" I asked.

The girl replied, "Where am I?"

"Where do you think you are?"

"The last thing I remember is being in Canada.

"Well, you are definitely no longer there. What is your name?"

"My name is Ashari Starr." She fell asleep.

Laura walked up. "All right, listen carefully, everyone. This is what happened. The woman here was a prisoner of the armored person; she and it were not the same.

We are going to take her back with us. When she wakes up, she will decide what she will do."

So, we packed up what little equipment we had and left, even though we knew the other helicopter was there to support us.

On the way back to base, I asked what actually happened, what the plan was, and where everyone went. As it turned out, Laura used Amelia and Rayshawn to place the rods all around the general area; Melena and the new recruit, who I honestly don't remember the name of, set up a good location for a short-range shot for Laura; as for Shorty, he was to wait by the plane to absorb the current of electricity, and I was bait. I was told it was my own fault; this was Laura's way of teaching me to listen when she tells me things. We returned to base with the girl named Ashari Starr, Ash for short. Later, Ash, John, and Commander Kim went through a station change. Shorty eventually up and left our base and more than likely found a way home. Cory was injected with an antibody that gave him an allergic reaction and killed him.

It was after this mission I realized I could no longer continue working for SUBWAY, for when it fell, it would be great.

# 11

# Never the Right Time...
# for the Right Thing

Fourteen months later, we hired more help due to the regular loss of people. Most of the new people didn't last more than a few days, a week, at most, of actual combat. As for these new recruits, they seemed to actually learn from their mistakes, as well as from others. I was glad, for training new people was getting tiring; the old recruits had set the bar so low you could step over it, honestly. It was good to see the recruits exceeded this low expectation.

Due to their bravery, all were promoted to sergeants, and one was assigned to a low-ranked Lieutenant, Sandra. She was not a particularly good lieutenant, although this may have been because she was often thrown into unfamiliar situations. Melena was forced to be the commander because of her experience; for whatever reason, they couldn't find any others capable of surviving this kind of work.

After about a month, O'Neal didn't like the idea of a woman being in charge, so he sent a covert party to locate and recover Dave. From what I heard, he had been hiding out on the south side of the island. When they got to the location, they could not find him. Instead, they found a young man by the name of Brad Summers who knew his location. Summers refused to share the location with that party until they agreed to let him work for SUBWAY as well. He was like a car dealer, very persuasive and slimy. He could've sold a cup of hot tea to a snowman, a hunter to a buck, and salt to a snail. Once, I even saw him sell powdered sugar to Rayshawn, who has a particularly intense hatred of powdered sugar. From what we collected, Dave was rumored to be recovered, and due to our history, I wasn't too happy. The only thing going through my mind was that I should have gotten on that plane with my brother-in-law. Then Laura would walk in, and I would forget about the stress of the job and my homesickness. Still, I kept thinking, *How long until I am framed again for a crime I did not commit?*

Around this time, Melena noticed the Jx3s were not fitting in too well, so she suggested to O'Neal a way to fix this and offered the idea of job trading until the situation could be resolved. They gave us one of theirs to train in the jobs we did, and they took one of ours. The purpose was to give a new perspective and help the two teams learn to respect each other, work more effectively as a unit, and eventually merge together. We traded Amelia for Ronda, a young lady on their team who barely looked out of high school and was known to make things happen "by accident," including making people disappear. I mean that literally; one day, she accidentally locked someone in a weapon locker, and we didn't find that person for three days. I digress... back to the point. With this, tactic peace was finally achieved. So, they sent Topaz as well. I watched as all this went down and said nothing; it had little to nothing to do with me.

When Topaz went in for training, Laura told me the next time I could leave would be in one month. The contacts' names were Eliana De Anastasia and her sister Cortney De Anastasia. They planned to leave by boat on the north point of the island. Since I was forced to wait, I decided to spend my last moments helping SUBWAY and waiting for the time when I would go back. Staying at SUBWAY, I expected to go and get myself killed for some guy who forgot how to be human, giving us missions that were pointless and difficult. This was where my story continued.

The recruits who were promoted included Dee, Reena, Mosby, Nathanial, and Emilio; the recruits named for the Jx3s were Riku, Jessie, Ilana, and Nelly. They were promoted through a process they called Roshital. I was uncertain on what it was exactly, but I guess as long as they knew, that was all that mattered. The confusing thing was every one of them was promoted to the same rank. What the recruits didn't know was the promotions were pointless, except to allow them to dump more work on you, poor noobs.

Due to Laura pulling some strings, I went on fewer missions. As a consequence, I was forced to go on night watch with my favorite person of all, Topaz—and yes, that is sarcasm. At first, it was unbearable, but because she was the only one to talk to, I was forced to get to know her better. Then it wasn't all that bad. She was still self-absorbed, but something was better than nothing.

I sat down while on guard duty and thought about life and the things I had wanted to accomplish by this point in my life. For example, I would have liked to be married, but even if I had the opportunity, I bet I wouldn't have the courage to tell a woman how I feel. I mean, I could use Laura as an example. I fell in love the moment I saw her, I had yet to tell her how I felt, and I had known for at least seven years. I knew I would have to say something soon, but the question was how I would go about doing it. I had never been good at... being serious about my emotions and dealing with the opposite sex.

One day, a mission came up, and they were short on personnel, so I had to fill in the shortage of people. Going with me were Mosby, Jessie, Dee, Anna, Nathanial, and Laura. According to the briefing, it was going to be a simple mission. I would be squad leader with Laura as my second in command. We later learned we went because no one else wanted to because it was a babysitting mission. Lucky me. For the love of all that is right, I sure had a lot of those moments during this time. The team and I would move out under the code name Zeta Squad. It was a code name they gave any team under my leadership. It was a meaningless title created to make me feel important, yeah. The title was just for seniority, so it meant nothing. The mission was set in an urban district that felt like an abandoned town.

The drop ship, also known as the MOTH, brought us in. When we landed, we gathered our equipment and drove for about a good four miles, until we eventually ran out of road. So, we got out and grabbed the equipment, for the tires weren't made for all terrain. Well, my vehicle was, but it could only seat two, so we left it. Surprisingly, we went the rest of the way without conflict. When we got to the location, we picked up a briefcase about the size of a guitar case. It looked to be double-plated, wasn't too heavy, and there wasn't a contact to get it from. It was just the case. From what I could see, the carrier was killed, and the case was still with his or her body. They must have died away from combat since the case was still with them and we didn't have to go to an actual enemy base. From looking at the body, I could see they had been dead for days. The enemy might have been looking for the body.

"Mosby, you're going to carry this package; Dee and Nathanial, cover him; Jessie, you cover the rear, we can't have our medic hurt. This should be an easy mission, but with this body here, there might be enemies in the area. Anything could happen at this moment. When we get back to the vehicles, Laura, I will need you to play recon and, if needed, a sniper. I will take point. If you die before the mission is over because of ignorance, cool, you are expendable. The package is not. I've seen good men and women die one day and be replaced the next. I do hope you guys can continue to break that cycle. If you have any questions, ask as we move. Now, let's go before things get worse." I pulled out a rifle.

"So, what is your plan?" Dee asked.

"We will head back to the cars and go back to point Alpha. That will be the most efficient way back."

"All right," Mosby said, heading the way we came.

Laura stopped him. "No, there has been a recent change of plans. Our eye in the sky tells us the vehicles have been compromised, so we are going to plan B. We are going to make it back to Rhonda and Anna at point Charlie."

Mosby was quick to reply, "Dang, that is a four-hour walk and a thirty-one mile drive. They don't have a closer extraction point?"

"The point is to lose any pursuers; it isn't made for convenience; you know that." Dee replied.

"Yes, I know that." Mosby said as Laura left the group.

When Laura was gone, Nathanial approached me, nudging me in the shoulder. "She is a beautiful girl; so are you ever going to make it official?"

"Wait, what do you mean?" I replied.

Mosby said, "Yeah, I've been here a month and can tell you're totally into her. And I can't blame you. In fact, when I first got here, I assumed you two were an item."

Dee said, "It's my second day, and that is so true. Rayshawn talks about you two and how you make a good couple."

"Rayshawn says that about everybody," I replied.

"Bro, I would have told her at least how I feel by now. The worse thing she can say is no," Mosby said.

"Why don't you try to tell her before the end of the day?" Dee suggested.

"Yeah, we could help if you want," Nathanial said.

"No, thank you," I replied softly. "I got this."

"If you can't, I can tell her instead," Mosby said.

"You know you can't assume anything. I don't know why you guys are listening to Rayshawn."

The radio went off in my ear. "Hey, Cross, I doubled back, and yes, the vehicles have been compromised, so we will have to go the other direction. I have looked ahead using a portable drone, and I think Melena's intel was spot on. Do you still want me to keep watching from the shadows?"

"Yes, please, you are the only one I know who can get the best shots from defensive positions," I replied, then cut the radio.

"Ah, your girlfriend still calls you with concern. How sweet." I don't remember who said that.

"All right," Laura said, "you can start to advance whenever you are ready."

So, we headed out. As we walked, what I thought would be serious talk turned out to be the latest gossip going on at base. Then somewhere out of all of this, the conversation turned back on me.

"Why don't you just say it in passing conversation?" Dee asked. "As random as your conversations are, it might just work."

"If I do, will you people get off my back and never talk about this again?" I asked.

The whole time, Jessie was just laughing, though she didn't say anything. She kept to herself for the most part. Everyone then replied, "Yes!"

"Fine." I used the radio. "Serenity, I would like to ask you a question, if you are not too busy."

"Right now, I don't see anybody in the area. So, I am not too busy, just waiting for something to happen. Go ahead."

"Could you possibly do—" We saw a shadow run past. "Did you see that?"

"Yes, I am trying to track it as we speak."

Jessie then suggested, "Should we keep diamond formation, holding Mosby in the middle?"

I said, "Yes, that is what we need to do, but we have to continue moving. Keep your eyes open and watch for any sudden movements."

So, we started moving in formation.

Laura said, "Look out, McNasty." She was talking to Dee; that was her code name. "There is a forest critter coming your way."

I turned toward Dee and saw a bear ran out of the woods from her side. I was going to fire my rifle as well, but I saw it was just running past, which I assumed was the reason Laura didn't fire. As for Dee, she unloaded a full clip and missed every shot. I turned to her and stopped her, but sadly she had already used the whole clip.

"Well, if there are any enemies in the area, they know our position now," Jessie said. She was speaking ironically, but lo and behold...

"Yeah, you're right." I interrupted, and then I asked, "Laura, do you think that was the figure?"

"Negative. That was not the same figure. Your first figure is heading toward the city; your second is moving away from the city."

"Great, nothing like a possible ambush. By the way, would you like to—"

"Cross, the original target is still on the move. The way he is moving, I can't get a shot on him."

"I can see some vehicles up ahead. They belong to the enemies in the area. When we get into the city, we are going to have to protect the vehicles so we can get out. I will be helping you from here. So, we can—" The radio cut out.

"Serenity...Serenity! Crap, she cut out."

"She must have cut off the radio," Jessie said, "so it doesn't give off her position."

"How do you know?"

"Because she is flagging me from her current position using a laser pointer." She pointed to Laura's location and I could see the laser going off.

"The hostiles in the area are unknown, as are their weapons and equipment. So, we are not sure if they have a way to track us," Mosby said.

"This is true. All right, keep an eye on Laura, Jessie. We are going to have to proceed with caution. Let's be quick and efficient; the sooner we get this mission done, the sooner we can go home," I said.

As we left the forest area, I heard gunfire from behind.

"She said keep moving," Jessie said. I looked behind and noticed she was looking toward the forest but not directly at Laura. "She said for you to tell us to hold position."

I raised my hand, giving the signal to stop.

"Contact in sight. Due north. Three hundred feet ahead," Nathanial said.

From where we were, there were a lot of buildings around us. The target was on a road with an intersection.

"Yes, I have another one in the building to our right, on the second floor," Dee said.

"Are there only two?" I asked, prepared to create a shield. "We might have stumbled upon a small scouting party, if that is the case. Mosby, Nathanial, eliminate the target in the building, and I will take out the target on the street corner."

"The rooftop?" Jessie asked. At the moment, I didn't understand why she said that. As it turned out, Laura was moving to a new position on a rooftop to keep from falling behind.

I knew one of the two were calling for backup, that was an inevitability, so we needed to move quickly before they finally arrived; if they arrived before we could get out of the city, it would get more complicated. As soon as the man popped his head around the corner, I shot him in the shoulder, the one above tried to open fire in response but was immediately dealt with. And if he didn't die from the gunshot, he died from the fall. I led the team to the location of the person I had shot.

As we approached, we saw that he was already running away, so we shot at him again, aiming at his other shoulder. This was when he dropped the radio, just as I needed him to. That way, I could keep tabs on the enemy's movements, at least until they changed broadcasting stations, and even then, I might be lucky enough to find the new station. I then heard gunfire coming from behind. I looked behind me and saw someone on the rooftop, then Jessie said, "Target down."

"Is that Serenity?" I asked.

"The person up there is still using the same codes we use to communicate, so I will assume so."

I looked back and saw a body pinned to a building. "All right, everyone, we move forward."

So we moved forward even faster than before. Now, with as fast as we moved, there was little resistance. As we ran into more and more enemies, we had to take cover in the nearest building. There was no one protecting the building to keep us out. We checked the building as we made our way up, and as we did, we saw no one in the building and found a path that led to another of the buildings, and we continued heading even further up the stairs. Once we went up a couple of floors, we had a little bit of time to recollect ourselves, so we did, put our backs to the wall, and waited. Strangely enough, from how much time we waited, the enemy was either far off or didn't know the buildings intersected.

I mapped out the area with my team, and then on the radio, Laura said, "Is everything all right in there?"

Nathanial yelled, "No, Cross was shot in the heart by cupid's arrow."

"Yes, everything is fine, we just needed to take a break," I said.

"OK, I saw you run into a building and at least seven ran in after you. What is your location so I can properly protect you?"

I tapped Jessie on the shoulder and said, "I am going to send Jessie and Nathanial to silently flag you. So, keep an eye out." The two of them moved out.

"You know that would have been a great way to tell her how you feel about her, right?" Dee said. "You were already halfway there."

"Yeah, man," Mosby replied.

"You guys make it sound so easy. Besides, we are in a hot zone, you know that, right?" I replied.

"That is your excuse for everything," Dee said.

"We are always in a combat zone," Mosby said, and honestly, he was right. We were always in a combat zone in one way or another.

Laura said, "All right, position confirmed. They are returning to you now." Nathanial and Jessie came back pretty quickly. "Hmm...if you go to the next building, cutting your way through the wall, you should be able to go into the next building undetected."

"I copy you, Serenity; we are moving now."

So, we moved to the end of the building. This led us into an old bathroom. I used my water reserve to cut a hole in the wall big enough for us to go through. Once everyone was through the hole, I picked the wall back up; this was only to slow them down. I knew if they were to see it, they could easily follow suit by pushing it down. So, we made our way down from there to the first floor. As I came out the other end, there were two soldiers there. They reached for their guns, and I created a shield barrier to cover the front of me. Before they could fire, I pushed them away. Nathanial, who was the second out, saw them and shot them. "Crap, they know we are here," I said.

"Sorry, I forgot," Nathanial said.

"Don't worry about it."

Laura yelled, "Everybody brace for impact!"

"From what?" I looked in front of me and saw a plane falling out of the sky, crashing directly into the building in front of us. So, I grabbed Nathanial and ran back inside. We waited a few seconds, and then ran outside, using the crash as a diversion. This didn't last too long; though it killed those in the immediate area, the others were in quick pursuit.

"Where did that plane come from?" Mosby asked.

"Not sure. Honestly, we should be glad it wasn't a bigger explosion; pilots don't usually fly that low," I replied. I needed to think of something that would slow them, and I remembered Jessie was in possession of a grenade launcher. "Jessie, hey, Jessie, I am going to need you to use that launcher two floors down and the third window to the left of where the plane crashed."

"I will see what I can do." Jessie turned, aimed the launcher into the air, and fired it. She did miss, but it did what I wanted it to do, which was to force at least one of the thrusters to fall.

As we ran, we came a across a sewer hatch. Then it was Dee's idea to use it to go underground. So, we did. Luckily, Laura had already left the rooftops and made her way to us.

I placed a grenade on the hatch, and after the top fell in, we jumped down. The sewer stench could have been a lot worse, but then again, I was wearing the helmet and was not about to take it off. Luckily it was dried up and easy to walk in. It must not have been used in at least ten years.

"So, where are we heading now?" Dee asked.

"We need to find a way back to the surface," I replied. "A safe area would be preferred; where we are now, if we go back up to the surface, we'll be in a dangerous area."

"Obviously, yes," Jessie said.

"So, where do we go?"

Laura put her rifle on her back. "Right now, we will go further into the sewer. It seems to be ventilated, so there might be a way out if we continue along our path."

"That seems like a good idea," Nathanial said.

So, we made our way through for about fifteen minutes before we found another way up. But we had to continue even further, for there might have been an ambush waiting. After another fifteen minutes, we found natural light in front of us, so Laura ran ahead to check the area.

When she was far enough away, Mosby whispered, "I think I would rather die from a gun wound then go through another sewer."

"Stop complaining," Dee said. "Just be glad we are not in an active sewer. If there is any smell while we have been down here, it has only been spotty." I watched as Laura climbed up to the top. "Hey, she's moving up. Do you think it is going to be safe?"

I replied, "Safe? Probably not; however, we do need to get back up there anyways, and she is the best at scouting the area." We continued our approach.

"Hey, you guys, get up here quickly, there is something wrong," Laura spoke down to us from above. So, we climbed up. I let everyone climb ahead of me then made my assent. As I climbed, I noticed the cracks in the sewer system caused by natural disasters, most possibly an earthquake. There was a massive hole that separated one side from the other, at least a hundred feet. I could see the different layers; first, concrete, dirt, then gravel and asphalt. When I reached the surface, I looked around and saw we were around vehicles.

"Dang, they left their vehicles unattended," Mosby whispered. "Is this some sort of trap?"

"If it is, then it is the most creative trap I have ever seen. They left their keys in the ignition and everything. I have scanned the area, and there isn't anybody around,"

Laura said. "What do you suggest, team leader?" She referred to me, of course.

"Well, they did steal our vehicles. I guess it is only fair to steal theirs," I replied. "Let's hurry up and go before they return."

So, we got into the cars. Jessie, Mosby, and Dee were in one car with Jessie driving; Nathanial, Laura, and I were in the other. Lucky for my car, Laura drove. I somehow ended up with the package in my car.

As we pulled off, Laura asked, "So, you wanted to talk to me about something?"

"Talk to you about something?" I said. By now, I had completely forgotten what it was; after all, it had been a couple of hours by this time.

"You know, that thing?" Jessie said over the radio, hinting.

"Ah, yes, that, how could I forget about that? I was wondering if you were interested in—" The phone rang loudly. I pulled it out and saw it was Rayshawn.

"You should take that call; it might be important," Laura said.

"I am sorry." I answered the phone. "Hello, Rayshawn. What is going on?"

"Hey, bro, I heard you were finally going to officially ask her out on a real date."

"How did you hear about that? You're not even on this mission."

"Rumors spread around here all the time. Bro, I heard it from Melena, who heard it from Amelia, who heard it from Anna, who heard it from Ronda, who heard it from Dee."

"Man, news travels fast. But I truly doubt that is the only reason you called."

"What, oh no, that was just one of the two reasons. I was calling to inform you the package is really a super-grade megaton bomb with enough power to take out all forces on the island."

"Wait, what?"

"Yeah, it's supposed to have enough power to destroy all life on this island and parts of the neighboring islands too, so try not to miscarry it."

"Who would ever need that kind of power?"

"I don't know; just be glad the thing isn't armed."

"Yeah, that doesn't make me feel any better."

"Well, you might be right. Good luck. I have to finish some paperwork." He hung up.

"Thanks," I said reluctantly. I put the phone down. "Well, the package is a bomb. It has enough power to completely destroy this island and parts of the neighboring islands."

"That isn't good," Nathanial replied. "I know I work for them, but I feel we should defuse it."

I looked at Laura, and she looked back at me through the rearview mirror.

"You mean dismantle?" Laura said. "I can't do that, not unless I was the one who made it. Guns are one thing, but explosives are completely different, and I am not trained for it." She pulled aside the other car, rolled down the window, and yelled, "Do you have anyone in your car who can dismantle a bomb?"

"That would be Dee. She should know, after all, she has received the most training with explosives," Jessie said.

"All right, we are going to pull over."

So, we pulled over. We took Dee with us and continued to drive.

"Dee, inside that case is a bomb. We need you to make the bomb inoperable; if not, it will do a lot of harm to everyone here, and this does include you as well."

"I thought this case looked like bad news and high in grade, like a fancy coffin."

She opened the case after checking the outside for anything that might trigger a secondary fuse. She opened it right after the double check. As she opened it, the bomb was pre-exposed, as though it was missing a cover piece or someone had tried to work on it beforehand.

"Hmm...that is strange. It looks as though the inner shell was stuck to the top of the case. After we are done, we will have to drill it back down, and you will not be able to tell the difference. To be honest, though, it seems the person who came before me was stopped at some point, and I must go in and clean the rest..." She paused for closer examination. "I don't know how to say this, but the bomb is unstable and could go off at any time. That is if I am looking at this correctly. Just give me some time."

"You know, that is just as bad as saying we have five minutes to get back to base," I said.

"Don't put more pressure on her than she already has," Laura said.

"You're right. Whoever assigned us to this mission might have already known about the bomb's condition."

"Do you think this might be why they called upon us for this mission?"

"I am starting to think they are really out to get us."

I am sure they want to go with the least number of casualties. So, what were you trying to ask me?"

"Oh, yes, I just was going to ask you—"

A rocket was launched in front of our vehicle, destroying the road ahead; this created a crater that launched the vehicle a few feet in the air. The second car was able to avoid the other incoming rockets and damage done to the road.

"Dang! I pressed the wrong button. That did it. Now that stupid thing is armed," Dee yelled. She pulled down the case so she could see the display of numbers. "Well, the timer is counting down from ten minutes. It should be plenty of time for me to unarm it and make it non-lethal. From what I have seen, the last person was very close to finishing the unarming process. I should be done in sixty seconds."

"Dang, these people picked the worst time to show up!" Laura yelled. "Shoot back at them or take the wheel, either way, make a choice."

I saw our team move toward our side, so I cut the leather off the car's roof. Doing this caused Laura to temporarily lose control, and the wind picked up the roof and launched it back into the cars behind us, but it had no effect because they just avoided it. I grabbed my two pistols from my hip and opened fire on the drivers behind us. After I emptied the chamber and hit to reload, I heard screeching coming from Jessie's vehicle. So, I looked over and saw them cut their car's leathers roof off. When the roof made contact, I heard a car behind us crashing. I finished reloading the pistols, stood back up, and fired at the car's tires. When one popped, the vehicle leaned forward and right. After that, Nathanial destroyed the engine on the other car.

"All right, guys, good work." Laura said. I saw the vehicle crushed and a tank rolling over it. "Crap! These people really want this case." The tank's barrel aimed at Jessie's vehicle. "Come on, you need to jump." Seeing that the tank was about to fire its cannon, I jumped over to them and shielded the car. Though it stopped the damage, there was still an impact that caused me to fall out. I rolled and quickly stood on my feet, pulling the sword off of my back. As it closed in, I leaped onto it using the sword's water PSI. As I cut, they used the barrel to try and knock me off, but as they turned, I ducked under and continued cutting. The way I cut was side to side from one end to the other. The vehicle stopped moving, and I heard the hatch open. As soon as I saw someone come out, I shot him before he shot me; if I had to be honest, I think I missed. I cut the rest of the way through, and the front part of the tank fell off. I put my sword on my back and dropped down in front of the tank, pistols drawn.

"Come on out, guys," I said loudly. "I promise you, no harm will come to you." I heard a loud noise come from the sky, so I turned and saw our MOTH-class drop ship head to the rendezvous point. "Looks like I missed my ride." The first person came out, and three others followed; they got down on their knees and lined up as though I would execute them. "Is there anyone else inside?"

"No, sir," one of them said. I put my pistols away.

"Good." I threw two grenades inside the empty tank. My plan was to use it as a signal. When they exploded, it was enough to pop the top off. "Sorry, guys, but you will be stuck with me for just a little while. As soon as I find my way out of here, I will allow you to call for backup."

"Hey, Cross, you out there?" Mosby said over the radio.

"Yes, I am. What is your status?"

"We are still being pursued by two more cars; Mac Nasty"—meaning Dee—"disarmed and defused the bomb, so it won't be used ever again. Our ride is inbound, and it is going to be a close call. If we can, we will pick you up. We don't have too many choices."

"Understood. Godspeed."

"Godspeed." I guess. I didn't make it to the rendezvous point. It was not the worst thing that had ever happened to me. I unarmed the four men and took their ammo and explosives away.

"Are you going to kill us?"

"No, not today at least."

"So, what do you plan to do with us?"

"Nothing. I just don't have the patience to deal with everyone's nonsense." I knew I had to find a way to be obtainable in case they flew overhead and could pick me up. "Here is a radio for you. Go ahead and tell them your position." I held the radio, pushing the button.

"JIB, this is Baby Giant unit."

"Go ahead, Baby Giant." Dispatch spoke, I assumed.

"We are stranded. The tank malfunctioned here. Our location is currently where the black smoke is, so roughly two miles from your location."

"That is a good copy, BG. We are sending someone to pick you up ASAP."

I dropped the radio and then shot it three times. "Good."

"You are the fierce warrior Cross's Neptune, are you not?"

"I guess...kind of a stupid name, but more than likely."

"Why don't you just end our lives already?"

"I don't need to."

Dee said, "We are going to your location now, so brace yourself."

I looked up and was pulled off the ground. I could not move my arms or feet. I noticed I was upside down and moving at an incredible speed. I was absorbed into the clouds. The wind slowed down. I saw what I could only describe as a frame surrounding the clouds, and the frame had begun to grow.

"See, I told you that would work. Tell the pilot the package is secure; we have him now."

The shutters closed, and I saw Mosby standing in front of me.

"So, what happened?"

"We picked you up with a powerful magnet."

I heard Laura laugh; she sat down Indian-style, poking me in the forehead. "So, do you wish to tell me what it is you were talking about earlier?"

"I would, but I think every time I do, something bad happens. I am also upside down just dangling here, so I don't think you want me to tell you right now anyways."

"You might have a point," Laura said. She signaled for them to drop me. As I fell, my armor retracted, and Laura caught me before I hurt myself. "I will be waiting for your message when we land." Laura set me down gently. "Until then." She left.

It was at this moment Nathanial tapped me on the shoulder and said, "Yeah, I'd rather not chance it. I want to get home in one piece."

Mosby added, "I am not a superstitious guy myself, but I, too, would like to make it back in one piece."

They helped me up. After I thanked them, I walked away, saying I had to prepare myself for what I had to say.

Once we landed, I felt a little stage fright. Luckily, Laura had already left to take the package back to Melena, which gave me enough time to collect my thoughts. As I walked by, I ran into Melena, who confirmed she had received the package, but she told me there was a rumor around the camp about the operations of SUBWAY and how we were needlessly wasting our lives. She wanted to know if I knew anything, but sadly, all I could do was confirm what she already knew. We talked quietly for about two hours to keep from eavesdroppers. I left the room and saw Laura, who called my name. She was sitting on the rooftop of Jx3's dormitory, which was just beyond the door I stood at.

I walked up to the building she sat on and asked her, "So, how did you get up there?"

"Leo, I am an expert at recon work. Getting up in high places is child's play, especially when there is a ladder on the side of the building. Are you coming up or what?"

"I am, just give me a moment." I walked around the building and saw the ladder. As I climbed, I felt my heart race. It got so bad the only thing I could do was look at the clouds and try to calm down.

"Laura, I know you have been waiting to hear what I been wanting to ask you all day. Honestly, I wanted to ask right before we joined SUBWAY's forces."

She sighed heavily, lying down on her back. "Are you still upset about how I choose to go about the mission?" She was referring to a pervious concern of mine about why we didn't need to kill everybody in combat. "The Webmaster would approve."

"No, she wouldn't. I am more than 84 percent sure she put us together to balance the other one out. You have the toughness I am lacking, and I have the kindness you still need to improve on."

She rolled to her side, facing away from me. "Well, my father would approve," she mumbled just loud enough for me to hear.

So, with that, I continued, "I knew there was something special about you the first time we met. I couldn't tell you what it was." She turned back toward me to make eye contact. I could tell she had mixed emotions and was unsure about what I was trying to say from her teal-colored eyes. "For about three years now, I have been trying to summon the courage to finally tell you." From the reflection in her eyes, I could see a crowd forming below.

"Oh, OK," she said, startled, though I wasn't sure why. It could have been because I wasn't very direct, but I almost never was.

"I hope to clarify this here and now, so I may know once and for all. I hope it doesn't ruin our friendship when I ask this question."

She stared at me as though she was looking at an executioner. "I hope so as well...Please proceed," she replied. But after looking at her eyes, I began to doubt if I should ask her the question to begin with. But I had made it this far, and she wanted me to continue.

"Laura, will you marry me?" I asked, closing my eyes, afraid of what she might say.

She paused, hugged me tightly, and made a loud sigh of relief. She kissed my forehead and said, "Of course. I have been waiting for you to ask me forever."

I could not reply because she answered differently than I had expected. The crowd cheered. I finally could hug her back.

I heard sparks, so I opened my eyes and saw Laura's face. She looked caught off guard. I turned around and saw the Lightning Bearer on another rooftop, holding a bolt of lightning as if he was getting ready to throw it like a spear. As he stood there, the bolt grew in size. When he threw the bolt, Laura pushed me to the side, standing between the lightning and me. We all heard thunder, which nearly deafened everyone's ears. I got back up, and Laura was unconscious on the roof. I looked to the other roof and noticed the Lightning Bearer was gone. I hugged Laura until the medics came.

# 12
## Is It Revenge...
## or Is It Despair?

**O**ne week had passed before Laura was cleared from the clinic. I visited her every day while she was there. When she finally could leave, I could not be there even though I wanted to. I had pulled a double shift on guard duty and agreed to do so because Laura was supposed to be released the next day. I woke up, and there she was, sleeping in a chair beside me.

The moment her eyes opened, I knew that I would have to take that lightning jerk down. I was not too sure what his relationship was with her, but what I did know was if he would do something like this to keep her from being happy, I needed to put a stop to this soon. I wanted to talk to her about how I planned to bring him down, but I wasn't sure how close they were as friends because they constantly worked together, even then. I knew because of this I would be on my own.

It was at that moment, I realized just how important Laura was in my life. I knew I would need help from several others to make up for the lack of Laura—at least three others. I talked to several others about my plan, and they actually agreed to assist. However, we would have to plan this out. Since there were no upcoming missions, we decided to meet in the mission briefing room. Melena, who was in charge at the time, didn't mind. In truth, she offered me the room.

Originally, I only wanted four to help me with my plan, but Rayshawn and Melena had talked me out of that idea. We continued planning until it was completely airtight. The only thing we lacked was an ideal location. For me, an ideal location would have been the beach or a swamp, heck, even a waterfall—any place with a constant amount of water. As things finally wrapped up, Mosby received a phone call that forced him to immediately leave, I heard later that he would not return to SUBWAY.

I had gotten in contact with Cayden, but he didn't want anything to do with this. Instead, he recommended I back down, if only just this one time. He didn't specify why, but I assumed it was because the chance of survival was less than 5 percent, even with the help of the others. I had fought this foe before and narrowly escaped with my life. I knew I should heed his advice, but I didn't listen to him.

We chose a beach, and with that, we had to find a way to draw him out, but the only way we could get in contact with him was through Laura, and I didn't want to place her in danger again in case I failed. So, my only way to contact him was out of the question. The only other way I could think of was putting a contract on myself, but as effective as he was, that would be a very stupid idea, so my options were limited, and no one knew what to do. As we were about to go with plan B, Laura agreed to get him for us, leading him to the location. However, the deal was I must try to talk it out first. Why she wanted me to talk to him, I couldn't say, but I agreed to the terms. Maybe she had feelings for the guy because during the agreement, Laura had looked distracted.

We spent hours on the beach that day just prepping. Though it seemed half the people didn't like each other and the other half were easily distracted, we did a lot in a shorter amount of time than expected by at least two hours. Maybe it was because everyone knew their jobs, maybe it was because they all secretly hated the same guy, or maybe since we were on the beach, they wanted to finish early so they could have fun with the remaining time. Whatever the reason, it worked.

As we closed the day out on the beach, Laura arrived, making an announcement. "Tomorrow, I wish you all well in the confrontation with the Lightning Bearer. Hopefully you can do it without any bloodshed from either side. As for tomorrow, that will be the last time your friend Leo and I will be with you all, so enjoy his company while you have this moment."

I asked, "Does that mean..."

"Yes, I was able to grant us safe passage to a southern country known as Cuba. From there, we can grab a flight to the US."

I got up and hugged her, lifting her into the air. "Words are not enough to express just how much I appreciate you. If you ever, ever want anything, you name it. I mean that." Of course, I would have done anything she wanted anyway, but that didn't click until right just then.

"Please don't worry about it. Soon, we will be away from this battlefield and returning to your home." She hugged me, kissing my forehead.

Rayshawn got up and held a mug into the air. "All right, tonight we celebrate our friend's last day with us. You have saved most of us at least once or twice, put yourself in danger for the sake of your teammates, not to mention despite being cast away, you were still willing to return to us. Here is to our friend and comrade, Leonardo."

The crowd cheered. When I looked again at Laura, I did not find her.

Nathanial walked up to me and said, "She has returned to her tent and did not want you to pursue. But we all know you will, so go ahead."

"Thanks." I saw the tent and made my way to her. "Laura, are you OK?"

"Nathanial told you not to come here and yet you do. I already knew that you would. Just so you know, I will be camping here tonight because I have one last early morning preparation before we can leave. The earlier I finish, the better our chances of leaving here without incident. Our point of contact is a Brittney Mace. One of the Webmaster's contacts hired her. I need to meet with her first thing."

"I don't think you should leave your people on the beach. There is a chance they could trigger one of your preparations."

"I expect nothing less than one or two traps being triggered."

I sat down in front of her tent and looked out at the horizon. The sun set, and the smell of sea salt filled the air. "So, how long were you planning to be gone tomorrow?"

"To be honest, I am not sure. If they are prepared for my arrival, then I'll be gone an hour at the most. If they are not, then it could take all day." I felt her arms around my shoulder. "Why, are you going to miss me?"

"It isn't that." It was kind of that. "I was just wondering." I felt her chin rest on the back of my head and felt her look up with me. "The sunset—sure is beautiful, isn't it?"

"Yes, it is. I hope that when you return home, it is exactly as you remember it."

"You and me both."

We sat like that for about an hour, then I completely lost track of time. I fell asleep like that. When I woke, Laura was already gone, and I was covered with a blanket. I stood up and walked around. I noticed people had slept here instead of going back to base. The first person I ran into was one of the new rookies. "Hey, kid, get up," I said.

He rolled over and wiped the sand off of his face. "Sir?"

"You are the sniper, right?"

"Yes, I was told I will be promoted to lead sniper if Lieutenant Laura does not return in time for the mission to start."

"Good, go ahead and set up. I don't think she will return in time...Wait, what is your name?"

He stood and began to stretch. "Cassie Martinez."

I walked away, not saying a thing. I was in shock because I thought she was a he and didn't want to be rude and say that. I continued waking everyone else up. Within an hour, we were ready in case something would go down. We waited there another hour before the Lightning Bearer arrived. During the wait, we discussed different movies we had seen, what the theme was, and what made them good. Once we heard lightning strike, the group went quiet.

"I am here as I promised," the Lightning Bearer said. "What did you want from me?"

I stood there speechless, for I wasn't sure myself.

"Did you summon me here so you can get revenge? You know you don't stand a chance against me, but if you think you do, then I encourage you to try."

I replied after much thinking, "Do you really think of me to be so pitiful? Holding a grudge will get us nowhere and will hurt more than it helps. No, I just have a few questions. Why did you attack Laura?"

"Laura? I never intended to attack Laura. You were the target. Attacking Laura would profit me little to nothing. You were just lucky she got in the way. As for killing you, that is something less difficult to explain. You had a bounty on your head. I was paid to assassinate you without harming those around you. Seeing as how I already failed by hurting your ...let's say bride to be, I didn't get paid, and the contract is now void." He folded his arm, and a surge of power physically wrapped around his body.

"It's just another job I took." "I guess that was a predictable response, considering who you are and the rumors that follow your path. It makes sense. I was hoping you considered us friends by now, or at least allies. I guess you are just as bad as Cayden when it comes to alliances. He literally only has one, his sister. I guess I don't blame him. Laura is an incredible person. I wouldn't be surprised if you felt the same way about her. The real reason you might have attacked me, the real reason you accepted the contract, is that you are jealous."

"Do you think of me as some simpleton? Jealousy is not something that motivates me."

"Is that so? Emotions are one of the few things that motivate us as humans. Not being good or bad, but rather how we feel about a situation."

"Get to the point. I do have other things to do."

"I guess there is no point but to say that you are still human, meaning one thing: you can still make mistakes. So, truthfully, you are in love with her. But if you are, then why haven't you told her? I guess you might just be jealous of her though you are not in love with her."

"So, you summoned me here to give me a piece of your idealistic bull—"

"No, I summoned you here because I would like to know and understand you. And so far, you remind me of an arrogant know-it-all. I don't think I have ever hated talking to someone so much. At first, I only wished to avenge Laura, but then, she and Cayden were against the idea. And I decided not to do that."

"Look, I do have other things to do, and from what I have heard, you and my former companions will be leaving soon, and you will never have to deal with or even see me ever again. I agreed to this meeting for a simple request. I want you to tell Laura and you that I apologize. That will be that last contract I take against her and her allies. Goodbye, Waterfalls."

I assumed he called me that because I was bringing down his spirit.

I turn around and was relieved there was no conflict, casualties, or even a need for a plan. "All right, so long then." I waved, saying goodbye. I saw a glimmer from what I assumed was the present sniper, Cassie. She fired, which was bad. I assumed she thought my wave gave her the signal to fire. I tried to stop the bullet but I failed. Knowing the next action was not going to be a good one, I stood in front of where the shooter was to redirect their attention.

"You were warned not to fight me, and yet you do not heed those warnings. Now I will make you regret your own existence."

He moved so fast I could have sworn he disappeared and reappeared. He punched me in the gut, launching me into the air at least one hundred feet. I could feel the jolt of electricity as his fist made contact with me. I tried to stop myself from falling, but my powers didn't activate. I fell headfirst. He punched me in the rib-cage and cracked my rib through the armor, sending me flying in the air. I immediately blacked out. When I came to, I saw Cassie standing over me. The sound of gunfire filled the air.

"Crap, I didn't know. I thought that you were signaling me. I didn't know you were waving goodbye."

I looked at where I laid and saw a dirt trail about twelve feet long. "What is our status?"

"La Bruja and Anna charged in to give you backup and pull attention off of me. As they ran in, he overcharged their radios, forcing them to explode. They were killed instantly. Luckily, their part of the plan was to roll out the red carpet in case things went wrong, so at the very least they succeeded on that part of the plan."

"He overcharged their radios?"

"Yes, and caused them to explode."

"Crap, I have to contact Laura." I pulled out my radio and tried to call her on a closed channel. "Laura, Laura, are you there?"

"I am sorry, but Laura will not be joining you in this. I gave her something to do that will keep her...preoccupied. I would let go of the radio if I were you. Otherwise, this battle you wanted will be over too quickly," said the Lightning Bearer.

I felt the radio warm up. As I threw it, a bolt of electricity melted the radio to gooey-looking plastic.

"Dang, hey, Cassie, you are going to have to master your skills with that rifle within the next five minutes. You will only have one more shot, and if you miss, everyone, including yourself, will die. This time, you will definitely know when I am telling you to shoot. Until you are 100 percent sure, do not fire."

"Understood." She ran to a new location. I didn't bother to tell her where to go; I knew that she understood her role and expectations.

I did not have a way to contact the rest of the team, so I slowly made my way toward the gunfire. I pulled out one of my two pistols and preloaded it. I knew that the chances of me actually shooting him were slim, but I had to try to draw his attention before he killed off the rest of my team. I saw craters caused from the grenades we were equipped with, and there were a few bodies lying on the ground, but that was to be expected. This was actual combat, after all. I checked around to see if I could find another radio. Of the ones I found, three of them were still intact, but they didn't have enough charge to communicate; it was possible they hadn't charged it the night before. As for the rest, they were broken beyond repair, so I had no choice but to continue going. As I got closer, the gunshots stopped.

"Stopped?" I whispered. "That's not a good sign." I stopped moving, then watched as a rock flew by, hitting the sand in front of me. I followed where it came from.

Turning around, I saw Rayshawn shushing me and flagging me to follow him. So, I ran over to him. "Glad to see a familiar face."

"Dang, what the heck happened out there? I saw you get launched in the air and then fly over us about thirty minutes ago. Then the Lightning Bearer started going on a random killing spree."

It seemed I was unconscious for about twenty minutes. That was a pretty long time. "Our sniper prematurely fired the shot. What is our current status?"

"We lost a third of our forces, including two of our leaders. We had to turn off our radios and find a way to regroup our remaining forces. Since we have no way for a radio transmission, we sent out a small group to gather the remaining forces. You and the sniper are the last of the team, so where is she?"

"She is repositioning."

"All right, as a fallback plan, from what we have gathered, we still have enough units and 70 percent of the props still placed to make the plan work. That is, if you still want to go that way. With you here, we can still proceed. I just hope it will be enough to end this before we lose too many more of our men."

"Well then, we better start moving. If we stay here, it is only a matter of time before he finds us here."

"All right, then follow me. We are meeting up at the cliff."

We moved. I thought to myself, *If the Bearer keeps this up, it is only a matter of time before he wipes us out completely. Being around this much water and the beach should give me an advantage, but with his speed, it is nearly impossible to stop him.* It was apparent who had the advantage here. As long as he hadn't destroyed those rods, we could stop him. Before I knew where I was, I realized our own people surrounded us, and Rayshawn walked toward me.

"From our observations, the Lightning Bearer is currently waiting by our vehicles," he said.

"Well, we either fight him or hike back to base," Melena said.

"Yeah, not a lot of options there," I replied. "Well, I guess we will have to proceed with the original plan, with minor alterations, of course. As stealthily as possible, everyone position yourselves according to plan C. However, those whose leaders were KIA, you are now with Big Girl's group. She will be creating an escape route for us in case things go south. Big Girl, you will be retaking our vehicles once we have lured him away. Once I know we are ready to proceed, I will reveal myself. I doubt that he thinks that I am dead because everything that he is doing seems more thought out than I would like to admit. Let's go."

From where I was, I could see the teams slowly make their way to the desired locations. It was about fifteen minutes before we were completely ready to attack. They used reflections from the sun to signal when they were ready. I took a deep breath and ran off the ledge. When I made contact with the sand, I shot my way up like a bottle rocket, pulled one of my pistols, and fired downward as I fell. As I hit the ground, I rolled out of the way, put the one pistol away because it ran out of bullets, and switched to the other. I fired a shot, and then the Bearer punched me in the gut. I recovered, fired once more, and he kicked me in the face. I went for a reload, and the gun and bullets were taken from me.

"Have you ever wondered how much of a kick her bullets would have while you are still wearing that armor?" he asked.

"Wait, what?" I said. He fired the gun. I tried to block it by shielding myself but I was too late. The force alone was like getting hit by a horse. He shot me in the shoulder, which forced me to land on my face because my body got turned around. "Crap, that hurt."

"Not as much as this will." He placed the gun right next to my cracked rib and shot again. I slid about three feet and knew it was broken for sure. I held onto it, yelling loudly, which was the trigger for Plan C. I'd known I wasn't going to win, and at some point, be forced to cry out in pain.

The first team to strike was Melena's. Her objective was to lay down some cover fire by tossing a grenade from behind the cars. If the injury looked bad, Nathanial was to come in and pull me out. To do so, he threw smoke grenades in what seemed like a random pattern but was not. I used the smoke as a distraction to crawl away. I admit it wasn't easy, but I knew I couldn't fall now. The next part of the plan required his team to slowly lift the rods just below the smoke point and get it to conduct downward. Rayshawn's team's job was the easiest but most dangerous; they were to keep him preoccupied and keep his attention off me. Ronda and Dee were on standby to pick up if there was any slack in the plan.

The Lightning Bearer yelled things like, "I have seen better shots from a blind man. What, you never hit a target like me before?" and "I used to think you were of the best, but now I realize your name was overhyped."

While he was distracted, I created massive tidal waves like the ones exaggerated in the old cartoons I watched as a kid. This was the only way I knew I could catch him. I looked and saw Rayshawn caught in the Lightning Bearer's hand. I flagged for the sniper to shoot, and when the bullet hit, Rayshawn was thrown straight up, landing on top of the tidal wave as it passed by. The top of the wave gently brought Rayshawn down while the middle trapped the Lightning Bearer in the water. Though he was trapped under water, I didn't even see the Lightning Bearer struggle or resist. He sat still floating in the center, sitting cross-legged.

"If you use your power at all, the air inside that is keeping you alive will escape, and you will die," I said, lying down on the ground, preparing to get up.

"So, you intend to make me suffer as I die."

"That is not the intent behind why this was built. It was a contingency plan in case you proved more hostile than expected. This device is one that I truly have no control over other than feeding it water."

"How stupid are you? Honestly, do you think killing indirectly is a way you keep your hands clean? No, you fool. You still killed them, though through other means. You really are not as guilt-free as you think you are. Though you are good in nature, it is only a matter of time before the darkness reveals itself. And then what will you do?" He placed fingers next to his head. "As far as your liquid taps go, if you remember nothing else about me, remember that I choose my own fate." He pointed his thumb out. "Bang!" He placed his thumb back down. A little lightning emitted from his hand, and the bubble that allowed him to breathe floated to the top. He remained seated and did not struggle or fight back. Was it possible his suit had an oxygen tank or something?

Rayshawn helped me up and kept my arm over his shoulder for balance. "Is this what you wanted?" he asked me.

"No, but I guess this is what he wanted." Truthfully, it was; I'd do anything to keep Laura safe. Everyone came out of hiding, including Cassie. Two minutes passed. Then a big bubble released, but he wasn't gasping, he just sat there, though a large amount of electricity began to surge. Then it just stopped. I knew he had died.

I heard an explosion coming from my left. When I turned to see what it was, I saw Cayden. He was not wearing his armor.

"Cayden, what are you doing here? I thought you had a mission or something to take care of."

"This time, you two have gone too far," he yelled.

"You two? Who are you talking about?" I asked.

Cayden punched the ground; a wave of fire skipped along the beach then exploded, which caused the device that kept our prisoner afloat to release. He ran over to me then pushed me to the ground.

"I believe that you are smart enough to understand why I told you not to challenge her," he said.

"Her?"

"Yes, her, you moron." As he finished, the helmet opened, and I saw it was Laura lying there lifeless and still. I fell to my knees, and my body was numb. Cayden immediately proceeded to give her CPR and mouth-to-mouth resuscitation.

What the crap had I done? I should have known it was her. All signs should have pointed in that direction. But how was I supposed to have known that she would go this far? This really wasn't out of the ordinary, at least not for her. I had killed the only woman that I had ever loved. I could do nothing but watch as Cayden tried to save her life. Melena and Dee helped Cayden in whatever way they could. Nathanial and at least three others formed a circle to keep everyone back.

Cassie said, "Did you know it was her?"

"No, nobody did," Rayshawn said. "She never shared that information with us."

"Do you know why she attacked and killed us if we are her friends?"

"Because of the bullet you shot, she saw that as a challenge. This was her way of accepting that challenge. I guess it might have only been a reflex at that point. She wasn't one to back down, no matter the odds. Hey, bro, it isn't your fault."

I watched her, quietly hoping to God that she pulled through. I heard her cough. Cayden flipped her over. Along with the water, which was so thick it looked like clear slime, she also coughed up chunks of vomit.

Ronda did a checkup status on Laura. When she was done, she said, "She will be fine as long as she can get some rest."

Cayden said, "Thank you. You guys may leave us, for your services are no longer required. I will be taking care of these two myself."

"All right, men, you heard him. We need to return to base." Rayshawn said. I assumed Laura must have told Rayshawn about her brother at one point when the two of them were hanging out, which explains why he was so quick to withdraw. "Maybe we will meet again. Hopefully under better circumstances than we are in right now. All this combat is a little much. Good luck, brother, I hope you return home soon enough."

"Godspeed, my friend." I shook his hand one last time. "Look, I have told you and your sister this on many occasions, but you need to leave SUBWAY before you two are also killed. We both know Conner would throw you under a tank just to make a profit."

"If the opportunity comes, we will. Thank you again for being our friend."

"Brother!" Melena yelled.

"Yes, I hope for the same. I hope that we meet again, if only once more." I would have hugged him, but my broken rib disagreed, so I shook his hand instead. Rayshawn hopped in the vehicle and drove off. SUBWAY and Jx3 left me there.

Cayden left to get some firewood, leaving me with Laura. The whole time he was gone, we said nothing. I wasn't sure what to say, and Laura was not good at being the center of attention in serious matters such as this. I heard Cayden come back.

"That is it." He dropped a tree between us. "You two need to talk because I am not dealing with your awkward silence."

Laura stood up and leaned against the tree. "There is nothing to talk about."

"What do you mean there is nothing to talk about?" I asked. "You just killed a third of our allies, and you used me to kill yourself."

Knowing Laura, first, she would claim it was just a test to see how well I could operate or something generic like that.

True enough, she said, "Look, it was nothing more than a field test gone wrong."

"Which part exactly?"

"Every part, duh!"

"That is a lie," I said. "Why are you lying? Can't you be serious for once?" Though I said it, I think I was talking more about myself at this point; it wasn't like all she did was joke with me.

"I am a very serious person all the time. Maybe it is because I know that I can relax when I am around you. Why do you care?"

"That is not what I meant to say. Look, just be honest with me. Why...Were you just so unhappy being with me that you would go so far as killing yourself, using me as your suicide assistant? If that were the case, you could have just said no instead. I would have eventually gotten over it."

"Shut up!" Laura said. "You want the truth, then here it is. Honestly, I knew that as long as you lived here on this island, you would eventually hear about the Lightning Bearer, and so I decided to keep that information from you, for it would not have profited you to know that information. And instead of helping you, I would be even more of a crutch hindering you from your full potential. Those killed were killed for a reason and targeted strategically. They were killed for being traitors with proof from Cayden. This was supposed to be my last job on the island. If it wasn't for you and your revenge plot, it would have been more efficient."

I was left with nothing to say. "You are right."

"So then, sister," Cayden interrupted. "Would you please explain why you nearly killed yourself?"

"Shut up, Cayden!"

"Please, I think you owe us both some kind of explanation."

She paused. "The truth isn't just because I was committed to playing the role of the Lightning Bearer but rather because I felt that I deserved that fate." She looked down as she talked. "Today, I tested out all of my theories that I had questions about. I was amazed just how well he did against what is considered an impossible enemy. My second question was answered last night as I watched him sleep and remembered all the good times we shared. When I was captured, those memories returned and had a different effect. I remembered you, Leo, and all the people I killed. You were returning home, and if I were to go with you, then I would have to eventually talk to your family about what we have done. It just became too much for me. I realized it would be easier to just erase myself."

So, in short, it was my fault for putting her in that predicament, not once but twice. Good job, Leo, you pressured her into nearly killing herself.

Cayden stood up and stretched. "So, you are trying to blame your relationship and commitment issues on Leo? You and I both know that couldn't be further from the truth. Though I don't want to admit it, I can see where she is coming from. I remember hearing a quote from an old shepherd who served in Vietnam; I believe his name was Myles. He said, 'As I've gotten older, I've always wondered why am I here? Was I meant to be great, to do something important here? Or am I just supposed to be an object for a bullet to pass through?' I only mention that because it seems to me that she too has gone that direction of just being unclear. Leonardo, I hope you can forgive my sister and her stupidity."

I replied, "Of course, I will. I just hope that something like this never happens again."

"I apologize. I just wasn't thinking before I pulled the trigger. Truthfully, I was more surprised that you never caught on to me living a double life."

"I have seen you walking side by side with him...I mean you."

"All the suits have that function," Cayden said, "including yours. It is an exoskeleton mode that allows you to project the suit's functions while not wearing it. It allows you to project all but the voice."

"What kinds of things were you doing?" I asked.

"Where to start...For one, I was told to survey SUBWAY before we sent you over there. It was located when my brother and I were out on a scouting mission. That was about a year before you left the BCC Village. It was a request from Anita and the Webmaster, for they could sense the village council member's disinterest in keeping you around the village. There was fear growing that the Webmaster might try to use you to overthrow the village or something ridiculous like that. Once the decision was made to relocate you, my brother did a little more digging and found out that the organization was corrupt; however, by that time, it was too late. You would have to find a new location soon or else place your fate in the hands and fear of the council. Since time was short and you were moving in with unfamiliar allies, I requested to assist you on your journey at least until you returned home. I was planning to relocate you at some point, but SUBWAY was better fortified and the lesser of the other evils."

Cayden said, "At some point, my sister noticed you getting used to the suit's abilities over water, but you weren't comfortable using it very well. So, she used a favor she acquired from Chief Vasconcellos to do special detail work, and as an extra insurance policy, I also acted as a personal bodyguard upon transport."

I raised my hand as if to politely cut in. "Wait, why didn't you just go to the base and train me then?"

"That is an easy question to answer. If the people around you caught wind that you lacked any kind of control, then that would invite trouble down the road. Traveling as personal detail to the chief was a beautiful façade."

"I thought for sure you knew I was a suit user as well once I didn't translate for the guard, for how would I know the armor would translate otherwise," said Laura.

Back then I didn't think about it because I was nervous about the mission.

"While he was training you, I kept the perimeter safe from unnecessary guests. When you lost contact with me, I was thanking my brother."

"What about that time we fought Becky and Daysen? What did you give me that day?"

"I was just giving you a boost of power, for my armor didn't need it."

"Wait, what about the time I was underground? The whole bit you were doing with the princess makes no sense."

"Actually, not true. As the Lightning Bearer, I take many contracts. That particular time, I had accepted a contract, but right after Anita called and informed me that it was a foul-play contract. Simply put, it is a contract that is placed on someone for the wrong reasons. That one was a power struggle contract. As it turned out, that young lady was a kind one and only dreamed about going home. That was an absolute distraction, and someone saw this as a risky situation. That was the reason they hired me. As the Lightning Bearer, I have never backed out of a contract, no matter what the situation was, even when SUBWAY was hired to rescue her and, more specifically, you. When I got out of the helicopter, I was starting another contract to severely cripple the enemy forces. I placed a tracer on your pistol so I could better locate you. Then when you 'ran into the Lightening Bearer,' that was a way to test your combat ability and give you an enemy much stronger than you. As for the underground shooting, I sent the empty suit down there and waited for your request to shoot the target."

"So, that jet that went down from the last mission..."

"Yeah, that was me too. Shot it down to keep detection minimal. It wasn't all that hard because they have to stay below two thousand feet or the field will mess up the electrical equipment, and it was hovering. I didn't calculate where it was going, and it crashed into the building. As for reasons for not wanting the case, I didn't want it to predetonate."

"What about after the mission? Why did you attack... yourself?"

"That is a little complicated to explain. From what I have understood, my armor's auto defenses misread my intent toward you. You see, I thought you figured out who I was, so I felt like I was backed into a corner. And when you popped the question, I went through a lot of emotions, which must have been what triggered the attack."

Cayden said, "My sister is complicated over thinking each situation, so that makes plenty of sense."

"Yeah, that makes sense as well," I replied. "What about today? I don't feel you were being completely honest. Why were you so short with me?"

Cayden said, "It is because she is sleep-deprived, mixed with the feeling of anger from you not heeding our warning not to fight."

"I had no intent to fight. My shooter somehow mixed up the signals for shooting. Why did you hire your sister to attack and kill some of the others who were with me?"

"Some of the people in your organization were planning to find out how you were going to escape this island and go the way of the pirates and hijack it. She was supposed to be stealthier, but the job is done. Placing unstable batteries and sending a surge to the radios is what triggered the explosions."

Laura said, "As for continuing to fight you, that was a test." She paused. "I needed to see how I felt about you when pushed to the edge. When I fight someone, I normally do so without holding back, but with you, I just couldn't. When I tried, I just kept feeling my heart drop. The first time I met you, I was so excited to talk to you that I was rambling. In my life, I have never experienced anything so demeaning. It wasn't until I talked to Krissy that I figured out what was going on."

Those were just a few of the things we talked about, but the list went on. By the time she finished, I was speechless. Thinking about it now, that might have meant she was passionate about me. Man, what a way to start off a relationship, right?

"Yes, those are not including the times that she was with me," Cayden said.

I saw she was lying in the sand by then, looking up toward the sky.

Cayden continued, "I guess that long speech took it out of her. I see that she went to sleep, which works out since I am going to tell you something. I was in a similar predicament."

"You were?" I asked, getting up to walk closer to him.

"Yes, there was a time our little assault team had three. The third member was a young woman named Keisha. While we were chasing down one of our targets, they managed to set the building on fire with my comrade still inside. I knew that my suit could manipulate the fire, but at the time, I wasn't familiar with it and the emotional reader it had installed. When I caught up to her, she was trapped, and her right arm was stuck under a beam. I saw the fire was trying to get her too, but I wasn't going to allow that, so I stepped in to put it out. But from what I had examined, I was only making the fire worse. I saved her from the fire, but she suffered third and fourth-degree burns.

"Within a week of recovery, she was turned over to a Dr. Kornegay. He promised he could treat her wounds to lessen the nerve and tissue damage. After we took her, she wasn't released for several days. When we saw her again, most of the burns were gone and reduced to first degree. It looked as though nothing had happened, as though there was never an incident. In fact, the first-degree burn was only visible on her right forearm. She said that she was ready to return to the fight, but I couldn't risk it. In return, I gave her my cut for the job and sent her to Ireland."

"Dang, man, I didn't know. Then again, it doesn't explain why you are so calm right now. If someone were to attack my family, I don't know what I'd do."

"We still talk, and in a few days, I can apologize in person and try to explain what happened. As for my sister, she can be pretty stupid sometimes, as younger siblings are known to be. I advise you to keep looking forward because she will not hold this against you. She loves you too much, so much that she didn't want you to know who she was. Besides, I told her to tell you the truth after you saved that princess from the tower. Tomorrow she'll be back on her feet, so no harm, no foul."

"I hope you are right," I said. I noticed fog fill the area. At first, I thought it was smoke, but there was no smoke coming from the fire.

"Here, take this." Cayden handed me a rifle, standing up. "We are not alone."

Looking at the thickness of the fog, I agreed it was manmade. I put my suit on, and we stood back to back, looking for who it could be. I pulled water from the ocean and created a shield around us, making it wider and wider. We heard something enter, which I just assumed was Laura's body entering the water. I felt Cayden's hands on my shoulder and turned around. There was armor that looked exactly like mine.

"What is going on?"

"I don't know, is it a malfunction or something?"

It took off its helmet, and underneath was another me, except he looked lifeless. He opened his eyes, and they were white. He spoke: "Hello, Leonardo, I am sad we haven't been formally introduced. Then again, my existence is an anomaly, so it doesn't matter. Gentlemen, before we have a repeat of what happened earlier today, I just want you to know now that Laura has a collar around her neck that will inject her with poison. If you try to get in my way tonight, then I will kill her. From what I have gathered, I am just a dark and evil version of yourself. So there is less confusion in conversation, you can call me Aristotle."

"You're going by my middle name. Yeah, that is real original," I said sarcastically.

"Yeah, I know how you feel. I'm running short on time. We don't really have time to discuss that right now. You will meet me in three days if you wish to see her alive." He picked Laura up and held his hands up, flying away. I looked in the direction he flew and noticed a plane fly away.

Cayden said, "We can't afford for you to miss your way home once again. Go home and leave this place. I will take care of this."

"No, I will not leave her in his possession."

We were about to follow suit, but he was moving too fast due to the plane, and it was hard to see because it was night. When we lost sight, I noticed Cayden's gauntlet blink yellow. "Hey Cayden, your wrist is blinking."

He turned and said, "So is yours." I looked and touched the part that blinked. We received instructions displayed in our helmets, telling us to appear at another location. These came directly from the Webmaster; they were to lead us to someone named Antonio Zimmerman. So, we packed our things and headed toward that location. It was not like I knew where to find the one who kidnapped Laura, but I had a feeling Antonio did and could help.

# 13
## So...Umm...Back Where We Started

**W**e finally arrived at the location we were told to go. From the way the environment looked, it was truthfully the most tranquil place I had ever seen in my life. There was a light waterfall that could be heard off in the distance. All around, there was nothing but beauty; it was like we were above a rainforest, and the scene was captivating. As we continued, we could view all the different regions with the naked eye, including the desert. Looking ahead, I saw a building that looked a little bit out of place because all we could see was a small portion, and the rest of it was...just gone. We went a little further and saw a young woman tend a garden. When she saw us, she stopped and came to greet us.

"Hello," she said. "You must be the two young men that my teacher was telling me about. Leonardo Winchester and Cayden Zastrow, if I am not mistaken. The Webmaster has told us of your coming. Though you are later than expected, you are still expected. Please follow me."

We followed her. As we walked closer, the building shifted and expanded until we could see the entire thing. The woman lingered behind. I turned to see what she was doing, you know, paranoia and all. As it turned out, she was moving a veil.

Cayden asked, "What is your name, ma'am?"

She replied, "Dr. Sara Bliss, why do you ask?"

"Just a little curious, I just thought that you looked a little familiar. Think nothing of it."

"Oh, sure thing. Please, this way." She walked in front of us and opened the door. "Hello, Mr. White. I have the two guests you were expecting."

As we entered the building, there was a man sitting down in a rocking chair. "Thank you, my dear. I have been waiting for these two for a while now."

"I thought there were three of them."

"That is because the third member is currently pre-occupied. I was told she might stop by later. Please, you two, come sit down. I've been expecting you for years now." He pointed to some seats across from where he sat. "How have you been these past few years? I bet you are wondering why you were summoned here and presented to some old man. I know I don't look like much."

"No, sir, my question isn't why," I replied calmly. "My only question is, 'how?' How can this man help me? I can assume right away that you have some answers, just like the princess I rescued from the tower. She explained to me her grandmother was one of the creators of the suits..."

"Ah yes, Lilly," he interrupted. "The daughter of Catherin, the daughter of Karoline. That young lady is a stubborn little one, just like her mother." He laughed. "I digress. I take it that the third member of your team is the real reason you are here, and she is really important to you; otherwise, climbing up this mountain to see me would be the last thing that came to mind."

"How did you..." I replied, stunned.

"First of all, you have a very honest voice. You are not here to try to bond with an old man, are you? Of course not; you would rather get to the point."

"I apologize, sir. Normally, I would love to sit down and listen to your stories, but I am unable to do so at this time."

Cayden sat down on the floor, saying, "I'm guessing this will actually take a while."

"So, what are you here for? Can you be more exact on what actually happened?" Mr. White asked.

"From what I was told, my suit replicated itself and me. In the process, the other me, he kidnapped my fiancée and is holding her hostage."

"Hmm, so the fallback plan worked after all."

"What do you mean by 'fallback plan'?"

"To explain it to where it makes sense, I have to start at the beginning with a history lesson. This will explain where the suits came from and your current situation. I understand you're in a hurry, but you won't understand if I don't explain the history a bit."

I looked over to Cayden and realized he was annoyed. I was going to decline but Cayden stopped me by saying, "We have time. Please go ahead, sir."

I would have said something, but I thought I might find something useful in his information, so I didn't say anything, just nodded my head.

"All right, then, from the beginning."

Sara placed refreshments in the middle of the room.

"Gentlemen, here are some refreshments." She handed each of us a cup. The other two drank right away. I set mine on the ground next to me. She stood next to the older man.

He continued, "Now, where was I? Ah yes, the beginning. In 1888, A young man named Charles Watts drew up the original suit's blueprints, about a hundred years before you were born, if I am not mistaken. He was actually trying to make armor for everyday soldiers while he was in Australia, but what he was asking seemed illogical at the time, and they didn't have the proper resources to proceed with his plans. So he went where all big dreamers go with an idea, to America, where they had the resources. When he arrived there, American welders and mechanics laughed at the idea.

One year later, he met friends named James Worthy, Jeremiah Harris, and Sherry Loveless. It was they who had seen the vision of what the armor could be. They were a small team, but they had ambition. Watts, of course, was the team leader. They got together and tried to build a bulletproof suit of armor. They finished in 1900. Everything about this armor was perfect. The armor was so perfect that even the armor-piercing rounds we had in the seventies deflected from it." He handed us a picture of the armor. I took it, and the first thing I noticed was that it was made for heavy protection, so much so it could probably take a blast from a tank and not harm the user.

"So, what happened?" I asked because everything seemed too perfect, and I never heard of them using such armor during World War I.

"Excellent question. I am guessing you ask this since you have never seen pictures of it in your history classes regarding World War I!" He continued, "They needed to test the abilities, so they made an obstacle course through the sewer systems of Orlando, Florida. It wasn't the best idea, but it inspired making a helmet with an air filter. Once it passed their expectations, there was one thing left to do—test it in live combat. They had a choice: either they could rob a bank and get unwanted attention for their project, or they could wait for a war to start. So, they chose to wait for a war to get a live combat reading.

"Luckily, World War I was on the way. This was the chance they were waiting for. The armor tested very well; using the armor without being detected wasn't easy. They were told to make sure there were no photographers around before they could test the armor. Everywhere they went, they aided in battles. Because the tests went so well, they presented it to different manufacturers, but no company would take it. They all said it would be expensive to manufacture. So, Dr.

Watts went to the Army and presented the idea to them, but sadly, there were no takers. They had all but given up hope. This, of course, was also during the Great Depression, so there was no money flow. When all hope seemed lost, a young man saw a vision for the armor. This young man's name was Jason Wolfe. He had the money and connections to do something with it, so he presented the money to Watts, who had little choice and felt as though Wolfe could do something with it. So, he took the offer on the condition that he'd still monitor the progress.

"Through the years, they put in time to make the inside of the armor and make it better. They completed the objective they had in mind in 1934. The next year, Dr. Watts officially retired from the project and lived quietly with his family on his farm in Oklahoma. World War II was on the way, and by this time, he was just waiting until America got involved. In 1941, Wolfe saw that World War II would lead us to a new testing ground."

"Sir, that doesn't make any sense. How come we have no history of ever using an armored warrior in combat?" I asked him again. "It would be hard to test this, not once, but twice without getting caught. World War I was one thing, but World War II is a little hard to believe."

"Yeah, something tells me that you couldn't easily hide something like that, especially not from freelance photographers," Cayden added.

"Of course, you couldn't hide that. We had to ask the US government for special permission to use one of their military personnel who could follow orders and stay covert. They sent us a marine by the name of Atrau Winchester. The way we got him in was by using the D-Day operation as our smokescreen to drop our tester into place. Winchester came to land from the underbelly of one of the ships. His main mission was to test the suit in combat while using the US forces' transmissions to avoid visual contact with them and any photographers. He tested the suit to its extremes. Wolfe's forces eventually picked him up in October 1944, when the war was slowly ending.

"Since the suit had passed the live combat test, Wolfe then wanted to push it to the next extreme, but he was unsure where to go. This was when Tony Grossman, one of his assistants, presented an idea to push the very elements themselves. As for Mr. Winchester, he returned to the military to finish his term, never to speak of the experiment. To do this, they needed a team of scientists with like minds to make this work. They searched for six months and found the team capable of pushing the very fabric of nature as much as they could without any glitches.

"The teams needed to be split into seven other teams, each with either slight differences or complete differences. How they achieved the goal was up to them. Of course, they needed to have suits to make the elements useable and controllable, and as you know, every team needs a team leader, so the team leaders were decided based off of what they knew about the science they were dealing with."

He stopped, looked at me, and then looked at Cayden. "I take it that you two have run into all the suits by now."

"Yes, sir!" I replied.

"Of course," Cayden replied.

"Good! Then you know there is strength, time warping, rapid healing, stealth, electricity, and, of course, fire and water."

Cayden interrupted, "I never ran into a stealth user. Who has stealth?"

"I know the scumbag who has that one. Please continue," I said.

"To reintegrate, the trick was to use nanotechnology to make most of these possible. The team leaders were as follows: strength went to Randall Prometheus, a true exercise nut; time warping to Dr. Caroline Trainor, a lady who was obsessed with perfection; rapid healing to Dr. Tim Brooks—he was the closest to completing this science; electricity to Katelyn Falls—she was actually considered the only one crazy enough to do the job..."

"Why?" I asked.

"Because she was. The electricity she worked with could fry brain cells in seconds if not used properly, and could very well incinerate the entire body. Fire went to Professor Kalem Hues, who was perfect for the job as he was a pyromaniac who was already experienced in that field. Lastly, water went to me, Dr. Joseph White. I was picked because of my experience with using the elements for my benefit. You would think it was our plan to make the stealth armor, but it was nothing more than a fluke. Stealth was never part of the original plan.

"So, the teams finally split off. Seeing as how controlling elements was something fire, lightning, and water had in common, we had to compare notes to make this as fast as possible. A year later, the other teams joined in their beneficial efforts. We finished the task in about ten years. The other team then officially broke into separate groups. I started experimenting with nanomachines to manipulate water, but something just wasn't made right. So, I focused on that.

"Toward the end of the Vietnam War, I gained an assistant by the name of Rodney Trotter; you know him as Ron Trotter. He was a creative young man who had just left the Army and wanted to be a teacher. I convinced him to work with me on his time off from college. He was what we called a guinea pig; I, however, called it an opportunity to be the first to try new science.

"We pushed the nanotechnology to its limits. We could get it to respond to human mind, which the nanomachines are in sync with, which is what we wanted. But this did more than we expected. The nanomachines would open a destructive doorway with the human mind. I saw this coming in advance and had an emergency shutdown switch if something went wrong, one for the suit's power and the other for the nanomachines. Once removed from the host, after about an hour, there was no long-term damage. Once we realized they linked with human minds, we had to find a way to make them more...what they called 'user friendly,' so the users still had control over their minds. Our project finally reached a conclusion. It was now we had to use Watts's original armor model to make our models the same as or better than his."

"May I ask why my suit had an armor facade when I first got it, and when it broke, the real armor was finally revealed?" I asked.

"'Facade,' I guess you could call it that. Honestly, it's a funny story. We finally had our armor delivered to us, and the one delivery girl, named Amanda Shrine, she forgot to tell me about the competition between the different groups. They wanted to see who could make their armored suits with the least number of remodels. I was disqualified because I never did this. I would have won, though. Since I had no idea of this, I placed the suit's extra material in the defensive aspect of the suit so there wouldn't be a surplus of material. This is the real reason you don't have anyone but you with water abilities. There were a few unneeded pieces, so I shipped the rest back when I was done. How I built the suit was to use the weak armor first to act as a trial version of what the suit could do. Then, soon after the exterior suit was destroyed, it would activate the real armor while repairing the old one for the next user, if there is ever another. You actually did better than I was expecting you to do, Leonardo. Your suit lasted three years, if I am correct."

"More or less."

"I was also impressed that you weren't accidentally killed when it fell to pieces thanks to your brother-in-law to be. Why is that?"

"I was told ahead of time by the time-warping user what would happen, so when your suit was destroyed, I knew to stop. Not only that, but he was the only one I have ever met to use that ability, and your suit would just put out any flame attempt."

"Once the real armor activated, so would the true suit's potential. That was the plan. Mr. Trotter actually came up with an idea to make the suit fold up. We shared the idea with the other groups. It quickly became a big thing. All suits can now fold because of this. Once our suit was foldable, we were finished, and we decided to assist the other groups with their projects to speed things along. This was ten years of progress.

"As you could guess, time warping took the longest. I couldn't tell you how we made it work, but we found a way. Once we finished, the new objective was to combine our thoughts and professions into a single suit, so we did. Unfortunately, the suit was more powerful but very corruptible, meaning the user was more easily susceptible to the nanomachines. We called this one the Beta. So we had to make another suit that could take the same ideas as the others. It worked as a practice suit; we called this one the Veda suit. It was later called the stealth suit because our scientist found out it was better for defense and not offense. But we only put a fraction of our abilities into the suit and adjusted accordingly.

"We knew we were ready for the AELFA suit, which was originally named the All Element Laced Fusion Ability Suit. You element users might know it as the Alpha suit. Once we knew what we were looking at, it didn't take us long to put our projects together into one suit. We finally finished our project.

"Not soon after, the founder Watt died after seeing his work come to completion. Mr. Wolfe and his assistant Dr. Grossman were originally going to sell the idea to the US or British government, but after having a long meeting with the rest of us, we all concluded that this was a horrible idea. The final assessment was that we hide them from the modern people and instead place them where they cannot be found.

"For the element users, we gave ours to the village where the young chief at the time was an eleven-year-old girl known to the people as the Webmaster. We trusted her because she was a really good judge of character, and she showed great wisdom for some one her age. Dr. Tim Brooks gave healing to a very young girl he saved from a fire; she would have died if not for him. Unfortunately, he died months later. A Russian spy stole the strength suit, which we found out later had it stolen from him. Caroline Trainor gave it to her nephew as a birthday gift. The Beta, Veda, and Alpha, we hid those collectively far from anyone. As for the corrupted suits, we sold those to pay for the project after we warned the handlers never to use them. Before the corrupted suits were handed out, their nanomachines were rewritten to fuse with the uncorrupted ones, kind of as an incentive. We managed to place one of the corrupted suits in a museum in England because it looked to be made from gold and rubies."

"Why isn't Amelia's armor corrupting her?" I asked.

"Yeah, I didn't understand that," Cayden added.

"I assume you are talking about Amelia Vandenberg. She came to me looking for a way to stop the corruption that was slowly consuming her. I was able to do this at the cost of her armor's ability. Her armor used to allow her to jump ten minutes into the past versus the five seconds she has now. It was all I could do since she seemed sincere.

"This brings me to the reason there is a clone of you. I made the armor to clone the user, so the user would have a chance to learn control, not just of the armor but also of life. I take it you recently had a mixture of confused emotions, then almost instantly you felt them leave. This was the trigger, which will only happen once per user. This was the only suit made like this. The good news is your clone will die in about a week if he hasn't died before then. Sadly, he is aware of this predicament due to a doom's day clock. His armor is a little weaker than yours. This must be the reason you are here. All you need to do is outsmart yourself, which doesn't sound easy, but right now, you have information that he doesn't. All I can say is think outside of your regular parameters. I believe you can do this. As for you, Walking Inferno, I have some extra nanomites left so you won't die too quickly from drowning. Please come with me. This will only take a minute."

As I sat there waiting, Sara asked, "Is there anything I can do to help you?"

"Please don't bother yourself with my needs. I am sure you have better things to do than worry about me. So, what is it you do exactly?"

"I am his assistant and student. Dr. White's current experiments consist of purifying polluted water using a detoxifier. I am not allowed to disclose too much, but the objective is to restructure the ozone layer that has been damaged over time, or at least that is the gist of how it is supposed to work."

I looked at her and noticed she was armed with a sword on her back. I wondered how I hadn't noticed this. She walked toward me.

"So, young man, were you done with your drink?"

"I am sorry, ma'am, I just haven't needed anything to drink in a long time." I took the drink and started to chug it to be polite. As I was close to finishing, she started to clear her throat.

"I understand your predicament, so you need not finish on my account."

I handed her my cup after I finished.

"I was unaware of just how powerful the armor was. Those nanomachines must be real handy. With that said, they must be a burden too," she said.

I looked at her. "Did you know before the project?"

"No, I met Dr. White when the project was coming to a close. It's a shame some of the brightest minds will never be known for their brilliance. Creating armor in the dark must take its toll on a human mind in one way or another."

"Is he your father?"

"Father, no. But he has been pretty close to one. He's taken care of me since I was fifteen. He gave me a job, a home to live in, and a car to drive, asking nothing in return."

"Then can you explain how it is you are his assistant? I am sure you are old enough to be doing your own projects."

"I could, but I lack the ideas and motivation to move onto my own projects."

Cayden and Dr. White walked back out to us. Cayden said, "While we were gone, I called Amelia, and she has agreed to aid us. I thought about it, and the more people we have to help us, the better our chances will be. I was going to call your other friend, but I was sure the clone would know how to fight him, so he might be a bit too predictable." I assumed he was referring to Rayshawn. "The only one who can change tactics on the fly is Amelia. She will meet us at the rally point. Thank you, again, Dr. White and Dr. Bliss. Let's go, Leonardo."

I waved goodbye and headed to the door. When we arrived, there was a jeep waiting in front of the house.

"When did this get here?" I asked.

"Don't worry about that. I need you to focus and figure out where we are supposed to go."

"If I were the clone, I would try to hide somewhere I felt I had a full advantage, so most likely a..." I paused. "I know where the water copy is. He's going to be close to a large body of water, like a riverbed."

There was only one location it could be, which was an abandoned canal that Laura always talked to me about.

Along the way to the canal, I realized what I was up against and who: a fight against myself—there was only a 50 percent chance of success even with Cayden's help. I thought about what I could do if I didn't survive. So, I wrote letters to certain individuals, people I had not seen in a long time. At some point, because I was quiet, Cayden asked me what I was doing, and I told him. After I finished the third letter, we arrived. Fortunately, or unfortunately, depending on how you look at the situation, we had to wait for Amelia to arrive before we could make our move. Though I had combat experience, I lacked hunting experience. Because of this, Cayden decided to scout alone. I continued to write letters as I waited for them. Out of all the fights I had been in, this one seemed to be the most realistic of all. Once I finished, I noticed I still had time to kill. I wrote one more letter to the one who mattered most. It was an hour before Amelia showed up, and another half hour before Cayden reappeared.

"His location is pretty well fortified. I was able to disable some of his traps, but not all of them. He has auto turrets in locations that make it hard to be careless. It looks like he wants to know our location the moment we show up but doesn't want to bother with anyone who just strays in here. The ones I deactivated I destroyed with a silenced sniper rifle. While I was at it, I set some traps of our own in the area. We don't have much of a plan to work with, but as long as she is here, we have more to work with than we originally had. Are you two ready?" We both nodded our heads. "All right, then let's get into position."

"Hey, Cayden. I have a favor to ask of you. If I fail this mission, I need you to give your sister these letters. Afterward, she should know what to do."

"Fine, just hurry up and get into position." He took the letters and secured them.

"I guess I must go in first to activate the traps," I said.

Cayden pointed in the direction that I was supposed to head in. After about two minutes into the walk, I saw destroyed turrets because sparks were shooting out of them. I made it to an opening, and there I saw Aristotle waiting, sharpening his sword. As I crossed into the opening, an onslaught of bullets fired in my direction. I formed a shield of water in front of me as I always did. I slowly walked backward because the number of bullets might have pushed the suit too far. Though it had taken shots from tanks, exploding planes, and rocket launchers, they were never fired from at least twenty different locations with such focused accuracy. As I hid behind a tree, the turrets stopped firing. "Do you have your shots?" I asked.

"Yes," Amelia said. "You will be free to move up in ten. Until then, stay put!"

So, I sat there quietly, counting to ten, then tried to re-enter the battlefield. Then explosions set off on the ground, but they were all in random locations.

"Ah, Leonardo, you are a little earlier than expected," Aristotle said, putting the sword into the ground and using it to stand up. When he was all the way up, he threw his sharpener to the side.

"Tell me, why?" I said.

"Why all this?" he replied, patting himself down. "Why attack you? Why kidnap the woman you love? I know that no one as smart as you could possibly be that stupid. Because you are no longer fit to live in a world like this. Because you have taken your position for granted. Because...I can. Because I can, I am going to kill you. We have the same mentality, so I am surprised you are asking such a ridiculous question. This will be the most intense battle of your life. Our memories and pasts are the same, our fighting style is the same; the only difference is I am pure evil. I wonder if you can return to our fiancée's side before the end of the day. Yes, I share the love you have for her. If I didn't, she would have been killed or at least beaten ruthlessly just to prove a point. I have tried everything that I can to bury it all as we did with Nichole, but it seems the feeling for this one is 100 percent pure. So, Leonardo, shall we begin?"

The ground under my feet shook. I almost lost my balance, and water shot up like a geyser, shooting me into the air. As I rose, two more turrets opened fire then exploded just as quickly. I grabbed the sword on my back and placed it on my hip. Water was shot to increase my speed. When I was within range, Aristotle formed a wall from the swamp water. The wall took all of the impact, but it was enough to destroy that wall at the cost of the blade. This left me open. As he used his momentum from the crushed wall to get a fast swing in, I returned the action and used my momentum to launch him like a catapult. I could feel his sword graze my armor as he launched over me. To avoid hitting the ground, he used water pressure—enough to send him through the wall and into the air above the trees. I rolled out of the way.

"Well, if we keep this up, the fight will last forever and a day!" I yelled, waiting for him to come back down.

I heard leaves shake; the top of the tree I was close to fell down behind me. He jumped down in front of me and said, "So then, do you just want to cut to the chase?" The sword he using now glowed a bright green, perhaps because he had been in a swamp a while ago. My sword began to shine white. "Well, now, this is more like it! Two men fighting to death over the love of a single woman! How poetic," he said with excitement.

"Shut up. You talk too much," I said.

"Let's proceed."

I rushed in, and he did the same. The sword never changed its katana shape, though it extended. It was possible the swords fed off each other. We parried each other, spinning away as we fought, just to charge once more. This time as I approached, he sidestepped and tried to expose an opening. Fighting him was very difficult because he thought the same way I did, which gave him a slight edge. He was stopped by one of his scattered turrets. The turret was destroyed, but after the blast, I heard more explosions go off in at least fifteen other locations around the swamp.

"It seems that your wannabe support has run into some of my traps. It's a real shame I cannot face them myself. Waste of a few soldiers, if you ask me. The only one that could survive that is our beloved brother-to-be, Cayden. I assure you that I have made the proper arrangements concerning him. Poor Cayden is here looking for his dear sister, but all because of me— oh, I am sorry, I meant to say you. Since I am feeling generous, I will inform you that your beloved is currently not here just yet, but she will be here pretty soon, dropped in like a bomb. I hope it doesn't explode when she finally hits the ground. That would be ever so annoying because I want her to watch you suffer."

"So, there is no reason for me to hold back?" I asked.

"Oh, my, for you to hold back now would just be an insult at this point. Shall we continue?"

As we were about to charge in one more time, we heard an explosion coming from our left. I saw something quickly approach out of the corner of my eye, and I turned to cut down. As I swung, I noticed that Aristotle did the same and struck the same the tree on the opposite side, so seeing that he also left himself open, I prepared to strike. I swung the sword and held onto it with my other hand. With my open hand, I blasted him with water. Needless to say, he had the same plan. This pushed us away from each other. Then another tree was launched, but this time, it was more directed toward Aristotle. Both of the trees flew as though they were shot out of a cannon. I leaped even further back to avoid any kind of friendly fire. Since I was out of the way, I watched as Aristotle sliced each tree in half. In total, there were ten trees cut. As he cut the logs, I collected water in my hand.

As the tenth and final tree was launched, I noticed Cayden riding the tree. When he got close enough, he jumped off before the tree was cut, holding a spear in the thrusting position, charging Aristotle. Laura had told me her brother was very skilled with the spear in one or two of our conversations, but this was the first time I'd seen him using it. Even in his meetings with me, he'd only used his bare hands. From the speed of the attack, Cayden was able to crack the armor's shoulder piece; a wall of water caught the rest of the attack. If not for the water, he could have possible ripped clean through the armor. Aristotle formed a shield with his free arm as though he anticipated what I had planned to do

"Your sister was right, your skill with the spear is astonishing. If I had not let go of my sword to redirect the spear, the blade might have gone through and I would no longer exist."

I couldn't help but look around and notice his sword was cast away. So, I rushed in with my own sword, seeing an opening. Without dropping the wall, he slid out of the way and kicked off, landing by his sword once more.

"Did you assume that I had forgotten about you?"

"Nice to know that you can foresee that much in the future," I replied.

I turned the sword and moved it in a thrusting position. Cayden and I charged in, attacking from opposite ends. How he fought reminded me of the times my brother and me would spar using our mom's brooms and mops. She didn't like it too much because we would end up breaking most of them. The clone fought both of us with little to no problem. Though the two of us should have easily overthrown him, he was too well defended for working by himself. Though the clone and I had the same training, he fought like another experienced fighter. There was no freaking way he should have defended himself so well.

As we fought, I thought of different ways that we could turn the tide. Then, before we knew it, Amelia ran up and punched him in his face, knocking him down. As this was another opportunity, Cayden struck him, but the blow only grazed Aristotle, sliding along his back. Aristotle rolled over to his feet and was greeted by Amelia's uppercut. I snuck up behind and hit him with the flat part of my sword. With that blow, my broken rib began to send pain signals, so I placed the sword on the ground. *Darn Laura's perfectionism*, I remember thinking to myself.

At this moment, I lost view of the fight and tried to recover. The only thing that I could come up with was trying to manipulate the water in my body and holding it like a cast. As I did this, I felt pain until it manipulated properly. I picked up my sword once more. I was about to move back into the fight when I heard the sound of a passing jet followed by a loud whistle.

"What was that?" I asked, and then went to go check it out, for it was close enough to cause the ground to shake. I arrived and saw what I thought was a bomb. Then I heard it explode, followed by coughing. I checked to see who it was and saw it was Laura, so I ran over to her. As I got closer to Laura, she was on her knees, choking from the smoke in the air.

"You shouldn't have come here. Why aren't you with the transport? It is your ticket off this stupid island," she coughed.

"I'm not leaving without you," I replied. "You have stayed by me all these years, and I will stay with you until the end."

"Are you trying to get stranded here?" Laura whispered. "I don't think you understand what position you are in right now."

I noticed her gauntlet was by her feet. "What happened? Are you all right?"

"He ripped off the gauntlet to forcefully take away my powers, then gave me back my power after he went into the building. He walked in and out within two minutes. He cleaned my wounds from our previous battle, and the whole time, I have been his prisoner. Leo, I don't know what his plans are with you here, but it is not good. Leave, and I promise you I will be right behind you, please."

But I couldn't get myself to leave, even though I knew what she said was right. I noticed she wore something on her chest; it looked like it could have been a bulletproof vest, but it was too big and bulky.

"Don't you love it?" Aristotle's voice was behind me. "This is a bulletproof bomb that I bought. It's amazing what you can buy on this island. You see, she cannot interfere, and you cannot rescue her until you have actually killed me. I hope you enjoy earning your pot of gold at the end of the rainbow—if you win, that is."

Cayden grabbed him and sent him soaring through the sky; and from the projected angle, he would land about a kilometer away from my estimate. "Do you think he is bluffing?" Cayden asked.

"If it were another person's clone, I would call it a bluff, but he's like me, and I don't see the use in mediocre, juvenile tactics like lying, no matter the situation. I don't respect liars, so why would I become one of them?"

Amelia said, "Yes, I doubt he has a reason to lie. At this point in the fight, it would be kind of too late to make any difference."

I placed a shield in front of us, and Aristotle rammed his sword into the shield. I allowed some of the blade to pass through to keep it in place, then I wrapped the shield around Aristotle, capturing him in place.

Cayden placed his hand over the water as Amelia said, "I will see if I can defuse the vest."

The orb began to boil and turned a light orange.

Aristotle began to laugh. "I hope you don't think I am finished."

"I do," Cayden said. The orb exploded from the immense heat, lasting about five seconds.

Cayden searched where the explosion came from; he looked for any trace of Aristotle, no matter how small. It was something he'd picked up while hunting.

"Do you think it was possible the explosion was strong enough to obliterate the body to nothing?" I asked.

"I am not sure it would be as simple as that. Then again, what we just did was also unheard of, so I guess it is a possibility. But here is one thing my sister told me about you. You will not fight unless your chance of success is more than seventy percent assured. I feel more than certain that our friend here is programmed the same way."

"Yes, I agree, but I thought that was the reason for the turrets."

"I guess that would be true, but I would like to eliminate the possibility of a mistake." He patted the ground. "Laura!" he yelled. "Have you ever seen something like this before?"

"No, brother," she yelled back.

"She has more experience than I do in the field of nanomachines, not just because she ran into a good majority of users but because she was taught by Mr. Trotter to use them and how they worked. It is one of the reasons she is really good with building things. How are things going over there, Amelia?"

"This is one of the most complicated pieces of technology I have ever seen," she replied. "No matter how we go about trying to disconnect this, it will explode. I have run seven scenarios. I feel as though it is triggered by an electrical interference that is transmitted from the suits. Maybe there is a metal detector that is detecting the metal? Whatever it is, I am being prevented from disarming it."

"Since my sister's device is still armed, according to our new friend, he is still alive."

"You're right," I mumbled. "We need to hurry up and find him. Right now, he has a huge advantage. Laura, do you see him?"

"No, but I can feel my hairs standing up. Brother, you need to get Leonardo out of this. It doesn't feel right."

"It might have something to do with what he picked up in the ruins, but what could it be?" I asked.

"Amelia!" Laura yelled. Next we heard the sound of cracking bones. When we looked to see what happened, we saw a long blade go through Amelia's chest. The blade was wide enough to reach from the top of her chest to the end of her belly button.

"Oh, my, I wonder what it is that he picked up as well," Aristotle's voice echoed. A surge of electricity gathered behind Amelia and struck the ground as he appeared. "It couldn't be he has the Beta suit!"

We saw he was right behind Amelia. He flung her off the blade to where we stood. Cayden, who placed her gently on the ground, caught her.

"Oh, you might want to treat her soon before she bleeds to death."

I quickly tried to find a way to make a tourniquet or something. Amelia began to cough up blood.

"What is the matter? Are you not able to time jump back and rewind? Oh yeah, I did scramble up your reader, making it useless with the bomb vest. Though the trap wasn't made for you, it was better than I anticipated. So, I guess you can do nothing but die."

As I franticly tried to keep her alive, Amelia looked at me, saying, "Stop, stop. It's too late now. Don't let this piece of turd kill you...Go home and..." She looked over to the clone, moved one of her hands in his direction, raised her middle finger, and smiled until she died; the smile stuck on her face.

"Ah, it seems as though I broke her. Too bad. I actually kind of liked her. Either way, I have finally gotten rid of the uninvited guest. Your little bomb thing would have worked perfectly in killing me if I didn't acquire the Beta. You did manage to break the copy of the water armor. Without that device, I would return to a puddle of water in the next twenty-four hours. Even though I have the Beta suit, there is no guarantee it will support my life. So, now there is nothing left holding me back from killing the two of you. So, which of you is going to be the next one to join Amelia?"

We stood there waiting for him to make the first move. He launched a bolt of electricity at the floor in front of us. "I am guessing that wasn't a choice." I pulled out my pistol and started to shoot Aristotle, hoping I could get one lucky shot in before I was forced to fight him in close range. With his strength being what it was with the Beta, he had the advantage. Dr. White did warn us that the Beta was a suit like the AELFA, but the biggest difference was the Beta was only allowed to use its abilities in short bursts.

I charged in and kept firing bullets, one after another until the clip was empty. When I got close enough, I stopped and threw it to the ground. I pulled out my sword from my back. Once I was within range of his sword, that was my only time to move back, and when I did, I used my blade like a geyser, pushing him back into a tree. As I did that, he sent an electrical jolt, doing the same. I then began to wonder how it was we could even defeat the copy, especially when he easily countered our elements with little effort. It was then I knew this would be my last battle, well, unless I joined the military when I got back.

Aristotle said, "You do know you're not going to win this?"

"That just may be, but if I never try, how will I ever know?"

A bolt of lightning next struck me. I tried to move but was unable. After that, I had a random flash of memories from the days when I was still in California. I remembered my dad trying to make me a better person, my mom waiting for my report card, Kat's interesting and not-so-interesting fun facts, Cheryl's medical tips on how to treat old people, and my brother Melvin, who consistently needed to be better than me. I remembered it all. I looked up and saw Laura's face. She was getting angrier about not being able to help Cayden, who was trapped in a ball of water.

"Leo, these is your favorite squad mates here," a voice over the radio said, "It took us a little while, but we finally found your frequency." That voice, Emilio— why was he on the radio? "We'll have to hit him with one attack. That's right, Mustachio, and I even brought Baby and Muscles. Just tell us where to hit him."

"Hey, Laura, hold this for me please." I tossed Laura the transceiver. There was no way I could miss a chance at finally having an advantage of a surprise attack. Though I was without a transmitter, I knew Laura would know what to do, so I would have to wait until they were ready. I began to lift and scatter little balls of water from the swamp. I watched Cayden, who was trapped inside the sphere of water, sitting calmly and boiling the water. From the way he sat, he was saying, "If I am going to die, at least I'll be comfortable."

I slammed some of the water into Aristotle, pushing him into a tree, and then let go of the water that connected to him. In turn, Cayden was freed. But the sphere Cayden was trapped in I kept intact, stretching it in different areas to grow large strings of water. All the strings attacked him at once. This forced him to completely let go of Cayden. Next, the floating water attacked him one by one, attaching until they had finally all collected into a war hammer. The hammer swung and pounded the copy into the tree. His body destroyed the tree from the impact.

Cayden grabbed my shoulders and said, "My sister said that the ground team is in position, and they will move according to your actions. My recommendation is you stay in Laura's line of sight."

Aristotle stood up, then almost as though he teleported, he appeared right next to us. He punched Cayden in the chest and picked me up by my helmet. "I am sorry, were you talking about something important? Oh, don't let me interrupt." He slowly tried to crush my helmet with one of his hands. I was about to retaliate, so in response to my actions, he sent an electrical current into my helmet. It was just enough current to relax my whole body. "Now that I have you holding on to dear life, how should I proceed in bringing you to your inevitable end? Should I boil you in your armor, cooking you until death? Electrocute you, forcing your body to shut down? Divert your sense of time, making your final moments feel like a twenty-four-hour death? Or maybe I should just break your little neck. What do you think I should do?" Before he could do any permanent damage, Cayden returned the attack from earlier.

"Are you all right?" Cayden asked me.

"I'll survive. I just need a moment to get feeling back in my body."

I kept clenching my fist over and over again until it finally became easier to move. I got up to see if Cayden was still fighting, but he was nowhere to be seen. Instead, there was Aristotle waiting. "So, are you ready to end this?" he asked.

I threw my head back. "Man, I never would have thought that I was this much of a prick."

"Yes, I know; it is amazing, isn't it?" He grabbed his sword from his back. "Say hello to our brother for me. I am sure you two will have much to talk about."

I next heard a loud bang; this was when he dropped his sword.

"He's not going to be visiting his brother today, but you can say hello in his stead," Mosby said.

The explosion didn't wound him but instead dented the armor inward around the elbow area. It was very possible that the weapons were loaded with some kind of high-caliber, armor-piercing round. It was the only thing that could possibly dent this guy's armor, but from the explosion, there must have been more. I then heard multiple different gunshots. Using them as a decoy, I formed the water into a club and slammed it into Aristotle's face while he was distracted. I knew it wasn't going to kill him, but I just knew Cayden would make his move soon enough. Though I was unsure where he was, I knew it would be a matter of time. I just needed to hold on and keep my reinforcements alive. The next shot fired was aimed in the rib, more specifically, where the ribs were broken. With the armor again denting, I targeted it, forging another war hammer. When it hit, I could feel a jolt of electricity leaving his body, and I saw his armor shatter where I hit it.

He started to fight back, but as he was about to hit me, Rayshawn shot him from point-blank range with a bazooka of some sort. The blast only caused Aristotle to fall backward. Rayshawn proceeded to shoot his helmet at point blank, barely being clear of the blast. Aristotle noticed that Rayshawn stood in the water at this point, and electrified it to an opening, but Rayshawn had already moved away. Aristotle returned to his feet and threw a ball of fire and protected himself with a shield of fire; this was when the fire split open. Cleared of being burned, Emilio shot him four more times in the back with a rifle. Cayden then appeared with his sword drawn and cut off his arm with the gauntlet, forcing his powers to stop. Then he stepped on it and melted it into a puddle.

"I thought I sent you further away so it would take you longer to return," Aristotle said.

"Since you don't have much experience with the other elements, this means that your understanding of how to use them is very limited," Cayden replied.

Before Cayden could get the killing blow, I yelled, "I think he's had enough." This stopped Cayden. There was no need for any more bloodshed, even if he was a clone.

"I have," Aristotle said.

I look at Emilio and asked, "Where is Mosby?"

"He is freeing Laura," he replied.

Aristotle pressed a button. "Your sister is free to move. I figure I had better do it instead of relying on another. They would spring one of the many traps I set to perform."

"Please go and assist Amelia. See if there is anything we can do for her." I turned to Rayshawn. "How did you guys know about this and where to show up?"

He threw down his bazooka. "Amelia told us everything. We would have been here sooner but her directions were imprecise on exactly where in the swamp we were going."

"Please tell Mosby and Emilio I said thank you."

"Congratulations, Leonardo, it seems you have defeated me not once but twice. So, why don't you just finish the job?" Aristotle asked.

"Why should I kill you? I have no real quarrel against you. Even if you killed one of my teammates, killing you for that reason will not bring them back. Besides, you will be dead in less than twenty-four hours, which means if you and me think alike, you will be reflecting on what you have done during your remaining hours. It seems you were wrong about who was going to fall today." Taking one last look at him, I then said, "I hope you can find peace in your final hours."

As Cayden and I walked away, I heard Aristotle mumbling, but it was unclear until I was five steps away from him. "You know that little moment that I wasn't around? I had jumped into the future and watched as you died, so you will not be going anywhere, same as me. It ends now."

I suddenly felt a pinching pain going through my chest. When I looked down, I saw a spear coming out of my chest where my heart was. The copy laughed manically. Since I knew the only things that could pierce the armor were like material, this meant it could change shape. I touched the spear to reshape it into an armed crossbow. I turned around, launching the arrow into his skull. He decomposed, turning back into water. I felt my armor retracting. I turned around, watching as Cayden began to prepare a blood clot from the environment around him.

"Man down," Cayden yelled. "He must have used a modified spear."

I thought to myself, *Who else is down? I am still standing.* I turned back around and took three more steps, ignoring the pain, for I have felt pain from battles before and shaken it off. This was when I fell to my knees because I had gotten lightheaded. I tried to get back up, but my body weighed three times its own weight. From what I could hear, it had begun to rain. I looked forward and began to crawl, trying to get close enough to see my friends, to see Laura one last time. If I only had one last thing to see before I died, I wanted it to be her. I could only imagine her.

My vision faded, but I could see shadows running toward me. Next was my hearing, for all I heard were muffled words, barely enough to understand who was talking. I felt dizzy listening to it all. I could hear Laura, but I couldn't tell what she was saying. I was guessing, maybe even hoping, it was, "Leonardo, please don't leave me." I felt a small jerk to my body as if someone had grabbed me, but I had lost all feeling in my body, so I couldn't tell. I smelled Laura's scent, so I assumed Laura was holding me.

"I love you, Laura..." I whispered. "I know I never told you...but I really do. I fell in love with you...the first time...I met you. Your eyes are the prettiest green...I've ever laid eyes on... I am sure they are a beautiful sky blue right now." I grew even more lightheaded. With my final breath, I said, "I love you...Laura."

If I knew then what I know now, I would have never been in that situation. But then again, if we all knew what would happen next, we could avoid a lot of problems. But if I could change one thing, only one thing, I would have told Laura I loved her all those years ago.

*To My Fiancée, Laura*
*From Leonardo*
*Dear Laura,*
*I don't know where to begin, but if you are reading this, I did not survive...well, myself. I was always curious why you stayed with me all these years. I know it wasn't for money; I didn't have any. It wasn't for my combat skills; you could easily beat me one on one. I truly doubt it was on the Webmaster and Anita's orders, for if that was the case, then you staying this long is a bit above and beyond any call of duty.*

*So, I, here and now, have decided to take a risk and play with a theory I have. Laura, I swore if I made it out of this battle alive I would tell you, but I have to be serious, unlike those movies I watched growing up, there is no guarantee I will get a final chance to talk to you. No matter what happens, I will be putting all my cards on the table. I have wanted to tell you for the longest time, but I was afraid you might not feel the same way. I never told you, but I have been in love with you since the first time we met back in that little hut.*

*You were the most beautiful woman I had ever laid eyes upon, and you still are. Of course, my second thought was that you were crazy, although that didn't last long. I know that if it weren't for you always being there with me, my life would be incomplete. Those mornings I would wake up and you weren't there was like a part of me was missing. The times your eyes turned blue, I wanted more than anything to solve the issue so it wouldn't bother you anymore.*

*Every time going home became a real possibility, I did not want to go without you. I am sorry I have always been so selfish; I was afraid I would never see you again, and I couldn't live with that.*

*You were always so strong, and I was too afraid of what you would say when I said just how much I love you, but since I am about to die anyway...I have no reason to hold back how I feel.*

*I thank God for every moment we spent together. Laura, I hope for nothing but the best in your life.*

*Goodbye.*

*Love,*

*Leonardo*


These are the letters I entrusted to my fiancée, Laura. I know without a shadow of a doubt they will be delivered appropriately. I told her to search for my sister Cheryl, who can locate the rest of my family so that Laura can deliver them to the right people.

*A Letter to Cheryl Rite, My Loving Sister*
*From Your Oldest Brother, Leonardo*
*Dear Cheryl,*

*I am writing these letters to you because the unfore-seen...no, in my line of work, it is most definitely fore-seen. As you must have heard by now from my fiancée, Laura, I am not coming home like I planned to do orig-inally. I knew it was possible that at any point I could fail to come home, though this was the first time I accepted this as a real possibility. I couldn't see you again, so I sent her in my stead. I don't exactly know if you still live in that desert town Barstow or if you've moved to some place like Hawaii or DC. Heck, I'll never know now. Regardless, I am sure Laura has found you, or at the very least, your husband. As far as the rest of the family, you should also know where to find them. I could have sent these to Mom, but you seemed to be the glue of our family, so this would be a lot quicker. Plus, you could get to know her, the woman of my dreams.*

*I take it you finally have your husband back home by now. You can thank our sister Kat for locating him, and you can thank me for saving him. He should have been home for about three years now. He told me while he was here that Willie Jr. is doing well. I hope all is well with you and your family. I hope your husband Willie D. has been acting better since the last time I saw you two in action. Oh yes, there was also a story of one I never met, Celestin, and I also heard you were preg-nant with your third child, who should have been born by now. Lily, he said the name would be. Tell your kids I loved them even though I will never meet most of them. I regret not being there.*

*I suspect that you're probably on your fourth child now, maybe your fifth. This is considering the rate at which you two have children and how much love you two had for each other before I left. There is only one thing I wish to tell you before I finish this letter. No matter what, stay strong and never stray too far from what the real decisions you know you need to*

*make for too long. I wish we could have met at least one more time. This is my final goodbye. I love you, sister. Godspeed.*
*Sincerely,*
*Leonardo*

*A Letter to My Youngest Sister, Kat*
*From Your Twin-Like Brother, Leonardo*
*Dear Kat,*

*I have written a letter to you not because you are my sister and not because I was forced to do so, but because I feel as though you could learn something from me for once. I usually learned from you while we were growing up.*

*My youngest sister, though you are older than me, I feel it relevant to call you by such a name. You see, I know that you have been on this island at least once, for at least two months and at most three. Even for the short time you were here, you left a big impact, not just with the Amazon tribes, but also with another group. You achieved so much in such a short time. You seem to have left a bit of your morals here. The sister I knew in the past would have never have left their brother here in a place like this. The only ones who have tried to get me home or even help me has been The Webmaster, Laura Cayden...and our brother-in-law Willie D.; he was a big eye-opener. But there were some things I was better off not knowing.*

*My sister, why didn't you tell us? Why didn't you even try? If no one else was there, wasn't I always there to try to help? If no one would listen, would I not lend an ear? If there wasn't anyone intelligent to talk to, was I not there to try to keep up? You have kept your life so closed that it would be easier for me to train all the animals in the world to talk out their problems.*

*Look, Kat, you and our sister are all that remain from Mom. All I ask is that you spend as much time*

*as you can with them while you can. You never know when they'll be gone. I wish we could have spent more time together before my untimely demise.*
*Goodbye forever.*
*Your Brother,*
*Leonardo*

*Dear Melvin,*

*Out of all the letters I have written, this one is the toughest. It's not because you're dead but rather because I know you'll never conventionally receive this letter.*

*I know I never showed or even said it; however, I will not take the blame for that. I do love you, little brother. We had some times where we could have literally killed each other, but honestly, we did have our good times. We'd played as sparring partners, we'd played video games, we'd shared jokes, had some laughs, we'd shared the belt, we'd shared our toys, we'd shared our desserts, we'd worked together, and even schooled together. Through it all, I can honestly say it's been fun more times than not. You are my little brother, the only one I have and will ever have. I know it seemed like we didn't get along all the time, unless we had to, of course.*

*My brother, through the years, I could only see all the bad, but now while I ride to my destination, I can finally see the good. Honestly, I will never admit this verbally, but I can admit it through this letter (after all, I seriously doubt I will survive this trial of my life). I have been a little jealous of your natural talent—being able to pick something up and almost instantly become good at it. You tried out for sports, and it was like second nature to you. We sparred, and you were naturally stronger than me. We competed for Mom's attention...though you won, I would compete in the same manner you did. You were never afraid to try something new or meet new people. It honestly seemed as though you lacked in common sense, but I just think you lacked in planning and preparation, so you improvised. Honestly, the thing that bothered me the most was you were the younger brother.*

*I wish the you from before that day could return, but things don't typically work that way. This is my final goodbye. Rest in peace, brother.*
*Sincerely,*
*Leonardo*

# 14
## So...Even Myths Can Turn Out To Be True

hear nothing and my body feels heavy. As I open my eyes, all I see is white. There are no lights, and there are no instruments, just white. I cannot tell if I am standing or lying down. What is going on? My mind starts flooding with memories of what happened to me. I remember fighting my clone and being stabbed through my heart. Hmm, the only thing that makes sense at this point is I must be dead, awaiting God's final judgment. The thing is, I don't see Him. Maybe I am in a waiting room of some kind, or maybe I was sent to another kind of heaven.

My feet are getting heavier. Crap, maybe I slept past His judgment and am now being sent to the fiery pits of hell. I can feel the temperature rise. Soon, I begin falling, so I clench my eyes tightly. I hear myself hit the ground. The fall wasn't as long as I thought it would be, but then again, why would God play games when it is time to be serious? The heat raises so much I think I am on fire.

"Leonardo, do you know why you are here?" A voice echoes all around me.

Humbly, I answer, "Yes, God, I know why I am here. I have killed, stolen things, even gambled, though I knew it was wrong..."

"God? What in the world are you talking about? My name is Dr. Zackary Kornegay. I am a doctor and nothing more. You might have suffered a little bit of brain damage if you think I am God."

"Dr. Kornegay?"

"Yes, that is my name. Let's skip the chitchat portion of this. You do have places to be. You were brought here because you were stabbed through the heart by what was described to me as a spear, but from what I saw in the autopsy, it was more or less like a shotgun. The room you are in is a decontamination room. My college built it years ago. Everything in the room is automatic. It was made to do surgeries, clean wounds, even cure diseases at their source. It can cure anything from common colds and fevers to more difficult ailments like Ebola and AIDS. They don't have them in the mainland hospitals because they are afraid it would make doctors obsolete."

"How did I get here?"

"He was a tall fellow accompanied by a man in his early forties named Trotter. They dropped you off by car This happened about two years ago. You have been here ever since. My job was to keep you safe here in this hospital. I was to also make sure the system was working properly; that way, you didn't die accidentally. This room has never had such a delicate procedure."

"This must not have been free. Who paid for it?"

"It was indeed free. You were the most delicate situation we have ever seen, especially since your organs were growing back slowly."

"Growing back?"

"Yes, in fact, I was going to replace your heart, but every time I tried, the computer would tell me you already had one in place. I took a look at your insides, but it must have been as small as a firefly's, as I could not see it. I know that seems weird, but you are not the first to be examined via this machine. There was another by the name Keisha, but that is not important right now. I have a message for your ears only, so I will play it now while we have the time to do so."

"Hello, Leonardo," a voice says, and on the screen was Peter. "I know it has been a while since we last met; from your perspective, three to four years, if I am not mistaken. However, from my own, it has been a while longer than that. By now, you must realize you're not dead. I have been doing well myself. After leaving SUBWAY, I headed back to the mainland using one of the trade routes on the island. As for what I am doing now, I have returned to the service of the German people. Sorry, but that is all I have time to explain at this moment. I have given the doctor instructions on what you need to do next." The recording closes, and the doctor returns to the scene.

"So, how long have I been like this?"

"You have been here for exactly nine months, four-teen days, eleven hours, forty-six minutes, and twen-ty-three seconds. Before that, you were in a white room from another part of the hospital waiting for your chest to close. Peter told me to tell you when you exit this building, you will be heading south. There you will find the evacuation point, which has been preplanned. When you get there, you will receive a radio transmis-sion telling you what to do next. That armor of yours is still on your person, so it will help you to get there safely. I was told that you will be familiar with using it, and you will notice some minor changes."

I try to get a feel for my suit but don't notice anything.

"Good luck, and I hope we meet again under better circumstances."

The screen turns off, and the door opens. I feel the ground shaking, and I can hear the sound of explo-sions. What is going on? I walk out of the door and see a window. I approach it. I am pretty high up. Out of the window I see a shell falling from the sky. The building starts to shake again, and I hear another explosion.

"Isn't this a hospital? Why would they do this?" I say. Looking out the window, I see I am at least twenty flights up. From above, two helicopters slowly lower down. Both of them are about to open fire, but both pilots go limp, and the helicopters crash into the building. I head back into the room I came from and brace for impact. The building shakes again.

"Hello..."

"Hello? Who is this?" I ask, but to my surprise, there is no response. Maybe I am getting someone else's broadcast; nevertheless, I will have to find a different way out. Now, considering the door is in front of a window, if I try to exit through the door, there should be a hallway or at the very least another room. This armor is pretty strong, so I should be able to break it down. I could use the water effect, but I am unsure if there is anything left in the reserves. I charge through the wall; to my surprise, it's like tearing through paper. I look back and notice the wall was pretty thick. Maybe really bad contractors built it. I make my way to the hallway and examine the area. Then I see another window

"I can't seem to get that signal." That voice again.

"Who is this?" I ask.

"Never mind, it seems that I have something, finally. Proceed according to the original plan."

"Are you going to answer or just keep me guessing?"

"Who? I don't think that question really matters right now. Whether I am your friend or foe will prove itself in time. All you need to know is I am a voice in your head and, if I so choose, your executioner. The helicopters are not the only ones after you. You are completely surrounded. Listen to me carefully, and you will avoid combat with most of them. The building you are in is rigged to blow upon your leaving, so you will have to make sure you are clear before the explosion."

"What do you mean?"

"Don't worry about getting caught in the blast; I doubt it can kill you. If I were you, I would continue in the same direction you are facing. And so you know, if you see a helicopter not shooting at you, I highly recommend you not shoot it."

"OK, simple enough." I run back to where the helicopters attacked me and jump out the window. From that high up, I shouldn't have too much of a problem with landing, right? As I am falling, I can see that I am higher than expected, and off in the distance, I can see smoke rising in several locations around the island. As I brace for impact, I hear the building exploding behind me. For a split second, it's like my heart has stopped, but then it continues and I am on the ground, but there isn't any kind of shock or resistance from the fall, which is kind of confusing.

I look around and see where the helicopters crashed. Off in the distance, I hear the sound of voices approaching, so I hide with the destroyed helicopters. My reasoning for doing so is to avoid confrontation; after all, I don't know what is going on here, and rushing in without a plan or an understanding is just dumb. As the people approach, I see there are three of them.

"Seems that we found the helicopters."

I hear them approaching but don't know how to proceed. Other than the suit, I am unarmed. Maybe if I steal a gun...

"Yeah, and we were lucky the building didn't cover it. We will have to report this back at command post after we check for survivors. So, what did you say happened to SUBWAY?"

"From the rumors, I heard another faction overtook it. It seems when they lost all of their big guns, it just collapsed. First, their special armor units disappeared, then the first and second in command followed in suit. That left their structure wide open and in need of replacements, but before it was done, they were attacked. Because of how the compound was run, it didn't require a lot of personnel." SUBWAY fell? But how, and when?

"What do you mean?"

"It's simple, the base was able to hold about a hundred or so people, but they only had minimum manning, something like forty-five. Once the command structure was broken, the base was easy pickings. Only a handful still remain."

"So where did the leader disappear to?"

Now they are passing by right on top of me. When they near me, I creep past them to further avoid conflict.

"That is an excellent question, but sadly, no one knows for sure."

I start running when I know I am in the clear. I have been asleep for almost a whole year; there couldn't be that much change.

To my left, I hear gunshots. Then my reflexes take over, and I grab my sword and form it into a shield on my back.

Over the radio, I began to hear chatter. "Muscles... McNasty...heading west...?"

So, some of them are still alive. That is a relief. I want to go and help them, but I might just end up getting in the way. I hear two shots, one from the man; I can't discern the other's location. When I see the man drop on the ground, I place my shield back and run over to him. I steal his guns—an assault rifle and a pistol, both stocked and full of ammunition.

"Keep moving, we don't have a lot of time," says the voice escorting me.

"I was just collecting some ammunition. I will be moving again soon." I can only collect one extra clip for the pistol and two for the rifle because I am so short on time. I continue heading south. "Hey, mister voice, could you tell me if you know a woman named Laura?"

"Laura? That is so nonspecific, for I know at least four of them, two who work for opposite agencies. Do you have a last name?"

Now, for the life of me, I could not remember it. "Never mind, it just isn't important right now." I can always ask when we are done here.

"Good, now just keep heading south; you'll see three tanks up ahead. Be warned, they'll fire if they think they have the shot. You are not to advance until you see one destroyed. That will be your signal to run until you get into the trenches. Once there, you will receive more directions on where to go."

"Understood."

I see a log that had fallen over, so I use that to approach quietly. From where I am positioned, I can see the trench. Now I just have to wait. Man, I wish Laura was here, but then again, this doesn't seem like a typical mission like we used to have. This seems even riskier than before. And for some reason, my suit seems different than before; maybe it's just lighter. I hear the explosion. I roll over the log and begin to sprint to the trench, holding my shield in front of me. The tank fires, so I jumped in the air to avoid the cannon fire. Once airborne, the shield manifests and I land on the tank, crushing it. This is impressive because of the jump itself; given I was comatose, my muscles should be weaker than they are now. Maybe it was something the doctor did to strengthen me. I leap backward and land in the trench. I hear another explosion. The voice replies, "Crap, you destroyed their tracker tank?"

"Tracker tank? I have been in endless combat for years now and I have never heard of this."

"That is true, but you have been asleep for two of those years, and as you know, technology likes to move forward. Tracker tank is an improper name. When it's destroyed, there is a drone that ruthlessly tracks and destroys the tank's destroyer."

I see a shadow and hear something pass by. I continue running, for it could be the drone. An explosion follows.

"I can't believe I gave up another day off I planned to use on playing video games for work. All right, you are currently heading southwest. Continue along that route, and you will see a hill. On the hill, there is an anti-air-rocket turret. If you wish to rid yourself of the drone, you will need it. After that, I'll need you to remove the turret; otherwise, we can't land."

"I understand."

I position the rifle in my hand and begin to attack. In total, I count ten soldiers protecting the AA rocket turret. The drone passes by again, dropping another explosion, so I get out of the way. The blast kills the soldiers and makes the AA turret obsolete. The only option I have at this point is to use the suit's abilities. I focus water in my hand and throw it. As it leaves my hand, I feel a little static as well. My throw misses because I don't have enough force behind it. As it comes underneath the drone, it shoots upward and blows up.

I hear a little bit of comm chatter. "Rayshawn, Ronda, and that Melena chick are all here at the main camp. I think they're using their comrade as a distraction. Can you hear me?"

"Yeah, we assumed once we made contact with the other two units. Capturing them and their friend is a high priority. If you don't think can defend against their units, just abandon the outpost. Our higher-ups will understand."

"I copy, sir."

Hmm...so they are still alive, but how did the enemy get their names?

The voice says, "I see that it is done. We will be there soon enough. So, stay alive. That is all."

I look around myself and see helicopters, infantry, and one tank.

"Surrender the Alpha suit to us," they yell.

I reply, "The Alpha? What are you talking about? I never had the Alpha. I was told years ago it is in a secure location. No one but the creator knows where it lies."

"Leo," the voice said. "You might want to get on your knees and put your hands up above your head."

So, this was all a set up. I really don't see how I will get out of this. I guess I will not get to see my family or Laura ever again. I proceed to do so. At this point, I am not surprised. I close my eyes and try to picture what Laura looks like one last time. When I do this, I hear lightning strike. I reopen my eyes to see one of the helicopters falling and destroying the tank; another bolt strikes and destroys the remaining helicopters. Dust forms around me, and I hear gunshots. The dust clears, and not a single soldier is left standing.

"Nice to see you can follow my directions on getting here. I was told you were a pacifist, so why did you grab a gun? You know that took some time away from the main operation, right?"

A hand taps my shoulder from behind. I turn to look but can't see anyone. I point the rifle where his head should be.

"Those guns are not very effective, even on me."

"Who are you? For real, Mr. Voice," I ask. "For there is already a user of invisibility, and I hate that guy."

"Indeed there is only one, and that is me. I have never met you before. As for the former user, he won't bother anyone ever again. My codename is the Ghost Wolf. I'm here to recover you," he said, becoming uncloaked. "My friend calls me Blue-Eyed Demon, but my name is Jay. Now, if that is all, we do have places to be, and I don't get paid by the hour." He presses a button, and the sky begins to blink like a beacon in the sky.

A hover copter begins to land. The back hatch opens, and three agents run out to secure the immediate area. The next to run out is Laura, who hugs me. It takes me a while to process. I must have died. I hear her say, "It was true. I am just so happy you made it here."

But if I've died, why can I feel her? She smells the same, if not better than before. I feel my suit coming off. I hug her as well. She kisses me, and I am left speechless for a second because this is the first time we have kissed. It seems out of character for her. This has to be a dream—or I'm still in the coma, right?

"Are you real?" I ask.

Cayden says, "Yeah, a real pain in the butt when you weren't around." I see him standing on the ramp with his arms folded. "It seems that the doctor's experiment worked very well."

Jay walks past. "If you two love birds are done, we do have places to be. The sooner you go home, the sooner I can enjoy my day off."

Cayden says, "You two heard him; let's go. You can continue this warm embrace when you get on board. Let's go before backup arrives."

As we make our way up the ramp, the other three come on board as well. I sit down, and Laura sits next to me. Cayden goes up to the cockpit. Two of the three agents sit down while the third remains on the ramp. We begin to take off.

"Can you tell me how I survived? Because I do remember taking a spear to the heart."

"That is complicated. Do you remember that day I saved you and Rayshawn from Daysen and Becky? Well, that item I gave you was a corrupted healing tool. I am not sure if you remember Dr. White telling you, but your suit can absorb abilities from malfunctioning ones. These can help enhance your suit's powers; however, though you can use the ability, you can only use whatever percent the broken one has. Most have a very strong output, but yours only has a fraction of the intended power, which was why you healed slowly, which might also explain why the fake armor took so long to break. A severe heart wound, like the one you had, should, in theory, have completely healed after the minimum of three days. But it took one and a half years to completely heal. This was one of the reasons it was deemed unusable but not useless. It had a weak output, but it still had an output. I felt it was important for you to have some kind of advantage, even if it was a small one."

I thought whatever she threw that day was destroyed; I didn't know it was absorbed.

"After we took you to the hospital, I delivered those letters to your sister, Cheryl. I was lucky she and Willie D. were still in Barstow and knew where everyone had moved. Before we left to deliver the letters, she showed me your brother's grave to read his letter out loud. Then we went to your other relatives. I have received status reports every day we were away."

"That does tell me a lot. I would ask you about their status, but I am sure I will find out soon enough." I feel my heart racing with excitement. It is finally going to happen. I am going home. "But wait a minute. Did someone on the island receive the Alpha suit? The people I ran into thought I had it."

Laura replies, "I heard rumors, but I assumed they were just that."

Cayden stands in the aisle. "That is because it is your new suit of armor that you are currently wearing. And though you didn't notice, you picked the color that best reflects you; in this case, the one that you were wearing before. When I was recovering the doctor for you, I ran into your former ally, Peter. Apparently, he remembered me from a photo Laura showed him years ago. Peter was serving as a bodyguard for an ambassador in Bern, Switzerland, which was where I was during that time. From my understanding, a civilian team uncovered it while they were looking for an anomaly on a farm to the north. He was able to recover the object without it becoming public. He told me to give it to you and said he was satisfied with the power he already has."

Cayden leaves us and switches places with the person in the back.

"Passengers, we will be leaving the island's airspace shortly," the pilot says over the intercom. "With those anti-airfields down, we can leave with little incident. Please bear with us."

"What is going on?"

Jay walks by and says, "The short version of this tale is the island is collapsing. Those anti-airfields didn't just offer camouflage from satellites, redirect ships at far distances, or keep people from escaping this horrid place. They kept the island afloat and together as well."

"Do the people know?" I ask.

"Some of them know; otherwise, there would be more air traffic. Anyone that has been a real ally to you has been informed. That might be why your pals have kept the radio busy today. According to the Webmaster's report, it is going to happen today or tomorrow. If you hadn't awoken when you did, this would have been a lot more difficult."

I hear three gunshots from the ramp. "What was that?" I ask.

"That is us holding up our end of the deal. Excuse me." He goes to join Cayden. I hear more gunfire. "All right, we can leave the area once we know they are airborne."

Laura places her hand on mine and says, "We are helping Melena and the others leave this cursed island."

"That's good. What about the Webmaster? How is she doing?"

"She has already left the area, she and the other Amazon tribe, as you called them. She foresaw this exact thing happening, and with Dr. White and Mr. Trotter's help, they built a device that carried the village away. Not sure exactly how, but there have been reports of a piece of land being lifted out of place several months back from the local people. After an hour, it disappeared. The only thing that remained was thick fog for twenty-four hours. From what I have been told, it sounds a lot like her ABOFNYS project."

"ABOFNYS project?"

"Aerial Barrier Operation from National (Y) Euthanization Sequence. It was described to me as a backup plan to escape this island in case something happened, like what is happening now."

Man, the Webmaster really likes to think ahead. That is one really prepared woman.

One of the other soldiers runs past me with more ammo. Wolf yells, "Bernice, tell the pilot we need to circle one more time; they are taking longer than expected. When I give the signal, pull off from this position and fly Route Echo 27."

"Laura, are they going to need help?"

"No, those two have told me I must keep an eye on you to make sure that you are well. I understand that you have enhanced strength, but you are still human and recovering. After half of the things you had done, it will take time."

The pilot speaks once more: "I am receiving a message from the remaining Special Unit Bravo. Patching it through."

"Hello, thanks again for your help, you guys. I hope that your package made it unharmed. We are taking off now and will be following your lead."

Is that Melena?

"That is a good copy, Big Girl." It is, I know that call sign and voice anywhere.

"Tell Mustachio that when we get there, I'll take care of the drinks."

"Hey, so what did SUBWAY actually stand for, Laura? The Webmaster never told me."

"Yeah, I doubt that she had time to tell you that day, but I thought I did when we first joined," Laura replies. "It is an acronym for Supplied Unit of Beta Weaponry and Yonder-tools. I am sure you noticed that we were using weapons and vehicles that have never been seen by the rest of the world. Well, that is how they received that title."

"Bravo team is in the air. We have the green light to move into position," Wolf says. "Hey, Leo, you should get one more look at this place, for you will never see it again."

I get up because Laura gets up, but she leaves to use the bathroom. I walk to the open ramp and take in the view and the relief of never seeing this place ever again. As we go by, I see a massive chunk of land missing from its resting place. That must be where the Webmaster used to be; and I can see the destroyed tower. Cayden gets up and leaves.

A voice says, "It is a beautiful sight indeed, and since we have further up to go, it will only get better."

I turn to see who it is, but I cannot identify him. I turn to Wolf, "So, who is he?"

Wolf answers, "I am not sure. He was aboard when we got the plane. I asked the pilot, and he said that he was a wanderer he picked up before the mission. For the most part, he keeps to himself. I am going now. I have seen enough of these in-sky moments." Then he leaves as well.

"What is your name?" I ask.

"If I told you, you wouldn't believe me," the wanderer replies.

"Try me."

"Quinn Ip Qintibli."

"You're right, I don't believe you."

"It's OK, no one ever does." He goes back to reading. I can see he's quick to get lost in the book. I got a closer look at the title, it was, *Cloud and the Tales of the Forgotten World*.

Laura sits next to me and asks, "Are you afraid to leave?"

"No. Just relieved." Taking a deep breath, I repeated myself, "Just relieved."

I am relieved I am finally free of this cursed land, relieved I am not dead, relieved I know my friends can go home as well, relieved I can see my family again, relieved I can go home and rest without looking over my shoulders, relieved that my love is coming home with me, relieved that it is all over. So, yeah, I am just relieved.

CPSIA information can be obtained
at www.ICGtesting.com
Printed in the USA
LVHW020222011021
699202LV00001B/26

9 781662 826436